Obeah
A Novel

Michael Eisele

Other books by Michael Eisele:
Without Tears And Other Tales
Twelve O'Clock Sharp
Odour Of Rectitude

Contents

Contents

Arrival

*T*he moment Wirt laid eyes on Murdoch he felt a slight resentment crawling up his spine, for reasons he could not have given. Because Murdoch, a man well turned out, seemed pleasant enough. Yet Wirt couldn't banish an inkling of discomfort near him. Something about the botanist, whose job he would soon acquire, dispirited him.

What caused it? His hail-fellow demeanour, the eager clasp of the hand, or perhaps his peppy manner of introduction? Or was it just an unworthy presentiment on Wirt's part? It took some time to decipher the underlying factors for this antipathy.

"Robert Murdoch, botanist of this godforsaken place. You are Mr Wirt, I take it?"

With these words Murdoch extended a hand which the other took.

"Hannes Wirt from Germany."

"No need to expound, we know everything about you," Murdoch interrupted, then hastened to add:

"Only what concerns us, of course."

Despite Wirt's misgivings about Murdoch, he welcomed his presence, because he felt at sea amid this jumble that resembled a regular babel. The few white faces among a host of black ones affected him strangely. The hubbub increased as more people arrived; so did the chatter. He could have sworn that every man and woman was graced with at least two tongues endeavouring to outtalk each other.

Ignoring the hurly-burly, Murdoch took Wirt in tow. Using both elbows freely, he forced his way through the prating, arm swinging crowd, in a manner of a supreme commander exercising a duty. Meanwhile he kept a lively conversation going, while looking occasionally over his shoulders.

"How was the crossing?"

"Agreeable, albeit a bit long."

"Well, at least you have arrived, good and ready I notice, to be put to the yoke."

Murdoch seemed to be known far and wide. The natives evidently tried to avoid him; their sideways glances bore a mixture of distaste and dread. After a fleeting glance they lowered their eyes and looked the other way. Giving directions appeared to be Murdoch's second nature. With peremptory gestures and gruff utterances he chased young and old around. An important shipment of equipment and plants, consigned to the botanical garden, needed to be unloaded. Emphatic orders were given like:

"Do this, leave that, put a move on."

In dealing with natives he neither showed solicitude nor social niceties.

"Hot, isn't it?" he remarked in between a scathing dressing-down given a stevedore.

"It certainly is," Wirt replied with conviction.

Indeed, he had never experienced such mugginess before. The burning sun high up in the sky, over ground kept moist by intermittent squalls, combined to create a hothouse condition. Wirt felt himself wrapped from head to toe in steaming towels.

Murdoch pointed to benches on the shore saying:

"You can sit there while I look after things. Believe me, these people cannot be left alone for a minute. Turn your back and see what happens; everything will be upside down. I won't be long, meanwhile enjoy the sight, not that there is much to see."

Wirt did not share Murdoch's assessment; quite the contrary. He felt awed by the scenery and intrigued by the motley crowd. Though an unholy confusion reigned from one end to the other, an atmosphere of goodwill prevailed. True, people jostled and spoke loud, but with not a hint of rancour. No one paid attention to him, all went their way while talking and gesticulating. He let his eyes wander from the Caribbean sea, a soothing sight, to the abruptly rising mountains, lush and forbidding, encircled by light clouds.

The nearby city of Roseau, a dismal scattering of shacks and shabby buildings, nevertheless attracted Wirt strangely. As he scanned the jungle-like growth, encroaching on upper-scale houses, and listened to the vociferous but friendly voices, Wirt felt transported to another world. A sensation bordering on bliss overwhelmed him. For the first time in his life he was touched by a sense of belonging.

"This is home," he murmured.

"Well, that's done," Murdoch announced. "I hope you weren't bored."

"Not in the least," Wirt assured him.

"Your belongings have been unloaded, they will soon arrive at the house."

"The house?" Wirt repeated.

"Yes, it's government property at your disposal till you find suitable accommodation."

Shielding his eyes with one hand, Murdoch pointed at a house across the river with the other.

"That's the one with the brown roof and white walls. I hope you like the place."

Looking at the indicated property Wirt nodded approvingly:

"I think I will."

It proved to be an older stone residence surrounded on three sides by fruit and palm trees and flowering shrubs, enclosed by high hedges. The Roseau River below, swift in parts, could be seen and heard from a nicely appointed veranda. Smiles lit up his face. The house, and more so the garden, made a pleasing impression. Particularly the tall, swaying palm trees replete with coconuts made his heart leap. The location, somewhat sequestered, satisfied his penchant for privacy. The only damper of his joy were the presence of natives milling about inside the house and out in the yard. Glancing at them inquiringly prompted Murdoch to explain:

"They are your helpers, Mr Wirt."

"Oh?"

Sensing a hint of disapproval, Murdoch raised his eyebrows.

"You don't seem to be enthused."

"Well, the fact is I don't really need help."

Misunderstanding Wirt's reaction, Murdoch declared:

"Have no fear, the government covers the costs."

Wirt cared not a hoot about expenses, he just resented anybody constantly around him, in particular domestics. They made him edgy, he perceived them as stiflers of his freedom. How can a man be himself, give his thoughts free rein, with people around him who continually covet his attention? He wanted to object, yet dared not. One glance at Murdoch's reproving frown set him right; he postponed the airing of his concerns.

Ultimately an agreement was reached whereby they would spend one day per week there, and five days somewhere else.

"I have stocked your larder with provisions, and the sideboard with liquor that will tide you over till you find your bearings. Should you need assistance of any kind, call me."

Before leaving, Murdoch said:

"By the way, there will be a dinner given in your honour."

"Tonight?" Wirt asked noticeable perturbed.

"No, no, on Wednesday evening at six o'clock."

"Is it formal?"

"Not at all. The premier and his wife will be there, myself of course, plus the chief of police."

"Any special dress requirements?"

Murdoch, shaking his head, chuckled:

"Just no shorts or short-sleeved shirts. Anything else, reasonable clean, will do. We are not so stiff and foppish here."

He described the location of his house where the dinner was going to be held with an exactitude that made Wirt chuckle under his breath. Even a man in his cups couldn't lose his way between here and the eye-catching building, a veritable landmark visible from Wirt's dwelling. No further elucidation was needed, but Murdoch for the third time painstakingly gave instructions, in the minutest details, how to find one's way.

After Murdoch and the domestics had left, Wirt heaved a deep sigh. Postponing unpacking, he reached for a bottle and a

glass, which he took outside. The view from the veranda
neither took his breath away, nor made his heart leap to his
throat. Something more profound happened. He gradually
gained an awareness that he never felt before. His mind started
to drift into a world hitherto unknown. As if captivated by a
spell, he felt deeply elated. In fact, the magic of the Caribbean
had engendered a sense of bliss in his heart. Despite visible
squalor in all directions, an enchantment lay in the air that
made him strangely happy.

In the river below women of all ages washed clothes,
making a din to wake the dead. They sure were an unruly lot;
certainly not of the demure Griselda type awaiting her lord's
bidding. What an odd sight they were, splashing about with the
vigour of warriors, in a spirit that neither privations nor
setbacks could subdue.

Wirt was unable to suppress a rising admiration for these
raven-black women, lusty and earthy, yet nevertheless exuding
an aura of femininity that confounded him. They gossiped
raucously, laughed uproariously at ribald jests, but their
clamour soothed rather than annoyed. In fact, the bustle below,
coupled with the rush and rustle in the trees and bushes, made
Wirt pensive. Leaning back he let his thoughts wander.

Almost by coincidence he ended up in England on his last
vacation, where an advertisement caught his eyes, which he
copied and promptly forgot. Only his companion's prodding
induced him to apply for the post offered. Ten days later a
contract warmed his pocket, which he valued greatly.

After bringing his affairs in order, he bordered the next
ship steaming to the Caribbean. After a long and tedious
voyage, then a transfer in Barbados, he finally arrived at his
destination. Chuckling in retrospect over his friends'
objections, he loudly recited some:

"It's a forsaken island, devoid of a single diversion for a
civilised man."

"Poor and unsightly," Wilhelm said.

"Still dabbling in black magic," his father reminded.

His mother, taking him aside, whispered in a sepulchral
voice:

"Hannes, I am told they practise obeah, which can bring disaster to an innocent man."

Their exhortations made him smile, albeit briefly, for the thought of Murdoch clouded his amusement. A strange man that is, he had to confess, rumoured by his colleagues at Kew Gardens to be a crow on the left hand none wished to encounter.

Murdoch intended to return to England, he was told by the Gardens' administrator, who seemed ill at ease when Murdoch's name was mentioned. Wirt couldn't banish a notion that the truth lay elsewhere. Kew Gardens did the hiring, in this case for the Dominican government, whose requirements for this post were rather stringent, especially concerning languages.

"They set a high value on a multilingual man," he was told.

Wirt's bewilderment grew after he visited the Garden, which he found shockingly neglected. That seemed odd in view of what he was told at the time of hiring. He distinctly recalled the administrator's words:

"The botanical garden is a pet project of the local government, every minister is bent on making it world famous. Don't forget the island is the home of unique plants, shrubs, and trees. Botanists from every corner of the globe are intensely interested in Dominica's flora, and fauna for that matter."

The dismal sight of these revered grounds made Wirt feel queasy; he resolved to quickly take remedial measures.

Informal Meeting

At six o'clock sharp Wirt was introduced to the premier and his wife. The chief of police had not arrived yet. They turned out to be somewhat affected and self-conscious, as opposed to Murdoch who was outgoing to a fault. His talk, meant to be didactic, touched Wirt unpleasantly. The premier and his wife he treated with benign condescension, which they accepted with an inner shrug. Their relationship suffered from constraints that neither side was able to conceal. Himself, Murdoch honoured with a patron's benevolence intended to put him at ease.

"How is your French, Mr Wirt?" the premier's wife asked.

"Quite fair," Wirt answered, glancing sideways at Murdoch as if to say: "I hope you don't mind."

The premier smiled:

"Well, then let's put it to the test."

Saying that, he and his wife started to converse in fluent French, to Murdoch's visible chagrin. Uttering not a word, he sat there glowering, pretending to admire the sunset.

Darkness descended rapidly, bringing to life the singular voices of a Caribbean night. The calls of whistling frogs, piercing yet strangely reassuring, almost instantly filled the air. The shrill cries of the pygmy owls, a mixture of whistles and trills, resounded from the foothills. The queerest sound ever heard by Wirt came from the back of the garden. Resembling rolling drumbeats growing louder, then dying away and ending in rapid-fire gabbles.

Seeing Wirt's questioning glances, the premier remarked:

"I see the weird clatter intrigues you?"

Wirt noddingly admitted:

"It's the strangest sound I have ever heard. What is it?"

Smiling broadly, he was told:

"Converse opinions prevail. Some say it is the voice of a crapaud, a toad in other words; others insist it belongs to the cuckoo manioc."

"A bird calling for rain the old-timers say," Mrs Burchard explained.

Wirt listened spellbound, he could have sworn that the earth had opened up and spat out weird creatures jubilant over their freedom.

Dinner was delayed on account of the police chief's tardiness. Time weighed heavy on everyone's mind. Conversation, perfunctory to begin with, proceeded haltingly. Not for lack of topics, mind you, since everybody shared an interest in botany. As it turned out the premier, as much as his wife, was deeply involved with the island's flora and fauna.

"It will be a pleasure working with you, Mr Wirt. Be assured of our undivided support, the well-being of the botanical garden is close to my heart."

"And mine too," his wife added, who was the honorary president of the facility.

Looking from Murdoch to Wirt, the premier expounded:

"Our future plans, which I shall be happy to lay before you, entail improvements and expansions that will enhance Dominica's prestige. Exciting days await us, gone will be the hobble of the past."

Did his perception play a trick on him, or had Mrs Burchard indeed cast rebuking glances at Murdoch while this was said? The premier, having undoubtedly noticed his wife's insinuative look, hastened to change the subject. Mentioning Wirt by name he inquired:

"I suppose you are acquainted with the island's history?"

"Through books only."

"Then you are probably better informed than most," Mrs Burchard quipped, while trying to avoid her husband's admonishing mien.

She had her knife in Murdoch alright, no two ways about it. The premier, anxious to maintain an atmosphere of civility, addressed Wirt ceremoniously:

"I hope you will feel at home here," he said.

Murdoch perked up.

"That will take time. In my case months went by before I became acclimatised," he remarked.

"It seems you find it difficult to divest yourself from it now," Mrs Burchard suggested with an innocent air.

If Murdoch noticed the tinge of irony in her remark, he showed no sign of it. He merely smiled graciously and inclined his head ever so lightly.

Wirt was about to make known his fascination with Dominica's enchantment, which grew by the hour, but the words remained stuck in his throat.

"Something is wrong here," it flashed through his mind, dreadfully wrong. The Burchards' and Murdoch pursue different agendas, which put them on guard with each other. Wirt felt they were trying to sidestep invisible squares, one party set for the other. The realisation put him on pins and needles, it marred the magic of the island. Even the indomitable voices of the Caribbean night appeared to lose their splendour; they suddenly sounded subdued.

Mrs Burchard interrupted the painful silence:

"Well, Mr Murdoch, you must be anxious to hand over the reins," she commented.

"Who can blame him after many years of service fraught with bitter disappointments," her husband commiserated.

Murdoch consented:

"Yes, the last one still grates on my nerves. That Alfred Nantes affair cut me to the quick, I must admit."

Noticing Wirt's raised eyebrows, the premier explained:

"Nantes, Mr Murdoch's intended successor, arrived two years ago, then suddenly disappeared without a trace."

Murdoch, turning to Wirt, explained:

"What a peculiar chap that was, a feigner of the first order. Pretending to be enthused about the job till the day when he absconded. He sure left us in the lurch, especially me who had already undertaken other obligations. As in your case three months had been allowed, giving my successor a chance, with my assistance, to become familiar with the Gardens' ins and outs."

Shaking his head disapprovingly, heaving a sigh of disgust, he exclaimed:

"Nantes' head-over-heels flight, as I call it, threw us in a dither. My bags were already packed, farewell dinners had been given, and travel arrangements were made. Of course leaving under the circumstances stood out of the question."

Mrs Burchard wondered aloud:

"It seems odd that we never heard from him again."

"Bizarre, really," her husband agreed.

Turning to Murdoch the premier declared:

"Your willingness to extend your tenure another two years deserves praise and thanks."

Wirt's bewilderment grew as he listened to these astounding revelations. He wondered why Murdoch signed on for another two years, being ostensibly anxious to leave the island. It should hardly require two full years to find a suitable replacement. Beyond that, how could someone, fairly prominent, a white man to boot, disappear among a sea of black people in a confined area?

His reflections were interrupted by rumbling noises outside. Someone stumped up the steps, snorting as if out of breath, hurling imprecations at these confounded inventions.

Murdoch heaved a sigh of relief:

"Finally," he expelled.

"Sorry, folks, I couldn't come sooner, the hussy acted up again," a stentorian voice announced.

The premier grimaced, as did his wife. Everyone but Wirt realised who was meant; none other than Caroline Brise, the terror of Dominica.

Howard Brunt, the chief of police, it couldn't be anyone else, revealed his origin by his accent. His cradle, without a doubt, stood within the sound of the bells of St. Mary-le-Bow-Church; in other words he was a cockney. Wirt gazed at the Falstaffian figure in dismay, for he doubted that the chief could squeeze through the door opening; not unless he sidled in.

"Murdoch, unlimber your refreshments, somewhat laced, if you please," he roared as he crossed the threshold.

Wirt instinctively liked the man. His rough-and-tumble manners affected him pleasantly; he was a breath of fresh air, wafting away the gossamer of genteel sarcasm.

The conversation soon became vivacious, contrasting sharply with the previous wariness. Brunt's raucous laughter filled the room, he possessed a gift to relate insignificant incidents with a Rabelaisian flair. Turning to Murdoch he remarked:

"Well, old boy, soon you will be on your way. When have you seen England last?"

"Seven years ago."

"A deuced long time, I grant."

Casting an eye at Wirt, he inquired:

"No doubt you have heard of Nantes?"

"Yes, just now."

"Believe me, sir, we moved heaven and earth to find him. Way up the Morne Diablotin I chased scouts, down into bottomless gullies I urged volunteers to scramble. All for naught I must confess. That Belgian, well liked I should add, had performed a vanishing act worthy of Houdini."

The premier expounded:

"We contacted his relatives and acquaintances in Belgium, and checked with every company and individual known to convey people to and from the island. All proved futile. To this day he remains untraceable."

"It is a mystery that might never be solved," the police chief sighed.

The premier, inclining his head towards Wirt, observed smilingly:

"I venture to say that this time we have no reason to fret."

"None at all," Brunt agreed.

Did anyone notice Murdoch's sneer? Probably Mrs Burchard had, judging by her reaction. She gasped, then looking at her husband she said:

"It's getting late, Raoul, remember our meeting with the Daniel's."

Evidently baffled he raised his head inquiringly, ready to protest. But something in her demeanour prompted him to acquiesce.

"Oh that, I plain forgot about it," he commented.

Refusing proffered coffee and cordials, the Burchards left after shaking hands with the others. Again Wirt couldn't banish an odd sensation of discomfort, he physically felt an undercurrent of enmity between the Burchards and Murdoch. Guarded, mind you, yet tangible and no less intense.

Raoul Burchard, the premier, being a politician accustomed to dissimulation, managed to suppress his inimical feelings. But not so his wife who as mentioned had her knife in Murdoch; she blanched on account of stifled anger. When he extended his hand, she instinctively hid hers behind her back, as if a viper was about to strike. Overcoming an impulse to cut and run, she offered her hand with an air of undisguised loathing.

Soon afterwards Brunt took his leave. Saying goodbye to Wirt he said in an undertone, contrasting with the bluff air shown so far:

"Should you need me, I can be reached at the Government House. Don't hesitate to call, be it for professional or personal reasons. No appointment is necessary, just knock and enter."

Then he added ominously:

"You might need me sooner than you think."

Being alone now an awkward silence descended upon them. Outside the voices of a Caribbean night resounded undiminished. Geckos scurried across the wall and the ceiling, stopping at times to gaze with raised heads and inflated throats at the two figures.

Wirt ended the silence. He rose and extended a hand:

"I shall see you tomorrow at the Gardens," he declared.

"I shall be there about nine o'clock," Murdoch replied.

Out on the road Wirt hastened his steps, as if quickly to lay a distance between him and Murdoch. He neither understood, nor approved his paradoxical perception of his colleague, although seemingly shared by the Burchards and Brunt. He thought of himself as an honourable man who rejected the notion of vindicating his own prejudices with those of others; at least he tried to. All the same what he just witnessed could not be circumvented; it heightened his intentions to be on guard.

Why did Murdoch's guests treat him with suspicion? Will the same dubiety be allotted him after takeover? Or was their mutual resentment a result of past rancour? The mysterious disappearance of Nantes caused him additional concern. According to the premier and his wife things were looking up. Nantes proved to be dedicated, knowledgeable, and amiable.

"A godsend," the premier had declared.

"A paragon," his wife, the figurehead, asserted.

Murdoch's faint praise received not the slightest consideration, for was he not on the way out? Not really, as it turned out.

"Many questions, few answers," Wirt murmured.

When he reached the main street, he halted his steps to glance at the house graciously assigned him. Both sides of the street leading to it were lined with skimpy dwellings, shacks really. Diffused light shone through sparsely draped windows, flickering ghostlike, casting grotesque shadows on the pavement. The piercing cries of whistling frogs echoed in his ears. These unrestrained sounds, Wirt had learned, no other force but the glimmer of dawn was able to silence. A pedestrian met him at times, more infrequently a rider on a donkey. On one side the ripple of the Roseau River could be heard, on the other the gentle sound of waves breaking rhythmically on the beach.

"The spell of the Caribbean," Wirt whispered.

Stirred by sentiments withered long ago, he started to hum. Growing bolder he sang in a subdued voice songs of his childhood and youth.

Suddenly the notes choked in his throat. Someone moved around inside his house. Who was it? One of the servants perhaps, he surmised, but repudiated the notion immediately. They always left before sunset, besides on Wednesdays, as agreed, they did not come.

Baffled by what he saw he instinctively walked faster, then stopped. A second person, a man judging by appearances, approached the other, whom Wirt also made out to be a man.

Sawing the air with both hands, they stood in the light of the wan moon arguing vehemently. What did it mean?

Despite growing apprehensions Wirt hastened forward. As he approached the house he coughed repeatedly with all the air in his lungs. The men perked up, then ran outside where they disappeared in the undergrowth.

Angry Dispute

*N*ext morning Wirt arrived at the Gardens ahead of time; he wanted to look around undisturbed. The sun came just around the mountains and climbed rapidly towards its highest point. The pleasing morning air buoyed up his spirit.

As he walked along, one eye aglow with joy, the other darkened by disapproval, he couldn't ward off a feeling of discomfort. The palm trees were the only bright spot amid the gone-to-seed facility, which obviously lacked a caring hand and discerning eye. The entire Gardens were in a deplorable condition.

"The paucity of money must be a contributing factor of this appalling neglect," Wirt said to himself.

Then quickly changed his mind, for the workmanship too left much to be desired. His reflections were interrupted by Murdoch's arrival.

"Good morning," he called out.

"Good morning," Wirt repeated.

Murdoch looked different today, more relaxed and purposeful. There was an upbeat air about him, indicative of a man with a mission. His devil-may-care attitude, whether feigned or real, affected Wirt pleasantly, although he cast an image of a ruthless machinator who brooked no opposition.

"Well, did you look around?"

"A bit," Wirt answered evasively.

Murdoch, stepping up to him, considered him closer. Was he mistaken, or did imps dance in his eyes that grinned and blinked at him?

"What do you think of it?" Murdoch wanted to know.

"The palm trees are beautiful," Wirt praised.

"And the rest?"

"Needs a little work," Wirt granted.

Murdoch understood. Pursing his lips mockingly, he remarked:

"No need to pretend, I realise that the Gardens should be in better condition. Whose fault is it? I let you guess, but remember what the eye sees does not always reflect reality."

Confounded by Murdoch's enigmatic observation, Wirt agreed:

"Yes, I know. There are always two sides to a coin."

Murdoch unlocked a building that had seen better days. Once inside he offered Wirt a seat and pulled up another chair for himself. As they talked Wirt felt discomfited by an annoying quirk Murdoch had. Despite his urbane manners one couldn't drive away the feeling of being continually sized up, weighed in the balance, and found wanting. Was this intrusive scrutiny meant to befuddle, or was it a mere personal caprice? Or had it a more sinister significance? In any case it bothered Wirt. Being condescendingly examined, having one's words silently dissected, rendered a conversation awkward. Wirt concluded that a cordial relationship was impossible with this mocking martinet.

Murdoch explained:

"As you know an initiation period of three months is stipulated during which time your responsibility is limited, as much as your authority. We ask you to be co-operative and willing to learn. I suggest to proceed step by step, starting with bureaucratic aspects before directing your attention towards the operation. Once that hurdle has been cleared, we tackle the matter of plants and trees."

"That suits me fine," Wirt declared.

Murdoch, squinting with one eye and raising the other, emphasised every word:

"There is the matter of government intervention, in particular by the premier's wife."

"She is the honorary president of the botanical garden, I understand."

"Yes, and we both know what that entails, but she does not. Her wishes and directions, as much as those of her husband, you may carry out at your discretion."

With a steely gaze, Murdoch added:

"After I am gone."

"In three months in other words," Wirt commented somewhat rattled by his colleague's icy, if not menacing tone.

Did he imagine it, or flitted a sneering grin across Murdoch's face who, glaring at him, repeated:

"In three months from today."

Then with a softening mien he declared:

"As far as I am concerned, the initiation may begin."

Files were shown, documents explained, drawings were perused till Murdoch, stifling a yawn, proposed:

"This is boring stuff, let's take a stroll through the Gardens."

Wirt rose with alacrity, for he too found the paper-shuffling tedious.

"Just to give you a general perspective," Murdoch remarked.

He appeared to be in a good mood again; the ill humour of a moment ago had evaporated. Trying to hide his bewilderment, Wirt asked perfunctory questions, to which he received cursory answers. Workers, who wielded rakes and shovels, seemed to avoid them deliberately. Not on account of indifference, Wirt surmised, but out of apprehension. Yes, they were being observed alright, furtively, mind you, for Wirt sensed their burning gazes on his back, which were quickly averted when noticed. A peculiar crew, Wirt granted; a weird, troubled boss, he concluded.

Murdoch, barking orders left and right, aimless and unduly emphatic, took evident pleasure in bossing them around. The workers spoke patois, a language Wirt did not understand. When he ask his colleague whether he comprehended what was said, he expelled indignantly:

"No! Why should I? Everyone working here must understand English. After all it is Dominica's official language. Everybody priding himself to have a midget of grey matter between his ears should be versed in it."

In the evening they met at Murdoch's house for a sundowner in accordance with an old Australian custom. Besides Wirt were present Harold Rintoul, bank manager, and Michael Mauch, newspaper publisher.

Darkness set in rapidly, bringing to life the voices of the night, which stir the heart and sharpen the intellect. As if a conductor had given the signal to an anxious chorus to start, the tiny frogs commenced their rousing tune.

To Wirt's surprise Murdoch disported himself with abandon. He behaved outright puckish. Out came the bottles, glass, and crushed ice. Unusually chipper, with hoorays on his tongue and mischief in his eyes, he filled everyone's glasses, which they raised to each other.

"Prost, skoal, to your health," could be repeatedly heard.

Soon the glasses were empty which delighted Murdoch, who refilled them with playful dexterity. Relieved from the day's heat and the vexing routine, they became outright frolicsome. The conversation, surprisingly versatile, flowed free and easy. No one put on airs; even Murdoch acted in a jocular manner, of which Wirt had never thought him capable of. Mauch's ribald banter was received with mock indignation, yet encouraged at the same time. He proved to be an intrepid freethinker; well read, widely travelled, and endowed with an enterprising spirit. He neither minced matters, nor showed any traces of hypocrisy. Setting his sails to the wind evidently never occurred to him.

It was a boisterous, yet congenial gathering, till the mood suddenly changed. Somehow the discussion drifted onto a controversial field, which quickly set Mauch and Murdoch at loggerheads. They soon monopolised the conversation, leaving Wirt and Rintoul on the sideline. Words and expressions were bandied about by the host and the Irishman, which were Greek to Wirt. True, he had read about voodoo and such matters, but paid little heed, and even less credence to it.

Mauch and Murdoch went at it tooth and nail; with gusto at first, degenerating gradually into doggedness. Wirt barely managed to conceal his amazement noticing his otherwise prim colleague breaking out in regular rants. He stubbornly stuck to opinions with a sourness of temper never suspected of the aloof botanist.

Mauch, evidently no slouch in the matter of the occult, gave tit for tat. Though shying away from outright verbal abuse, Wirt deemed their behaviour offensive. He and Rintoul couldn't get a word in, they just sat there in bewilderment, listening to the others' strident argument.

Murdoch bridled up:

"Are you saying that you actually believe such mumbo-jumbo like voodoo or obeah?" he snorted derisively.

Mauch, affecting an air of shocking incredulity, wanted to know:

"Don't you?"

Feeling twitted, Murdoch half rose and bellowed while throwing both hands in the air:

"Old wives' tales, nothing but skulduggery, spread by fools or opportunists intending to lend mystique upon the island, in order to attract adventurers with deep pockets and shallow brainpans."

Looking at Rintoul he asked:

"Am I correct?"

Rintoul nodded eagerly; not because he agreed, but for the sake of peace, since Murdoch had reached a state of temple madness, a blind zealotry unbefitting the occasion. To tell the truth he, and Wirt no less, felt perturbed by the acrimony displayed. Mauch too showed traces of deprecation, judging by his reluctance to continue the discourse.

Afterwards the mood of the party changed; the previous hilarity became overshadowed by a painful awkwardness none could dispel. Murdoch, and to a lesser degree Mauch, remained visibly petulant, especially with each other. Both spoke guardedly about trifling topics; they realised that they had stepped beyond the pale. Observing the others with sheepish eyes and guilty grins, they searched for traces of rebuke. Mauch's the-devil-a-bit attitude gave way to conciliatory inclinations. Being men of the world the previous spirit of good fellowship returned. Murdoch, remembering the duty of a host, regaled the company with his wonted flair. By degrees their festive mood returned; the former exuberance dispersed the remnants of lingering animosity.

Rintoul said it first:

"Time to go, fellows. One for the road, and that's it for me."

The others followed suit; they soon shook hands and left. Rintoul's dwelling stood in an opposite direction to Mauch's and Wirt's, who silently walked side by side, lost in thought, thinking of what should be said. Noticing Mauch's sideways glances, seemingly wrestling with the notion to bridge the silence, Wirt spoke first:

"What is obeah?" he asked.

Mauch, regarding him obliquely, answered evasively:

"It's quite a subject, spectral, and no less disputatious."

"I noticed that while listening to you and Murdoch."

"I warrant you did," Mauch chuckled.

Wirt declared:

"I find it odd that Murdoch, whom I consider to be cool-headed, got all worked up over an innocent debate."

"I wonder," Mauch remarked deliberately.

"Hm, how should that be taken?" Wirt conjectured.

Mauch, halting his steps, thereby compelling Wirt to do the same, cleared his throat several times, then observed:

"As mentioned, obeah is a fascinating, albeit controversial topic, best discussed quietly in a peaceful surrounding."

"Is that an invitation?"

"It's meant to be."

"Well, where shall we meet?"

"At my house, if it suits you."

Seeing Wirt's inquiring look, he added:

"I am a bachelor."

"When?" Wirt asked.

After setting a date and time, and Mauch had explained where he lived, they shook hands and went their ways.

Mysterious Crates

*N*ext morning at sunrise Wirt strolled towards the market. After crossing the bridge the surrounding took on an aspect of a shantytown. Yet, odd to say, the dismal sight did not convey misery; poverty, yes, but not misery. Did the friendly sky over the smiling sea convey an aura of wealth not visible but felt? Was it the unaffected, shy demeanour of the children that overshadowed the shabbiness of the surrounding? Or were the open smiles and animal spirit of young and old causing this delusion? Wirt avowed that he never encountered such laughing eyes and glowing faces in children. They were a treat to watch; observing him from a distance, speaking in whispers, giggling while holding on to each other. When he tried approaching them, they broke out in embarrassed laughter, and scurried off in every direction.

The market was teeming with people, voices resounded from one end to the other. Under temporary shelters sat or stood women of all ages displaying fruits, produce, and handmade wares. They were a noisy, lively lot, devoid of any traces of meekness. Their infectious vivacity brought a smile to Wirt's lips. Most wore hats of various shapes and colours. Their skirts and dresses, sewed invariably with their own hands, embroidered at times, were worn with the air of self-confident women. Not a few were talking with themselves, others exchanged words with passers-by or idle men forever lolling about. The hubbub, as much as the talk in a local dialect, which Wirt did not understand, nevertheless affected him pleasantly. Although he was pretty well the only white person amid a throng of Negroes, no one paid undue attention to him. Curiosity seemed not to be one of their bad habits. Besides, they were too busy to occupy themselves with an unfamiliar face. Making a sale, or wangling a bargain, they found more alluring. Many of the women had walked from their mountain homes, laden with baskets on their heads and under their arms. How they managed to be so chipper amid grinding want and never-ending hardship puzzled Wirt.

His sense of well-being, engendered by the scenery and the peculiar agreeable bustle, was marred by a presentiment of being followed, that refused to yield to reason. Ever since he crossed the bridge he was convinced, or convinced himself, of being furtively pursued. Barely had he reached the southern abutment when he felt a stinging sensation crawling up his spine. Hastening his steps, suppressing an urge to turn around, he continued on his way. Then curiosity got the upper hand; an irresistible impulse induced him to stop and spin around. Nothing suspicious met his eyes; just a few pedestrians, chiefly women and children, were walking behind him. Chuckling to himself for giving in to a baseless notion, he nevertheless hurried towards safer ground.

Having arrived at the market, mingling among people, he heaved an involuntary sigh of relief. As his eyes passed over the displayed products, and his ears perceived the lilt of voices, he forgot his self-delusion. Seeing a native working on a boat at the beach, he decided to take a closer look. Scarcely had he turned his back, when the previous misgiving assailed him again. Someone shadowed him.

"What the deuce," he muttered as he whirled around.

Sure enough, two men unmistakably had him under surveillance. Their feigned concern with the banana boat did not deceive Wirt; they were enjoined to spy on him, by whom he could not even guess. Determined to confront them on the spot, he bridled up. But before he made the first step they scampered. To his chagrin he was unable to obtain a good impression of their features.

Meanwhile the time had arrived to go to the Gardens, which he wanted to reach before Murdoch showed up. To his surprise he was already there, giving instructions to several workers in his inimitable fashion. Wirt was completely ignored; some large boxes claimed Murdoch's undivided attention. His eyes were fixed on one of the crates being opened. Observing his colleague's scowl, his cold stare, and rigid posture, again invoked images of impending dread. There was something ominous about Murdoch's glare that foreshadowed evil intentions. Barking helter-skelter commands in a menacing tone supported Wirt's nascent speculation that Murdoch possibly suffered from untreated psychosis. These bellicose orders, in his opinion, were not given to be carried out, but to assert dominance.

Seeing that he stood in Murdoch's way, Wirt hesitated to ask questions, or offer his assistance. He walked away to attend to unfinished work started yesterday. Yet he couldn't resist casting furtive glances at the little group belaboured by Murdoch, who grew visibly more peevish. He didn't fret and fume, that was not his style, although his frosty bearing and displayed petulance distraught the workers more than a dictator's rant.

Succumbing to an impulse Wirt took another glimpse at the activities beyond. What he saw fanned his curiosity to a level that overshadowed a desire to remain aloof. As if inadvertently he approached Murdoch and the crew. Pretending to be engrossed in work that made him oblivious to his whereabouts, he inched up to them. Why he acted with such circumspection he could not have said, for he was certainly entitled to walk around freely anywhere on the premises; in fact, it was a prerequisite of his job.

As he approached the last crate was being opened. He was struck dumb by what he saw; all were empty, each one had its entire inside lined with copper sheathing. Even the undersides of the plywood lids were treated similar. Murdoch never said a word to him. When he looked up once or twice his face was a mask of animosity, distorted with frightening resentment that spoke louder than words. No doubt he wanted him to go away, but dared not say it. Daunted by his colleague's inimical attitude, Wirt suppressed a desire to talk, then walked towards the other end.

Wirt Is Being Frustrated

*F*ive weeks had passed since his arrival, tedious and nerve-racking weeks, that deemed him like five months, if not longer. He pined for the day when the reins were officially handed to him, and Murdoch had left the island.

Looking at the situation with all the optimism he could gather, Wirt had to admit that he was facing a Sisyphean task. For whatever he did, or attempted to do, Murdoch opposed or countermanded. His good intentions, unstinting dedication, and applied skill, seemed to offend Murdoch more than they pleased him. Wirt's endeavour to give satisfaction was met with disdain and undisguised mockery, of all things. Try as he may to ingratiate himself, Murdoch increasingly rebuffed him, and treated him like an underling. What baffled Wirt particularly was his overt reluctance to acquaint him with the operation. According to him his colleague actually strove to prevent it. This flew in the face of repeated avowals that he looked forward to the day of his departure. He distinctly recalled Murdoch's frequent remarks:

"My dear colleague, I do hope you learn fast."

Not quite comprehending, Wirt initially stated:

"Oh well, the allotted three months should be more than enough to learn the ins and outs of the operation."

Murdoch chuckled:

"I wish you could take over sooner."

"You mean prior to the agreed time?"

"That's my fondest wish," Murdoch reiterated.

Such sentiments, purporting a keen desire to hand over the reins earlier than scheduled, were expressed until recently. But these assertions stood diametrically opposed to Murdoch's puzzling behaviour. Wirt could have sworn that he was intentionally kept in the dark, perhaps in order to prolong a dependence on him. The more Wirt reflected, the more his conviction grew that Murdoch pursued an ulterior motive. Instead of eagerly acquainting him with the Gardens' management, he impeded the progress. Were personal dislikes an underlying factor of this absurdity? Could Murdoch's paradoxical conduct be attributed to a quirk? Or did he have an agenda that Wirt's presence imperilled? No doubt his proximity caused Murdoch undeniable grief, which no amount of studied civility and pretentious gentility managed to conceal. What perturbed Wirt in particular was a sneer etched on Murdoch's countenance when dealing with him lately. He could not banish an impression that he was looked upon as a transient, an unwelcome guest on his way out.

Not a word was uttered anymore about his departure, ostensibly hankered after with every fibre of his being. He acted as if the Gardens would remain under his management for a long time. This was intimated through gestures, insinuations, and eye language. The linchpin and master of the Gardens he was, and would remain, his demeanour expressed.

Wirt grew out of sorts, he felt thrown to the wolves. His views received scant consideration, his recommendations even less. Questions, increasingly asked with heightened shyness, received short shrift, or were ignored. Strange to say the incident with the crates honed Wirt's mettle, he resolved to be more assertive. It irked him to be shown the cold shoulder and driven off with scowls and growls from something that concerned him more than anyone else. True, an innocent explanation might exist for the presence of these mysterious crates, but, nevertheless, he should have been in the know. Especially in view of the considerable costs involved to a small island lacking mineral resources. Copper is not cheap, Wirt knew, especially if formed into sheets. Thinking about Murdoch's secretive conduct raised his hackle; besides, what possible benefit could these crates be to the Gardens? No, he was not going to accept being sent off that easily anymore. As future manager of the facilities, he owed the owners a duty.

When he raised the subject with Murdoch he gaped at him as if dumbfounded by so much temerity. But seeing Wirt's set face, he quickly caught himself. With pursed lips and creased brow, he explained:

"These crates have nothing to do with the premises, they belong to Kew Gardens, whose interest I safeguard.

"But didn't they cede everything to the government?"

"Not so, just the Roseau facilities."

"They own other properties then?"

"They do," followed a brusque answer in a tone of finality.

Despite Murdoch's vexatious attitude Wirt found consolation in the knowledge that he would soon see the last of him. The realisation revived his spirit, as did the assurance that in less than seven weeks he would be the sole manager of the Gardens. Meeting all requirements should not be a concern, for he came well equipped in more than one way. His education and training were known to measure up to the highest standards. Although still relatively young, he had gained practical experience at home and abroad.

Wirt had two major attributes in his make-up: One, moulded by empirical knowledge, the other by the world of books. His ability to instinctively assess situations and events helped him to act promptly and decisively, overly so at times. Unfortunately he had a penchant to enter conflicts head over heels, which sometimes landed him in hot water. Yet so far he always surfaced again, not unscathed, mind you, but he survived. Would he this time? No two ways about it, his dratted enthusiasm had once again landed him in a boiling maelstrom from which he must extricate himself or drown. Forces were lining up against him which he neither completely recognised nor comprehended.

One thing was crystal clear: Someone wanted him to leave the island. Did Murdoch conspire against him on his own volition? Or had he been made a cat's paw? Who could say in view of his colleague's habit of looking one way, yet walk in another direction. His inbred urbanity, one might have thought, should obviate any inclination towards deceit. But what about his eyes, if not his whole mien, which suddenly breaks out in a devilish sneer?

There is only one way to lighten up this murky situation, Wirt decided. Yes, he would take the bull by the horns, confront Murdoch in other words, right now before quitting time. It made no sense to aggravate each other's lives.

"What's your agenda, my dear colleague?" he intended to ask him.

"Am I in your or your handler's way? Then tell me straight what you expect of me. Out with it, we cannot go on like this," he resolved to inform him.

It never got that far, because as he aimed his steps towards the office, a fortuitous sidewise glance diverted his plan. Two figures caught his eyes, who reminded him of the encounter at the market. He felt an impulse to rush at them, but he restrained himself on time. What could he say or do since they were on a public road which, as much as the botanical garden, could be used by anyone, any time. As long as they conducted themselves properly, no one had the authority to shoo them away.

Just the same he couldn't resist strolling inconspicuously towards them. Feigning undivided interest in a row of flower beds, he stepped closer. He wanted to obtain a mental image of their features previously denied him.

With one eye furtively fixed at the two natives, the other scanning the office building and its surrounding, he moved on gingerly. Sure enough he soon perceived Murdoch standing half hidden behind a cluster of shrubs.

"I am being spied on from two sides," whispered Wirt.

Scarcely did the notion enter his mind, when he repudiated it as a paradoxical idea unworthy of consideration. A man of Murdoch's stature would not possibly lower himself to such a level.

"Are these two fellows here again?" Murdoch called out.

"Do you know them?" Wirt asked.

"Not in the least, I thought they were acquainted with you."

"Perish the thought, I have never seen them before," Wirt replied with conviction while turning his head.

The two natives had disappeared.

"Am I seeing you later at sundown?" Murdoch inquired on his way out.

"Sorry, not today, I must catch up on my studies."

"As you wish."

Wirt Visits Mauch

*E*very Friday after work Wirt delved, in a manner of speaking, into Dominica's world of flora and fauna. He felt remiss in his duties, because of over a thousand known species he could barely name two hundred so far. A paltry achievement in his estimation that needed remedy. Like Socrates, he too became painfully aware that the more one learns, the more a man becomes conscious of his ignorance. The island's vegetation possessed a rare diversity not readily found anywhere else in the western world. He resolved not to rest his feet and hands, nor spare his faculties, till most species are represented in the Gardens. He had drawn up workable schemes towards that end which he intended to apply after Murdoch's departure. For he couldn't help thinking that his colleague acted more like a detractor than a supporter of the Gardens' affairs. Despite a far-reaching reputation as an expert in tropical botany, the facilities left much to be desired; in fact, they were in dire strait. Why this overt negligence existed Wirt could not rightly imagine; it might have been attributable to a peculiarity in Murdoch's character, inexplicable as much as unexplainable.

On his way home Wirt felt generally at ease, but not today. He was plagued by a perception of riding on a merry-go-round, trying desperately to get off. Voices rang in his ears, fretful one moment, soothing the next. Presentiments assailed him that made his head spin. What did it all mean? Notions of imminent perils rattled his nerves, sensations of being pursued harried him. All in all he imagined to be dragged towards an inescapable abyss. Once or twice he considered flight; an ignominious retreat deemed him more honourable than this harrowing existence. What induced Murdoch to act so enigmatically? Was he friend or foe? Was his Janus-faced deportment inherent, or simply the precept of a whimsical fate?

Prior to next day's sunset, Wirt knocked at Mauch's door. The house, somewhat apart from the others, stood high above the sea on level ground at the edge of a jungle-like growth. Nothing obstructed the southern view; neither houses nor trees. About a dozen stately palm trees, surrounded by blooming shrubs and bushes stirred in the wind, causing a rustle and sough that touched Wirt agreeably. Below, on the calm, shimmering Caribbean Sea, several sailboats approached the beach. The grounds around the house, lovingly cultivated, engendered a peaceful ambience.

Mauch appeared to be glad to see Wirt, judging by his beaming face and hearty handshake. Despite being greeted effusively, like a long lost son almost, Wirt noticed a measure of decorum appealing to the sympathies. Wirt felt instinctively at home in the publisher's proximity. His mercurial wit, though caustic at times, revived his sorely dampened spirit. An unmistakable sincerity, though tinged with sarcasm, was balm to his heart. Compared to Murdoch's Olympian indifference, Mauch's eagerness felt like a breath of fresh air. He proved to be an enigmatic host, inclined towards Socratic irony one moment, then, as if ruing this, he quickly changed and spoke without a trace of dissemblance. But just the same he couldn't resist to draw the long bow, it was part of his nature.

After preliminary exchanges about trifling matters and observations concerning life in Dominica, Mauch inquired:

"How is the work going?"

"Not too well," Wirt felt tempted to reply, but something in Mauch's manners startled him, for which reason he held his tongue.

What induced him to deliberate and weigh his host's harmless question, posed most likely out of courtesy, puzzled Wirt. Was it a loaded query perhaps serving a sinister purpose? Or was Mauch honestly concerned with his well-being? A prompt reply would have been more appropriate than this embarrassing shilly-shallying, Wirt concluded. Yet he gave an evasive answer:

"Actually not so bad."

"That doesn't sound too convincing," his host remarked.

With a sheepish grin Wirt glanced in every direction except at Mauch.

The unfailing voices of the Dominican night had meanwhile set in. Wirt, still searching for a more suitable answer, found them strident and intrusive this evening. Though desirous to vent his misgivings about his perplexing relations with Murdoch, he remained silent. A little voice from the depth of his being cautioned against telling the truth. Trying to gloss over what secretly bothered him, he changed the subject.

He didn't deceive his host for an instant. While Wirt strove to distract Mauch with small talk, the publisher, in his inimitable fashion, cocked his head and raised his eyebrows. It disconcerted Wirt, who saw images of mischievous imps dancing over his countenance, taunting him to speak of what is burning holes in his tongue.

"Tell us, tell us," the little spectres seemed to wail.

One side of him wanted to unburden his heart, the other counselled to desist. Feeling guilty he reverted to the previous topic:

"I reckon the remark about my work at the Gardens' hasn't impressed you," he offered.

"Not really, I must admit."

"I realise it sounded cryptic and elusive, but in all due respect I'm at a loss what to say. I can no longer separate reality from imagery. The most fitting answer to your initial question would be, I don't know."

Mauch heaved a sigh, indicating that his guest's veiled language fell short of expectation, especially since the circumstances involving Murdoch and the botanical garden were known to him. The grapevine, seldom static in Dominica, was astir for many years with astounding revelations. Murdoch and the Gardens were the talk of Dominica's elite. Something was brewing there, had been for some time, that disconcerted the government and others concerned with the island's reputation.

Mauch, the publisher, felt incumbent to stay abreast with happenings, local and offshore. His profession compelled him to keep his eyes peeled and ears pricked. He had runners on the road whom he called news-sniffers. No doubt, many reports that landed on his desk could be termed spurious, but he had learned long ago to sift the chaff from the wheat. At times he did print dubious articles, yet always with discernible tongue in cheek.

Vile gossip followed Murdoch and the Gardens like the devil pursues a sinner's soul. Wirt, though leery of his colleague, moreover aware of the friction between him and the Burchards, had no inkling of the dire resentment directed towards Murdoch. Not understanding the local dialect, nor being in the confidence of the island's leaders, he was oblivious to what he later learned. The government, businessmen and intellectuals had combined forces to rid Dominica of Murdoch's presence. That wasn't all, he learned; far from it. Accusations were circulating; some covertly, others openly, that Murdoch was up to his eyebrows in the obeah cult, which Wirt, having heard and read about , deemed nothing but arrant nonsense.

To his relief his host interrupted his musing.

"The other evening you inquired about obeah and voodoo," he commented.

"I did," Wirt admitted.

"Are you still interested?"

"Not particularly," he would have liked to respond, but noticing Mauch's eagerness to expound, he prevaricated:

"More than ever," he emphasised with forced enthusiasm.

"Do you read French?"

"With ease."

"In that case I shall procure some books for you on my next trip to Haiti."

"Oh, you are visiting there sometimes?"

"Quite frequently," Mauch assured, then added with a smile:

"Actually I lived there for eight years prior to settling in Dominica. Do you know the place?"

"Only from hearsay and books."

While Mauch signified understanding by nodding several times, Wirt observed:

"Haiti is called the dark island, isn't it?"

Mauch bristled almost imperceptibly. He observed coolly:

"Haiti is not an island, Mr Wirt. As far as darkness goes I suppose you are inferring that the inhabitants are ignorant and wicked. I will defer to someone's judgement that they are poor and ignorant, as far as school learning is concerned, but wicked? I strenuously disagree."

Realising that he had put his foot in it, Wirt grimaced. Annoyed at himself he tried to make amends:

"Of course Haiti is not an island anymore, my tongue hurried on ahead of my brain. But as it may be, I remember reading, not just in one book, mind you, that Haitians practise devil worship, and also that it is the home of voodoo."

A smile hovered around Mauch's lips, ironic in part, but also tinged with condescension. He expounded:

"Don't be so sure about it, these assertions are usually made by people who never set foot on the land, or go there with preconceived notions. Most, if not all, are on guided tours, doing the place on the run, with rum in their veins, and air in their craniums. Driven by desire for exotic experiences, they haste from one tourist attraction to the next. The hotels, recognising a fool when they see one, provide cheap entertainment they call adventure. These speed travellers have neither eyes nor ears for the country's beauty, nor its singular inhabitants. Anyone wishing to savour the unique character of Haiti must live in the mountains for awhile among the peasants. I grant they are poor, but they possess riches no amount of money can equal; they have a soul."

As Mauch talked a peculiar glow illuminated his features; he became transfigured by heartfelt emotions. Wirt, bewildered by his host's mysterious excitement, did not know what to say. But Mauch's prolonged sojourn in Haiti awakened an interest rising above mere curiosity.

"Do you speak Creole?" Wirt asked.

"Most certainly."

"Is it the same as spoken here?"

"Not exactly the same, but quite similar."

Mauch was getting into his stride, he related experiences that took Wirt's breath away.

"I must tell you one thing. For years I scoffed at the idea of voodoo, or anything connected with primitive ceremonies. Of course while living in Haiti I heard and read about it, but didn't give a hoot whether it existed or was just a bugaboo. For a long time I shared Murdoch's denials; not as frenzied, mind you, but I too deemed it nothing but hocus-pocus."

"But no longer, I take it."

"No, no longer," Mauch admitted.

"Hm, could you tell me why?"

Mauch didn't respond straightway. Judging by facial expressions he weighed in his mind what to say. Not wishing to appear overly eager to receive an explanation, Wirt diverted his attention from his host. He pretended to be engrossed with banana shrubs swaying in the wind. Casting glances from the sea to the encroaching jungle, he did not neglect to observe Mauch now and then stealthily from the corners of his eyes. Evidence of Mauch's inner struggle was written on his face. He seemed to vacillate between a desire to speak and the wish to say nothing. Considering his guest closer, as if taking his measure, Mauch spoke slowly:

"A fitting reply to your question cannot be given absolutely, beyond asserting that voodoo does exist in Haiti, and other parts of the West Indies."

"Is it not really a religion?"

"Quite so in my opinion. A strange religion no doubt, unfortunately often associated with sorcery, like obeah and zombiism, thereby degrading it."

"Obeah, zombiism, what is it exactly?" Wirt queried in a deprecatory manner, signifying amusement rather than curiosity.

He appeared to have touched a raw nerve, gathering from his host's reaction, who visibly winced. His countenance acquired an aspect of apprehension. Frowning, his eyes dilated, fidgeting in his chair, he seemed to nerve himself to stave off an attack. Wirt was taken aback by this sudden transformation. He observed Mauch mutely, albeit anxiously. His host's challenging gaze made him uncomfortable, more so when he explained:

"Indeed, do such things exist, one may ask. To take it for the gospel truth overstretches reason, if not sanity. But not everything is mythical that is empirically unexplainable. We accept and repudiate in accordance with our moods, determined by fears, joy, or hope. What one man hails as reality the other deems nothing but fancy."

Wirt was thoroughly baffled by Mauch's ramblings, he listened only with half an ear. As his host kept talking in turns and twists, a disquieting thought befell Wirt: Mauch pursued a hidden agenda, which his convoluted discourse was meant to disguise. He strove to set him onto a path diametrically opposed to his beliefs. No doubt the intention to mislead him lay before him like an open book.

Looking at Mauch closer, pangs of guilt could be gleaned from his countenance. Was he harbouring an awful secret that could harm Wirt? As Mauch went on and on Wirt gained the impression that he was gearing up to give him a hint under the rose, but dared not, for fear to incriminate himself. What a muddle this seemed to be, Wirt told himself.

Facing his host fully, he still heard him talking about incomprehensible things, albeit with more emphasis.

"I often ask myself whether I really saw or heard what indelibly lingers in my memory. I repeatedly catechised, soberly dissected with razor-sharp logic my experiences, to no avail."

Wirt, now as then clueless what his host was aiming at, interrupted slightly irritated:

"What occurrences are you alluding to?"

"Be patient, I will get to it, just bear with me."

Heaving a deep sigh, chortling in overt discomfort, Mauch continued:

"You see, Mr Wirt, what I wish to relate does not roll easily over one's tongue. Don't be shocked, what you are going to hear boggles the mind and strains belief. Coming back to what I said about disproving with ratiocination what I saw. As mentioned it led nowhere. The fact remains I encountered men and women, glassy eyed, moving like robots, tilling the fields of Haiti. They reminded one of mechanical men, paralysed by terror, devoid of a will, being remotely controlled. Ah, I see you bridle. Who can blame you, certainly not I. But hear the rest. If spoken to, these automatons gazed hollow-eyed into space with an expression presaging the beyond, predicting a world only known to themselves. Doctor Janin, my frequent companion, called them the living dead."

"Living dead?" Wirt repeated louder than intended.

"Yes, that's what these deplorable creatures are called. Dr Janin explained everything to me in the comfort of his study. You should be aware that he is not only an esteemed physician, but also an expert in voodooism. He opened the door to an uncanny world, engulfed by hate, ignorance, and wickedness, difficult to describe, saying nothing about believing it. I shall repeat the gist of his narration. Zombies, he said, are dead men walking."

"What do you mean?" Wirt cried.

"They are corpses, buried like others, but there is one significant difference."

"There is?" Wirt expelled.

"They are not dead."

"Are you implying that they are interred while still alive, or have I heard wrong?"

"You heard right. These people are inanimate, but not physically dead. They are in a state of suspended animation. Within forty-eight hours someone disinters and reanimates them with substances prepared by bocors."

"Fiddlesticks, I say," interrupted Wirt.

"I don't blame you for being incredulous, but let me continue with Dr Janin's amazing revelation," Mauch implored.

Wirt, unsure whether the puckish Irishman was making sport of him, squinted while commenting:

"Are you seriously insinuating that such practices exist?"

"I believe they do. How successful these stratagems are, I cannot say."

Noticing Wirt's doubting stare, he advised:

"Remember, I saw these ghostlike beings. Where they came from I do not profess to know, but I can convincingly state that they were working in the fields."

Wirt, raising both hands in protest, remonstrated with his host:

"What possible purpose could these – these machinations serve?"

"Revenge is one consideration; acquiring cheap labour another, according to Dr Janin."

Sawing the air as if miffed, Wirt expostulated:

"You are putting me on, how can dead men work?"

Casting a sympathetic glance at his guest, Mauch remarked:

"That's exactly what I said to Dr Janin."

"What did he answer?"

"His answer was:

" 'They are not dead, just bereft of a soul, so people maintain. Even men of learning do concur with that interpretation.' "

"Does the Doctor believe this rising from the grave?"

"I asked him that."

"What was his reply?"

" 'I take it with a grain of salt, but if obliged to repudiate it I should balk.'

"When I suggested that these workers might be peasants suffering from catatonia, he gestured as if to say:

" 'I have heard that one before.' "

Wirt had heard enough. Fidgeting in his chair he inwardly prepared to leave at the first propitious moment. A growing suspicion grated at his nerves that Mauch meant to lead him astray; he was guided by an ulterior motive. The weird subject didn't make Wirt leery, but his host's fervid style of speech sure did.

Upon noticing Wirt's discomfort, Mauch reached over and put a hand on his arm:

"Make no mistake, not all what you call fiddlesticks is chaff before the wind, otherwise Haiti's criminal code would not contain a most astounding paragraph."

"Which is?"

"Whoever induces suspended animation in someone with drugs, or any other means, is liable to criminal prosecution. Even if that someone is reanimated, it is considered as murder."

Wirt shook his head so vigorously that his whole body trembled. Leaning forward, he queried:

"Are you seriously maintaining that ways and means exist to cause a deathlike condition in a living being, bury him, disinter him several days later, and bring him back to life again?"

"That's what Dr Janin implied."

"But for what reason?"

"As I mentioned already sometimes for revenge, in which case an exhumation is not made; other times for gain."

"To work in the fields without pay?" Wirt suggested with tongue in cheek.

"So it seems," agreed Mauch, a bit nettled by his guest's sarcasm.

Expelling air audibly, Wirt rose. It was time to leave; his head throbbed, and his ears buzzed. Extending his hand, thanking his host for an entertaining and informative evening, they said goodbye. Mauch's parting words stayed with him for a long time.

"Believe what you want, or dare for that matter. Just remember, I saw these so-called walking dead. I shall never forget those vacant stares and wooden movements. The eerie silence that has no name haunts me to this day."

On his way home Wirt could barely put his thoughts in order. Images of spectral shapes, like latter-day golems, stone dead once, brought to life by sorcery, flitted through his mind. Mental pictures arose of men and women, dug from their graves, more phantom than human, on the prowl. He could almost hear stealthy footsteps, see shadowy figures approaching, and feel their fetid breath on his bare neck. Yes, the walking dead were searching for him, to be taken to the sugar cane fields of Haiti.

To divert his attention from these ghastly apparitions, he called Murdoch to mind, particularly that vehement dispute with Mauch. Why did he almost jump out of his skin at the mention of obeah? How could a man, elaborately formal, suddenly lose his composure because of another man's opinion that could not possibly affect him, certainly not deleteriously? Wirt had neither seen his colleague in such a flurried state, nor thought him capable of it. Something was amiss here, terribly so.

A premonition of looming disaster seized him, he felt drawn towards an inescapable vortex. What is this obeah cult at whose hint a staid scientist turns into a ranting Herod? No doubt the wily Irishman goaded him, but still, for a man settled in habit and manner to fly into a rage over a trivial matter, egged on or not, seemed worrisome. But is it a trivial matter? Wirt expostulated with himself. More than likely not, he presumed. Take Mauch's cryptic remark: 'I wonder,' made in an insinuating tone, resonant with mockery.

In retrospect he rued his precipitate departure just now. Mauch, surely in the know, would have gladly elaborated. He did mention in passing that Dominica, especially the remote mountainous regions, is haunted by bizarre rites and observances. Obeah is one of them, more insidious than the others, which the government is trying to root out. Well, there would be other opportunities to query the publisher, or even Murdoch.

"How dark it is tonight," Wirt suddenly noticed.

Neither the moon nor a single star shed a ray of light. His inner gloom of course accentuated the blackness around him.

The notion of turning around struck him. Going back to Mauch, excuse his hasty retreat, and broach the subject of obeah. After all the hour was not late yet; besides, he felt apprehensive to be alone in his house.

It was not meant to happen, because when he turned around he saw scurrying shadows, barely discernible in the dim light, yet raising his anxiety. Hardly did he try to get a closer look, when they disappeared.

What did this mean? Was he being spied on again, or did his overwrought mind play him a trick? Not so, he soon found out. The perceived silhouettes proved to be natives who hesitantly stepped forth. Were they about to attack him?

"Perish the thought," he murmured, for he remembered that assaults or hold-ups were pretty rare in this peaceful island.

Anyway, trying to rob him would have been senseless, as anybody with half an eye could see. A man scantily clad, holding neither bag nor purse would hardly warrant the risk to commit robbery upon. No, Wirt surmised, their lurking served a more sinister purpose.

Suddenly he felt a column of hot anger rising within him. Engendered no doubt by his initial apprehension, spurred by the effects of copious liquor consumption, his ire could not be contained. Casting caution into the wind, he snortingly hurled himself towards his presumed pursuers, who fled with surprising alacrity. In no time they vanished amid a cluster of houses.

Wirt, getting into his stride, could not be deterred; like an enraged bull he roared after them. He raced around every house within sight, while uttering bloodcurdling threats. Gradually doors and windows opened, angry voices demanded what was going on. Stimulated by his own clamour, Wirt got all keyed up. Forgetting good manners, dignity, and shame, he bellowed at the top of his lungs:

"Come on out, you cowards, show your faces like a man, you miserable cravens."

Seemingly from nowhere appeared a portly woman, no longer young, raven-black, who approached him resolutely. Stopping at some distance, gazing at him inquiringly, she started to sway her hips in a provocative fashion.

Wirt's first impulse was to take to his heels, thinking the woman was either unsound or drunk. While he still wavered whether to walk away or remain, more women, mostly elderly, showed up, who also commenced swinging in that alluring rhythm. While never ceasing to shake their hips and move their arms in the hula-hula fashion of Hawaiian dancers, they formed a circle around him. Some started to sing in their local dialect, while others encouraged him to join in. Struck dumb, Wirt cast bewildered glances in every direction. He felt strange sensations crawling up his back, especially when a woman, younger than the rest, stepped forward with flashing eyes and sparkling teeth. Her seductive demeanour attracted and repulsed him simultaneously. While tempting him with suggestive gestures and movements, she spread her arms wide:

"Come to my bosom, darling, don't be shy."

Wirt, uncertain what to do or say, dared not look at the seemingly enraptured woman, ostensibly trying to seduce him. Ill at ease, beset by bashfulness and trepidation, he searched for a place to hide. Was he dreaming, or did this Messalina indeed invite him to her boudoir? Were they merely teasing him out of impishness, perhaps trying to fluster the white man? Or did they attempt to send a more ominous message?

As the swaying and singing women continued their strangely sensuous performance, Wirt felt an eerie prickle getting the better of him. The cool, soft night air took on a stifling sultriness, the voices of the Caribbean sounded like Cassandra's warning cries. Turning abruptly he fled. Ignoring the guffaws sent after him, dead to the alluring calls of the women, he hastened towards his house on the hill, where he speedily locked doors and shut windows.

In the morning things looked friendlier. Surrounded by sweet scents, blooming vegetation, and pleasant expectations, his spirit rose. By the time the sun had climbed over the mountains his misgivings vanished like gossamer in autumnal winds.

Today was Sunday; time to rest and contemplate, and seek a reunion with one's better self. He resolved to confront happenings with shrugs and smiles today, no matter how unpleasant they might appear to be. Disquieting thoughts he determined to make short shrift of. Only notions on the wings of joy and hope were allowed to enter his mind. His brow, he vowed, would remain unruffled from now on, and his lips uncurled.

Feeling buoyed up by this resolution, his sight became keener, and his hearing more acute. He ate breakfast on the veranda overlooking the river and the city. Eating leisurely, he savoured every morsel that touched his palate. While revelling in the wondrous world of contentment, the sough in the trees and bushes, the rush of the river carried his thoughts to lofty heights. He spent the entire day walking around the garden, humming to himself. At times, sitting in his favoured chair under rustling palm trees, he reminisced about the past. Odd it seemed, but his hometown where he spent his formative years, which he left only three months ago, had almost fallen into oblivion. The realisation made him feel guilty. Pangs of disloyalty beset him; his conscience tried to make amends, but failed dismally. How can one not pine for the land of one's birth, kith and kin left behind, and sacred memories after an absence of so short a time? he was reminded. Plagued alternately by guilt and angry rationalisation, Wirt shooed such reveries away.

Murdoch Flip-Flops

*M*onday turned out to be a day as most others, with one difference: Murdoch conducted himself surprisingly conciliatory, a fact that eased Wirt's mind. All will go well, he told himself, while attempting to fend off recurring scruples. Shortly before quitting time, he asked Murdoch:

"Does your invitation for sundowners still stand?"

"Most certainly, you are welcome every evening."

"How about tonight?"

"I shall keep the glasses tempered."

About thirty minutes prior to sundown Wirt walked up the steps to Murdoch's house, which might soon be his. After the usual preambles their conversation drifted from politics to local occurrences as reported in the weekly newspaper.

Finally they ended up speaking about the work at the botanical garden. Immediately Murdoch's attitude changed; he became formal, ruminant, and generally frosty. When the talk touched on his impending departure, Murdoch drew himself up as if stung. Frowning down on Wirt, he let it be known that the subject couldn't possibly be of any interest to anyone. Confused, and somewhat cowed, Wirt avoided the topic, he talked of less sensitive matters.

"Can you give me some directions how to conduct myself after takeover? Are there any set rules to be heeded?" he inquired.

Murdoch's response to this innocuous query could best be described as peculiar. Making a wry face as if annoyed, startled at first, then squinting as though imposed upon, he uttered not a word. A sardonic smile appeared on his countenance while obviously weighing an answer. Deciding to put a good face upon whatever bothered him, he said:

"No set rules I know of govern, one must take things as they arise, use one's own judgement in other words. Some days nothing turns out well, everything undertaken goes awry. But that can't be helped."

Reflecting for a moment, he continued:

"Of course, without the ongoing meddling by unqualified busybodies, life would be easier."

"Who is meddling?"

"A few know-it-all, foremost the honourable president," Murdoch grumbled.

"Mrs Burchard?" Wirt inquired overtly at sea.

"No other. It's a vexing fact. Since the government took over the Gardens, torrents of difficulties have been cascading onto my shoulders. My joy and interest in the property took a nose dive, and I am not the only one saddled with that predicament. To make matters worse, they appointed the premier's wife honorary president. Honorary my eye," Murdoch snorted.

"I don't understand," Wirt remarked.

"It's a slap in the face," Murdoch emphasised.

Noticing Wirt's eagerness to hear more, he expounded:

"She treats the Gardens as a private fief to be used at her discretion, sole discretion I should say."

Wirt, seemingly not agreeing with this assessment, protested quickly:

"I haven't noticed any interference on Mrs Burchard's part."

The comment evoked a snicker from Murdoch:

"Of course not. First, she is accompanying her husband on an extended trip overseas; second, she is not going to show her claws before they get you tied down good-and-ready. Anyway, let me continue. Barely did the ink dry on the announcement of her nomination as honorary president, when she came rummaging through the grounds like a Caledonian Boar. Talk about the nose this woman has, she pokes into every nook and cranny looking for evidence."

"Evidence?" Wirt echoed.

"Exactly. She acts like a sleuth on an assignment."

"That sounds odd, since to my knowledge honorary titles exist in name only, entailing limited authority and duties," Wirt commented.

"I quite agree, but someone should inform Mrs Burchard of this fact," Murdoch stated irately.

Try as he may, Wirt couldn't banish the impression that his colleague's diatribe, besides venting his spite on the minister's wife, served another, weightier purpose, somehow aimed at him. Yet he failed to see a connection, nor did he have an inkling what Murdoch was driving at. But, by jingo, he was aiming at something, and strenuously so, gathering from his arcane deportment.

"You said a moment ago that Mrs Burchard is looking for evidence," Wirt reminded.

"Indeed, I did."

"Could you elaborate?"

"She snoops around the property expecting to find proof supporting vile suspicions she, among others, entertains."

"Suspicions about what?" Wirt asked puzzled.

"A presumed scheme aimed at Dominica's vilification, as far as I understand. One cannot help thinking otherwise. She rifles through files, ransacks drawers and boxes trying to find what?" Murdoch spat while staring at Wirt defiantly.

"Hm, search me," Wirt replied.

Dissatisfied with the noncommittal response, Murdoch fired another broadside at his presumed nemesis:

"You may think I am drawing the long bow, but let me tell you, Mauch and I are betting that one day she will climb up those tall palm trees to tap the coconuts for hollow spots. To what purpose you ask? Perhaps to find inside evidence of a cabal directed against the island."

Wirt, though at sixes and sevens, couldn't help smiling at the thought of a stout, dignified woman of middle years, clambering up slender trunks of palm trees. Picturing the matronly Mrs Burchard dangling from limbs high above

ground, holding on for dear life with one hand, sounding
coconuts with the other, made him break out in laughter. Even
Murdoch, cross as he was, couldn't suppress a chuckle.

"Am I wrong in suggesting that Mrs Burchard is not one
of your favourites?"

"You are not," Murdoch answered morosely.

Both men remained silent for a while, keeping their
thoughts to themselves. Wirt sensed that Murdoch had
something on his mind, judging by appearances. His awkward
movements, clearing of throat, and unsteady glances intimated
as much. He manifestly tried to overcome his inherent
reticence, as much as an acquired reluctance to speak his mind.

Visibly embarrassed he cast sideways glances from Wirt
to the sea, where rolling waves broke rhythmically on the
beach. Any attempt to steer the halting talk towards his
impending retirement was met with icy stares and furrowed
brow. At the slightest attempt to speak about Wirt's upcoming
takeover, Murdoch bristled. He grew fidgety, rose from his
chair, and started to walk around aimlessly, pretending to
stretch his legs.

Wirt realised that his manoeuvre was meant to divert
attention from himself and the Gardens. Smiling inwardly he
reluctantly obliged; he switched to a more innocuous topic.
Murdoch, as if by chance, returned to his seat. There and then it
occurred to Wirt that his colleague harboured no intention to
leave the island soon, if at all.

Meanwhile rain started to fall. It quickly came down in
buckets, then stopped suddenly. Shortly after a cool breeze
wafted down from the mountains, carrying in its wake a
fragrance reminiscent of Mauch's garden.

"Ah, there is that sweet scent again," Wirt remarked,
while glancing inquiringly at his host, who said that it derives
from the cashimar tree.

"Are you referring to the cashimar zombi?" Wirt asked.

Did his eyes deceive him, or had Murdoch indeed
recoiled? Averting Wirt's surprised look, lowering his head,
shifting from side to side as if trying to avoid a blow, he
temporised:

"That's what the peasants up in the mountains call it, but I wouldn't pay any heed to their prattle, if I were you."

That's a curious reply, I would say, Wirt thought, rendered more peculiar by Murdoch's grimace indicating closing of the subject.

Wirt had no intention to back down, instinctively he sensed the reason for his host's punishing glances.

"I bet the word zombie makes him fretful," he mused.

"Does the tree bear fruit?" Wirt asked.

Annoyed, yet desirous of being a good host, Murdoch explained:

"Yes. Sort of apples not fit for human consumption, not to white men anyway. Some birds even avoid them."

Wirt was set to pursue the subject despite Murdoch's defensive stance. He posed another question:

"What does zombie actually mean? Is it in any way connected with that notorious cult you and Mauch were arguing about?" Wirt inquired with a cherubic air, knowing full well his host's repugnance towards even a whiff of the supernatural.

Murdoch shook his head emphatically. Dropping the corners of his mouth disdainfully, he vented scathing condemnation:

"It's supposedly a West African deity, according to the lore of the locals, who in my opinion don't know tip from tap. In any case the cashimar zombi tree is in no way linked with voodoo or obeah, which is nothing but a fancy nesting in soft brains. Such mummery is utterly unseemly for a European to dabble or believe in. Mauch has been duped by unscrupulous operators, and too much Haitian absinthe."

Silence reigned for a short while, it hung heavily in the room. Murdoch straightened himself up at times, slumped down again, hemmed and hawed, but said not a word. Then he blurted out what lay on his tongue all evening:

"By the way, I have a favour to ask of you."

"Aha," Wirt said to himself, "he is finally going to spit out the bone in his craw."

"I will gladly grant it, provided it's within my power."

"You remember those crates, I take it?"

"You mean the copper lined ones?"

"The same."

Murdoch came to the point:

"I should appreciate if the incident remained between us. The reason, quite insignificant, can be explained if you wish. Anyway, it was a wrong shipment which has been returned promptly. Making that erroneous delivery hawkers news, while seemingly irrelevant, can cause considerable harm in this case."

Wirt unhesitatingly assented. Then assured his colleague that he neither mentioned it to a single soul so far, nor harboured a thought to do so. Seeing Murdoch heaving a sigh of relief, he added:

"I am not a tattler by nature anyway, nor a dissembler. Admittedly those crates troubled me a bit, as can be readily understood. But since they are on the way to the intended consignee, I have no more compunctions."

Murdoch, pretending to be nonchalant about the matter, nevertheless appeared to be self-conscious, judging by his next words:

"Why I concern myself with such trifling matters you will soon find out, when the scales fall from your eyes."

"Oh, when might that be?"

"At the impending committee meeting. You will be asked a hundred asinine and intrusive questions. Mark my word, when the Burchards return they will pump you dry."

"Pumping me, about what?"

"Myself mainly, I suspect."

Noticing his guest's searching gaze, Murdoch elaborated:

"They are frantically seeking a scapegoat, a whipping boy to hide their own incompetence. Every adversity befalling the botanical garden, no matter how trivial, is attributed to my supposed inadequacy, if not nefariousness. No doubt you have noticed the grounds' neglected condition, but the circumstances responsible for it have probably eluded you. Money, plus other considerations are essential to maintain, let alone improve an operation like this, especially if no revenue accrues from it. Co-operation by various factions is necessary, good will even more. Nothing prospers in an atmosphere of malevolence."

"The property has only recently been acquired by the government, I understand."

"About a year ago. A very tedious, long year, I might add."

"It's been taken over from Kew Gardens, I think."

"Yes, I am still under contract with them; in fact, I manage all their concerns on the island. As you are properly aware Kew Gardens is obliged to maintain a capable administrator at the site, till the government finds a suitable replacement.

"Which they have done now, I hope," interrupted Wirt.

Murdoch's response surprised and dismayed Wirt. He tilted his head from side to side while raising his eyebrows, as if to say: "I am not so sure."

What a tactless gesture that is, Wirt thought, unworthy of a mature scientist. A notion took hold of Wirt which he wanted to verify.

"Are you not employed with the government?" he asked.

"Never have been."

"Hm, I will be the first government administrator then of the Gardens."

Murdoch's behaviour, incomprehensible at the time, soon acquired significance. Lifting his head abruptly he considered Wirt with an expression on his face that could only mean one thing: "You are not there yet."

Then his host screwed up one eye, lowered the other, while his lips curled in a sneer. Taken aback, Wirt instinctively looked aside. Were the sibilant sounds real or a figment of his imagination? Did Murdoch whisper: "Not on your life," or had the wind sighed in the bushes? Glossing over his arcane and rude conduct just now, Murdoch became more agreeable. He talked about trifles in an affable manner. Showing a flicker of resentment, Wirt commented:

"What you say is all well and good, but I would like to find out more about Dominica's vegetation, that's were my interest lies."

"Perhaps so, but maintaining that interest may be difficult," Murdoch suggested.

"I suppose," Wirt granted unconvinced.

"True, the island is blessed with a unique flora, which regrettably thrives mostly in remote and inaccessible places. Finding and transplanting them can be toilsome and time-consuming."

Wirt, unable to repress a deprecating smile, gave his opinion:

"Well, tenacity and tirelessness are requisite to a botanist, aren't they?"

"No doubt, but eagerness flags in the best of us if harried by incessant carping and interference. But enough of that, let's turn to more agreeable matters, like heaving a few."

Murdoch appeared to have divested himself of a burden; he became lively and talkative. To Wirt's astonishment he steered the conversation towards obeah and voodoo.

"You are aware of my views concerning these mummeries, but just the same I'm willing to expound their meaning, should you wish."

Staring at his colleague in disbelief, Wirt commented carefully:

"Your views have been emphatically stated. I do share your sentiments to some degree, albeit with less fervour. Nevertheless, I'm anxious to learn more about these mysteries. Mauch promised to secure some books for me dealing with these topics."

"He might forget," his host suggested in a significant tone.

"Quite possible, besides, he may not take another trip to Haiti for a long time. Anyway, you were going to explain that obeah cult to me."

"How about a draught or two first, because what you are going to hear requires advance fortification."

Wirt, wondering why Murdoch offered to speak of things declared loathsome a moment ago, considered him closer. What could have possibly induced him to overcome the fierce resentment towards anything smacking of obiism, he couldn't imagine offhand. Just hinting at the subject enraged him; till now that is. Yet all of a sudden he volunteered to go into details about it, with unconcealed glee to boot. Wirt couldn't help thinking that Murdoch was struck by an idea that contained the solution to a vexing problem. It rendered him more amenable, smoothened his brow, and made his eyes light up.

"I am all ear," reminded Wirt.

"Obeah is a curse, intended to do away with enemies by heinous methods. It may be nothing but a laughable superstition to everyone, except the victim, who suffers a slow and painful death."

Wirt couldn't resist raising his eyebrows and cocking his head. Murdoch, pretending not to have noticed his guest's manifestation of incredulity, posed a question:

"Did you ever hear of secouyas?"

"Not that I recall. Who, or what are they?"

"Old women, wrinkled from head to toe, merciless and vicious as only beldams dare to be, with a reputation eclipsing that of Beelzebub. Up in the mountains the peasants swear that she throws a shadow of evil, which brings a slow and tortuous death to anyone coming into its influence."

"Influence?" echoed Wirt.

Yes. It is a bit involved, I will explain it another time. The secouya hawks charms, portends omens, and generally keeps the community in awe."

"Sounds innocent so far," remarked Wirt.

"No doubt it does. It's been done for ages on a much larger scale. But here is the salient feature."

Murdoch cast sidewise glances at his guest, testing him as it were, whether he could handle the revelations he was about to hear:

"Let's suppose you wished somebody dead."

"Don't we all at times?" Wirt chuckled.

"Perhaps so, but it seldom leads anywhere, except to our own grief, contrary to the obeah practice, where the wish can become the father to the deed. I will expound how it works. Someone, desiring a person's demise, obtains an article of clothing worn close to the victim's skin and takes it to a secouya, who does the rest."

"She dabbles in fetishism in other words," Wirt observed.

"Not exactly, but wait till you hear the rest. That piece of clothing is offered as a charm bestowing eternal bliss to a deceased if taken to her or his grave. I see you shrugging your shoulders indicating boredom, or diffidence perhaps. Here is the meat of the matter. From the moment the garment lies with the corpse in the coffin, the intended victim falls ill, terribly so. It soon becomes apparent that he or she suffers from a wasting malady which no doctor, quack, or holistic practitioner can diagnose, not to mention cure. As the corpse decays in its grave, so does the life drain from the accursed person's body. They always die a miserable death."

"But that's impossible," Wirt cried.

The outburst earned him a rebuking glance that made him cower. Murdoch had more to say:

"Of course corpses aren't always available, in which case the secouya soaks the garment in a tincture of her own brew that decomposes the fabric fairly quick, thereby producing the same effect as if buried with the corpse; with one difference, however."

"Which is?" Wirt asked against his better judgement.

"An element of uncertainty plagues that method, because the afflicted person finds and unearthes the buried pot at times."

Wirt felt like bursting out in peals of laughter, but desisted.

"I must hand it to you, that's quite a tale, worthy of a rollicking Munchauseade."

Seeing his host's stern look, Wirt tried to smoothen things over:

"Does any reasonable man lend credence to such shenanigans?" he inquired.

Murdoch examined his colleague with unabashed distaste. He was sizing him up prior to continuing. As he delved back into the same theme, Wirt sat there like a man riveted to the spot. An inner struggle ensued between reality and phantasm that gradually gained the upper hand. Common sense took a back seat to imagery. Murdoch's demeanour acquired an eagerness difficult to describe, even more so the cause of his opinion's reversal. He acted like a man with a mission, anxious to convince rather than enlighten. Glaring at his guest he exclaimed:

"It might seem absurd to you, yet it happens all over the island."

Noticing Wirt's sceptical look and intention to say something, Murdoch raised a hand:

"I am speaking from experience, these practices exist, they are performed right under our noses."

Wirt felt his flesh creep; not on account of Murdoch's absurd narration, but his feverish effort to defend this sudden contradictory conviction. Gripped by an eagerness, deemed messianic by Wirt, Murdoch plunged deeper and deeper into the muddle of obiism.

Thoroughly bewildered, transfixed would describe it better, Wirt listened. How the same man, who vehemently denounced esoteric notions a short while ago, now ardently proclaimed their existence, boggled his mind. What had turned the furious denier of anything occult into an instant mystic? Murdoch didn't relent, nothing short of a thunderbolt could have stopped him. His voice, one moment high-pitched, the next sepulchral, made Wirt uncomfortable. Worse, he felt a stinging sensation crawling up his spine, while a growing desire urged him to flee.

Sitting there awe-struck, he endured his host's attempt to convince him of obeah's reality. Appalled at Murdoch's about-face Wirt's thoughts reverted to his heated dispute with Mauch, when he rabidly negated what he now zealously vindicated. More than once he wanted to ask:

"What is happening here? A moment ago you decried obeah as arrant mummery, and now you declare it factual."

Yes, Wirt wanted to pose that question; yet, as strange as it appears, he dared not. Was Murdoch trying to be sportive? Had he taken a drop too much, or perhaps become delirious? None of it, Wirt decided. No, his host's sudden turnabout is the result of a brain wave which had just entered his head. Murdoch is setting me up, he concluded, the whole spectacle serves but one purpose: to soften me up, as it were; for what, he couldn't imagine.

"The fear, terror I should say, of becoming a victim of obiism is real. Some take their own life upon sensing the curse's sting; others flee to the remotest corner of the island, hoping distance will mitigate or remove the bane."

Wirt, unable to restrain his curiosity, asked a question that lay burning on his tongue. At the first lapse of Murdoch's verbosity, he said with tongue in cheek:

"Perhaps my predecessor's disappearance is attributable to this obeah business?"

Murdoch showed no signs of having heard. Wirt had to repeat it twice, plus more emphatically, before his host reacted; with scarce enthusiasm, it should be added. Nevertheless, he made an effort to tear himself from a trance-like state. Like a medium casting off the effects of a séance, his face mirrored disorientation. Glowering at Wirt, he responded irritably:

"What did you just say?"

"It was meant to be a quip, but on second thought it might have substance. I implied that there may be a connection between Nantes' vanishing act and this obiism."

"The possibility exists."

"Has he ever voiced any complaints?"

"Not to me," came a brusque reply.

He is up to something, it flashed through Wirt's mind. My upright, stuck-up colleague is hatching a nefarious scheme, which out of the blue occurred to him an hour ago.

Conspirators Meet

*B*y far the most imposing structures in Dominica are the government buildings. On either side of the impressive mansion are attached three small, round-roofed buildings. The little complex exudes an old-world charm, balm to the soul. The perimeter lawn, always green and well cared for, is covered with trees, flowering shrubs, and blossoming flowers. The view from anywhere on the property invites one to linger. The open, park-like grounds exude an unforgettable serenity. The stately palm trees, stretching boldly towards the sky, give the spirit a lift. The never failing trade wind makes the fronds tilt and lift in regular intervals, producing a rustle soothing to the mind.

A conference was about to take place in one of the government's offices. Mrs Burchard, the honorary president of the botanical garden, had invited Brunt, the chief of police, for coffee, to discuss pressing concerns she could not banish from her mind. She had a lot on her mind; her woman's intuition, that inner voice, spoke louder than cold reasoning. Ominous incidents nudged her into action. She had no confidence in Robert Murdoch, and even less trust. He lacked ability in her opinion, plus uprightness of character. Wherever one looked, she maintained, glaring neglect and signs of mismanagement of the Gardens stared one in the eyes. Even more worrisome she considered blatant irregularities, pointing to fraudulent manipulations. Despite her husband's suggestion that she divined more than what could be seen, she felt incumbent to investigate.

Mr Brunt stood by her, although his suspicions too rested on flimsy evidence, unable to weather closer scrutiny. He disliked his countryman wholeheartedly. The reason, kept to himself, could easily be guessed at. Their divergent characters, as much as physical appearances, could have been the culprits. Contrary to Murdoch, Brunt looked and behaved un-British. Besides being portly, blustery, and expansive, he called a spade a spade to his countryman's chagrin, who winced at the notion. His language, couched and deliberate, stood in crass contrast to the chief's off the cuff expressions. Brunt liked an earthy joke, as did Mrs Burchard. Back-slapping amity and railleries were the chief's trademarks. Needless to say Murdoch turned up his nose at such bucolic deportment.

Like two conspirators Brunt and Mrs Burchard furtively glanced in every direction, as though suspecting an eavesdropper hidden somewhere. Ignoring the rush in the bushes and trees, they turned to the business at hand. Mrs Burchard poured coffee, then pointing at a bottle of brandy said:

"I haven't forgotten."

Yes, she was aware of the chief's predilection for strong drink which, he maintained, enlivens the spirit. Mrs Burchard explained the reason for their get-together.

"My concern is a property in Sylvania," she stated.

"I know the area," Brunt acknowledged.

"But not the spot I am alluding to, I take it."

"Not really," the chief admitted, feeling somewhat sheepish, since the location had been pointed out to him several times.

"Who owns it?" he asked.

"Kew Gardens of London, England."

"You are interested in it, I presume?"

"The government is, they intend to purchase the land."

Screwing up his face, the chief inquired:

"What's the hurdle?"

"Robert Murdoch who, to our dismay, has an option on the place, which he stubbornly refuses to forego."

"Has he been made an offer?"

"More than one, but they all fall on deaf ears. The most generous terms suggested meet with a cold shoulder."

"I wonder why?"

"So do we, since the property, being remote, and barely accessible, has no commercial value worth mentioning."

"Why is the government interested then?"

Mrs Burchard reflected, seemingly unsure what to say. Reaching for her handbag wherein she thumped through, she fished out some papers, which she handed to Brunt with the words:

"Here is a copy of an agreement between Kew Gardens and our illustrious botanist. Peruse it and tell me what you think."

Brunt, a slow reader, took his time. He read with little enthusiasm; at first that is. Soon he became more engrossed, as evidenced by his facial expressions, altering from indifference to eagerness. Cocking his head, drawing his brow into folds, he murmured:

"That's an odd agreement."

"A sweetheart deal in my opinion," Mrs Burchard emphasised.

Bending forward, reaching for the bottle, pouring himself a liberal measure, the chief wondered:

"Why has the property not been transferred yet to Murdoch's name?"

"Because the government blocks it."

Casting a knowing glance at her, Brunt proposed:

"It wouldn't be on your behest perchance?"

"Now, now, Mr Brunt," she chuckled, more pleased than offended.

As pointed out the chief of police liked to call a spade a spade, and a fig a fig. Besides, he dotted his i's and crossed his t's.

"I'm baffled, to say the least, perhaps you can enlighten me. But first, how did you get hold of these papers, surely not meant to be blazoned abroad?"

Mrs Burchard hemmed and hawed in obvious embarrassment.

"Does the premier know about this?"

Sensing her reluctance to answer, Brunt barked:

"I am honourable you should know. Besides, in my profession a telltale would soon become a lame duck."

"He is using me as a proxy," Mrs Burchard advised.

"To what end?"

"To prevent Murdoch from acquiring the Sylvania property."

Brunt, a fair man, and easily approachable, abhorred secretiveness. Looking squarely at Mrs Burchard he demanded to know:

"What do you want from me?"

"I will come to that. But may I first ask your opinion about Murdoch's options?"

"It's not an option, but a transfer of ownership, incontestable to my mind, as your legal department undoubtedly knows."

Mrs Burchard winced under the chief's reproving stare that seemed to say:

"You are not so ignorant, madam, to be oblivious to the fact."

She wasn't. Yet feigning obtuseness in legal matters deemed her an appropriate stratagem to draw Brunt out, who ceased frowning as he commented:

"Even though the conveyance does seem suspect, it is valid."

"What do you find debatable?"

"The transfer neither mentions a purchase price nor a time-limit, which I find unusual."

"Suspiciously so," Mrs Burchard agreed.

"You are drawing inferences, by the sound of it," Brunt commented.

"Yes, we do," she granted, yet did not elaborate.

Brunt, growing more bewildered by the minute, barely able to contain his impatience nor irritation because of Mrs Burchard's beating about the bush, came to the point:

"The government is blocking the takeover you say. I therefore presume that Murdoch is unable to obtain legal title to the property."

"So far, yes."

Brunt, shaking his head, reflecting for a moment, asked:
"How did they manage it?"

"By declaring the Sylvania holding a historic site, thereby negating ownership by non-permanent residents."

"When was this ordinance introduced?"

"Prior to the issuing of the transfer."

Brunt, quick on the uptake, cast an approving glance at the premier's wife, who lowered her eyes in feigned modesty. They both smiled; Brunt out of respect, Mrs Burchard because of the silent homage paid her.

"In other words over four years ago."

"Four years and four months, to be exact."

Brunt started the devils tattoo on the table. He observed matter-of-factly:

"Permanent residency is acquired after five years continuous legal domicile."

"Of course," Mrs Burchard agreed.

"But Murdoch, a British subject, is not effected by this rule, or at least shouldn't be," Brunt protested.

Mrs Burchard, observing him shrewdly, remarked quietly:

"No matter, the transfer remains blocked."

"The whole thing looks like trumpery to me," Brunt intimated.

"Maybe so, but it is nevertheless effective."

"What is Murdoch saying to all this?"

"Quite a bit."

"I mean what is he doing about it?"

"He threatens with litigation of course which, according to our lawyers, he would win hands down."

Brunt concurred:

"I reckon so."

Mrs Burchard tilted her head in the manner of a slyboots, she seemed to think otherwise:

"Perhaps you and the lawyers have a point, but let me remind you we are not exactly shooting with wet powder."

"Meaning?"

"We got an ace or two up our sleeves, evidenced by a simple fact."

"Which is?"

The interdiction is in force over four years. I ask you, why is Murdoch not trying to have it annulled?"

"Hm, you have a point there," the chief granted.

"Anyway, Murdoch has given us a deadline now to have the restriction removed within four weeks, or suffer the consequences."

"He is going to sue, in other words."

"Yes," Mrs Burchard replied.

The chief's countenance expressed dubiousness.

"Frankly, I believe the man is bluffing. For reasons known to him he dares not to proceed. I can tell you from experience court cases can be stressful, if not dangerous to one's health."

"Especially if one has skeletons in the closet," Mrs Burchard assented.

"No doubt," Brunt agreed.

Mrs Burchard reflected on the chief's opinion, then said:

"You may be right, but we are averse to take that chance. We must ensure that the Sylvania property does not end up in Murdoch's hands."

Brunt signalled consent by nodding several times. He divined which way the wind blew. Mrs Burchard, the government's unofficial representative, has been enjoined to engage him in devious activities. Raising a hand as if asking for time out, he declared:

"I have to stir up my brain a bit."

Saying so, he reached for the brandy bottle, which he lifted invitingly towards Mrs Burchard, who shook her head.

"Are you sure you don't want to share my pleasure? Drinking by oneself is boring," he commented, while tempting her again in a prankish manner that made her break out in soft laughter.

She was partial to Brunt. She liked roguish men who knew how to court a woman; discretely that is.

Having emptied the first snifter, smacking his lips, glancing appreciatively at Mrs Burchard, he poured himself a second one. Again he raised the bottle and tilted it towards her, then bowed gallantly when she refused. Shrugging his shoulders he said:

"I take it you are out to enlist my help?"

"That's correct."

"To do what?"

"Get Murdoch off the island."

"That's a tall order. To begin with he has contravened no laws, nor is declared an undesirable. What shall I impute him with, except arrogance and incompetence perhaps? That will not suffice, as little as innuendoes or baseless allegations."

"What about moral turpitude?" she suggested.

Raising his eyebrows while observing her closer, he demurred:

"I don't understand."

"Isn't he a proponent of obeah?" she insinuated.

Brunt snorted:

"Claptrap! nothing but malicious rumours. His hands may not be clean in that respect, but what of it? Dabbling in necromancy is not a crime in Dominica. Accusing him thus would make the lawyers laugh; charging him might engender merriment in the dourest judge."

"But isn't practising obeah an indictable offence?" she wondered.

"Not really. Our laws are rather vague concerning voodoo, or any form of black magic. Unless of course someone has been, or demonstrable will be harmed by such practices. But I can tell you no crown prosecutor will charge anyone who supports or performs obiism."

"But isn't obeah synonymous with murder?" she protested.

"Not in itself. We must proof malicious intent to injure, or to have injured someone with this abracadabra. How can we do that, I ask you?"

Receiving no reply, the chief continued:

"Take the case in Bassinville five years ago, where a youngster by the name of Medvil died under mysterious circumstances. Our investigation unearthed some curious facts: Medvil, a picture of health, vigorous mentally, robust physically, suddenly became ill and quickly wasted away. Neither medicine nor physician's care were able to arrest the sickness, let alone heal it."

"I remember, he died," fell in Mrs Burchard.

"Contentions that he was done away with the help of obeah by a rival became so insistent, that an autopsy was made in the hope to clear up the mystery, but more so to stem the rumours that meanwhile had grown to a roar. It turned out to be a fool's errand. We had engaged a renowned surgeon from England. Sir Horrace presided at the post-mortem examination. Flanked by two assistants, he proceeded with utmost meticulousness, as if England's salvation depended on his findings. The outcome? Not a trace of poison could be detected, nor any signs pointing at a malady or other abuse. Just the same, rumours persisted, opinions were voiced more vociferously than before. Medvil was a victim of obeah, the consensus was."

"Yes, I recall the hubbub, not only in Bassinville, but also right here in Roseau," Mrs Burchard confirmed.

"Like a barrel organ's tune, played over and over again, the same talk could be heard. Wherever I went I was accosted and bombarded with words like: obeah, secouya, poor Medvil, cursed to die young, cursed to die," the chief complained.

"As I deduce, Mr Brunt, you pay little credence to obeah," Mrs Burchard commented.

"None at all," Brunt assured her.

"How do you explain the mysterious death after a sudden, unexpected illness?"

"Natural occurrences, madam, nothing else," he grumbled.

"In other words you are convinced that obeah cannot detrimentally affect anyone?"

"Aren't you?" Brunt exclaimed with more vehemence than intended.

Celia Burchard stood up and walked to an open window. While observing the swaying palm trees she thought about a suitable answer to the chief's query. What should she tell this well-meaning, prosaic man from a faraway land? She knew of his world, which after a sojourn of three months remained vividly anchored in her memory. At the mere thought of England, foreign and cold, filled with spiritless people, she felt chilled to the bones, despite the sultry heat. Yes, after returning home, she recalled starting from sleep in the middle of the night, bathed in cold sweat, terrified to be taken back there. In her dreams she sometimes heard voices urging her:

"Run Celia, run for dear life."

She had to tear herself from the gloomy memories before facing Brunt again. No doubt he could neither sense, nor submit to the dark forces brought over the ocean by her ancestors, and kept alive by their descendants.

She sat down wordlessly trying to arrange her thoughts. Brunt started his wonted finger drumming, despite Mrs Burchard's censorious glances.

"You haven't answered my question," he prodded.

"I know. I can tell you this: obeah does exist in Dominica, to what extent it can, or does harm anyone, I am unable to say. Secouyas do trade in charms, lay curses on people, and engage in exorcism. It happens all the time, particularly in the back country. Whether it spreads misery, is criminal, or just a sham, I wouldn't venture to guess."

Brunt realised that Mrs Burchard lectured him; it put his back up.

"Why is that remote unproductive piece of land significant to the government?" he inquired frowningly.

"It is essential to the botanical garden on account of the rich plant life found there, unique not merely to Dominica, but the entire western hemisphere."

Brunt, confounded, was about to commence the devil's tattoo again, when a sharp glance by Mrs Burchard made him decide otherwise. Rising groaningly from his chair, stamping twice around the table, clearing his throat several times, he stopped opposite Mrs Burchard.

"You said you made Murdoch an offer?"

"Yes. It's been done more often than once," she assured him. "He categorically refuses even the most generous ones."

Brunt, starting his walk again, flared up:

"I don't understand the man. Hang it, he knows the situation. He is a thorn in the side of most expatriates, not to mention the government. So why not cash in and leave?"

Mrs Burchard shared the chief's exacerbation, she concurred readily:

"Your guess is as good as mine."

Squinting, wagging his head, the chief conjectured:

"There must be more to it than mere obduracy. Has sweetening the pot been tried?"

"In more than one way," she assured him.

"Strange, strange," the chief grumbled.

"That's what we think too. Is it just plain contrariness on his part, vindictiveness, or inherent in his nature to rebuff anything not originating from him? We can't figure it out. At every approach he puffs himself up like a fighting cock. One cannot do business with the man, he is set to obtain title to Sylvania, nothing less will do."

"That endeavour will ultimately be successful," Brunt intimated.

"Unless we thwart it," she implied with an impish grin.

"The question is how, and no less, why?"

"Now, Mr Brunt, that's why I invited you, to discuss ways and means. After all you are more conversant with the law than I."

"La-di-da," he almost expelled, for surely the government's lawyers, by far more erudite than he, were advising her. He uttered the obvious:

"Let's be on the up and up here, madam, you want me to do something underhanded, is that it?"

Taken aback by his forthright statement, she prevaricated:

"Not exactly. But then again what could be wrong with a bit of skulduggery if it benefits Dominica without harming Murdoch, who will be amply remunerated?"

Brunt shook his head indignantly, indicating that the whole affair was not to his taste. They tried to entangle him in something neither tailored to his nature nor inclination. He voiced his displeasure:

"Before we go any further, let me sum up. In about eight weeks Murdoch obtains clear title to the holdings, barring any unforeseen hurdles of course. The registrar can no longer postpone the entry. Doing so, perhaps even now, in my opinion is nothing less than usurpation on the government's part. Murdoch can squash that in a twinkle."

"But he hasn't," Mrs Burchard commented.

"Not so far, but he will now, according to you. Am I correct?"

"Yes."

"Alright. Lets look at the possibilities. The government ban is toothless, an exercise in futility, in my estimation. Hoping that Murdoch's life will soon end is whimsical in view of his exuberant health. So, what else is left?"

"Obeah," she almost exclaimed, but bit her tongue in time. Instead she posed a question:

"Isn't his stubbornness suspect?"

"Maybe, but not criminal," the chief quipped.

"Doesn't his morbid insistence to own the property, neither fertile, nor of any commercial value beyond some unusual trees and shrubs, connote sinister intent? Don't forget, he would be recompensed for something which will never be his."

"I regret to differ," Brunt declared.

"Something else seems strange. A man, professing undying love for his homeland, nevertheless shuns it like the plague."

Bending halfway across the table, she observed:

"Do you know he has lived here uninterruptedly for over seven years? During that time he not once took a home leave, granted and fully paid for by the employer. I see you shrugging your shoulders, yet all I say, isn't that peculiar for a homesick man?"

"Not to me," came a baffling reply.

"Oh! how should that be taken?" she inquired with a creased brow.

"Quite simple. I'm not astonished that he avoids England," the chief responded.

"Would you care to elaborate?"

"I would not," he declared.

"Aha, police secrets," she quipped.

"Professional discretion, madam," he enlightened.

Though slightly vexed on account of his evasiveness, she secretly paid respect to him. A wily smile lit up her face, bespeaking startling news. Reaching for her handbag again, she riffled through it while muttering:

"Where the deuce are you, where are you hiding? Aha, there it is."

With these words she pulled out a piece of paper which she handed Brunt with a triumphant grin.

"Read paragraph three," she bid.

The chief skimmed over it twice, then read it again with rising interest. Evidently chagrined by the tortuous lines, intended to confuse, he grimaced; for next to physical exercise he abhorred intricate writing. Lifting his head, he observed the premier's wife closer, while signs of admiration scurried across his countenance. Kew Gardens' transfer appeared no longer straight forward; it was encumbered by restrictions. The chief realised it could be finagled to the government's advantage. Howard Brunt initially chuckled under his breath, then broke out in a guffaw.

Taken aback for an instant, Mrs Burchard chimed in. After both had vented a heartfelt merriment, they combed through the document with undisguised glee. Brunt read aloud, stopping frequently to allow evaluation and discussion. They perused the attachment word for word, sentence by sentence to the last letter. They quickly recognised its significance and advantage accruing to the government.

Mrs Burchard saw the stipulation as a vehicle to deliver Sylvania into their hands. Brunt entertained different sentiments; he hoped what lay before their eyes will be the medium to administer a decisive blow to his unsympathetic countryman, which would chase him headlong off the island.

In response to his inquiry how she came by this document, she replied smilingly:

"Contrary to your secretiveness, I have no compunction to disclose the fact that I procured it from Kew Gardens in London, England. Let me say this: from the onset of my request, hurdles needed to be overcome which surprised and vexed me. Persistent inquiries fell on deaf ears and cold shoulders, as did the petitions of Mr Garneau, the minister. He was treated with utter nonchalance, bordering on disdain. Finally my husband entered the fray. Using diplomatic channels initially led nowhere. Only after harnessing the foreign office's influence, did the paper arrive."

"I presume someone at Kew Gardens tried to prevent the disclosure," Brunt conjectured.

"With a vengeance, it appears. Anyway, here it is. What do you think?"

"It's good news. The restrictive clause can be applied to our advantage. This covenant confers chattel rights to the government till Murdoch obtains title to it. It empowers us, at our botanist's discretion, to exploit the holdings for the benefit of Dominica."

"That's also our interpretation. Our botanist, Hannes Wirt, approved by Kew Gardens even, is entitled to make use of Sylvania's facilities for the enhancement of the botanical garden and Dominica's prestige," she exalted.

"After the official takeover," the chief objected.

Mrs Burchard cast a rebuking glance at Brunt as if to say:

"Don't be a spoilsport."

"Which will be soon," she countered.

"Quite true, but what advantage will that bring?"

"Advantage? Very simple. Mr Wirt shall have unrestricted access to Sylvania, which under Murdoch's control received amazing ameliorations."

"I thought it was only a tract of wilderness, possessing neither commercial nor other value, or did I misunderstand you?"

"Yes and no. My evaluation of the holdings, stated a moment ago, described the condition at the time of transfer," she expounded.

"It is no longer a neglected parcel then?"

"Far from it. To begin with the entire area is walled or fenced in; the inside looks like a park now, containing plants and trees that would enhance the botanical garden."

"In what way?"

"There now, we are getting to the meat of the matter."

"Which is?"

"The uras trees."

"Did you say uras trees?"

Seeing her nodding, he observed:

"Never heard anything about them."

"You are not the only one. Even Dr Beckmann, the eccentric loner and world-renowned botanist, had to profess ignorance about them. Dr Beckmann, you may know, has been tramping, still is for that matter, all over Haiti and Cuba, searching for unusual plants. Subsequent to a standing invitation by Alec Baldwin, he arrived one day with a knapsack on his back, a rolled-up sleeping bag under one arm, and the inevitable wooden box under the other. With a machete as always tied to his belt, he criss-crossed Dominica for months."

"His name sounds familiar," Brunt declared.

"I have met him only once, yet I will never forget that queerest of men; small in stature, but huge in erudition."

She paused, then chuckled:

"What a scrounger he turned out to be."

"A scrounger?" the chief echoed, evidently not fully comprehending.

"As he wandered untiringly about, he was not averse to importune the peasants for food and shelter. Surprisingly they obliged unreservedly, despite his gruff and quarrelsome inclinations. Being crotchety and artless themselves, I suppose they felt an affinity with this errant, quirky man of nature; particularly when they discovered that he appeared to be colour-blind. Strange to say, these poor people in the interior shared their last crumbs with him; in fact, they looked forward to his visits. He was called Le Blanc; they revered this selfish, imperious straggler with an arcane shyness. Of course he speaks our patois fluently, although that was not the main reason for his popularity."

"What did endear him to them, could you explain it?"

"I can. He was, still is I take it, implicitly genuine, which are attributes that instinctively stir the heartstrings of uncorrupted people. His blue eyes, I can tell you, scrutinise one unabashedly from head to toe. I am told of an incident, which may be amusing, but also telling."

"What is it?" Brunt interrupted.

"When he met Murdoch he examined him full thirty seconds, then turning on his heels walked snortingly away."

"I can't blame him," Brunt commented.

"Anyway, country folk respect obstinacy in a man. I also suspect they admired his pluck. Stamping about in the wilderness, utterly alone, in weather no dog would want to be abroad, just to collect plants, made them snicker no doubt, but also raised their awe."

"You just mentioned Alec Baldwin, of whom I heard a lot, but never met," Brunt stated; then added:

"What was he like?"

"That was another odd customer. The two got on famously. Beckmann, a Swede I believe, almost half Baldwin's age, is still roving about."

"What is Baldwin doing?" the chief inquired.

"Shortly after Dr Beckmann left, he gave up field work. The latest I heard, he died recently. As I said, those two inveterate loners were quite a team. One loquacious, the other taciturn. Both unworldly, they formed an instant alliance, despite their divergent personalities. Beckmann gives not a hoot about conventions, he literally thumbs his nose at society's mores; whereas Baldwin, a countryman of yours, valued propriety. What presumably united them was an inner restlessness, and unquenchable thirst for empirical knowledge."

"It appears that you know them both."

"Dr Beckmann only fleetingly; Baldwin, however, quite well. My mother kept house for him some time ago."

"Hm, sounds interesting, can you tell me more?"

"Another time, it's getting late," she reminded.

"Very well, I shall wait for your call, for I'm not so dense as not to realise that Baldwin and Beckmann are, or were, somehow entangled with that mysterious Sylvania property."

"They were at one time. Baldwin, dead now, is out of it of course."

"And Dr Beckmann?"

The question made her raise her head. Brunt noticed a flicker of dubiousness in her eyes, as though unsure what to reply.

"To my knowledge he hasn't stepped onto our shores for ages. He seems to avoid Dominica like the devil avoids holy water, chiefly on account of Murdoch, I think. But he is alive and kicking, from what I hear, probably digging and mooching in the wild mountains of Haiti."

If the chief grinned on account of her prevarication, he was unaware of it, but he could barely disguise his disappointment. Although having more than an inkling what she was leading to, he was still in the dark what role she meant him to play.

As he prepared to leave, she said:

"I cannot overemphasise the importance of the uras trees at the Sylvania holdings. They bear an evil that I cannot explain; yet a hunch tells me there is something satanical about them. That property, Mr Brunt, must come into our possession. I repeat, a fateful devilry is secreted in those buildings."

Brunt nodded assent, bowed gallantly, and left.

Mrs Burchard accompanied him past the door, from where she watched the lumbering chief walking pantingly down the few concrete steps.

Entering a pathway lined on both sides with flowering shrubs and swaying palm trees, Brunt moved on. At the droll sight of the clumsy figure trying to maintain its balance and dignity, she smiled openly. Imagining the parakinetic policeman chasing a putative criminal, nimble as a weasel, she had to clap a hand over her mouth to stifle an outbreak of laughter. What a spectacle that would be; watching the corpulent chief trying to catch a zigzagging youngster suspected of a crime. She could almost see him gasping for breath, with insufficient air in his lungs to cry halt, chasing an agile native. Rumours circulated that some prankish young men, pretending to be conscience-stricken, scamper at the sight of him, hoping to be pursued. Invariably the chief, nothing loath, would stumble after them, crying:

"Stop! stop him!"

Upon finding that the prankster had led him on a wild chase, Brunt merely chuckled. With the threat:

"Next time you get your ears boxed," he let the culprit go.

The chief, no slouch as a wag, appreciated a good caper, even if he was the butt.

Celia Reminisces

*H*er glance wandered from the disappearing chief to a bench below a flowering cashimar zombi tree. A broad smile lit up her face, partially on account of the seductive fragrance emanating from it, but more so because of childhood memories.

Alec Baldwin had planted that tree a long time ago, when she was still a gangling schoolgirl with round eyes and knobby knees. Being exceedingly shy, especially in the presence of white men, she often observed him from afar planting and pruning trees and bushes at his homestead in Sylvania. She distinctly recalled watching him set this cashimar tree. It was small, a mere sapling.

She guided her steps towards the tree, while reminiscing about the past. She could see herself accompanying her mother, rain or shine, on her way to the market in Roseau. It was a long toilsome trek; two hours down-road, three hours back. Complaining repeatedly, she tried to keep up with her mother's sturdy legs, which at times seemed impossible in view of her extraordinary stamina. Swinging her hips, a heavy basket on her head, lighter ones hanging from the crook of each arm, her mother stumped along the rough path, singing, laughing, and talking. The daughter's complaints were answered with words like:

"Celia, Celia, next year we will buy a donkey."

Next year arrived; the donkey failed to show up. Yes, she remembered those walks as if it were yesterday's occurrence. Inquiring about the songs her mother sang, she was told:

"They are voodoo and obeah airs, brought all the way from Africa by our ancestors. Ah, Celia, one of these days we are going to buy two donkeys and ride over to Portsmouth catching a ship that will take us across the ocean to our ancestral lands. Patience, child, we soon will have three donkeys; one for you, the other for me, and the third to carry our baskets."

Celia sensed that her mother had no clue where Portsmouth was, nor in what direction faraway Africa could be. Her world was small; it stretched no farther than a day's journey on foot. When she touched on the subject of voodoo or obeah, her mother halted her steps. Only after looking left, right, and behind her, did she mention mysterious incidents in a low voice. Celia learned about astounding secrets that disturbed her sleep and troubled many a dream. Later, when she mingled within sophisticated circles, sojourned in Europe, and ultimately married, the gloomy recollection faded gradually. Only the memory of her mother remained fixed in her mind, as did the songs, the unfailing cheerfulness, and even the worrisome narrations about obeah and voodoo, which to this day haunted her.

After setting up house in Roseau, where she rapidly climbed up the ladder of success, and increasingly associated with Europeans, she experienced a clash of emotions. Anxious to step onto the path leading to a bright future, yet unable to dislodge her feet entirely from the past, she spent many tortuous hours. She lay in the grip of a quandary. Reason demanded to look ahead; remorse bid to step back. Two forces knocked her about; two opposing voices rang in her ears. One bellowed to forget, the other hissed to remember. She felt miserable, especially after visiting the little hut occupied by her mother.

The day arrived when she had saved some money. She would never forget how she ran up a good portion of the way, calling out from afar:

"Mother, I have the money for two donkeys; one for you, the other for the baskets."

The old woman laughed:

"Child, a woman does not ride on a donkey," she declared.

"But you can lead him," Celia protested.

"Celia, Celia, who ever heard of a woman handling a donkey?"

"But–but," Celia interposed.

Her mother observed smilingly:

"I know what you want to say. Didn't I once desire a donkey or two? Not at all, I just talked nonsense, trying to buoy up your flagging spirit."

Urging her to acquiesce led nowhere. Entreaties she met with chuckles and banter. Age, toil, and hardship had seemingly not weakened her resolve.

The message of her death reached Celia late one afternoon at her workplace. She died suddenly; not a word of complaint had crossed her lips, her spirit remained upbeat to the end. Celia was told that one early morning she went to see joiner Masden.

"Carpenter, make my coffin, I will not see another sunrise," she stated calmly.

Hearing about her prophecies, the younger folks poked fun at them.

"Just another whimsical notion of that maroon," they said.

"She is getting more erratic by the day," many scoffed.

Not carpenter Masden. Without uttering a word he started cutting and nailing. Before Celia received information about her mother's announcement, she lay forever silent in her newly framed coffin. Celia's aunt Ruthie stayed with her sister till she drew the last breath.

"How did mother die?" Celia asked, nagged by guilt.

"As she lived. She laughed, joked, and sang till sundown; then sat quietly in her chair, which you know so well."

Indeed, Celia did. That makeshift seat, inseparable as a shadow from oneself, had been a silent witness of her mother's sorrows and joy, from the day she could remember.

"What did she say prior to her death?" she asked her aunt.

"Not a word. At the first shimmer of dawn she turned her head sideways, then died smilingly."

Even in her coffin the coal-black face seemed suffused by an impish grin; wan, but content, as if she had just outwitted fate.

Her mother's death engendered conflicting feelings in Celia. Gratification, which she tried to hide from the world and repress in herself, and sadness openly shown. She bid the inner voice to be silent that whispered about rejoicing and savouring the newly-found freedom. Her subconscious told her that she must tear off the gloomy drapes of the past wherein her mother and many others of her generation found refuge amid eternal backwardness and poverty.

Life in Roseau among Europeans and educated Negroes agreed with Celia. She earned money and acquired an education. The newly-found liberty from the excruciating days of yore, albeit tempered by culpability, opened vistas she never knew existed. She started to dress with more care, honed her manners, and polished her language. She gradually lost her natural simplicity; meaning she became superficial. When she married Raoul Burchard the pinnacle of her ambition had been reached.

Meanwhile the sun dipped rapidly towards the Caribbean Sea. In the distance, across the Martinique Passage, mountains loomed high above the water. She and her husband liked to visit the charming island of Martinique, where they could practise their French.

Looking around the pleasant ground, forever in full bloom and fragrance, always had a soothing effect on her. In contrast to the cloud-ringed mountains due north, that made her scowl whenever her head turned towards them. There, at the foothills of Morne Trois Piton lay Sylvania, the place of her birth she wished to forget. She wanted to leave her past behind without remorse, in order to enjoy the present and look optimistically towards the future.

As she prepared to go back inside she was startled by strange cries coming from the interior reminiscent of her childhood and youth. A smile stole around her lips while thinking about incidents difficult to forget. The arguments between Masden, the carpenter, and Bovil, his helper, were a treat to witness. At the call that sounded like quak-quakiwack coming from somewhere in the distance, they stared at each other defiantly, both daring each other to say what lay on their tongues. Often, as a girl, she ran towards their workshop to hear the inevitable upcoming dispute. A lively exchange it always proved to be. Bovil generally made the first remark:

"Aha, there is that frog again," he would say in a stage whisper.

Masden, putting down his saw and square, looked at his assistant with eyes that knew how to punish and mock. Emphasising every word, he said incisively:

"Lordie, some people can't tell their knees from their elbows, let alone frogs from birds."

Appraising his helper with a pitiful mien expressing feigned worry, Bovil was informed:

"Frog? Fiddlesticks! That's the cuckoo manioc calling for rain," he said patiently, as one does with a slow learning child.

The bickering always took place in patois, thereby rendering it saltier. On it went, sometimes for a mortal hour, while the work stopped completely. Before you knew it others joined in, mostly older men of various opinions and degrees of belligerence. All were blessed, according to themselves, with infallible erudition, which was nothing but hearsay, Celia realised.

Raftan, the elder, didn't keep one waiting long. As soon as he got wind of the argument, he unfailingly appeared. Seemingly imbued with irrefutable knowledge, venerated on account of his grey hair, he jumped into the fray with gusto. First he glanced at Masden approvingly; then turning to Bovil gazed at him scathingly. Snickering as only an old man can, snorting several times while rolling his eyes in mock disgust, he expounded:

"It's the cuckoo manioc, Bovil, how often must I tell you that. I repeat, it's the cuckoo manioc."

Observing the carpenter assistant with withering looks, Raftan declared:

"Here, watch this."

Saying so he put a hollowed hand to his mouth and called in a tremulous voice:

"Quak-quakiwack-wack-wack."

Sure enough the call was not only answered, but the caller came closer, perhaps mistaking old Raftan for one of his own kind.

"There he is. Do you see the big grey bird on that mango bough? It's the cuckoo manioc," Raftan crowed, whereafter he explained:

"Cuckoo manioc is a haughty bird that finds it beneath his dignity searching for water on the ground. Perching on a mango branch and a leaf, he calls for rain. He orders the rain to come, then opens his beak and lets the drops from the leaf roll down his throat."

The bystanders, though having heard a hundred times what none believed, nevertheless pretended to listen.

As Mrs Burchard reached the office she vowed to look up Hannes Wirt today. I must sound him out with a woman's adroitness, elicit from him secrets about Murdoch, she told herself.

Inside the building Michael Mauch emerged before her inner eyes. She could almost hear his inveigling voice and see the roguish face and mocking eyes.

"How can a man live in such grand style on a small income?" she mused.

Alone his two ocean-going yachts were worth a king's ransom, in her opinion. The house he owned, a manor really, surrounded by splendid gardens, having a view second to none, must have cost a bundle. Where did the money come from to lead the life of a Lydian king?

She didn't trust Mauch, never did. Even less since she discovered his connection with the disputed Sylvania property. Upon checking the land title registry she unearthed a disquieting fact: Mauch had purchased a part of Baldwin's property some time ago. Oddly enough at the same time as did Kew Gardens; in fact, their respective titles were registered simultaneously to almost a minute. Ten of the original hectares were now owned by Mauch; ten still belonged to Kew Gardens, and the balance had been transferred to a Mrs Joan Gibson. The Kew Gardens' property of course contained the mysterious uras trees. Mrs Burchard could not understand Mauch's interest in seemingly useless land, situated in the middle of nowhere. Why would a sedentary newspaper publisher, patently indifferent to nature, fauna, and flora, covet an overgrown, almost inaccessible property?

To cultivate and plant trees and shrubs indigenous to that area? Not Michael Mauch, she decided, who was known to be averse to any kind of physical activities. Wasn't one of his favourite quips:

"Even observing anyone working tires me out."

Something else made Mrs Burchard leery: Mauch's frequent boat trips due north. According to the chief of police, Murdoch usually accompanied him on these long journeys. What were they up to? Hatching sinister plans, or pursuing legitimate business? No one appeared to know; even the chief remained in the dark. When she apprised him of her discoveries, he promised to keep an eye on Mauch.

Alec Baldwin

*A*lec Baldwin, the reclusive Englishman, grew chummier in advancing age, thus more communicative. Approaching the end of his life, he spoke and wrote increasingly about the island's plants and animals, especially the ones found on, and around his land, which originally consisted of thirty hectares. After Celia Burchard had been entrusted with the honorary presidency of the botanical garden, she went to see Baldwin. He seemed older than she remembered; he evidently had lost his wonted zest, yet he now as then retained an upright posture, as much as that annoying reticence. She made no bones about the purpose of her visit; the source of her vexation and worry lay with Murdoch, and to a lesser degree Mauch. When she asked about the land purchases, he raised his eyebrows and stared past her, as if to say:

"Celia, I don't hear so good today."

Even though she had become the first minister's wife, he continued calling her Celia. He had a gift for punishing burdensome questioners with crushing silence. She knew that stare only too well; it made her shrink in herself even now. She had learned a lot from the taciturn hermit. Since the day her mother introduced her, and insisted that her girl with the shaking knees make a curtsy, she felt awed by the stiff Englishman.

In her formative years that reverential fear subsided, but a strange ambivalence lingered. She felt drawn towards the solitary man, yet once near him she wanted to run away. He frequently sent her on errands, which in time she thought of as futile exercises. They served no other purpose, she sensed, then to be rid of her for awhile. As mentioned she lost her awe of him, thus asked questions he must have deemed pesky.

Baldwin possessed prodigious knowledge, particularly concerning nature, but he was loath to blazon it abroad. Of his own accomplishments he seldom talked, and if he did, they were treated condescendingly. He appeared to have been everywhere. Botanists and biologists were known to him from every corner of the globe. Scientists from Canada, the United States, and Europe sought him out. His extensive reading was impressive, more so his empirical acumen. He preferred experimenting to book learning; results arrived at by trial and error deemed him far superior to erudition. His visitors, renowned scientists mostly, asserted that they learned more from him than the other way around; certainly about Dominica's flora and fauna.

The uras tree, a name coined by Baldwin, was unanimously proclaimed the most singular growth ever seen or heard of. They were amazed upon being told that try as he may, Baldwin was unable to transplant these specimen anywhere else in the island.

"Not even a mile distance from this spot," he maintained. "They wilt almost before one's eyes if planted in other places," he assured his visitors.

The background of the uras tree is this: Baldwin sort of stumbled on it by accident. From the day he arrived at Sylvania he had a predilection for the cashimar trees growing around the house. Their pleasant scent lulled him to sleep, and bestowed agreeable dreams. For that reason he ordered part of his land to be cleared, and transplanted a number of smaller trees thereon. The natives, steeped to their gills in superstition and magic, called these fruit-bearing trees cashimar zombi.

"Only the devil can make them grow," they affirmed.

Attempts to drive such silly notions from their frizzled heads met with stubborn opposition.

"It's the zombie, a devil and none other that makes the tree bloom. Every third night he comes down from Morne Trois Piton and blazes the trunks," they countered with the conviction of someone possessing incontrovertible proof.

"Where are these scores? show me," Baldwin demanded to know; at the beginning that is.

Later on he just nodded and let them talk. He knew their response by rote:

"There they are, sir, without them blazes the tree dies."

"Bunkum, arrant nonsense," he felt like saying, but kept his tongue in check.

After ten years forty of these fragrant trees bore fruit; little apples not particularly tasty. At about the fifth year Baldwin noticed shoots pushing through the ground all over the cleared land. At first he had them cut down, but to no avail, they grew back within days, with increasing vigour to boot. At last he dug up a few, roots and all, crated them carefully, and sent everything to a friend in San Francisco, requesting to have a thorough examination made. Four months later a report arrived, stating that the specimen could not be recognised.

"We looked and inquired everywhere in vain. The plants sent us appear to be unique, you can therefore name them at your own discretion. Keep us posted how it goes," his friend wrote.

From thereon Baldwin let the uras, as he called them now, grow at will; cultivated them however with the same care as his beloved cashimar trees. Within two years buds appeared, and blossoms broke out. At the end of the third year most bore small, nut-shaped fruits.

One morning Rasmus, the gardener, approached Baldwin, evidently nonplussed. Tapping his temples, shaking his head, and talking to himself, as always when he felt at sea, he waited to be spoken to.

"What is it, Rasmus?" Baldwin obliged.

"Zombie is stealing the bark," the gardener said in a muffled voice.

"What kind of blatherskite is that again?" Baldwin snapped.

"Zombies are stealing the bark off the new trees," Rasmus insisted.

When Baldwin consented to investigate, he stopped in his tracks. Something was amiss here; the trunks had changed overnight. Someone had peeled strips of bark from every tree.

Looking closer, however, revealed the fact that theft was not the cause of these bare spots, for the removed bark lay on the ground. Examining the damage more minutely, two significant discoveries were made: one, visible; the other, odorous.   New skins started to form already on the naked spots; very thin, but perceivable to the eye. As the myopic Baldwin bent forward to obtain a better look, he reeled back. A pungent smell, outright offensive, attacked his nose. Had he not instinctively recoiled, who knows, he might have fainted on the spot. Rasmus of course stood in no danger to be choked by that terrible smell, since he steadfastly refused to go near this piece of devilry, as he called it.

As it turned out, these extraordinary trees cast off their bark and retained their leaves. In no time did the trees replace the lost bark, which to Baldwin's astonishment grew denser after every renewal. He informed several international botanists of the surprising occurrence. A few, intrigued, and of a roving disposition, paid him a visit, to see with their own eyes Baldwin's curious trees. Dr Beckmann was among them. Captivated by his friend's communication, he interrupted his rumble over Haiti's Morne La Salle, and started the long journey southward.

Some of the scientists stayed awhile, others returned the following day. Without exception they filled boxes, either brought with them or procured from Baldwin, with twigs, leaves and bark from the singular uras trees. At home in their laboratories they intended to subject everything to a thorough examination.

It wasn't meant to be. The contents of the small wooden cases remained in the jungle of Dominica; with one notable exception that is. What happened can be explained in a few words. An odour, a stench really, emanated from the boxes that grew ranker by the minute. Before they reached Roseau, the botanists were forced to empty them on the way; not Dr Beckmann however. As soon as the execrable smell assailed his olfactory nerve, he acted with alacrity. Cursing his friend's twisted sense of humour, who undoubtedly knew about the vile odour, he buried the offensive contents along the path, then continued on his way to Roseau. He knew what needed to be done. As he walked on, he stopped now and then, turning in the presumed direction of Baldwin's home, and bellowed:

"Ha, you sneaky Englishman, ha, to you! Tricks like this don't swerve a resourceful Swede from his course. Go ahead, snicker, old man, chortle away."

Dr Beckmann calmed down quickly, whereupon he started to laugh. To tell the truth, he appreciated innovative pranks, especially if played on some of his dour colleagues. He could picture his old comrade chortling wickedly at the thought of these stiffly neat and proper scientists being caught in a delicate situation. Dr Beckmann was not unacquainted with exotic and vile odours. Take the durian fruit for instance, that smells like rotted fish, yet tastes heavenly; he liked them enormously. The smell? he contained it the same way as he intended to do with Baldwin's uras bark.

With the little wooden crate under his arm, he arrived in Roseau before lunch time. Asking for direction, he soon found a tinsmith, whom he enjoined to line the inside with copper sheathing. As luck would have it, the tradesman appeared to be well versed in these matters.

"Do you stock the material?" Dr Beckmann asked.

"More than enough," he was advised.

"Don't forget the lid and the top edges, everything must be perfectly airtight."

If the artisan found the request odd, he betrayed his surprise with neither words nor gestures.

"When can I collect the box?"

"Tomorrow afternoon," the tinsmith replied.

Next day with the finished product in hand, Dr Beckmann hastened to the hiding place and retrieved the concealed plants. Then sealing the box with utmost care that not even an agouti would be attracted by the scent, he returned to Roseau. A few days later he embarked on a voyage to Haiti.

Celia Burchard remained unaware of these events, although she met some of the visiting botanists who spoke freely about every subject, except the uras. Upon being prodded about the purpose of their sojourn in Dominica, they answered evasively:

"Just a social call."

"We haven't seen Baldwin for a long time," were some of the excuses.

She believed none of them, since the grapevine hummed with news of these mysterious trees at Sylvania, apparently propagated by Alec Baldwin. But she did not divine their significance; not yet anyhow. The bearers of the tidings were mostly natives from the area, whom she knew as masters of concocted and bully stories. Trying to worm out information from Baldwin proved to be a task beyond her ability.

After reading in Mauch's newspaper a spurious anecdote touching on the so-called uras tree, she accosted him on one of his rare visits to Roseau. Baldwin, hardly a fountain of information at best of times, behaved outright ornery. He responded in monosyllables to her inquiry, then claiming to be in a hurry, left her standing in the middle of the road.

Disquieting Revelations

Celia Burchard, on her way to the Gardens, deep in thought, gave no heed to the rain, till it came down in streams. Having covered only about a third of the distance she decided to return to the offices. Vexed on the one hand, she was also glad to have the cobwebs of recurring thoughts washed away.

While she changed into dry clothes the rain stopped. As the clouds dispersed, the inevitable sun shone again. Despite making haste she arrived too late at the Gardens; Wirt and the workers had already called it a day. Murdoch couldn't be seen anywhere. Several people, tourists judging by their deportment, were milling about. Mrs Burchard couldn't help thinking that they were talking too loud, and moving too fast. They also huddled as if fearing an attack.

At the other end she caught sight of Dr Brodeur, the widely known physician. She was about to hail him when something held her back. Seemingly lost in thought he walked around a mangosteen tree, nodding and shaking his head alternatively, and making entries in a notebook.

Dr Brodeur hailed from Haiti, he had moved some years ago to Dominica, where he gradually established a practice. It wasn't easy in view of the vile gossip nipping at his heels. He was a man of mixed blood, neither white nor black; a Creole perhaps. His demeanour resembled a Frenchman's. He spoke with his hands in a flowery fashion, besides being fastidious in many ways, he aimed to please. The most conspicuous feature about him must have been his secretiveness. Ill rumours hadn't spared him to this day, although time did mitigate the mordant bile and venom. He had to flee from Haiti in the middle of the night, malicious tongues whispered; the law is still at his heels, backbiters trumpeted behind his back. Dr Brodeur seldom, if at all, took a position against these scandalmongers.

"Let them talk," he countered any well-meaning advice.

But when Mauch's newspaper published a calumnious report about him, he pulled off the gloves.

One sultry afternoon he paid the publisher a visit. Friends and acquaintances who encountered him professed never to have seen him so determined. With a voluminous bag in his hand he strode purposefully towards the newsman's office. Brodeur and Mauch knew each other from way back; the discreet man from Haiti and the rash Irishman had a long history together. Their relations were amiable till that dire incident occurred which caused one as much as the other untold grief. Mauch blamed the doctor for the mishap, or rather his sense of honour; moronic in his estimation. The episode took place many years ago.

What happened that day in Mauch's office never came to light. The air was filled with wild speculations. Rumours circulated of drawn pistols, murderous threats, and loud thuds suggesting a violent struggle. What actually did take place only the two participants knew, who said not a word about their impetuous encounter.

In the next issue a retraction appeared on the front page of the newspaper, which raised the eyebrows of more than one reader. Mauch, known for his straightforward reporting, had never disavowed what he wrote; certainly not in recent years. He apologised to Dr Brodeur and his readers for the baseless accusations, innuendoes, and aspersions cast.

Yes, Mauch and Dr Brodeur were old acquaintances and friends, although they shunned one another now; like Satan shuns a crucifix. It sure wasn't an easy feat in the confined area of Roseau. Should they meet accidentally a farcical situation arose, a skit worth watching. Turning their heads sideways, staring transfixed at something seemingly enthralling, they sidled away in opposite directions.

Finally Dr Brodeur noticed Mrs Burchard. Was she mistaken, or did he indeed prepare to hide from her? Both hands were behind his back, evidently trying to conceal something. She hesitated to approach him for fear of causing the doctor embarrassment who, with a juggler's dexterity, slipped into a bag what lay in his hands. Only then did he welcome her with feigned heartiness.

"Madam, you look charming as always," he said while bowing gallantly and extending a hand.

"Doctor, doctor, you are trying to confound an old woman," she chuckled; then added:

"I didn't intend to disturb you, I came to see Mr Wirt, but missed him by the looks of it."

"Hannes Wirt?"

"Yes, our new botanist," she confirmed.

Dr Brodeur's countenance darkened, it expressed conflicting sentiments, strong misgivings appeared to be one of them.

"Hm, hm, the new botanist, you say?"

"That is right."

"Is he replacing Murdoch?"

"Of course."

The doctor became restless, visibly fidgety. He stepped from foot to foot, then stared vacantly past her, seemingly preoccupied with disquieting thoughts which he tried anxiously to suppress. Letting his eyes wander from the mountains to the sea, endeavouring to avoid her inquiring glances, he said not a word. Something appeared to disturb his wonted equanimity. He gave the impression of a man riven by contrary emotions. His eyes revealed apprehensions which his tongue wished to conceal.

After several throat-clearings he spoke up:

"Could you spare some time?"

"As much as you need," she replied eagerly, for his puzzling behaviour had aroused her curiosity.

"Do you have a key to the buildings?" he inquired.

"Most certainly," she declared.

"Could we go inside? I wish to apprise you of a matter, trifling perhaps, but nevertheless disconcerting to me."

"Well, what are we waiting for?"

Once inside, though consumed by a desire to learn about what the doctor had on his mind, she assumed a nonchalant air. She neither rushed him with words, nor did she insinuate by a flutter of eyelids or suggestive facial expressions, the least bit of impatience.

Dr Brodeur appeared to be standing at the crossroads of a decision; whether to talk, or walk out. She let him collect his thoughts without betraying a flicker of eagerness. Judging by his behaviour, a struggle took place in the worthy man, between conscience and duty. After heaving several deep sighs, he posed a question:

"When will Mr Wirt take over Murdoch's position?"

Caught by surprise she hedged for an instant:

"I believe in about four weeks," she advised.

His brow creased as he reached inside his voluminous bag from which he retrieved a little book, through which he leafed. Expelling a loud "aha," he skimmed a page.

"I see, I see," he repeated, then turning fully towards Mrs Burchard, he inquired:

"You haven't forgotten Alfred Nantes, I take it?"

"Murdoch's designated successor? how could I."

Drawing a loud breath, he commented:

"I must tell you something remarkable and disconcerting. Nantes consulted me three weeks prior to the scheduled takeover, not as patient, mind you."

"Oh!" Mrs Burchard exclaimed.

"He seemed at the end of his tether; a human wreck would better describe his condition. What he revealed disturbed me greatly, enough to request a thorough medical examination, which he at first declined. But he talked wildly, madam, did he ever talk and tremble. I remember him well. He spoke French fluently, which in itself endeared him to me to begin with. The main reason, however, why he remains indelibly etched on my mind is this: His narration revived memories I had dearly hoped to forget."

When Dr Brodeur paused for a moment, Mrs Burchard had to constrain herself not to ask ten questions at once. Her curiosity being aroused beyond endurance, she felt tempted to plead:

"Doctor, go on, please don't stop."

Yet knowing his character somewhat, she bit her tongue. No, Dr Brodeur did not take kindly to any form of inducement. He took up the thread of the narration again.

"Nantes' complaints vividly brought back to me that weird event in Haiti. He felt beset by a puzzling anxiety that disturbed his sleep at night, and made him dread his waking hours. Try as he may, he couldn't stave off a foreboding that assailed him with increasing intensity, which neither work, extended walks, nor alcohol managed to assuage. Terror had now culminated to sheer panic. As I concluded later, Alfred Nantes seemed to be racked by nothing more than a presentiment, which had totally ensnared him. His demeanour bore symptoms of abject misery, that much a layman could have diagnosed. The man suffered agonies, triggered by nameless sorrow. His eyes bulged from sheer horror. All in all his deportment resembled that other man's who consulted me in Haiti."

Noticing Mrs Burchard's puzzling glance, the doctor commented:

"I will tell you about him shortly. For now I wish to say that both men conveyed an aura of extreme fear that made my spine tingle. I urged Nantes a second time to submit to a medical examination, to which he consented. What I found was this: My patient, still fairly young, blessed with a physique an athlete would have been proud of, was neither befallen by injuries nor any physical ailments."

"It was all in his head, in other words," Mrs Burchard suggested.

"One could say that perhaps, but I wasn't so sure then, and am even less now, after subsequent occurrences opened my eyes. You see, madam, anxiety can be a destructive force; mixed with rampant imagination, fanned by fear, it does at times engender physical pain and mental anguish which changes personalities; in fact, anxiety can cripple. That's what happened with Nantes and the other man. Nantes moved erratically, jerkily, to be exact. His knees literally wobbled; his complexion was deathly wan, and his voice quavered. But the most appalling features were his eyes; they had a catatonic glossy stare, which neither a flutter of eyelids, nor a flicker of the iris disrupted. For an instant delirium tremens entered my mind, but I rejected that notion quicker than I had formed it."

Mrs Burchard interrupted:

"I concur, doctor, Nantes, whom I met quite regularly, bore no signs of an alcoholic, or drug addict."

"Quite so. But then, why were his nerves shattered beyond control? What made him look like death's-head on a mopstick? Having met Nantes occasionally, in fact, a week prior to his visit, my judgement of him contrasted sharply with his bizarre behaviour. He always impressed me as being intrepid, calm, and sober. What had driven him into the fangs of desperation that appeared to consume his vital forces, I dared not think of, let alone mention to anyone the notion that gradually entered my mind. Nantes' next words made me gasp; it was my turn now to stare wildly."

"What did he say?"

" 'Every night I witness my own burial. I see myself being lowered into a grave, and hear someone snickering in derision:

" 'You want to be the leading botanist, do you? It will never happen! never happen!'

" 'Then just as the crazed being on top starts shovelling earth onto me, I sit up and scream.'

"When I asked him whether he recognised the voice, Nantes answered:

" 'Robert Murdoch.' "

Mrs Burchard shrugged her shoulders:

"A nightmare, nothing more," she declared.

"I would agree but for one reason."

"Which is?"

"The man who consulted me in Port-au-Prince had similar delusions, except the name of the man trying to entomb him was different."

Glancing at her sheepishly, Dr Brodeur burst out:

"The name mentioned was Michael Mauch."

Undecided what to make of the doctor's narration, Mrs Burchard posed a question:

"What happened finally with Nantes?"

"He disappeared, as we all know."

"I am referring to his visit," she declared.

"He left in a dither."

"Did he consult you a second time?"

"Yes," came a reluctant reply.

Seeing her inquiring glance, Dr Brodeur hastened to say:

"Let me first relate my horrendous experience at that time in Port-au-Prince. You will notice the similarity between Nantes' case and the other fellow's. It might even help to lift the clouds from the Belgian's mysterious departure."

Though her interest lay in Nantes' fate, she encouraged him:

"I am anxious to hear about it."

Dr Brodeur grew hesitant, as if uncertain what, or how much to relate. Strange, Mrs Burchard thought, a moment ago he seemed eager to talk about something that now remains stuck in his throat. He gave an impression of someone reluctant to reveal what should remain untold. He moved his head from side to side, wiped his brow with the back of his hand, and generally behaved irresolute. He evidently wished to change the subject, but knew not how.

Trying to conceal an embarrassment written across his face, Dr Brodeur prepared to retract his slip of the tongue, when Mrs Burchard made a comment:

"Dr Brodeur, in case you intend to disclose something confidential, rest assured it will not reach another ear; not even my husband's."

The promise appeared to ease his conscience; he started to talk:

"As you are aware I had a flourishing practice in Haiti. Prospective patients tumbled over each other to be on my roster. My waiting rooms were filled with men, women, and children from morning till night. From the humblest peasant to pretentious snob, they jostled for my attention. Even the president and his staff vied with each other to be treated by me. I can consciably say that I travelled on the road leading to riches and renown."

Dr Brodeur fell silent; ugly memories stifled his voice. Moaning like a man reliving a nightmare, he lamented:

"All ended abruptly. One day I soared on the wings of fame, the next I plunged into an abyss of disgrace. What a fall that was! The eulogised physician of yesterday became a disparaged quacksalver over night. In no time did I become fair game for anyone's scorn, and the police's target for their little tyrannies. One day even the notorious Tonton Macouts came storming through my rooms."

"But why, doctor, why?"

As the doctor cast a long glance at her, a flicker of a smile hovered around his lips.

"Don't you know human nature?" it seemed to mean.

"One morning a benefactor and patron of the government practically forced his way into my consultation rooms, without an appointment that is. He behaved imperiously from the moment he arrived. Loudmouthed he was from the onset; he demanded to see the doctor without delay. When my secretary denied his request, he pushed her aside and stormed right in. By a stroke of luck I had no patient with me at that moment. I recognised the ruffian instantly as a notorious toady; dreaded and despised. He was a dangerous man, best to be given a wide berth.

"The fixer, as he was known, deemed his moniker a title of honour. The basis of his influence and power were collections of documents and photographs of the government elite, highly revealing, and no less damaging. Anyway, this fixer, by the name of Andrew Vezina, gushingly explained the reason for his unceremonious entry. He related his problem in detail, which resembled Nantes' to a tee; with one notable difference. Whereas your botanist had no clue what ailed him, the fixer, as I prefer to call him, named the source of his malady unequivocally."

"What was it?"

" 'Obeah,' he moaned in a rasping voice, 'a curse has been flung at me that eats the marrow from my bones,' he maintained. 'I feel the fetid breath of death, from which only you, doctor, can save me.'

"I asked the secretary to admit no more patients till further notice, for Andrew Vezina, the fixer, acted stranger by the second. Without permission he lowered the venetian blinds

with shaking knees and trembling hands. While doing so, a
wary expression scurried over his face. With a Hippocratic
mien, meant to elicit pity, he petitioned me to mix a concoction
to counter the obeah curse laid on him.

" 'Be quick about it,' he urged; then made another request.

" 'Here, invoke the same obeah curse upon these
scallawags.'

"With these words he handed me an envelope which he
held in both hands. I wasted no time telling him that he had
knocked at the wrong door. I am neither a bocor mixing
tinctures, nor do I dabble in obeah, I advised. The fellow stared
at me aghast, his eyes almost popped from their sockets. He
looked like a man for whom death was calling. When he started
to move around aimlessly while uttering wild imprecations, I
furtively removed all sharp instruments from sight, while at the
same time looking for a weapon.

As I walked towards a sideboard were some of my
trophies stood, I was jolted by a piercing scream, followed by
an inhuman throat-rattle. It came from the fixer, who virtually
leaped through the doorway and disappeared. The man
standing in the door opening seemed to have frightened my
visitor out of his wits."

Acquiring a speculative air, Dr Brodeur observed Mrs
Burchard reflectively, prior to saying:

"For an instant I dared not trust my eyes; it was no other
than Michael Mauch who put the fear of God into the fixer."

Mrs Burchard started:

"Our Michael Mauch?"

"The same."

"You knew him already in those days?"

"Not intimately, but that changed from thereon."

Visibly stirred, Mrs Burchard begged to hear more:

"This is getting more intriguing by the minute. Please do
go on."

Dr Brodeur hesitated, fresh doubts appeared to assail him.
With pursed lips, indicative of indecision, he stepped up to an
open window. The sun, dipping towards the horizon, would
soon disappear in the shimmering water of the Caribbean Sea.

A gust of wind blew down from the mountains that made the palm trees sway, and caused a rustle in the bushes.

Evidently still uncertain how much, or what to say, he pretended to be captivated by the sough of the wind and the swell of the sea breaking on the shore. He realised by elaborating on his knowledge about Nantes, he is exposing himself to reproaches by Mrs Burchard and the premier.

What of it? the doctor must have decided. He perked up and resumed his narration:

"As indicated Mauch's unannounced emergence made the fixer bound out of sight. What did the publisher want? Why did he visit me? I asked him, thoroughly annoyed at the intrusion. I dearly wished to query him about the fixer's flight upon catching a glance of him, but recognising the futility of such an inquiry, I desisted.

"Hemming and hawing, treating my insistent questions with disregard, he started to interrogate me. What brought the fixer here? What did he say? How come the consultation room is kept in semi-darkness? When he steered his probing queries towards the politicians mentioned by Vezina, I grew alarmed. Mauch, I would say, besides being a newspaper publisher, was active in politics. The grapevine also had it that he was up to his elbows in voodoo and obeah."

"He still is in my opinion," Mrs Burchard suggested.

"He might be, but more on the sly than hitherto in Haiti."

Shrugging her shoulders, tilting her head, thus signifying lack of conviction, Mrs Burchard gave no answer.

"I alluded to the grapevine, but that is not the whole story. In my opinion, and others at the time, Mauch did have his fingers in occult practices. But back to that unsettling encounter in Port-au-Prince. Mauch became exceedingly obtrusive, offensively so, consequently I showed him the door. Would you believe it, madam, the fellow brazenly refused to go. I am not averse to confess that I lost my composure."

"What happened?"

"I lifted him by the scruff of the neck and made him walk Spanish."

Mrs Burchard raised a hand to her lips to hide the grin that forced itself upon her. The perception of the mild and urbane doctor displaying atavistic tendencies tickled her fancy.

"What made you believe that Mauch practised obeah?"

"I don't say he practised it, but his conduct pointed with all ten fingers in that direction, meaning a vested interest. True, he made an effort to hide that fact by pretending to be an iconoclast."

"In what way?"

"For one, his newspaper railed against obeah, which he described as humbug that not only brought Haiti disrepute, but undermined good sense. His mission, he never tired to proclaim, was nothing less than obliterating that heathen worship from Haiti and beyond. He denounced obeah with particular venom, suspiciously so. He declared it Satan's work, with no redeeming value, but deleterious consequences. The consistent brouhaha invited suspicion."

"You think it was a sham?"

"Nothing else. Why write and talk so much about spurious practices? one is entitled to ask. It's a petty artifice, as old as the hills, to conjure up a nonexistent evil for the sole reason to inveigh against it."

"Yes, doctor, I know all about that ruse," she concurred.

"Let me tell you, Mauch described hypothetical incidents, which he spun and twisted till in the mind of the confused reader they acquired an air of reality. The sequel of these so-called incidents, self-serving in my estimation, invariably reeked of disaster. Something else I should mention. A number of people wrote to him asking about the meaning of obeah."

Dr Brodeur, drawing himself up, cast a sideways glance at Mrs Burchard prior to saying more:

"Mauch's explanations, usually withheld till the questioner became irate, invariably were nothing but amateurish attempts at obfuscation."

"In other words he wouldn't, or couldn't expound on the sorcery which he denounced so vigorously," Mrs Burchard commented.

"Exactly. To conclude, Mauch ran a racket to his, and possibly others, benefit."

"Well, he still is, doctor."

Since she didn't elaborate, Dr Brodeur, tactful to his fingertips, refrained from inquiring.

"After unceremoniously expelling Mauch, I heaved a sigh of relief. Pulling up the venetian blinds again, my eyes fell on the envelope left behind. Knowing whom the fixer wanted, I was nevertheless curious what the envelope contained. Upon opening it, a piece of paper plus three photographs fell out, on whose back were written the names of my close acquaintances. The half-length pictures confirmed their identities; they were some of my most valued patients. They were in the fixer's, as much as in Mauch's cross hair, judging by his strident inquiries about them. What is going on? I asked myself. Why did the fixer wish to invoke evil on these men? moreover, of what interest were they to Mauch?"

Dr Brodeur cast significant glances at Mrs Burchard who hung upon his lips, anxious to hear more. She felt induced to prod him, but bit her tongue. Mauch had long ago roused her suspicion. She, as much as her husband, didn't trust him out of their sight. His pretence to be devoted with body and soul to that unprofitable newspaper business, both found suspect. For good reasons; for how could a spendthrift of Mauch's magnitude survive on such paltry returns? His association with Murdoch fanned their distrust even more. They, among others, had concluded long ago that he derived extraneous income from illicit sources; secret and undeclared. To her husband's chagrin she maintained that the origin of his major earnings is somehow connected with the defamed obeah. Perhaps, she mused, Dr Brodeur's fascinating disclosure will shed light on the mystery.

But he seemed reluctant to say more, for reasons she couldn't fathom. What was holding him back? Fear to be rebuked for not having advised the police about Nantes' dilemma? Or his inherent reserve?

Dr Brodeur started to hedge, then gradually fell silent. He prepared to rise, yet changing his mind decided to speak. Nothing came of it, something held him back.

Mrs Burchard, sensing that the doctor's experience in Port-au-Prince might throw light on Nantes' fate, waited with bated breath for further information. She never believed that he left on his own volition. Nantes either met with a fatal accident out on the sea or up in the mountains, or became a victim of violence. But now a third possibility had reared its head. Listening to Dr Brodeur's astounding account, the notion took anchor that he may have divined an impending peril from which he fled head over heels. Yet she quickly rejected that idea, for Alfred Nantes, an honourable man, would surely have sent word upon reaching safety.

Dr Brodeur straightened up, he was ready to speak. But not a word was uttered, because Murdoch appeared seemingly from nowhere.

Mrs Burchard, visibly annoyed on account of the disturbance, realised an awful truth that made her gasp audibly. Murdoch had eavesdropped! Every word that was said he clearly must have heard. Did he stand under the open window, or nearby, pretending to be busy with pruning? Or cower perhaps in the grass feigning absorption in a flower bed? He greeted them cordially, then excused himself effusively:

"I noticed the open window which I believed to have neglected to close. Good night, Mrs Burchard, good night doctor," he wished, then walked out to the road.

Afterwards no force on earth could have induced Dr Brodeur to utter another word despite her repeated prodding.

"Madam, I have nothing more to say," he remarked.

Bowing lightly, extending his hand, he bid her goodbye.

On his way back Dr Brodeur was unable to shake off memories of that momentous encounter with Nantes, which he wished to have kept secret. In a way he thanked his stars for Murdoch's timely interference, which prevented further disclosures. Just the same he regretted his abrupt departure, which in retrospect deemed him lack of good manners. But the stings of remorse were mitigated by the soft air and the exuberant voices of the night. He was unable to decide whether to tell Mrs Burchard the sequel concerning Nantes' uncanny flight of fancy. Much more had taken place prior to the Belgian's putative flight.

As already mentioned, they met again; rather Nantes paid him another visit. It happened about a week prior to his puzzling disappearance. One glimpse said it all; the man stood in the shadow of death; his movements resembled that of a sleepwalker. An eerie meeting that was, even today goose pimples covered his skin at the thought of it. What cruel demon inhabited that sound body and stout soul of some weeks ago? What fiend could transform a spunky individual into a quailing craven? Nantes lay in the fangs of a terror which Dr Brodeur divined, but dared not name. The aspect of the Belgian, utterly disoriented, tormented to the marrow, followed him to this day. How could any man with a breath of compassion in his breast forget the moment when Nantes staggered up the few steps to his, Dr Brodeur's rooms, moaning as if beset by Dante's twelve devils. Darkness had already descended over an hour ago; the world was astir with sounds that enlivens one's spirit. Indeed, Nantes was a sight to remember. Aghast, pale below the skin, he stood before Dr Brodeur, so haggard that he resembled a walking corpse. Asking for forgiveness on account of the late hour, he groaned:

"Doctor, help me, I'm at the end of my tether."

"How can I help, Mr Nantes, you underwent a thorough medical examination a week ago, you know the results; there is nothing amiss with your state of health."

His visitor looked at him fixedly, evidently doubting his diagnosis. When pressed to submit to another checkup, Nantes almost bolted:

"No, no, there is nothing wrong with me physically," he lamented.

Dr Brodeur, as stated, was partial to the Belgian, wherefore he took utmost pains to be of assistance. He suggested hypnosis, which the other rejected vehemently. An awful realisation gripped the doctor; it sounded far-fetched, yet possible. Nantes tried to shield the source of his grief, which he knew or guessed, but intentionally obfuscated. What, or who could it be?

Dr Brodeur heaved a sigh, indicating that he had more than an inkling who was behind it. But the method employed to create such a morbid state of mind in an otherwise wholesome man eluded his comprehension. Nantes suffered from hysteria, caused by fear of the unknown, possibly somehow instilled by Murdoch or Mauch, perhaps even both.

Obeying an instinct Dr Brodeur inquired:

"Have you mentioned your condition to Murdoch?"

As suspected, that suggestion touched a nerve. Nantes' head bound up, while staring at him as if the poisoned cup had been proffered. His accusing gaze made the doctor feel uncomfortable. Nantes appeared to be thunderstruck; he trembled in every limb. Surprised at the arcane reaction, Dr Brodeur inquired:

"Have I said something out of bounds, Mr Nantes?"

His visitor made no reply; he had risen to his feet upon hearing Murdoch's name mentioned. There he stood now as if rooted to the floor, and examined the doctor from head to toe with a furrowed brow, and mistrust written all over his face.

The mere thought of speaking to Murdoch seemed to aggrieve him. Urging his patient to explain in detail the symptoms of his anguish led nowhere; he remained tongue-tied, seemingly afraid to utter another word.

Dr Brodeur, disconcerted to the core, baffled as seldom before, could well imagine what tormented his visitor. He recalled the adage that the troubled mind perceives the weight of a feather as a ton of iron crushing him. Haunted by dismal imageries, in a tremulous voice, Nantes insinuated that he was being poisoned.

"By whom?" Dr Brodeur demanded to know.

Instead giving an answer, he turned sideways, muttering repeatedly:

"I must leave the island without delay."

"Well, what's hindering you?"

Nantes' eyes distended as he said, rather croaked:

"They–they will never let me get away."

Dr Brodeur bristled annoyed, besides, he was losing his patience. He burst out:

"Who are you talking about, Mr Nantes? tell me."

Casting a pained glance at the doctor, the Belgian gaped, swallowed several times, then left while muttering to himself.

Seeing that sorry wreck of a man tottering down the steps, rattled the doctors equanimity. He was in a quandary; his conscience demanded to make a full report to the government, perhaps even to the police. Yet a doctor's pledge to secrecy should not be breached, especially in a case where a patient showed no inclination towards violence, or a tendency to harm himself.

In hindsight, that is presently, as he came near his home, he wished to have alerted Mrs Burchard after Nantes' first consultation, in which case he might still be here, and Murdoch, finally unmasked, would surely be gone forever.

As he walked along the rushing river, contradictory sentiments played havoc with his mind. Guilt, that monster with a thousand claws, assailed him relentlessly, till vindication, the antidote to remorse, staved off the growling beast. Of course there was a downside to a belated disclosure, similar to the one in Haiti, that ultimately forced him to leave. Would he not be treated likewise once his professional relations with Nantes became hawker's news? Now as then he might be blamed for the Belgian's misfortune, as happened in the case of Vezina, the fixer, back in Port-au-Prince, who disappeared without a trace three days after visiting him.

"I should not have said a word to Mrs Burchard about Nantes' condition, or even his consultation," he deplored. "It will only cast aspersions onto me, without bringing him back," he surmised.

The thought of being imputed with that abominable obeah cult made him shudder. To be stung with disgrace again, ostracised by friends and acquaintances, and persecuted by the police, thoroughly dismayed him. He was well aware that the latent ugly rumours about his amoral conduct were still circulating; they could flare up once more at the slightest provocation. Moving again deemed him abhorrent. Nevertheless, by the time he reached the house, he resolved to make a clean breast of it, and the devil fetch the hindmost. As always, once decisions are made, the inner turmoil subsides.

After Nantes' second visit nothing more was heard of him, nor had he been seen again.

"The earth has swallowed him," remarked chief Howard Brunt after months of investigations.

Two weeks after his inexplicable disappearance, a short announcement appeared in the Dominican Weekly that Nantes had left the island without informing a soul. Astonishment was expressed by the editor about the secretiveness surrounding his departure; in fact, Mauch deplored the botanist's caprice, as he called it, especially since he had been accorded a princely treatment by all concerned. Mr Murdoch, he wrote separately, has voiced dismay at his slated successor's highhanded action.

"I feel betrayed. After all I have done for him I didn't expect to be left in the lurch like this," were his exact words.

More was written about Mr Murdoch's woes.

"My suitcases were packed already. One can imagine the anticipated joy of seeing the white cliffs of Dover again, after more than five years."

The article waxed angrily:

"Lucky for us, Mr Murdoch is putting a brave face on a bleak situation. Being a gentleman of the old school, he offered to remain at his post till a suitable replacement is found. 'Duty before self-interest', he told us in a voice quivering with shattered hopes. How long is he prepared to stay? If need be another two years, our local botanist promised."

Mrs Burchard snorted unrestrained when she read the exercise of dissimulation, as she termed the write-up.

"The whole scribble reeks," she remarked to her husband, who nodded and grinned.

"Of what, dear?" he asked.

"Of rancid lard, Raoul."

She was not the only one harbouring misgivings about Mauch's efforts at window-dressing. Upon reading it, Dr Brodeur's face creased, a sardonic smile hovered around his lips, which turned to a grimace. For he recalled Nantes' mien, distorted by terror, when asked to confide in Murdoch, who after all was not only a colleague but had a vested interest in his well-being. Yes, his thunderstruck gaze was like a stab in the doctor's heart, negating Murdoch's insinuation, bandied about by Mauch, of a friendly relationship between the botanists. At the end of the article Murdoch's merits were accentuated; lavishly so.

Dr Brodeur's twinges of conscience had not ceased; he now as then felt incumbent to have a word with Murdoch, despite a growing aversion with the scientist. Why did he feel the need to approach him? Not on account of Nantes, which would only open scarred wounds. Anyway, like an arrow in flight, the Belgian cannot be brought back, neither could the past be undone. The present and future concerned Dr Brodeur; in other words, Hannes Wirt's fate. Could it be similar to his predecessor's? Ought he be forewarned? But most of all should Murdoch be made aware of Nantes' silent accusations directed towards him?

A premonition had gripped the doctor that swelled out like a mazzikeen ass. He was fairly certain that Murdoch had a hand in the Belgian's misery; exactly how, he couldn't say. Yet the notion of harmful substances, administered clandestinely, entered his mind more and more. Obeah, that invocation of evil, soaring on the wings of superstition and dread, inexorably pushed to the foreground. He was no stranger to the sibylline whispers about obeah, attributed with supernatural powers. Wirt stood in mortal danger, Dr Brodeur surmised; in his pessimistic moods that is, but once his spirit rose, he chased such thoughts away. Just the same he owed Wirt a duty not to be shirked. Very well, he told himself, after speaking with Murdoch I shall attend to the new botanist.

Wirt Visits Rintoul

Yesterday Wirt learned about the contested Sylvania property. He decided to investigate on the coming weekend. Harold Rintoul, the bank manager, who apprised him of the mystery-shrouded parcel, had invited him for a little get-together at his house tonight. Wirt accepted with alacrity, since it was a welcome diversion from his grind at the botanical garden. No sense denying it any longer; Murdoch went out of his way to make his life miserable, he became more insufferable by the day. The bond, supposedly woven by the lisles of common interest, slackened at an alarming rate. To tell the truth, these ties no longer existed.

Wirt felt increasingly uneasy in his colleague's presence, if not outright menaced. At the sight of him, gloomy presentiments made his body stoop, and eyes alert. Murdoch appeared to hatch schemes squarely directed against him. His leering glances, imbued with burning disdain, made him shudder despite the sultry air. He didn't understand how a man, a senior scientist of all things, could harbour so much malice towards anybody. The energy expended to keep a successor in the dark, and no less at bay, defied the realms of reason, especially considering his imminent departure. A gnawing suspicion of an impending disaster overwhelmed Wirt, of a calamity somehow connected with those copper-lined crates.

Yet, what drove him to distraction was the matter of the keys. Increasingly doors, filing cabinets, and drawers remained locked solidly. Why? Wirt asked himself at the beginning, before he broached the subject with his colleague who, hurling a vitriolic glance at him, sneered deprecatingly:

"Safety measures, old boy, security concerns."

"Fair enough, but how about getting me duplicate keys?"

Murdoch bristled as if attacked; he neither deigned to look at Wirt, nor vouchsafed an answer. Thereafter ensued a regular tug of war concerning these keys. Wirt had to get almost on his knees to gain access to the Gardens' facilities or documents. Murdoch, should he condescend to heed his colleague's requests, offered some lame excuses about his inability to disentangle a particular key from the ring which, he maintained, may not leave his person. Thus he felt obliged to personally open and close every lock, he assured Wirt.

His repeated declarations to have duplicates made rang hollow; apologies tendered concerning his forgetfulness sounded contrived, as did promises to make good. Murdoch's intentions were dishonourable, he pursued an agenda which made no sense to him. The small favour, a matter of course one should have thought, besides, if granted, would benefit the Gardens, was denied him intentionally, Wirt concluded.

His colleague's attitude, while bewildering, deemed him a detriment to the project. Murdoch paid scant attention to the Gardens anymore. His increasing absences were a source of vexation to Wirt, chiefly on account of the shenanigans with the keys. Curious notions occupied Wirt's mind. One of them, considered unworthy, nevertheless clung to him tenaciously. Murdoch's aim appeared to be two-pronged; one, to stymie the Gardens' progress; two, to get rid of him. Yet this was not Wirt's sole problem. Besides Murdoch's arcane conduct, quickly reaching inimical dimensions, another misgiving had arisen. The two mulattoes spied on him again; not clandestinely as previously, but quite openly. They showed up at the Gardens almost daily, where they wandered around for hours, pretending to be enamoured with the grounds.

Wirt wasn't deceived for an instant, he knew how the wind blew. Someone engaged them to keep an eye on him. Who, and why? Wherever he happened to be these two men showed up. Whether he went to town, the market, or the wharf, they were not far behind him, pretending to be lost in thought or conversation. Should he sidle up to them, they ambled off, seemingly inadvertently. Attempts to strike up a conversation, from afar that is, failed every time; they simply ignored him and walked away.

As if that didn't fill his cup other worrisome occurrences faced him. Of late the servants acted strange, especially the maid and cook, whom Murdoch had chosen despite his protest. He never liked these two; from day one he could barely hide his resentment. Yet, browbeaten by his colleague's insistence, he acquiesced. Neither one seemed able to look him straight in the face. Whenever he addressed them, their eyes grew shifty, and heads turned away from him. No doubt a guilty conscience caused such restless behaviour, alien to the native's character. What made them so skittish he soon found out.

They spoke in whispers now, chuckled nervously while casting oblique glances in his direction. Wirt couldn't banish the impression they were in a flutter with expectations he was unable to conceive. Surprising them at times leering furtively at him, he tried to make out what they were after. Did they anticipate an unusual incident, detrimental to him? It certainly looked like it. In any case their odd, and no less rude deportment worsened visibly. But Wirt, being a just and reasonable man, gave them the benefit of doubt. Might he not evoke spectres dwelling in his distraught mind? More likely than not, he decided.

Thus he resolved to rein in such galloping fancies, and step out of his ivory tower. Consistently eyeing Murdoch, drawing puerile inferences from mere idiosyncrasies, he declared a practice of the past. Yes, he would draw the line at such scrutinies, which benefited no one, but dragged him deeper into the proverbial Serbonian bog. This whimsical imagery must be suppressed, and wholly so. The chase after nameless ghosts had to cease. Wherever he looked, behind every tree, he imagined grimacing imps daunting him. At the call of a mockingbird hidden in the foliage of a breadfruit tree, he felt himself derided and challenged. Should workers converse in patois, their native tongue, which he did not understand, he perceived disdainful allusions directed towards him. At the sight of Murdoch he detected, or thought he did, signs of silent mockery with which his colleague considered him. As said, this could not continue; from today on he vouched to free himself of these chimeras.

"I shall seek the society of men who prefer action to soul searching, who don't give a rap about complex relationships," he promised himself. "Tonight will be a good opportunity to start; Harold Rintoul shall get to know the real Hannes Wirt. Let Murdoch scheme and fret to his heart's content, he would stand aloof from his shenanigans."

As he prepared for his visit, Wirt hesitated while musing:

"Is Mr Rintoul a music lover perchance? Who knows, he might enjoy listening to my favourite pieces. Just in case, I shall take my accordion along."

No sooner said, he slung it over his shoulder and headed out. He arrived at Rintoul's house shortly before sundown. After a friendly, yet measured reception, they took their seats at a table in the garden. Rintoul appeared to be a bachelor, judging by missing signs of a woman's presence. Wirt asked no questions, nor did he hint at anything in that respect. He had learned to accept the peculiar mores among expatriates concerning marital matters. Most men were married, but quite a few led separate lives. Some left their wives behind; others were abandoned by them, after an existence fraught with squabbles and resentment. Wirt had a hunch that the grounds for this antagonism causing the women to return home, had a lot to do with their men's slide into moral turpitude.

After the second cheers the sun dipped behind the horizon. The following, almost instant darkness, surprised Wirt, although he had witnessed it quite often. As the city below lit up, the frogs started their nightly concert. Ushered in by sporadic, cautious whistles, their mighty chorus soon filled the air.

"Am I mistaken, or do the frogs sound louder than usual?" Wirt asked his host.

"Frogs?" Rintoul repeated.

Uncertain whether he had been understood, or if he was made sport of, Wirt said:

"Don't you hear them?"

"Oh, that." Rintoul chuckled.

Seeing Wirt's quizzical gaze he added apologetically:

"To tell the truth, one pays no attention to it after a while. Unless reminded we don't hear them anymore. No doubt it will happen also to you in about six months."

As an afterthought he added:

"Provided you last that long."

"Oh, I will," Wirt assured his host, who remarked:

"Your contract, I take it, is for five years?"

"Yes, initially, but it can be extended for another five years by mutual consent."

Rintoul, seemingly not guided by a desire to pry, nevertheless inquired:

"By the looks of it you intend to remain with us for a long time then?"

"I might die here," Wirt chuckled.

Rintoul, nodding several times, observed his visitor with a significance that touched Wirt unpleasantly. He is doubting my word, it flashed through his mind, thus feeling obliged to make another comment:

"I hope you don't think I'm going to vanish like my predecessor Alfred Nantes."

Shaking his head vigorously, Rintoul asserted:

"No, I don't think so for a moment. By the way, Nantes did not flee helter-skelter as the grapevine says."

"You seem to know something about it," Wirt commented.

"More than I appreciate," Rintoul burst out.

"Do you know his whereabouts?" Wirt inquired with widened eyes.

"Not exactly, but I can well imagine why he left suddenly and furtively."

"Would you be willing to share your thoughts?"

"Most certainly, after all it's the main reason why I invited you. This is what I wish to tell you."

With these words Rintoul straightened up and replenished what had been consumed. Then both leaned back; Wirt in a flutter of expectation, Rintoul with the mien of a harbinger ready to impart gripping news.

"I had two interesting discussions with Nantes. Remember now, I'm referring to confidential conversations that took place between us, aside from fortuitous meetings. I found Nantes exceptionally outgoing, albeit a bit formal. To be sure he thawed with time, though he never lost his decorum. At one of these meetings that took place about two months after his arrival, I detected an irritability indicating strong misgivings. His fidgetiness implied what deep sighs confirmed. There is a man quarrelling with fate, I surmised then, and am sure of now. Tossing discretion into the wind, ignoring his reluctance to talk about himself, I gradually steered the conversation towards his job."

Since Rintoul paused while looking at him queerly, Wirt felt compelled to say something:

"Did Nantes take the bait?"

"Not at first, yet sensing my sincere sympathy his demeanour softened. He became communicative, then eager to talk. Although still talking in a roundabout way, I decided that he considered Murdoch the bane of his existence. He deemed him unfriendly, inimical actually, and morbidly secretive. Matters of utmost importance to Nantes, essential to him to be versed with, were intentionally obfuscated by Murdoch or kept concealed. His inquiries about the Gardens' intricacies were not only treated with offending silence, but were increasingly insolently rebuffed."

When Wirt displayed signs of irritation, Rintoul looked up.

"You want to say something?" he inquired.

Frowning, his eyes becoming unsteady, avoiding to look at his host, he explained:

"Only this: Imagination can play havoc with a person's sensibility in unfamiliar surrounding among strangers, plus unaccustomed heat."

"That's what I thought at the time," Rintoul agreed.

"But no longer?" Wirt asked.

"No," came a clipped reply.

Silence ensued during which Rintoul let his eyes stray from the sea to his visitor, who appeared to struggle with a desire to say something, and the wish to keep quiet. Meanwhile Rintoul resumed his narration:

"My assumption that Nantes merely suffered from overstrained nerves, was quickly shattered."

Rintoul raised and turned his head from side to side. His features acquired a portentous expression which no amount of restraint was able to hide. While sizing up Wirt, who divined that disagreeable tidings were coming to light, he continued:

"Nantes had cogent reasons to be alarmed, as quickly became evident. You probable are acquainted with the notorious Sylvania property, I presume?"

"Not really, although I heard about it. If you tell me the location I shall visit it on the weekend."

Rintoul's head bound up. He half rose from his seat, then sat down again. Agitated he raised a hand in disapproval.

"Listen to me first before you undertake that trip," he admonished.

Wirt, uncertain how to react, just nodded, indicating acquiescence.

"Are you aware that Murdoch has a valid claim against that property?"

"No. I was told he manages it for Kew Gardens." Wirt replied.

Rintoul examined Wirt closer. He made a curious remark:

"Kew Gardens is far away, but Murdoch and Mauch are here."

"Mauch, is he connected with it?"

"I believe so, in any case he owns the adjacent parcel."

Wirt pricked his ears.

"Sounds interesting, please do go on," he encouraged.

Rintoul, not waiting to be told twice, looking at his guest in a meaningful way, emphasising every word, commented slowly:

"Nantes' serious difficulties started right after his visit."

"To the Sylvania property?"

"Yes. This is what he told me:

" 'One sunny morning I set out with a hired donkey, a tent, plus provisions for two days. I knew the approximate location and the way leading to it. As I walked on, gnawing doubts encumbered my steps. Doubts about what? you may ask; about whom? you may wonder. Well, about Murdoch, primarily, especially his hostile attitude towards me. I exaggerate not an iota by declaring that my inquiry, innocent I should add, about the property at Sylvania was answered with nothing but a growl. Anyway, second thoughts assailed me as I neared my destination. What would Murdoch's reaction be should he find out about my visit? Just the same, I decided that it was too late to be concerned about him; thus I plodded forward. I arrived there by mid-morning. You could have knocked me over with a feather at the surprising sight. I tell you, the intoxicating scent made the donkey frisk his tail. What met my widened eyes can only be described as a splendour in the wilderness.'

"Those were Nantes' exact words. He instantly realised that this was no ordinary layout; it served a useful purpose. The grounds were meticulously kept; the buildings, though small, were tastefully appointed, and surprisingly sturdily constructed. The entire installation would have done honour to an architect of repute; it pleased the eye and comforted the mind. But, strange to say, it also had a frightening aspect, so much so, that he felt inclined to bolt, he told me."

"What perturbed him?" Wirt asked.

"I too asked that question."

"Did he tell you?"

"No. He shrugged his shoulders, indicating an inability to explain what repelled him. In any case he described the facilities in detail.

"Amid blossoming trees that emit a sweet odour, stand others, fruit-bearing, whose bark is peeled off to various degrees. Surrounding the entire park are dense hedges, interrupted by a single opening, barred by sturdy iron gates, guarded by two brawny natives. Visible inside is a small building encircled by a high fence. His inquiries were answered reluctantly, and no less morosely in patois, which of course he didn't understand."

"Hm, sounds odd," remarked Wirt.

"That's what Nantes thought at first till the next episode took place."

"Next episode?" Wirt echoed.

"A surprising one it turned out to be. Two men appeared from the fenced area, who resembled characters from an exhibition. They were muffled up from head to toe in rubber suits. Full masks covered their faces, and gloves protected their hands. One can imagine how Nantes felt as he stood beside his donkey, scantily clad, but nevertheless bathed in perspiration, whereas these men wandered about in rubber suits. Scarcely had they stepped from the enclosure, when the guards hailed them in patois. They ran back and disappeared in a flash inside the building. The guards' attitude changed drastically; they became gruffer and louder, while assuming a menacing stance. Stamping to and fro, shaking their arms at him, pointing towards Rosseau, they tried to chase him away. That was easier said than done; in fact, they reckoned without their host. Nantes was anything but a trembling leaf, besides, he resented being harangued. This is what he said to me:

" 'As these two put on a front of bravado to frighten me, I saw red. Pictures of my forbears appeared before my inner eye as they dashed across the plains of Flanders; heads down, spears up, prepared to do battle. Without uttering a word I rushed upon the guards, who scurried inside and locked the gates with one movement. Having reached safety, a mighty clamour ensued, accompanied by feint attacks. One fellow shook the bars with both hands, the other dealt them successive kicks, no doubt meant for me. Finally I had enough; I left. Believe me, the donkey seemed glad to be led away.' "

"Did he return to the city?" Wirt inquired.

"Not our Nantes, he was carved from hardier wood than that. The inexplicable hostility shown by the guards, plus the ominous masquerade of the others, not only made him curious but honed his mettle. He resolved to investigate further. 'Sealed rubber suits in this sultry weather; high security fences in the middle of nowhere, guarded by belligerent attendants? Indeed, what next?' Nantes scoffed.

"He set up his tent nearby, then waited till darkness descended. Leaving the donkey behind he walked towards the compound, which he had no difficulty finding in the diffused light of the moon and stars. Nearing the hedges, he saw lights moving around inside, resembling friars' lanterns. After finding a small opening in the otherwise dense hedges, he positioned himself there and looked through.

" 'Almost instantly I perceived the grotesquely clad figures. They were no longer alone however.'

"Pausing, Nantes eyed me with an air I can only call anticipatory. Straightening up, leaning back, he remarked in a mysterious tone:

" 'Two white men had joined them, whose identities stunned me to the core. Guess, who they were.'

" 'Murdoch and Mauch,' I offered.

" 'None other,' the Belgian asserted.

"By the way, are you aware that the two are old acquaintances from days in England?"

"I had no idea," Wirt replied.

"Let me expound what Nantes told me:

" 'The mummies, as I christened them, were busy peeling off the remaining bark from the trees, which they laid, along with pieces strewn on the ground, into small crates visible in the starlit night.' "

Wirt, starting involuntarily, interposed:

"Crates? Were the insides lined?"

Taken aback by his guest's outburst, Rintoul replied haltingly:

"Nantes didn't say. Why are you asking?"

"Just a thought for an instant."

"Come to think of it, Nantes did mention that the insides of these wooden boxes reflected the dim light of the moon in a manner incongruous with wood."

Noticing Wirt's strained demeanour, Rintoul fell silent, he waited for his visitor's response. Wirt was on the verge of disclosing his experience at the Gardens', but reined his tongue, for he recalled the promise given to Murdoch. He merely asked:

"What happened next?"

Disappointed about his guest's reluctance to reveal what evidently occupied his mind, Rintoul explained:

"Nantes watched the crates being filled with bark. As the covers were fastened, he noticed that they too reflected the light in the manner of shiny metal."

"Yes, I know," Wirt thought, then asked:

"Did Nantes discover anything else?"

"Not on that evening, he spent an uneventful night in the tent, under a darkening sky, whose clouds soon burst. Next morning he loaded his donkey and headed back."

"A peculiar story," Wirt granted.

"More than that, wait till you hear the rest," Rintoul asserted.

"A week after Nantes came to see me again. What a changed man he was. I greeted him effusively, but regret to say my breath was wasted. To tell the truth, I might as well have hailed a ghost. Standing at the bottom landing, exuding utter doom, Nantes resembled a man stuck to his neck in a slough of despondence. At first I hardly recognised the hollow-eyed, haggard figure, who looked more like a scarecrow than a man. As he staggered up the stairs, a cry of pity almost broke from my lips, for a more smitten man had never crossed my path. Two unspeakable sad eyes gazed at me from sockets of a gruesome hue. The man, bursting with strength a week ago, now resembled someone who had kissed the gunner's daughter. Before me stood a wizened old man about to breathe his last."

"What was wrong with him?" Wirt queried.

"Nothing, he insisted. Despite my entreaties to confide in me, he remained noncommittal, if not outright evasive. Finally he thawed somewhat, perhaps obeying a need not understood by himself. What he tried to explain, a sound mind could not have grasped. He lamented about a fear gnawing at his vitals, and moaned about dark forces dragging him inexorably into an early grave. As he drivelled on, weird notions entered my mind. Was the man on a spree? Had he gone temporarily insane? Or did he suffer from a trauma? Getting into his stride he whispered hoarsely:

" 'Even in my waking hours I see a gaping grave beckoning, with a tombstone bearing my name. A persistent voice from within bids me to find that grave.'

" 'Mr Nantes, you are hallucinating,' I protested. 'Did you hear what I said?' I practically barked, since he totally ignored my comments.

"As mentioned, the man was in his stride, not even a thunderbolt could have distracted or stopped him.

" 'Yes, yes, the bidding gets more urgent, shriller, my ears are ringing from the roaring sounds,' Nantes complained.

"Getting rather impatient, I chided:

" 'Sounds, voices, what are you talking about?'

" 'This: I am commanded to find and lie myself down in that grave, for only then shall I find deliverance from my torments,' Nantes reiterated."

"He had entered a state of dementia, by the looks of it," offered Wirt, while wiping his brow with the back of his hand, as if trying to brush away a creeping foreboding.

"Yes, he was in a terrifying frame of mind. I am not averse to admit my own rising anxiety. Having someone in the house scarcely known to me, who might momentarily have a fit, was not a pleasant experience," Rintoul said apologetically.

"No one can fault you for that, just listening to the story makes my flesh creep," Wirt commiserated.

"As mentioned I neither knew Nantes well, nor had I ever encountered a man so distraught. My house, as you may have noticed, is hidden by tall trees and dense bushes, thereby rendering it quite secluded. That evening neither the moon nor a single star lit up an Egyptian darkness. It may sound silly in retrospect, but scruples assailed me about my safety. The shimmering lights of Roseau in the distance never before glowed with such warmth and reassurance."

When Rintoul cast expectant glances at him, Wirt felt obliged to respond:

"I can sympathise with you," he comforted his host, who resumed his narrative:

"I have never seen a man in a fluster like Nantes that evening. My nerves became frayed, I had to get a grip on myself to keep them under control. Assuming a fatherly tone I tried to calm him with soothing words.

" 'Go home, take a good night's rest, in the morning everything will look brighter,' I consoled."

"Where you successful?" Wirt inquired.

"Far from it. He bolted upright, sheer terror distorted his face as he groaned:

" 'I can't go back to that house, not tonight, perhaps never again.'

"Seeing him ashen, and trembling like aspen leaves, I invited him to stay with me overnight."

"Did he accept?"

"With an astounding alacrity; in fact, I feared he would fall on my neck."

Wirt chuckled under his breath, picturing the standoffish bank manager being ardently embraced. What a compromise that would have been to a staid man invested with an official position.

"How did the night go?" Wirt asked.

After taking two ample draughts from his glass, Rintoul shook his head in a manner that expressed utter dismay.

"I would not wish that experience onto my mortal enemy. Although the guest room is located at the opposite end from my bedroom, I was kept awake by rumblings of a frightening intensity. Sleep was out of the question; a presentiment befell me of impending evil. Nantes' stomping and clattering I could have endured perhaps, but not the lamenting and moaning, interrupted by occasional murderous shrieks."

Looking straight at his guest, Rintoul inquired:

"Did you ever hear the weird cries of the kookaburra?"

"Not that I remember," Wirt replied.

"How about the uncanny call of the loon?"

"I know it quite well."

"Well, take those two, add a hyena's maniacal laughter, and you get the idea of Nantes' ravings. Screaming 'no, no' repeatedly, cackling hysterically in between, he pounded on the walls and belaboured the floor. I can say with justification that I am not a craven, but his conduct made me shudder."

"Did it last all night?" Wirt queried.

"Pretty well, till I stopped it. After listening for hours to this unearthly wailing, I had enough. More infuriated than sympathetic or scared, I confronted Nantes. What happened defies description. When I knocked on the door, he raised a murderous hue and cry.

" 'Stay away, be gone,' he screamed in a voice choked with terror.

"If you think that he just acted like a moon-struck, temporarily mindless fellow, think again. Finding the door unlocked, I entered the room. Nantes gazed at me with dilated eyes as if confronted by the basilisk with the fatal breath and look. I barely recognised him. He staggered backwards with bulging eyes, pointing in every direction while moaning piteously. He upset me so much that I would have dearly loved to box his ears; but taking pity on that heap of misery, I desisted.

"Finally he calmed down and laid himself fully clothed on the bed. Seeing him somewhat composed, I went back to my room. In the morning when the sun had climbed over the mountains, I awoke from a trance-like sleep. Nantes sat already on the veranda, looking sheepishly at me as I approached him. Manifestly embarrassed, he wanted to know how he behaved during the night.

" ' I had a terrible nightmare,' he confessed.

" 'Nightmare? You conducted yourself like a maniac,' I almost burst out, but in view of his hangdog bearing I consoled him with words like:

" 'Don't worry about it, it wasn't so bad.'

"Did I blush? Probably yes, I certainly am shamefaced in retrospect."

"How did it end?"

"I urged him to visit Dr Brodeur, our able physician, whom Nantes knew. Given my uncompromising stance, he must have sensed that my cup was overflowing, thus dousing the remnants of a waning sympathy. No man in my opinion, no matter what ails him, should lose control of himself. Nantes' suffering, no doubt genuinely perceived, nevertheless deemed me a chimera of an overwrought mind. Such wild fancies, then as now, find scant resonance with me. Nantes had given rein to extravagant images, as subsequent events manifested."

"What happened?" Wirt asked.

"He mumbled something about voodoo, obeah, missing shirts, and curses. This babbling infuriated me, for I utterly resent even a breath of superstition. I stormed and railed at him mercilessly. Was he devoid of common sense? I inveighed. Had he no pride in our European heritage whose reputation such twaddle sullied? How can a scientist pay credence to devil worship? I reprimanded."

"What did he answer?"

"Ha, the man had gone beyond the pale. Though somewhat cowed, he droned on about stuffed dolls, spitting images of himself, placed on his bed, sneering maliciously. When he added that these images had a thorn piercing the heart's region, I lost all patience. As I gave him a dressing-down, he nodded uneasily, while promising to visit Dr Brodeur without delay."

"Did he?"

Rintoul nodded assent. Then suddenly growing drowsy, he rested his head in both his hands. Heartfelt sighs escaped from his lips as he recalled the dreadful incident of that night.

"As I learned later he saw the doctor on his way home."

Raising his head, expelling another sigh, a moan really, Rintoul remarked:

"When Nantes left, more sure-footed than at his arrival, he slowly turned at the bottom of the stairs. In a quavering voice and challenging mien he said something that nearly made me run after him."

"Oh, did he get abusive?' Wirt inquired.

"Worse than that," Rintoul chuckled, "he became delusional. Standing there, assuming a defiant posture, he exclaimed:

" 'Do you know what else is inscribed on my gravestone?'

"I shook my head indignantly, meaning to express my growing irritation; for I declare the fellow began to stick in my craw. Paying little heed to my fierce stare, Nantes groaned:

" 'The day of my death.'

" 'Nonsense, man,' I barked.

" 'Do you want to know what it is, Mr Rintoul?'

" 'No,' I burst out.

" 'It's the day when I am supposed to take over the Gardens' management,' Nantes informed me, before he disappeared behind a row of hedges."

Silence reigned for several minutes. Rintoul appeared to be stricken by the memory of that momentous experience. Wirt had a hunch that his host wished him to leave. Yet, when he prepared to rise, Rintoul signalled that he should remain seated. Seemingly wrestling with contradictory emotions, he glimpsed at him several times in a significant manner, prior to continuing:

"I felt tempted to bound after him, but a strange weakness made my limbs tremble. As I wobbled towards the stairs I almost blacked out. A terrifying thought occurred to me: I had been infected with Nantes' morbid fantasies. Whatever ailed him was transferred onto me, I told myself. I had to grip the railing with both hands, so as not to fall headlong down the steps."

"I am sorry to hear it," Wirt condoled dutifully, but no less half-heartedly, for weightier matters occupied his mind.

He wished to call it an evening, for listening to his host's horrid narration cast a pall over his spirit. A strange foreboding made his spine tingle; an inner voice bid him to be on guard. According to Rintoul his predecessor endured excruciating anguish; whether self-induced by runaway imageries, or empirical knowledge, made little difference. Unsettling occurrences had taken place, if half of Rintoul's narration be taken for granted. What made him fear for his safety that drove him into the arms of frenzy? Wirt's thoughts turned to himself. Could he expect a similar fate? Judging by the state of affairs, especially Murdoch's arcane conduct and unsettling utterances, the possibility could not be ruled out.

Wirt observed his host furtively. He fervently wished to have been blessed with a mind-reader's gift. Something seemed amiss with Rintoul's story; it sounded contrived, undeserving of credence. But then again, why would a man of rank make a point to inform him of occurrences that took place two years ago? Did he pursue a secret agenda? Was it meant to chase him away and leave the field to Murdoch once more? Or had Rintoul a penchant for roguery coupled with anecdotal propensities? No, Wirt decided, his host's recital, fictional or truthful, served a more sinister purpose. Whatever it turned out to be, he made a silent vow not to knuckle under.

As he reflected, Rintoul waited patiently, loath to interrupt his train of thought. Noticing him touching the accordion several times, Rintoul asked:

"Would you like to play something?"

Chuckling self-consciously, Wirt replied:

"I don't think so after what I just heard."

"Admittedly it's a scary story, yet entirely true," Rintoul assured.

"One thing I don't understand," Wirt exclaimed.

"Only one?" his host quipped.

"Why did Nantes not report these alarming incidents to the police, or did he?"

"The answer is no," Rintoul advised.

"Hm, that sounds odd," Wirt remarked.

"It sure does. When I urged him to have a talk with Howard Brunt, the chief, he grew restive, if not decidedly recalcitrant. He practically moaned:

" 'No, not that.' "

Turning towards his host, squinting and knitting his brow, Wirt wanted to know:

"No offence, Mr Rintoul, why are you telling me this?"

"Concerning Nantes, you mean?"

"Yes."

"To make you aware of lurking dangers. Do believe me, there are malevolent forces at play in connection with the botanical garden, involving a number of highly placed men and women."

"Would you care to mention their names?" Wirt requested.

"I like to, but dare not on account of prevailing defamation laws. But let me exhort you to be on guard. Machinations are afoot again that bode no good."

Shaking his head suggestively, Rintoul repeated:

"They sure don't."

Wirt didn't ask for details, he changed the subject:

"You had a sudden attack of faintness, I understand."

"Yes, but it abated gradually. After Nantes disappeared beyond the hedges, I cast off my anxiety, or rather tried to. It proved easier said than done. I needed to harness every fibre of willpower to tame recurring thoughts of having contracted Nantes' malady. It took all morning to shake off a galloping queasiness that bore no name."

"When was the last time you saw Nantes?"

"On that sunny morning when he left my house in a dither."

"No one heard about him since, I understand," Wirt remarked.

"In a way yes, although Mauch's newspaper printed an article about him about two weeks after his disappearance, implying that Nantes had returned to his homeland, abruptly and clandestinely."

Recalling the police chief's comments at Murdoch's house, Wirt, raising his eyebrows, protested:

"I was told by no less an authority than Howard Brunt that Nantes had not returned to Belgium."

"The chief is probably correct," Rintoul agreed; then explained:

"That newspaper article, besides being slipshod, was also slanted.

"In what way?"

"Mauch labelled Nantes a flighty character, which in my estimation amounted to nothing less than a slur. Praising in the same breath Murdoch's reliability and loyalty bordered on base flattery, if not worse."

"What are you referring to?"

"It seemed to me a ruse, a cover intended to divert attention."

Wirt would have liked to ask what his host meant, but noticing his defensive mien made a statement instead:

"From what you told me one could deduce that Nantes suspected Mauch and Murdoch to collude in some devious scheme."

"He did. Strongly so, as did, still do, many others," Rintoul advised with a yawn and a glimpse at the clock.

"Time to go," Wirt told himself.

The Biter Bit

O n his way back many disquieting notions thronged upon him. For the first time since his arrival he paid scant attention to the wondrous voices of the Caribbean night, whose magic left him untouched. He halted his steps on the bridge. Listening to the rushing water below steadied his nerves, allowing him to think more rational.

As usually at this time the streets outside the city were empty. While watching the coursing water, Wirt meditated on Rintoul's revelation. Nantes' adverse fate made him feel uneasy, especially in view of his own misgivings, which gave no cause for jubilation. Murdoch's Olympian attitude he neither understood nor appreciated. Even though it were mere posturing or a harmless quirk, it caused a lot of grief. No doubt his inscrutable attitute impeded the Gardens' development, plus created untenable conditions for everyone connected with the project. Besides, what possible benefits could Murdoch reap through his contrariness?

Suddenly it dawned on him. His colleague, colluding with others, had devised a method to remain in control of the Gardens for a predetermined time. Wirt couldn't imagine the reason, contrary to the means employed, which he began to understand. Two years ago Alfred Nantes stood in his, or someone else's way; today he was the bone in that schemer's craw. How was Nantes gotten rid of? What induced a responsible scientist, after pulling up stakes thousands of miles away, to forsake his work under cover of night? Of course he might have been the victim of an accident, though foul play couldn't be ruled out, as opposed to heedless flight, such a belief no reasonable person would harbour. Perhaps he undertook a second trip to Sylvania when, spurred by curiosity and stung by guilt, he plunged to his death into one of the omnipresent ravines. He could have been pushed, or otherwise done away with, for all one knows.

Many suppositions obtruded themselves on Wirt's mind, for which answers were wanting. Realising that no amount of pondering would unravel the mystery, he directed his thoughts towards his intended trip to Sylvania. He wanted to see with his own eyes what Nantes had described to Rintoul. Doubt dampened his ardour when he called to mind Rintoul's veiled warning, meant to dissuade him to go near that property. Those oracular remarks rang in his ears:

"After Nantes' trip to Sylvania his troubles began in earnest."

It might be advisable to quell his curiosity for a while, at least till Murdoch has left the island. His colleague might take umbrage, perhaps deem a visit as meddling, thereby fanning discontent.

As he prepared to continue on his way, he remembered that he had left his accordion behind. In his eagerness to escape the atmosphere of gloom, created by Rintoul's narration, he had forgotten about it. Oh well, he told himself, the evening is still young, so why not go back and collect it.

After the first steps he noticed two dark figures at the end of the bridge, leaning over the railing, seemingly absorbed in conversation. Surprised to see anyone about, feeling a vague discomfort, he hesitated. While struggling with indecision, the corner of his eyes caught a glimpse of his house on the hill. The sight reassured him as a nearby fortress calms the nerves of a beleaguered man. Instinctively he looked again, longer and more intensively. At first he couldn't determine what attracted his attention. Only after a prolonged gaze did he identify the source of his bewilderment. The lights in the house were on; but that couldn't be, for he had ensured that they were extinguished prior to leaving. He treated such matters with solicitude; his thrifty nature abhorred any form of waste. Although the government paid the energy bills, his inbred propensity to parsimony refused to take advantage of the fact. Every morning before he left the house he ascertained that all lights were switched off. How could they be on now? The servants were not due till the day after tomorrow, besides, no reason existed for them to light up the entire house. They arrived after sunrise, and always left an hour before dusk.

While still trying to unravel the puzzle, the lights went out progressively. Someone rummaged through the house. Who could it be? Something else flashed through his mind. Recalling the previous incident where strangers gadded about the property, he locked all outside doors before setting out.

Torn between an urge to rush to the house, or walk towards the two men, who meanwhile appeared to be embroiled in a heated discussion, Wirt stood rooted to the spot. Things turned livelier by the second. Judging by the swell of sound, angry stomping and wild gesticulations, the discussion took on aspects of an argument. The two men encircled each other like fighting cocks ready to fly at each other.

Watching their antics with increasing consternation, it dawned on Wirt that something seemed fishy, almost comical. He soon realised that their ballyhoo served no other purpose than stoking a flagging courage, towards what end only the angels knew. Their war dance was surely directed at him, Wirt granted. Were they enjoined with a mission for which they lacked aptitude as much as resoluteness, thus attempting to pep themselves up with bluster? Stealing sidelong glances from the house to the clamouring men, Wirt remained indecisive. Should he hurry to his house or walk back to Rintoul's place? Hardly had he resolved to do one thing, when a countermanding voice from within told him:

"No, do the other."

His feet appeared to be stuck in blocks of concrete. He remained of two minds till the lights in the house came on again. That put him in his mettle. Garnering every ounce of strength that his body and mind possessed, he started to move forward. Obeying an irresistible urge to turn around repeatedly, he noticed that the two men followed him. The realisation awakened emotions that refused to be restraint. First came anger which fanned his sagging spirit. With a suppressed curse on his lips, both fists clenched, he turned around. Ready to show these sneakers a thing or two, he walked towards them. He fully intended to collar one after the other and shake a confession out of their pelts. His cup was filled to the brim, they better be prepared to own up.

Nothing of the sort happened, for hardly had he advanced a few steps when they vanished. Baffled, Wirt stopped for a moment. Scanning the dimly lit huts beyond the bridge, he didn't detect any movement, not even a shadow could be seen. Hesitating not another second he ran, rather leaped, across the bridge. Like an irate bull he charged through the narrow lanes, hollering at the top of his lungs. He was no longer himself; his nerves, grown taut by Rintoul's ill-boding narrative, stretched to the limit by the mystery of the lights in his house, were ready to snap. As once before he cast caution to the wind and transgressed the tenets of propriety. His rambunctious behaviour caused young and old to come outside.

"What's going on here?" people demanded to know.

Wirt, beside himself, bellowed at the gathering crowd:

"Don't play possum with me, turn them out this minute."

The commanding voice, meant to intimidate, produced general merriment instead.

"What is the man looking for?" someone asked.

"Probably his shadow," a woman suggested who, like most of her sex, refused to be cowed as readily as their men.

"I demand to see them," Wirt barked.

"Who are you talking about?"

"Quit dissembling, the two scoundrels who are following me around for weeks. Tell them to come out and face me like men," Wirt thundered.

His imperious manner achieved the opposite result than anticipated. Rather then throwing a scare into the rapidly swelling crowd, his threatening bluster made them coarsely jocular. In no time did a country fair mood enliven the surrounding.

"He is drunk," a woman announced.

"Cracked up," another one conjectured.

"Both, I say," someone chimed in.

"Wait, isn't that the new botanist?" an older man called out, who worked at the Gardens.

"Botanist or not, the fellow is causing a disturbance, he should be reported to the police."

That suggestion made the gathering break out in peals of laughter; for the natives, one and all, avoided the authorities like the devil avoids holy water.

The unexpected guffaw made Wirt stop in his tracks. Letting his wary eyes wander from here to there, a disquieting thought raced through his mind. No doubt these people looked upon him as a besotten rowdy, deficient of mental faculties, who rather deserved pity than mockery.

It suddenly dawned on him that someone endeavoured to cast a shadow on his sanity. Cognisant of his penchant to flare up if provoked, unknown adversaries lured him into compromising situations; in other words they wanted to brand him a hotspur who cannot possibly be entrusted with the Gardens' management. That was it! Those men were commissioned to follow him around, goading him as it were, into rash behaviour unseemly for a botanist in charge. A neat ruse, Wirt granted, but these shenanigans would be dealt a crushing blow, starting right now.

"Just watch," he murmured.

Acquiring a conciliatory stance, he announced in a voice dripping with humility:

"Yes, I am the new botanist, Hannes Wirt is the name. Don't be alarmed, I'm a little out of sorts, I will tell you why in a minute."

Talking in a similar vein he mentioned his good intentions, and expressed heartfelt thanks to the people of Dominica, and appreciation for their kindness and generosity.

"I'm looking for two men among you for two reasons; first, I want to convey a message, nothing unpleasant mind you; second, I have a gift for them, a payment for services rendered," Wirt lied.

He put on a commendable performance, worthy of a Thespian divinely inspired. Judging by the crowd's changing mood, his plan appeared to be crowned with success. The women started talking among themselves, in patois of course.

A matron, built like an amazon, called out several times. Her peremptory utterances induced two men to come forth haltingly. Egged on by a few bystanders, they peered cautiously around before proceeding. Getting a glimpse of Wirt, they made ready to disappear from view again. But having instantly recognised them, Wirt hailed the two like long lost companions. Despite their sneering, defying demeanour, he extended his hand smilingly. Nodding appreciatively, winking with one eye, fixing the other on the crowd, he announced for all to hear his joy at the reunion:

"Am I ever glad to see you again."

Revelling in their visible consternation, Wirt exclaimed:

"Forgive my rashness, folks, but friends, albeit nearly forgotten in the march of time, deserve to be greeted with a measure of exuberance."

His stratagem seemed to be working; snickers and chuckles abated, then died down completely. The crowd's deprecating scorn directed at him, now shifted towards the two men whom a moment ago they wanted to protect.

"You scheming scallawags," the matron cried.

Turning towards the others she exclaimed:

"To think what lies they have been telling us, my goodness, the insolence of it."

Approaching the two men, all in a dither by now, she planted herself before them. Arms akimbo, looking daggers, she inveighed:

"Blackening a gentleman's reputation, will you?"

"Who means well," another woman fell in.

"Be gone! Be gone!" they were told.

Wirt chuckled under his hand, things were shaping up. The hirelings, which they surely were, didn't know what to do. Obviously cowed, trying to avoid the merciless scolding, they sent imploring glances in every direction, which helped them not a whit. For the crowd, women mostly, vixenish to the marrow, self-righteous by nature, needed to vent their roused indignation. As the men made a retreat, Wirt drove home his advantage:

"Now fellows, don't go away, I got something for you."

His request fell on deaf ears, the putative agents were anxious to be out of sight.

An air of consternation reigned. Men and women, angry with themselves on account of the harsh and unjust treatment accorded Wirt, shook their heads and grinned sheepishly, while telling the young ones roughly to be quiet and get back inside.

Wirt beamed from ear to ear, for he realised that the grapevine would soon be whirring, singing his praise. Wishing everyone a good night, he set out for home. Though not knowing the time, he felt tired, spent in body and soul. More so upon remembering the disquieting occurrences at the house. Who could be rummaging about, moreover, for what purpose? True, the spooky incident might have an innocent connotation, but Wirt didn't think so. To him it possessed a portentous, albeit inexplicable significance. Anxiety winged his steps, apprehension weighed on his mind which conjured up dark forces lying in wait, set to pounce.

The bridge, shrouded in semi-darkness, barely visible from afar, was deserted. While crossing it with quickening strides, Wirt caught a glimpse of the house looming at the foothills. The lights were out, implying that whoever stole through the house might have left. He halted his steps, undecided whether he should continue on his way, or return to the city. As he tried to shake off a creeping uneasiness, haunting notions raced through his mind. Despite an effort to convince himself that all is well, he instinctively looked around for a weapon, be it only a stick or small rock. When he moved on and drew near to the house, a blast of wind shook the trees and shrubs in the yard, making them bend and creak ominously. Beset by flickers of dread, he nevertheless walked on.

Nothing stirred in the house, which Wirt approached with trepidation. On the stairs he rattled the railing, dragged his feet noisily over the steps, and cleared his throat repeatedly. The racket, admittedly intended to buoy up, or rather sustain, his courage, was chiefly meant to chase an intruder away.

"Is someone there?" he called out several times in a rasping voice, before he entered the house.

Going from room to room, while growling menacingly, he switched on every lamp. Finding no one inside, he proceeded to the yard. After the first step he nearly jumped back inside and locked the door behind him. Yet he managed to contain himself, albeit with considerable effort. For what he saw and heard almost induced him to run helter-skelter back to town. The wind played havoc with anything moveable. Trees and shrubs, moaning eerily, creaking suspiciously, cast weird shadows resembling ghostly dancers leaping about. Despite nagging misgivings, Wirt inspected bushes and shrubs, while suppressing an urge to cringe at every rush and clatter.

Opposed to his habit, he did not immediately retire for the night, fearing that his rattled equanimity would prevent him to fall asleep. Besides, the usual joyous anticipation eluded him; to lie on his bed under an open window, feeling the cooling breeze on his face, while listening to the voices of the forest. The river's ripple and the rhythmic splash of falling surf never failed to raise a blissful smile to his lips. Every evening he vowed to stay awake, reading, and listening to the sounds of the night. But scarcely had he stretched his legs, when slumber overwhelmed him. Not lately, however, for anxiety kept him awake till late into the night.

Wirt decided to sit on the veranda for a while and reflect on past events. He never ceased marvelling at the view, which captivated one's senses, especially on starlit nights. Often he sat there, sending a silent hymn to the fates above. The sight he found incomparable to anything encountered before. The city of Roseau below, not beautiful by any stretch of the imagination, nevertheless exuded a charm, at night that is, not readily forgotten. What made the feeling memorable Wirt was unable to pinpoint. He tried to describe it several times in letters sent home, but always gave up with a sigh. Could it be the soft light of Roseau, the faint reflection on the shimmering surface of the sea? Whatever made the sight noteworthy, tonight Wirt had neither eyes for the smiling beauty, nor ears for the wondrous sounds of the night.

His thoughts wandered to past and present events, foreshadowing an inglorious future for him. He didn't blame Nantes for his purported flight; not a bit, when considering his own plight. Granted, he most likely rid himself of one worry, but others still remained. The spying will cease, he surmised, while chuckling in afterthoughts. What a crude notion to evoke paroxysms of rage, thereby stigmatising him a firebrand, unworthy to occupy a lofty office, requiring discretion, plus a measure of dignity. Well, he sure managed to put a spoke in their wheel, for now in any case.

"I settled their hash, no argument about it," he remarked smugly, not really knowing who they were.

Notions upon notions raced through his head; some reassuring, yet most disquieting. No amount of sighing, self-ridiculing, or anger was able to dispel this growing dismay. A presentiment of evil, a lurking spectre, refusing to leave his thoughts, spun a stifling web around him. Life cannot go on like this, not for another day, Wirt told himself. Yes, he must take the bull by the horn and force the issue.

Suppressing the profane oath on his lips, he conjectured, rather groaned:

"What is the issue, how can it be forced?"

Calling in question that an ill wind was blowing in his direction seemed infantile. How to stem, or possibly reverse it, however, is a horse of a different colour, he conceded. Again Wirt made assumptions about the identities of his detractors, but one after the other collapsed like a house of cards in a breeze. A similar fate awaited the hypotheses concerning the reasons for these machinations. Many questions arose, few answers were found. One thing appeared to be incontestable: someone wanted him off the island. He needed no oracle to tell him this simple fact; either you pull up stakes, or suffer the Belgian's destiny. The mere notion of returning to the land of his birth disheartened him, for he hoped to draw his last breath in Dominica. Because for the first time in his life he felt a tingling sensation of contentment, despite the nagging vexation about the future. Unencumbered by convention, free and footloose as never before, he was enamoured with the Lonely Island. Returning to an environment devoid of a breath of individuality, where even thoughts are regulated, and opinions and demeanour receive undue scrutiny, made him shudder. Living among stereotypes who not only think and act alike, but resemble each other to a tee, was not in the cards. He would fight tooth and nail to prevent it.

But against whom should he aim this challenge since his detractors bore neither face nor name? Start with Murdoch, his inner voice commanded, face him squarely.

"Yes, yes," Wirt murmured, "but what should I say? That he stands in my way, intentionally renders my existence untenable?"

He could just imagine his colleague straighten up, exhibiting haughty indifference, towering over him with a puckered brow and drooping corners of the mouth, asking in a supercilious tone:

"My dear fellow, pray, what are you referring to?"

What, indeed? His high-handedness, lack of co-operation, or dearth of heartiness perhaps? Confronting Murdoch evoked the spectres of sniffs, sarcastic remarks, and sardonic smirks, which Wirt dreaded more than a sound thrashing. Nevertheless, he decided to have it out with him. Not immediately, however; first he must hone his faltering spirit. Extended, strenuous walks should give him the moral strength required to face Murdoch. Learning patois will also help, Wirt thought, to invigorate his waning morale. The desire to learn the local dialect, stifled amid nagging concerns about imagined calamities lurking at his threshold, must be revived. Dominica was his home now, the only and final one, he hoped. Ten wild horses could not drag him away from here, he vowed, let alone vile machinations of his enemies.

Suddenly he remembered tomorrow's meeting with Mrs Burchard and Howard Brunt. Why the chief of police wished to attend puzzled him, since he was not connected with the Gardens. Then again, Wirt welcomed the portly, expansive cockney's presence for several reasons. He liked his breezy manner; besides, rumours circulated that, to use police parlance, the chief had the goods on Murdoch which he might reveal tomorrow.

A Momentous Meeting

After a tumultuous night, plagued by horrible and frightening dreams, Wirt went to the Gardens early. The workers hadn't shown up yet, but to his surprise Murdoch was there. He seemed preoccupied, pensive beyond his wont; absorbed in thought, judging by the bowed head and perplexed demeanour. What occupied his mind, Wirt could not guess, except that something disagreeable disturbed his equanimity.

Suppressing an urge to call out, Wirt approached with measured steps. To all appearances Murdoch was oblivious to his presence. Staring at the ground with a wrinkled brow, shaking his head as if of two minds about something, he gave an impression of a man in need of reassurance.

"Good morning, Mr Murdoch," Wirt offered haltingly.

Murdoch bridled involuntarily. He responded with unconcealed aversion:

"Ah, there you are."

His scowl deepened while gazing at Wirt dripping with annoyance. But this inimical bearing changed in a twinkle, it assumed a conciliatory expression.

"I came early," he remarked.

"I wonder why," Wirt almost asked, but commented instead:

"So I see."

Sizing him up with eyes that knew not how to hide acquired condescension, Murdoch declared:

"Today looks opportune to show you the ropes, if it suits you of course."

Wirt couldn't help frowning, for two reasons; first, because his colleague's suggestion to spend time together, possibly all day, conflicted with his scheduled meeting, but more so on account of the proposal itself. Since for nearly three months his mere hints in that direction were either ignored, or quite openly repulsed. So out of the blue comes an offer that had lost its lustre and heightened his nagging suspicion about Murdoch's sincerity.

Trying to conceal his astonishment as much as rising doubts, Wirt replied:

"It's a laudable idea, but unfortunately I cannot oblige."

"Oh," Murdoch expelled as if on cue.

He somehow managed to accentuate his short exclamation with devastating reproof, bordering on condemnation. But strange to say an element of surprise was lacking. He is aware of our gathering, Wirt decided, he wants to sabotage it, since presumably he has not been invited.

Concealing his astonishment, Wirt suggested:

"How about tomorrow, or any other day for that matter?"

Without another word Murdoch turned on his heels and walked away. Things are coming to a head, rapidly so, Wirt admitted.

At the agreed time he called at Mrs Burchard's office. Prior to entering the premises he halted his steps and looked around. As always the sight affected him deeply; it made him pensive, and in a peculiar way also content. The tranquillity, strangely accentuated by the rustle of palm trees and banana shrubs, turned his thoughts away from temporal worries. He felt tempted to sit down on one of the benches and savour the mind-stirring impression till eternity. Whispers filled the air, hinting at secrets that could be divined, but neither understood nor expressed.

A booming voice tore him out of his reveries. Howard Brunt, leaning from a window, cried out:

"Look at the German, forever observing, never idle where the enrichment of erudition is concerned. Upon my word, madam, have we not made a splendid catch?"

Wirt couldn't help chuckling at the unorthodox, albeit uproarious reception. Hastening his steps, he quickly entered the meeting room. Mrs Burchard, smiling broadly, extended a hand. The chief appeared to be in high spirits, he patted Wirt's shoulder and announced in a chest voice:

"It's a pleasure, my dear fellow, to meet you again. How about a little refreshment, something alcoholic I mean?"

Brunt's hearty manner and Celia Burchard's well-disposed attitude touched Wirt; it salved his ebbing self-confidence. Though the chief's remark may have been made with tongue in cheek, it nevertheless buoyed his spirit. The vaguest hints of appreciation of his job were difficult to come by, which was not surprising, since he contributed so little. He felt like a hanger-on, a parasite sitting at a table provided for others.

When Wirt glanced from here to there, he noticed a stack of files on a sideboard within easy reach of Mrs Burchard. They must contain information about the Gardens, Wirt reckoned; erroneously, as it turned out. Celia Burchard, while alternately considering the two men who were still talking, tried to suppress a flicker of impatience. Her furrowed brow indicated a desire to proceed to more momentous matters than exchanges of pleasantries.

An odd sensation seized Wirt, her presence caused a warm prickle to rise within him. She exuded a womanly aura that confused and attracted him. Though lacking a smidgen of coquetry, he found her strangely seductive.

"How is that possible?" he had asked himself, after spending time in her presence at Murdoch's place.

Later, in the comfort of his house, he found the answer. Despite advancing years, a proclivity to stoutness, and total lack of affectation, she made him feel alive. Her awareness of being, and no less desiring to be a woman, influenced this perception. Of course the matter of clothes could not be ignored. Like all natives of her sex she wore colourful dresses, richly embroidered, which accentuated her femininity

Brunt, squeezed in his inevitable tropical uniform, sporting neither a badge nor insignia, beamed at Wirt. He didn't beat about the bush, that was not his style.

"Don't deny it, sir, you are wondering why a policeman, the chief to boot, should attend a meeting that could not possibly concern him."

When Wirt made a gesture of denial, the chief cut him short:

"Tut, tut, my friend, your thoughts are etched on your face. Well, here it is in a nutshell: Murdoch is at loggerheads with us, me, to be exact, concerning a property at Sylvania, probably known to you."

Upon Wirt's affirmative nod, Brunt went on:

"We want to engage in some horse trading."

"With Murdoch," Mrs Burchard fell in.

"Yes, but that compatriot of mine sets our teeth on edge; he is not only wily, but unpredictable like a bear with a sore head."

"So I noticed," Wirt agreed.

Brunt continued:

"We have reached an impasse, help is needed."

"Yours, that is," Mrs Burchard remarked as she turned towards Wirt, who now as before remained in the dark about their expectations of him.

Looking quizzically from one to the other, he said nothing.

The chief explained:

"The law dictates that once a property has been proclaimed a historic site, transference of a title is impossible without government approval, which requires the police's consent. This is usually a mere formality."

"But not in this case," Mrs Burchard stressed.

"May I inquire why not?" Wirt asked.

Two faces turned towards him, four eyes locked with his. Their miens expressed what they were reluctant to utter. Something irregular, improper perhaps, stood on the agenda, for which his assistance was needed. They meant to induct him, as it were, but didn't exactly know how to go about it.

Howard Brunt started to explain:

"Here is the point. We are blocking Murdoch's attempt to obtain title to the property mentioned, for reasons I cannot divulge at the present. If I have my way, this interdiction remains in force forever. But, as implied, we are skating on thin ice."

"It's getting thinner by the day," Mrs Burchard added.

Although Wirt failed to understand what all this had to do with him, he feigned interest by nodding assent.

Mrs Burchard reached behind her and removed a file from the stack through which she slowly riffled. With the words:

"There you are," she removed a sheet of paper, which she handed to the chief.

Brunt read it with evident chagrin, indicating that he objected to the contents. His brow furrowed and his eyes contracted, while he searched for a particular clause. Tapping the paper with a sigh, he commented:

"Here it is in black and white."

Raising the sheet to his eyes, he started to read:

"Should a title transfer be legally forestalled, reasons must be given within an appropriate time, but no later than ten working days after the petitioner's request for a disclosure."

"What happens in case of default?" Wirt asked.

"The title must be registered in the petitioner's name."

Wirt, who sensed the drift of things, posed a question:

"What is the present status?"

"The clock is ticking," the chief growled.

"To tell the truth, Mr Wirt, we ran out of excuses," explained Mrs Burchard.

"What does that mean?" Wirt inquired.

"Murdoch will obtain clear title," the chief declared.

"When?" Wirt asked.

"In less than two weeks," Brunt replied morosely.

"Unless…" Mrs Burchard insinuated cryptically.

Wirt, still in the dark, felt it incumbent upon him to feign interest. Wondering what they were up to, utterly mystified about his own intended involvement, he queried half-heartedly:

"Why are you so keen to thwart Murdoch's intention to gain legitimate ownership of an insignificant parcel of land in the wilderness, barely accessible as I understand?"

The question, surely justified, plus no less innocuous, made their heads snap up. Exchanging quizzical glances, then lowering their eyes as if caught with both hands in the cookie jar, they shook their heads.

"We will tell you in due time," Mrs Burchard stalled.

"Something else I find difficult to comprehend."

"Let's hear it," the chief encouraged.

"Why would a man cling to a worthless property, located in an out-of-the-way place, in dispute to boot?"

"Why, indeed," Mrs Burchard sneered.

"Besides, is he not anxious to return to England at the drop of a hat? How does he put it? 'Not even a promise of eternal bliss would keep me here a day beyond my tenure.' "

While Mrs Burchard chuckled, Brunt observed Wirt with an air resembling commiseration.

"Fiddle-de-dee, my dear sir, nothing but stuff and nonsense," he snorted.

"Are you implying that Murdoch intends to stay here?" Wirt asked thoroughly bewildered.

"He has no choice," Brunt burst out quicker than discretion could prevent it.

"That's news to me. Would you care to elaborate?" Wirt asked.

"Regrettably no. Professional prudence demands that I keep mum about it. But be assured that Murdoch will not set foot on British soil in the foreseeable future."

Wirt, hearing the disturbing information, winced visibly. Because if Brunt's assertion were true, as it most likely was, it would affect his own existence profoundly. Murdoch, averse to his presence, will surely fuel a never-ending enmity towards him.

At a loss of anything else to say, he posed a question whose answer he already knew:

"So in less than two weeks Murdoch will obtain legal ownership of the Sylvania property?"

"It looks that way," the chief replied with a Hippocratic mien.

The puzzle started to unravel. The government, with Mrs Burchard in the lead, was embroiled in a bitter feud with Murdoch, into which they endeavoured to drag him.

Wirt smiled imperceptibly, for he began to understand. No wonder Murdoch doesn't trust me, he thought. Who could blame the man for his reluctance to co-operate with a presumed antagonist? He surely must see in him a stool pigeon enjoined to keep the government informed about his movements. Yes,

Wirt saw his colleague's moroseness in a different light now. He might well deem him a partner in a scheme meant to do harm. I must be cautious, he exhorted himself.

Brunt asked for another file, which Mrs Burchard selected and handed him.

"I have no wish to weigh you down with trifles; nevertheless, here is the bone of contention," the chief remarked.

Raising his head he added:

"Would you like to hear it?"

"Most certainly," Wirt affirmed.

"The uras trees are the apple of discord," Mrs Burchard observed.

Noticing Wirt's bewildered look, Brunt explained:

"These remarkable trees, shrouded in mystery, highly valued by some, judged pernicious by us, are the reason for the police's intervention."

Blinking in surprise, Wirt turned towards Mrs Burchard:

"Did you say uras trees?"

"Yes, I did."

Glancing from her to Brunt, cocking his head sideways, he wondered:

"Are you referring to the poison tree of Macassar?"

"The upas? No, they might be equally baneful but that is where the similarity ends," she advised.

Wirt, at the threshold of yawns till now, perked up. Trying to hide a sceptical frown, he commented:

"You do mean uras?"

When both nodded unhesitatingly, he declared:

"Hm, I never heard of such a plant before."

The chief snorted derisively:

"Small wonder, the people interested in these trees don't exactly blazon their existence abroad" he exclaimed.

"Are you intimating that these uras trees, as you call them, grow only in Dominica?" Wirt asked, still dubious about their existence.

"More than that. We are quite sure they are found nowhere else except on the property claimed by Murdoch.

Assurances to that end were given by renowned botanists from every corner of the globe," Mrs Burchard maintained.

Wirt puckered his brow, indicating a state of confusion.

"You say that Murdoch claims the property. Is he not the actual owner then?"

"In a way, yes, but he still lacks possession, as we explained," the chief growled.

"That might soon change," Mrs Burchard suggested.

Wirt had no idea what all that meant, yet he sensed that his assistance was expected. They were hatching out a plot under Mrs Burchard's tutelage to gain an advantage over Murdoch by methods not exactly above board. An ongoing tussle had ensued which Murdoch seemed about to win.

"What do you want from me?" Wirt burst out.

Looking at each other for a moment, Mrs Burchard encouraged the chief:

"You tell him, Mr Brunt."

"I shall, but first I must digress. My acquaintance with Murdoch reaches far back. It originated in England, was renewed in Haiti, and I hope will soon be ended. Based on my experience with Murdoch, professional as much as social, I consider it my duty to rid the island of his presence. The man is driven by impulses imputable to the prince of demons and his adherents. I know what I am talking of, everyday language lacks depictive power to evince a portrait of this Janus-faced fake. Knowing him as I do, it is incumbent upon me to stand between him and that property at Sylvania."

Wirt, noticeably startled, first glanced at Mrs Burchard, then looking fully at the chief, made a comment:

"Did I hear you say fake?"

"Yes, and I mean it. He is neither an accredited botanist, nor worthy of the title. As Mrs Burchard will confirm, he receives no acclaim from even a single scientist of merit; in fact, they almost avoid him like an impending calamity."

Mrs Burchard nodded affirmatively:

"If the truth be known, I have seen some wince at the mention of his name, while others fled at the sight of him."

Observing Wirt, the chief conjectured:

"What do I read in your face? Wait, let me guess. I see astonishment being overshadowed by a dawning realisation. Graced with an expert's eye, you of course noticed the dismal state, not to mention the paucity of plant life, in our vaunted Gardens."

"I did at first sight, but my censorious tendencies were softened by Murdoch's avowals."

"What are they?" Mrs Burchard asked sharply.

"Shortage of money, lack of co-operation, plus undue meddling," Wirt advised.

Mrs Burchard harrumphed such assertions; chief Brunt sniffed in disgust.

"Make no mistake, sir, Murdoch, in connivance or collusion with others, whom I wish not to name, are propagating these singular trees for base and criminal purposes. Granted, concrete evidence is wanting that warrants indictment, but circumstances do justify vigilance."

Mrs Burchard chuckled:

"Spoken like a policeman. I am not governed by such principles. In my opinion Murdoch is either the kingpin of a felonious group, or an important part thereof. I am convinced that the uras trees serve a nefarious objective."

The chief assented:

"I wholeheartedly agree, these trees are a curse of nature. I support the government's aim to either keep their propagation under strict control, but better yet eliminate each and everyone to their last root; legally of course."

"If possible; by trickery if need be," Mrs Burchard offered with a goading grin.

Brunt, drumming on the table, looked straight at Wirt:

"You wish to know what we want from you?"

As an answer Wirt nodded several times. Spreading out the sheets given him, the chief expounded:

"We are walking a thin line here, I freely admit. Yet our endeavours shall be crowned by success, provided we each play our parts."

Tapping one of the sheets before him, he continued:

"This is a copy of a document prepared by Kew Gardens, bearing a notary's seal and signature, ceding the Sylvania property to Robert Murdoch; fair and square, I do concede."

"But he hasn't obtained clear title yet," reminded Wirt.

"Not so far," Mrs Burchard concurred.

"Kew Gardens are now as before named in the register as owners," Brunt declared.

"For another week or two by the looks of it," Wirt interposed.

His comment evoked an unexpected reaction from the others. Mrs Burchard cast an archy glance at him, the chief sported a mischievous grin which seemed to fill the room.

Raising one of the sheets above his head, fanning it while squinting at Wirt, Brunt announced gleefully:

"The crucial point is clear title, with an emphasis on the word clear. Murdoch will most likely obtain title to the property, but let me tell you, it will be encumbered by a caveat."

"Which is?" Wirt inquired with scant interest.

"I'm glad you asked," Brunt remarked, as he flipped the document across the table.

Pushing out his chin, he proclaimed:

"This appendix, which recently came into our possession, confers an indefeasible right to the government. It allows us to make use of the Sylvania property, provided that certain stipulations are adhered to."

Observing Wirt reflectively, the chief expounded:

"Transplanting, permitted at our discretion, may only benefit Roseau's botanical garden. Furthermore, it must be done under the control of a recognised botanist."

"Which is you, Mr Wirt," Mrs Burchard called out.

Wirt, no wiser by all this verbiage, asked again, more insistent this time:

"You must tell me how, and where I fit in."

Mrs Burchard looked him full in the face as if to say:

"Can't you see that with half an eye?"

Yet, she nevertheless elucidated:

"Quite simple. As our botanist we ask you to transplant the uras trees within the allotted time."

Construing Wirt's inquiring mien, Brunt, pointing at the paper on the table, declared in his grumbling manner:

"We have a month to complete the task, in compliance with Kew Gardens' article of sales."

"Has this – this caveat been duly registered yet?" Wirt wanted to know.

"The minister will do it tomorrow," he was told.

"Is Murdoch aware of this charge?" was Wirt's next question, which evoked a prolonged snort from Brunt, and an exclamation of derision from Mrs Burchard.

"Most certainly. It was he, and no other, who removed it from the file," the chief bellowed.

"He also doctored Kew Gardens' instrument, in our opinion," Mrs Burchard added.

The chief, in his stride now, proclaimed:

"That rascal loaded the dice in his favour."

"Tried to, chief, tried to," Mrs Burchard corrected.

"It's a fact, madam, a bitter reality that came to haunt him."

Although nobody questioned his allegation, Brunt rumbled on:

"How, you want to know? It spoiled his appetite for litigation. As I said previously he wouldn't dare stepping onto the witness stand."

Wirt cleared his throat several times while casting glances from Brunt to Mrs Burchard. He commented haltingly:

"If I understand correctly, you want to uproot these uras trees from Murdoch's deeded property, and replant them at the botanical garden."

"Not exactly. For security reasons they need to be set in the ground at our protected compound, which is fenced in and guarded, till a safe area has been set up at the Gardens," Brunt noted.

"Aren't these trees too large for transplantation?"

Mrs Burchard quickly allayed Wirt's concerns:

"Not to worry, they are rather small, I am told; moreover, their roots appear to be surprisingly shallow."

The chief concurred:

"That is my understanding also. I venture a guess that a simple rig, consisting of an a-frame plus blocks and tackles, will do the job."

"Won't they die in the process?" Wirt objected.

Mrs Burchard sniffed at the idea:

"Let them, I for one would not shed a single tear if that happens."

Brunt qualified her statement:

"A few should be preserved to be exhibited in the Gardens. The rest can be used as firewood, as far as I am concerned."

Wirt's head was in a spin. A presentiment of impending grief overwhelmed him, which he couldn't name, yet divined nevertheless. Despite the midday heat he felt chilled to the bones. What he heard so far baffled and worried him; it made little sense. Why anyone, invested with an elevated position to boot, should be at sixes and sevens about trees growing in the sticks, boggled his mind. What was going on here? Were they trying to inveigle him into holding a candle to the devil? Well, anyone even trying can go to blazes, he wouldn't be roped in that easy.

Addressing himself to no one in particular, he commented:

"I heard it said that a thin line was being walked. What exactly is meant by that?"

Brunt replied:

"Legally we are skating on thin ice; morally we are on solid ground. Although not provable beyond a reasonable doubt, it's clear to us that these uras trees play a prominent role in a dastardly trade."

"You are not referring to that spurious voodoo or obeah cult?" Wirt asked in a voice tremulous with scepticism.

"He is," Mrs Burchard responded decisively.

Brunt bridled almost imperceptibly at Wirt's tongue in cheek remark. He asserted peevishly:

"These plants are used for one thing only."

"To spread misery, and fan superstition," Mrs Burchard noted.

Brunt nodded as he explained:

"I learned from reliable sources that unscrupulous minds and skilful hands can prepare a concoction from the bark of these trees, more deleterious than the sap obtained from the infamous upas."

Drawing himself up the chief reiterated that all concerned ought to go the extra mile in order to gain control over these trees; quickly and irrevocably.

Noticing Wirt's apprehension written across his face, Mrs Burchard assured him:

"You may rely on it, we expect nothing untoward from you, just a willingness to observe the work for the Gardens' benefit ."

"Which shouldn't take more than two weeks," Brunt stressed.

Wirt, loath to offend, yet also reluctant to appear eager about a questionable venture, tried to sidetrack:

"Wouldn't it be more conducive to continue, perhaps intensify, negotiations with Murdoch, aiming at an amicable solution?" he suggested.

"Of course. As explained we even attempted old-fashioned horse-trading," Wirt was told.

"For instance the government offered him a similar tract at the outskirts of town which trade, without batting an eyelash, anyone with an iota of business sense would call a bargain," Mrs Burchard remarked.

"But he refuses?" Wirt frowned.

Brunt snickered:

"He doesn't even deign to respond. All offers, written I should emphasise, remain unanswered to date."

Screwing up his face, signifying vexation tempered by incredulity, Wirt observed:

"Hm, it does seem arcane, but I suppose that property, though remote and lacking commercial worth, bears a sentimental attachment for Murdoch."

Pooh-poohing that notion Mrs Burchard voiced different opinions. Her womanly insight, she maintained, supported by years of association with Murdoch, qualified her to be a fair judge of his character.

She explained:

"Mr Murdoch is a stiff-necked opportunist, plus no less a grudge-bearing dissimulator. I told Mr Garneau, the minister responsible for the Gardens, repeatedly that he is pulling the wool over our eyes; deliberately and sneeringly. You might say that I have my knifes in him; perhaps so, yet, considering circumstances, I proclaim they are not in deep enough."

Wirt, on pins and needles, wanted to leave; he needed time and solitude to think, for he felt cornered. Wishing to be compliant on the one hand, apprehensive of the consequences on the other, he pined for the security of his home. Should he sing placebo to his employers, thereby incurring his colleague's wrath, or wriggle out of the task they tried to enjoin him with?

"Why don't you try another tack?" he suggested.

"What?" they burst out in unison.

Taken aback by their vehement reaction, Wirt managed to stammer:

"Declare these trees a national asset, protected by law."

"Phooey," Mrs Burchard protested.

The chief, more self-possessed, uttered not a syllable. When he was about to start the devil's tattoo again, Mrs Burchard's frown set him right.

He exclaimed:

"It cannot be done, old chap, not on private property. Believe me, even going through many hoops, while putting up a song and dance that could make a Hawaiian hula-hula pale in comparison, prospects of success are dim. No, that game is not worth the candle."

Mrs Burchard concurred:

"Our plan, admittedly fraught with a few kinks, is the only solution, provided we act in unison, and instantly."

The chief seconded her comment:

"Irresolution would be synonymous with dereliction of duty."

"What about Murdoch, will he not balk at my interference, lock us out, perhaps even resort to threats and violence?" Wirt cautioned.

Reaching in his pocket, Brunt produced an official-looking paper which he raised for everyone to see.

"It's a valid point but of little consequence."

Fanning the sheet in his hands, he remarked gleefully:

"By virtue of this injunction, anyone appointed by the ministry must be accorded unhindered access to the property. Any attempts to obstruct an authorised person in his work within those premises, faces arrest and possible indictment."

"Have no fear about meddling, the chief has promised to station two policemen at the site from the moment the work begins till it finishes."

"Make no mistake, should anyone mouth, or wag a finger at you, I will personally march them to the local lock-up by the seat of their trousers, and scruff of their necks to boot," Brunt growled.

Mrs Burchard jumped up unexpectedly. Stomping a foot on the floor, her wonted impish eyes spitting sparks and flashing fire, she started to scold like a fishwife:

"It's more than Boccaccio's Griselda could submit to. Look at our position, consider and try not to weep tears of rage. Here we are, trumpeting about Dominica's unique flora, crowing over an unrivalled plant life, loud enough to be heard across two continents:

"This way, botanists of the world, make our island your hunting ground for plants that thrill an expert's heart. Only in Dominica will you find the mysterious uras trees, a singular growth, justifying an odyssey to behold. Take home a few saplings for future study. Help us to unriddle the secrets of these wondrous plants."

Looking daggers at no one in particular, she almost shouted:

"What a letdown awaits the visitors who arrive on the wings of awe, but depart in the talons of disappointment. Why? Our botanist cannot be found, because he skipped town.

" 'When is he expected back?' they ask.

"Ha, dare we tell them the truth that he will show up right after they have left the island?

" 'Can we examine the uras trees?' they inquire.

" 'Hm, hm,' we flounder, strenuously searching for face-saving excuses; for who is bold enough to own up to the fact that it is impossible, since they are kept under lock and key by our absent botanist, who stations guards at the gate to prevent anyone from entering."

Stamping her foot again, more furiously this time, she cried out:

"What makes him do it? What dark forces compel him to bite the hand that feeds him?"

Wirt, who had the wind up, was unpleasantly affected by Mrs Burchard's tirade. Reflecting how to leave without causing offence, he hit upon a ruse:

"May I speak freely?"

"We demand it," they replied in one voice.

"Can I peruse those documents, take them home perhaps?"

Answering the chief's questioning glance, Mrs Burchard acquiesced:

"Most certainly, here are copies of all the originals."

Accepting the folder with a sheepish mien on account of his artful dodge, Wirt felt obliged to explain:

"Do not misunderstand me, I fully intend to enhance the Gardens' reputation, but have no wish to become entangled in a controversy that I do not rightly comprehend."

"That's understandable," Brunt granted.

"Don't act so high and mighty," Mrs Burchard's frown insinuated.

Wirt felt impelled to elucidate:

"I abhor litigation, and the ensuing rancour even more. To tell you the truth, good fellowship is like the sap of life to me. At signs of enmity I retreat within myself. Such is my nature, I confess. What I'm saying is this: I feel bound to perform any task, provided it does not invite vindictiveness or burdens my conscience."

Brunt, pulling himself up abruptly, took Wirt's hand:

"I am with you, sir, indeed, I am."

Saying this he left.

Hardly had the door closed behind him, when Mrs Burchard started to query:

"Between us, Mr Wirt, how are things shaping up between you and Murdoch? We hear a lot, nothing exactly pleasant, I might add. After that debacle with Nantes, even a whiff of ugly news upsets us."

Wirt heaved a deep sigh. What should he say, rather what could he tell her after what he had just learned. Could Murdoch's inimical attitude be attributable to his dealings with the government? Did he pursue a villainous plot aimed at him, his successor? Or was his behaviour characteristic perhaps? Besides, Mrs Burchard's inquiry had a spurious ring which he could not identify. Did idle curiosity compel her to draw him out? Or was she motivated by genuine concerns affecting himself and the Gardens? Wavering between a desire to leave and the code of polite society, Wirt spoke evasively:

"Murdoch is a queer fellow, no denying it. He is neither obliging nor co-operative, but in my estimation upright and competent."

Hearing that, Mrs Burchard almost had a coughing fit, prior to bursting out:

"Upright? I hardly think so. Competent? Hm, who could have guessed."

Wirt stuck to his guns:

"His surly deportment, while disconcerting, cannot serve as a measure of the man. After all, seeing his plans thwarted, seemingly with my endorsement, if not assistance, could make even Job cantankerous. Besides, he must consider me an upstart, and foreigner to boot."

Mrs Burchard rose wearily, then walked, rather shuffled to an open window. Signs of the night were rapidly approaching; in no time mountains and forest would be swallowed by darkness, thereby calling to life nocturnal voices that never cease to beguile. The well-kept lawn surrounding the buildings shimmered in the soft glow of artificial lights, placed ingeniously under shrubs and bushes. Most people had left the buildings, yet one could still hear the odd good night, or good evening.

Closing the window halfway, Mrs Burchard returned to the table and sat down again. She glanced at Wirt with a nervous flicker in her eyes, as if uncertain whether to utter what occupied her mind.

Drawing a deep breath, exhaling audibly, she came right out with it:

"Are you aware of the backbiting directed at you?"

"I hope they have good teeth," he chuckled.

Taken aback by his flippant reply, she said haltingly:

"I thought you liked to know."

"Not really, madam, I have learned a long time ago to ignore tattles. Gossipmongers tell us more about themselves than others, whom they wish to injure."

"You may be right, but believe me, in a small place like Dominica, infested by an expatriate elite, whispers can acquire deafening proportions if not checked."

"Well then, what does the rumour mill say about me?"

"That you are inclined to be irascible, are markedly negligent with your work, aloof ..."

"And speak with a foreign accent," Wirt interrupted with tongue in cheek.

Mrs Burchard, realising the folly of giving second thoughts to such matters, sported a broad grin, then broke out in hilarious laughter. She had liked Hannes Wirt from the moment their eyes met, but now she adored him. Her predilection for quick-witted men, well known by acquaintances and friends, gained the upper hand.

As Wirt stood up to say good night his eyes caught sight of two shadowy figures outside. Blinking in surprise, frowning in dismay, his eyes contracted. Was he seeing ghosts that hovered along the dimly lit pathway? No, Murdoch in the flesh, seemingly absorbed in thought, strolled about. At his side he clearly recognised Michael Mauch.

Mrs Burchard, noticing his astonished gaze, said not a word. She was aware of their presence from the moment they had entered the grounds.

As Wirt was about to point them out to her, a din arose that made his earlobes tingle. Someone started to sing; rather blare out at the top of his voice. Rattled, he hastened to open the window fully again to obtain a better view. He couldn't decide what baffled him more; the ruckus outside cleaving the tranquil evening air, or Mrs Burchard's unconcern. She neither craned her neck, wrinkled her brow, or even raised an eyebrow.

Indifferent, somewhat amused, she observed the strange spectacle, which grew more arcane by the minute.

Mauch had planted himself underneath a swaying palm tree where, acquiring a pugnacious bearing, he let go with Irish rebel songs.

In response to his glances, more indignant than inquiring, she shrugged her shoulders while remarking:

"Probably drunk again."

Wirt couldn't avert his eyes from the singing and stomping Mauch, egged on by Murdoch who clapped and shouted lustily. Transfixed, he watched the weird exhibition that appeared to leave Mrs Burchard untouched.

Mauch, getting into the swing of things, shouted at Murdoch, who handed him a staff, which he shouldered like a rifle. Thus rigged out he marched around a nearby tree while belting out one fiery ballad after another. Murdoch, walking behind him, shouted encouragement:

"Louder, Mike, show us your mettle, me lad."

What happened next made Wirt wince and hold his breath. Mauch, stepping backwards a short distance, swung the staff from his shoulder, which he extended in the fashion of a jouster. Tilting his head, neighing with full lungs, pawing the ground, he waited. Murdoch, raising an arm, then lowering it with as swish, cried out in a voice deemed to be an Irish agitator:

"Charge, me hearty, charge!"

Mauch did exactly that. With a mighty hooray he charged the tree. Alarmed at the presumed impending mishap, Wirt glanced at Mrs Burchard who, to his chagrin, appeared to be quite unaffected. He didn't trust his eyes when she lifted a hand to hide a yawn.

"But–but, he is going to hurt himself," he stuttered.

"You are trying to cheer me up, are you? I wish they both smash their heads to smithereens," she said amid roaring laughter from outside, manifesting a well-turned-out prank.

After Mauch bowed like a Spanish grandee, and Murdoch invited applause from all sides, they left the grounds.

Wirt felt offended by Mrs Burchard's offish attitude, he could barely conceal his indignation. Realising that he was taken in by mere horseplay, disconcerted him as much as Mrs Burchard's veiled irony. When she made a comment praising their weird performance, he could almost hear the laughter up her sleeve. No doubt she made fun of him; albeit good-natured, it nevertheless pierced the core of his being.

While trying to douse a rising sentiment and smoothen the wrinkles of annoyance on his brow, he began to understand a simple fact; his outlook needed to be changed. He must relax, learn to take things in stride, balance his humour as it were, substitute bile with phlegm, and choler with cool blood. Yes, take a cue from the natives like Mrs Burchard who was amused by an episode which mortified him. Why take umbrage at an escapade probably meant to rattle him?

"How did you like Mauch's singing?"

"Hm, I have heard better and less strident voices," Wirt answered.

Ruing the caustic reply, he remarked in a softer tone:

"You mentioned that the takeover might be possible sooner than planned."

"Certainly, provided you are ready."

"Anytime," he assured her.

"Very well, I shall make the necessary arrangements without delay."

"Arrangements?" he echoed.

"Of course. An official dinner in Murdoch's honour will be held, it's an opportunity to thank him for the many years of dedicated service, also to extend our good wishes for his future, and do anything else required by decorum."

Her mocking eyes gave the lie to her kind words, Wirt couldn't help thinking.

"By the way, your presence will be essential," she advised.

"Oh, is that necessary?" he burst out against his better judgement.

"Most certainly. After all, many people want to see you face to face, and listen to your maiden speech. Moreover, it's an ideal occasion to hand you the Gardens' symbol; namely, a golden key."

"Which I presume is in Murdoch's possession."

"It is."

Wirt cast a wary look at her. Tilting his head sideways, he made a conjecture:

"Will he not refuse to part with it?"

The mere idea made her titter. With wrinkles of laughter on her cheeks, and a sharp harrumph in her throat, she exclaimed:

"He wouldn't dare to disoblige, believe me, it's the last thing he would do."

Wirt made no further comment. He folded the papers given him, then bid Mrs Burchard good night and left.

Murdoch Shows His True Colour

*I*n the next few days not much happened. A notice reached him that come Monday he will be in sole charge of the Gardens. Murdoch has been advised accordingly, the missive stated, he must hand over keys and anything else pertaining to the Gardens. A good roar, lion, as Schiller quoted, Wirt found out quickly, for it was easier said than done. The ceremonial dinner? postponed until further notice, he was told.

A veritable tug of war ensued now between them. Having a word with Murdoch proved to be difficult, if not impossible. Wirt's attempts to engage his colleague in conversation foundered on the latter's curtness. Murdoch avoided him as though he were afflicted with leprosy. Should their path accidentally cross, Wirt was met with a basilisk-like stare, and a brief nod.

Then everything changed abruptly. Murdoch's deportment took a surprising about-face; he appeared to be transformed. Arriving unwontedly early at the Gardens, he approached Wirt in a conciliatory manner. It happened on a Friday, three days prior to the takeover. Having been rebuffed repeatedly, Wirt bridled in distrust. He turned and walked away, muttering excuses about having to perform an errant that brooked no delay.

So it went most of the morning. Murdoch's eagerness to be chummy strengthened Wirt's resolve to avoid him. There is something amiss, he thought. Murdoch's behaviour, the sudden transformation, reeks of evil presage.

Later in the afternoon Murdoch sort of cornered Wirt. Approaching him with an outstretched hand and a mien purporting glad tidings, he called out:

"My dear colleague, I have lately been uncivil to you, unpardonably so. I don't know what induced me to be uncooperative, if not inimical. I can plead undue duress, mental strain in recent months that could be called a veritable Golgotha. Anyway, these Caudine Forks have been crossed, from here on I'm on your side heart and soul."

As Wirt struggled to douse the flames of distrust kept alive by discernible shadows of mischief in Murdoch's eyes, he received an invitation:

"Have you got time for a draught tonight?"

"At your place?"

"Yes."

"The usual hour?"

"Suits me. I shall expect you then," Murdoch said in a hearty tone.

Shortly after six o'clock Wirt arrived at the house of his colleague, whom he had never known to be so jovial. Cheerful, as if freed from an onerous burden, he met Wirt on the steps, who felt self-conscious on account of the effusive reception. With a radiant face and demonstrative gestures, Murdoch insisted to show him every nook and corner of the house. It surprised Wirt, who was aware of his colleague's aversion towards affability. After the house and yard were shown, they sat down on the veranda.

Murdoch inquired with a diffident glance:

"I presume you know the reason for my festive mood."

"Not really," Wirt admitted.

In a twinkle Murdoch fished out a paper from a briefcase which he offered his guest.

"Here is the source of my joy. A particularly rancorous squabble, ending in my favour, has been laid to rest by a stroke of the pen and an official stamp."

Wirt started to read, not out of interest, but to please his colleague. Soon, however, he perked up, signifying increased attentiveness. Despite the document's tortuous language, bombastic if not absurd, he understood a simple fact: a pall lay over Murdoch's delight which he tried to conceal. Wirt raised his head and cast a furtive glance at him as if to say:

"Don't rejoice yet, your swans might turn out to be geese."

While Wirt's perception of property laws were rather dim, he surmised that his colleague's professed victory amounted to gilding the pill. True, the document revealed that Murdoch had been granted first refusal by the court; it also mentioned restrictions that must be fulfilled prior to the title transfer. The property lines, contested by Mrs Gibson, Baldwin's legatee, needed confirmation in accordance with her registered charge. Thus a survey by an accredited land surveyor had to be made, before Murdoch could obtain the title so eagerly coveted.

Wirt sensed a lengthy delay which suited him to a tee. He heaved a deep sigh of relief that made Murdoch raise his head in surprise. Squinting, his brow puckering, he appeared on the verge to make a remark. Swallowing the words that lay on his tongue, he punished Wirt with a withering look instead. Lowering his eyes quickly, he exclaimed:

"What a careless host I am."

Saying so he literally bound up. Commenting about dwindling refreshments and tidbits, he went inside. Wirt welcomed the interruption, it gave him a chance to reflect. His thoughts didn't wander far; they hovered around Murdoch and his presumable triumph. Strange to say he alluded not once to the property's encumbrance, nor the government's rights. How could that be, Wirt muttered, in view of possible consequences that might endanger, if not negate his plans, whatever they were. Was he in the dark about the government's intentions, or were they treated with that upper crust disdain he, Wirt, knew so well? Surely Murdoch must be aware of Mrs Burchard's rankling resentment against him that was relentlessly on the prowl. She would not miss an occasion to settle his hash generally, but especially in this case. For she made no secret of her suspicion that Murdoch, along with others, was involved up to his eyebrows in a murky business, detrimental to Dominica's reputation. As mentioned, she had her knife in him, which didn't mind twisting when an opportunity presented itself.

Murdoch was still rummaging and muttering in the house, seemingly disgruntled over something. Wirt tried to collect his thoughts which were riven by conflicting sentiments. Loath to dampen his colleague's high spirit, plagued by an increased sense of fair play, he felt like a prisoner of his own conscience. His host, he realised, had imbibed a drop or two too many prior to his arrival, thus putting him in a devil-may-care mood, quite unwontedly so. He wanted to celebrate, plus give his tongue free rein. His putative success went to his head; it rendered him sneeringly sportive. The rancorous struggle with Mrs Burchard and others, gingered up with spite and spiced with malice on both sides, had sapped Murdoch's strength. But having gained the upper hand, his vital forces surged again, his host demonstrated when he returned.

"Not so fast," Wirt felt tempted to say, but just nodded instead.

"Be easy on the rum," he would have liked to admonish, yet again held his tongue.

Murdoch appeared to have digested his whiff of a moment ago, judging by his bearing. Setting down a tray laden with liquors and alluring morsels, he invited his guest to fall into it with both hands. He resumed talking as if vying with a professional orator.

Wirt barely said a word, he listened with only half an ear; weightier matters occupied his mind, more far-reaching than mere etiquette. What might Murdoch's reaction be upon learning of their scheme? After all, uprooting his treasured uras trees will certainly make him see red. Wrecking his source of income and power may well unleash more than a battle of wits. If the truth be told, Wirt dreaded Murdoch. The first impression of him lingered vividly in his mind. Who could forget the stiff imperious figure, the peremptory voice and haughty bearing? Should that not evoke the lord of fear fortress in one's mind, listening to him ordering people around certainly will. From the moment he had met Murdoch, Wirt felt unpleasantly affected by his manner of issuing instructions. Trying to describe it, made him stumble over his own words. Was it the glacial stare, or the sibilant commands expelled through clenched teeth? No matter what, the whole man exuded unbridled menace. No, Wirt did not relish to cross swords with him; neither in deed nor thought.

As Murdoch continued to ramble, Wirt reflected on his situation. Beset by conflicting emotions, which he could not drive away, he paid less and less attention to his soliloquy. One ear resounded with reminders of loyalty towards one's colleagues, the other reverberated with urgings to do one's duty. Despite these wavering sentiments he resolved to act in accordance with his contractual obligations. While he would have preferred to work harmoniously with Murdoch, listen to his advise and gain knowledge, especially about the propagation of uras trees, he realised that such notions were pipe dreams. Murdoch's inimical stance thwarted any attempt at friendly coexistence, not to mention teamwork. The man must have been born Janus-faced, Wirt often thought. For short periods he brimmed with good will towards him, then suddenly bristled with malignity. Those were the circumstances at the beginning of their acquaintance, but for some time now naked enmity on Murdoch's part reigned supreme.

So why had he been invited to a convivial evening by him? To ring in a new area of co-operative spirit? Hardly, Wirt decided, for he had learned to distrust his capricious colleague, who would change in a flash from a smiling benefactor to a demon of the pit, whom no sop was able to pacify.

Wirt's reflections were interrupted by the mention of a name deeply anchored in his psyche. He instinctively perked up when Murdoch spat out:

"That Nantes, what a lame excuse for a scientist."

Wirt, baffled to the core, scarcely hid his astonishment.

"What do you mean?" he asked.

"This: Had that bogus botanist expended half as much time and energy at his job as he did making conquests, we both wouldn't be here."

"I don't understand," Wirt intimated.

"You don't? Well, let me explain. He was not only an unmitigated libertine, but a skilled schemer who from day one agitated against me."

"But why?"

"To oblige Celia Burchard."

Noticing Wirt's perplexed look, Murdoch chuckled:

"You are not quick on the uptake, are you?"

"Admittedly no."

Contemplating his guest with ill-concealed disdain, Murdoch commented:

"You must be familiar with Rowe's Lothario?"

Wirt nodded, still at sea.

Murdoch scoffed:

"Ha, that fellow was a duffer compared to Nantes in matters of licentiousness. I always maintained that the Belgian deserves a monument for services rendered."

"Services rendered?" Wirt echoed.

The remark made Murdoch break out in Abderitan laughter. He seemed bereft of his usual reserve, beset by a heedlessness that made Wirt self-conscious. The purported triumph stoked some smouldering embers of emotions in him, that Wirt had no inkling existed.

Instead of an explanation Murdoch observed his guest with a Mephistophelian sneer, which made Wirt shrink into himself. For an instant he felt transported to a world of grinning and hooting spectres hovering around Murdoch, who appeared to enter a trance-like state. His face turned into a mask of naked malevolence, his half-closed eyes acquired a faraway look. Just as Wirt concluded that rum and his host were not compatible, Murdoch snapped out of his momentary transfixion. He chuckled:

"Yes, erect him a monument, right in the centre of town, I say. He earned it twofold as an inveterate agitator and philanderer."

Wirt, raising his eyebrows, protested:

"I didn't think Nantes fits that description."

"To a tee. Ask the belles of the island, and don't forget our matronly Celia, who never could hide a blush under her dark skin in the Belgian's presence."

"You are not insinuating ..."

"I am, my dear colleague, I sure am."

A roguish leer appeared on Murdoch's face when he continued:

"But he got his comeuppance, the unavoidable happened."

"What was that?"

"He got caught in his own net; in other words he hoisted his own petard."

"What do you mean?"

"What, indeed! The man had more enemies than hair on his head."

Wirt instinctively puckered his brow while cocking his head. Murdoch seemed to misunderstand his guest's involuntary movement. He ask brusquely:

"Don't you believe me?"

Feeling guilty, Wirt assured quickly:

"I do, but I am surprised to hear what you say."

"You are? I wonder why."

"I thought he was generally esteemed and welcomed."

"Fiddlesticks! I say. Such manifestations sound like utterances made by Celia Burchard," Murdoch remarked contemptuously.

Wirt protested:

"Not at all, everyone who knew Nantes praised him roundly."

Noticeably miffed, Murdoch, undecided what to say, grew sullen. Contradictions were not to his liking; he expected his assertions to be endorsed, not questioned.

Irritated he demanded to know:

"Do you seriously believe that cuckolded husbands appreciate or laud the seducer of their wives? Remember, the island is small, news travels fast and far among the coterie of expatriates. Among women especially, whose beer and skittle existence welcomes whispers, more so if they incline towards prurience."

"What are you saying?"

"Just this, my worthy colleague, that one or more of the deceived husbands probably spoiled Nantes' spooning fun."

"How?" Wirt questioned.

"That, I am unable to say."

Smiling suggestively in the manner of someone about to make far-reaching revelations, Murdoch bent forward.

"Nantes had an ardent love affair with the wife of a local trader by the name of Turcotte, who is an ugly customer at the best of times. When rumours reached his ears of a dalliance between Lorrain, his wife, and Nantes, it hit a raw nerve in the irascible Frenchman.

" 'I will settle his hash,' he vowed openly."

"Why not hers?" Wirt almost queried, but recalling the mystifying point of an honour code, so important to men, he held his tongue.

What Murdoch told him about Nantes he took with more than just a grain of salt. Willing or not, he had to listen to more, he seemed anxious to portray Nantes as a villain deserving the witch's bridle. He related how another cuckold, English to the fingertips, haughtily pretending not to be affected by his wife's treachery, vented his spite on the Belgian.

Here is how:

"One day, while eating lunch at the Fort Young Hotel with friends, he invited Nantes to join them. Ethics forbid to divulge the fellow's name, for he is well-known and respected throughout the island. After lunch, while drinking coffee laced with brandy, tongues loosened, minds relaxed."

"Where you present at that gathering?" Wirt interrupted, for no other reason than to show attentiveness.

This innocent question, casually voiced, triggered a reaction on Murdoch's part best described as arcane, and no less disturbing. Squirming perceptibly, casting reproving glances at Wirt, frowning from temple to temple, he sat there as if stung to the quick. Before Wirt's eyes, so it seemed, Murdoch turned into a pillar of aversion. He knew that look, it expressed abysmal disdain, and a silent command to be on guard.

Wirt thanked his guardian angel for the rattling noise made by toads coming to life down near the river.

"Ah, listen to that," he exclaimed, hoping to divert his host's attention.

He succeeded in a way. Murdoch, though still in a huff, lowered his eyes, cleared his throat, prior to reverting to Wirt's inquiry.

"Of course I was there, how else should I know what took place," he declared gruffly.

Wirt made no comment, he acquired a demure disposition while waiting for his host to continue his narrative.

"Out of the blue the man, I cannot name, announced for all to hear:

" 'Did you know that I possess the gift of second sight?'

" 'No, we didn't,' some intimated in a jocular vein.

"Others, raising their eyebrows, tried to look erudite. To mince no words their miens evinced ignorance, they more than likely had no inkling what this meant."

Saying so, Murdoch observed Wirt with a probing glance, which the other interpreted correctly.

"Clairvoyance, the French call it," he offered nodding.

Murdoch spoke again:

"The man repeated: 'Yes, I can see future events far away. Watch this.'

"Lowering his head, swaying lightly while uttering what sounded like incantations, he appeared to mesmerise himself. We weren't sure whether to laugh or pretend to be impressed. People, sitting at neighbouring tables, stared in disbelief. I venture a guess that patrons of the entire dining room were watching by now."

"I'm not surprised," Wirt remarked somewhat tartly.

He looked askance at Murdoch's narration, which he thought entertaining but contrived. Why he told him that tale of the tub he was unable to imagine. For such it was in Wirt's opinion; nothing but a Munchausiade containing a hidden allegory, directed at him for some reason. Anyway, there was no need to shroud the presumed clairvoyant in anonymity. Hm, a dyed-in-the-wool English man, a prominent businessman married to a woman on the make? Doesn't that description fit Kenneth Reid to a tee? He was known alright, but more laughed at than esteemed. His fame rested chiefly with his wife's notorious profligacy. Wirt knew and avoided her. He would have walked extra miles to evade that modern-day Messalina, who wore a love-starved heart on her sleeve. Nantes, a seducer? Not with Jenny Reid, he concluded.

"It was quite a performance," Wirt heard his host say.

"Lifting his head slowly, opening first one, then the other eye, which he fixed on the diners with glassy stares, prompted someone to murmur:

" 'He is overdoing it.'

"Undoubtedly it was a memorable presentation, crowned by a surprising sequel. In a sepulchral tone he announced:

" 'I see a man prostrate in a gully near Trafalgar Falls with a knife in his back. What else do I see? He is turning around, moaning like a man breathing his last.'

"Nantes, strangely agitated, squirmed as if expecting apocalyptic revelations. Trying to hide his discomfort behind a mask of irony, he asked in a playful manner:

" 'Do you recognise him?'

" 'I do.'

" 'Well, who is it?'

"Tearing himself from his trance, or whatever it was, he looked bewildered about. Then considering the Belgian with a steely gaze, he said deliberately:

" 'It is you, Mr Nantes.'

"Did anybody chuckle or laugh, you might ask? Nothing of the sort happened, a deathlike silence reigned, all eyes were riveted at Nantes whose sardonic grimace vanished under the withering stare of the soothsayer."

"What did Nantes say?" Wirt asked.

"Not a word, a pall appeared to be descending over him. Turning pale, visibly cowering, unable to avert the other's piercing eyes, he sat there as if transfixed. Just then one of the patrons at a nearby table knocked over some glasses. The resulting clatter broke up the anxious mood, it jilted Nantes into action."

"What did he do?"

"He rose and walked away."

Wirt felt decidedly uncomfortable. One side of him wanted to call it an evening, the other bid him to stay; wary looks, appraising glances followed by throat clearing and foot tapping, indicated as much. It increased Wirt's discomfort. The heat of the day, cooled down by the sun's disappearance, tempered by intermittent blasts of wind, nonetheless oppressed him as never before. The sounds of the night, which failed to enliven his spirit, grated on his nerves. His entire being acquired a state of alertness.

Why did Murdoch relate an incident that couldn't stand a ray of reality, which in addition bore all the marks of a raconteur? Murdoch might be called this or that, but never a story teller, not even in his cups. What Wirt just heard sounded like one of Michael Mauch's inventions from beginning to end. What purpose Murdoch's narrative served he couldn't imagine. Was it meant to impress him, or as a broad hint to be on guard? Let's find out, he told himself. Chortling appreciatively, he commented:

"Quite a story, I admit, albeit a bit crude, don't you think?"

"Not in my opinion," Murdoch remarked curtly.

"It's intended to be allegorical, of course," Wirt suggested.

"Perhaps not," his host intimated.

"You are not insinuating that this–this crystal gazing deserves to be taken serious?"

"I do," Murdoch replied with a meaningful look directed squarely at his guest.

It made Wirt squirm. For an instant he thought that his colleague took measure of his mettle. He burst out angrily:

"Nonsense! Besides, nothing of the sort envisioned by your dubious clairvoyant happens in this peaceful place."

"You are wrong. Murders do occur, ritual ones or otherwise, which are neither reported nor detected. The laxness of the police, coupled with the government's nonchalance, leaves most homicides, and accidents for that matter, unsolved. Nantes had a penchant for roving, nosing around I call it. His outings, surely known to some of these deceived husbands, must have given them an idea or two.

"Ambushing a hated rival blemishing one's honour? Nothing easier than that. One thrust with a finely honed dagger, there, his self-respect is restored."

Wirt shook his head involuntarily, while comparing Murdoch's description of Nantes' character, which was diametrically opposed to Rintoul's assessment, which deserved more credence in his estimation. What was Murdoch aiming at? He had reached a state of excitement Wirt thought odd in view of his habitual diffidence. Seeing his colleague, the embodiment of calmness, a pre-eminent stick-in-the-mud, impatient and outright convivial, affected Wirt to no small degree; it made him edgy. Something evidently weighed on Murdoch's mind that he wished to impart, but knew not how. He appeared to be disjointed, befuddled on account of the undue attention paid the bottle, which dulled his mind, yet strangely stimulated his emotions.

"One more won't do any harm," Wirt heard him say again.

To his host's chagrin, his guest raised a hand, indicating that he wished to pass, for he proved to be no match for Murdoch's drinking prowess. Yes, the man's wonted composure gradually fell by the wayside; it yielded to a devil-may-care attitude. Though imbibing liberally, he remained coherent; yet his throat, well oiled, allowed the tongue to wag freely. His facial contortions would have done honour to a pantomimist. Squinting one moment, puckering his brow the next, sniffing at heaven knows what, he appeared to be in a flurry. The cool reckoner had turned into a blatherskite of no mean proportion. It was eerie to behold and deal with. Equally annoying were those leering glances accompanied by smirks, pregnant with hidden meaning, which to Wirt implied a just wait-and-see attitude; a menace in other words.

Wirt wished to ask a question, which lay on his tongue and weighed on his mind. He didn't quite know how to pose it, but finally decided on a roundabout way.

"You are inferring that Nantes was attacked by one or more of the duped husbands laying in wait."

"I and others do exactly that."

"Could he not have been poisoned?"

"By whom?"

"A jealous lady friend," Wirt suggested.

"We don't think so," Murdoch replied hesitatingly.

"What about that obeah curse, could it have been invoked by one of those ... how do you call them?"

Murdoch's head bound up, an ominous shadow flitted across his brow. With pursed lips and a scowl he sprang to his feet. Wirt, recoiling instinctively, looked up in surprise. His colleague's sudden impetuosity, provoked by an innocuous remark, besides causing astonishment, made him wary. What followed took his breath away. Incredible as it may sound, his host's inebriation, in an advanced state it must be added, dissipated before Wirt's eyes; he stood there sobered in a twinkle.

Stretching to his full height Murdoch snapped:

"Man alive, whoever gave you that idea?"

For an instant Wirt was tempted to relate Rintoul's odd experience with Nantes, but a closer look at Murdoch, his hostile attitude, bid him to be silent about those episodes. Unwilling to compromise the bank manager, averse to unleash Murdoch's wrath upon him, he answered evasively:

"No one in particular, it just occurred to me on the spur of the moment."

His host seemed not appeased, judging by his angry stare, which seemingly carried a message. Be on guard! Anyway, the festive mood ended abruptly, a sore point had been touched, that raised Murdoch's dander. It was time to leave, the welcome rug had been whisked away. First, however, an important matter needed to be broached; the tricky subject of the uras trees. Let him frown and seethe with antagonism, Wirt thought. Come hell or high water, he is going to hear what I have to say. Starting to lead up to it in a roundabout way, he came to the meat of the matter.

"As you are aware I shall assume the Gardens' management shortly, next Monday already, by the looks of it."

Hardly had the last word slipped over his tongue, when Murdoch assumed a diabolical air. A sardonic smile hovered around his lips, a cynical scowl distorted his features, yet he neither flinched nor spoke. Turning up his nose his head moved sideways, as if trying to evade an offensive odour.

It was an insulting display of arrogance, mixed with gloating, that raised Wirt's eyebrows in annoyance. Mitigated annoyance one should say, in view of Murdoch's anticipated chagrin upon learning the news which Wirt had intended to introduce gently, with a sympathetic mien. Not anymore, he decided, after that resentful display. Sneer all you want, Wirt exulted inwardly, your dessert is about to be served.

"There is something else I want to say," Wirt intimated.

"Well?"

How a simple everyday remark could possibly be packed with such venom, Wirt could have never imagined. Anyway, it reinforced his intention to let him have it hip and thigh.

"Sometimes next week we are going to dig up the uras trees at the Kew Gardens' Sylvania property, and transplant them at the government compound in town."

Murdoch, still on his feet, strutting in the fashion of a fighting cock ready to pounce, pretended not to have heard. Yet his facial expression belied the dissimulation. Telltale signs foreshadowed a reality he endeavoured to hide. But despite a studied stiff upper-lip pose, Wirt envisioned a column of rage rising behind the facade of diffidence.

Feigning sudden recall, Murdoch remarked:

"I'm sorry, I didn't catch what you just said."

"Let me repeat it then. We are going to transplant every uras tree within the Sylvania property."

Expanding his chest, snorting contemptuously, Murdoch expelled:

"I will make a prediction."

"Tell me."

"Neither you nor anyone under your superintendence shall thrust a spade into that ground."

From his host's inimical bearing Wirt deduced that his presence was no longer desired. Nodding curtly, saying good night on the run, as it were, he hastened down the steps.

Arriving at the road below he heard Murdoch's gravelly voice resounding in his ears, loud enough to induce neighbours to rush outside. On he went:

"I repeat, sooner will hell freeze over before you or anyone else disgraces that property. You shall not see the day when this will happen," he hollered quite beside himself now.

What Murdoch bellowed into the night had an ominous ring, like Odin's promise that never failed to come true.

Wirt hurried along, endeavouring to lay a distance between himself and those prophetic exclamations, which sounded like a declaration of evil intent. Murdoch's blatant utterances were not meant to be oracular, he decided as he quickened his steps, neither were they expelled in a flight of passion, he concluded.

In a flash he realised, rather guessed, an awful truth about Alfred Nantes. Didn't Rintoul mention that after Nantes scouted around the Sylvania property he was riven by mental torment and racked by bodily pain? The Belgian's tale of woe, a veritable jeremiad as related by Rintoul, rang loud in his ears. He ostensibly fought a losing battle with forces sinister and incomprehensible that clawed at his sanity. As he approached the bridge Wirt vividly remembered what Rintoul had said.

"Nantes appeared to be at the end of his tether, he was devoid of the last vestiges of reserve. Misery had undermined his sense of pride and decorum. This is what he said:

" 'Since that fateful day of my visit to the Kew Gardens' property up in the mountains, I feel tormented by an anguish that slowly drags me into the jaws of a beast I cannot name. Mortal terror racks and ruins my waking hours. I kid you not, Mr Rintoul, at night in bed I feel the crushing weight of an incubus squatting on my chest, alternatively gnashing its teeth and shrieking like a fiend from hell. I need help, something is happening to me, I feel like a dead man walking.' "

Halfway across the bridge Wirt halted his steps. He felt a pang of remorse, accompanied by a painful sense of guilt on account of his hasty retreat.

"I have a good mind to go back and set the record straight," he encouraged himself.

But then quickly dismissed the notion for he abhorred any form of confrontation. His nature, neither combative nor ostentatious, spurned impetuous displays. Besides, the thought of curious, cackling natives, unfailingly attracted by quarrels between expatriates, induced him to desist.

As he continued on his way he couldn't help chuckling while imagining the natives' bustle, eager to witness the strange spectacle of two irate white men reviling each other with raised fists and execrable curses. How disappointed they must be upon learning that the new botanist took to his heels rather than confronting the man they disliked.

"So be it," Wirt murmured, for the notion of exchanging insults with Murdoch, or anyone else, made him cringe. Let him savour his triumph, which Wirt intended to turn into a Pyrrhic victory, come what may. For his innate forbearance had been ruptured by Murdoch's offensive exhibition. Whereas till now he treated his colleague's waywardness with smiles and a shrug of the shoulders, this rude flare up taught him otherwise. Shaking a fist at him removed the last vestige of tolerance and sympathy. Mrs Burchard's scheme would now be carried out to the letter, no longer reluctantly, but with unconcealed joy.

Wirt In A Dither

On the following Monday Murdoch remained conspicuously absent. In the morning a missive arrived confirming Wirt's position as botanist in charge, effective immediately. Succinct directions, aimed at Murdoch, were given, to hand over keys, files, and all documents pertaining to the botanical garden. A copy of this directive, a footnote stated, had been delivered to Murdoch. An inauguration dinner will be held upon the premier's return; date and time shall be announced in due course.

Strange to say, Wirt harboured second thoughts about the notice. Though welcoming the announcement, it set him on tenterhooks. Uncertain whether to consider the message as glad tidings or a letter of Bellerophon, he read it again. Why he felt increasingly queasy puzzled him, till a muffled sound from the cloud-ringed mountains provided a clue. Startled, Wirt scanned the peak of Morne Trois Pitons, shrouded as usually in layers of vapour, from which a voice, so it appeared, suppressed, yet emphatically urged:

"Run, Hannes, leave the island today, and never come back, flee for your life."

Straining every nerve he tried to make sense of these peculiar sounds, resembling oracular utterances, seemingly aimed at him. How could that be? Did his overwrought perception call into life chimeras unworthy of a pragmatic mind? Hurling imprecations at the imaginary soothsayer, Wirt turned his back. The sea was a friendlier sight to a harried man. Yet he couldn't control an impulse to glance occasionally in the direction of the portentous mountains, albeit furtively, as though fearing scathing rebukes from his own lips.

Trying to control a growing apprehension remained a futile exercise. Rustles in the ferns, or a rush in the palm trees evoked notions of an impending disaster. Gritting his teeth, however, he resolved to stand firm, and proceed with unyielding determination.

Nantes' fate entered his thoughts again. Could a man, conspicuous, belonging to a distinct coterie, vanish without a trace in a small, scarcely inhabited island? Not likely, Wirt concluded; yet, that's what happened. The prominent scientist, who crossed an ocean to commence a new life, has seemingly absconded into oblivion, arbitrarily and suddenly; or did he? The mere notion startled Wirt; at first that is. Could this not be a setup staged by him and Murdoch perhaps? Was Nantes the cog in a machinery constructed for evil purposes? Recalling Rintoul's remarkable narration, Wirt instantly pooh-poohed the idea. The man's anguish, according to the banker, should obviate such musings. No, Nantes waded into a bog of misery, towards an abyss of no return. He remembered Rintoul's very words:

"On his second visit Nantes resembled death's-head on a mopstick. Ghastly pale, haggard to the marrow, despair oozing from every visible pore of his skin, he impressed me as a man attending his own funeral. Never had I witnessed such abject wretchedness staring at me. There he stood, gaping with dilated eyes that seemed to mirror visions he neither could nor dared to name."

What racked his predecessor's body and tantalised his soul, Wirt couldn't imagine, but he instinctively knew who caused it; Murdoch, and no mistake about it. All day his image hovered before his mind's eye, sneering derisively one instant, growling menacingly the next. Trying to dismiss images of Murdoch baring his fangs, Wirt got ensnared with thoughts about his own situation. Why was he being followed and spied on? At whose behest did these men shadow him, and for what purpose? Disturbing thoughts raced through his head, for which he found neither answers nor justification. Nantes' mysterious disappearance, whether contrived or involuntary, cast a dark shadow over him, as did his colleague's portentous utterances, despite being deemed frivolous and pretentious. Yes, bluff or not, those auguries rattled him. True, they were made in the heat of passion, fanned by an alcoholic vapour, but just the same Wirt couldn't shoo them from his mind. Well, he said to himself, we will soon find out if it was mere intemperance of the tongue, or borne by reality; for come what may, he determined to give a Roland for Murdoch's Oliver; tit for tat in other words. No mistake, Wirt was on his mettle, the mere hint of retreat invited scathing scorn. Murdoch's outbreak, meant to intimidate, strengthened his resolve to carry out the government's will beyond the call of duty.

This new-found resolve calmed his nerves. As fickleness, the beast that gnaws at one's vital forces, reluctantly slunk away, Wirt's heart filled with joy. Despite a lingering apprehension he became imbued with hitherto unknown bliss. How wonderful life can be to a man whose mind is set and thoughts are clear, he mused. A seldom experienced contentment pervaded his whole being. Taking a deep breath, he raised his head towards the sky which before his eyes took on a dazzling brightness. The mountains, forbidding a moment ago, acquired an alluring aspect. The sea, flooded with sunlight, smiled approvingly at the man who was about to step onto a path fraught with uncertainty, if not danger, yet enter he would.

The messenger, a government official, had handed Wirt a small cabinet with keys clearly tagged. He seemed reluctant to leave, something weighed on his mind by the looks of it. Recalling the official's peculiar deportment brought a frown to Wirt's brow. He remembered asking:

"Do you wish to say something?"

Hemming and hawing for an instant, trying to overcome an evident embarrassment, he explained:

"When I advised the workers that you will be in complete and sole charge from hereon, they looked at me nonplussed, and absolutely dismayed at each other. I couldn't, still cannot, understand their reaction."

"Where they surprised?" Wirt asked.

"Surprised is not the word, they literally cringed as if expecting to be cuffed. How odd, I thought, unmanning really."

So did Wirt, who was not only perplexed but somewhat apprehensive. Why should they become fidgety upon learning that he will be their supervisor henceforth? They knew him as a forbearing man, exacting admittedly, but neither overly demanding, nor in the least abusive. What a peculiar lot, Wirt concluded as he turned towards more pressing matters.

First he intended to peruse the files and, if necessary, put them in order. Selecting the appropriate key, he unlocked the door and entered the office building. In a twinkle he opened one of the cabinets, which he shut even quicker. Going, rather bounding to the next one, he found it as bare as the other. It contained not a single file, just empty rails met his squinting eyes. Thoroughly baffled, he examined the rest, which also contained not even a chit of paper. Rubbing his eyes, shaken to the core, Wirt slumped onto a chair from which he quickly rose again. Murmuring repeatedly:

"It cannot be, it cannot be," he examined the cabinets once more, then searched through every room in the building with deepening frowns and pounding temples. Nothing could be found; every document, information collected over decades, had disappeared.

"I must be hallucinating," he moaned.

Then kicking himself, mentally that is, he exclaimed:

"Don't be daft, Hannes, these files were here yesterday."

But today they are missing, someone has removed them, Wirt concluded; who?

"Murdoch," he gasped, "but why?"

An awfully realisation revealed itself. This whole thing reeked of entrapment; his that is. Murdoch tried to impute him with gross negligence, if not theft. Disgrace and suspicion could already be perceived; one snapping at his heels, the other's fetid breath hovering around him.

"I am ruined," he groaned.

Though unable to think clearly, he understood that the loss must be reported immediately. While fingering his throat, as if trying to loosen a choking collar, Alfred Nantes came to his mind. Was the Belgian a victim of similar chicaneries that drove him to distraction and ultimately off the island?

This train of thought was rudely interrupted by a commotion outside. Somebody, evidently winded, came lumbering and wheezing up the steps. At a glance Wirt recognised the chief of police accompanied by two constables. They are coming to detain me it flashed through his mind. Should he abscond, or stay put? The mere notion of flight elicited involuntary sniggers. Running away? Why, and where to in this small island? Better to accept the inevitable.

Resigned, yet strangely roused, Wirt awaited the men, who midway on the steps stopped, then turned their heads as if searching for stragglers. Wirt, gripped by an odd emotion, a mixture of defiance and regret, observed them nonchalantly. Something hitherto unthinkable occurred; his apprehension gave way to blind recklessness that surprised him. Grievances of past months seemed to wind into a ball, ready to burst. Let them come and be shocked, finding a presumed embodiment of urbanity transformed into a raucous disputant. Like a solitary wasp with an angry sting he awaited the lawmen's approach.

"Be on guard, Mr Brunt," he silently cautioned. "I know your game. You are part of a conspiracy to chase me off the island. Ha, ha, and ha again."

Meanwhile four locals, black to the fingertips, turned around the bend, pulling and pushing a cart laden with boxes. Did they heed the chief's vociferous exhortations, accompanied by frantic hand signals? Wirt neither knew nor cared, his mind being set to have a showdown, nothing would divert him from it. His countenance, a mask of resolve, every limb brimming with vigour, he stepped outside.

"Ah, good afternoon, Mr Wirt, glad to see you again," Brunt called out.

To Wirt's surprise the chief appeared to be his jovial best, marred by not even a trace of sternness or officiousness. His whole Falstaffian being radiated genuine benevolence, tinged, however, by a breath of awkwardness. He went on:

"Sorry, sorry, my dear fellow, for the inconvenience. I meant to give you advance warning, but others decided against it. Not for mistrust, mind you, far from it, but simply not to compromise you. Anyway, here we are. First, how are you?"

Pointing at the stacked boxes, Wirt replied with acerbity:

"It depends what's in there."

"I understand. You must have been distraught finding the cabinets empty. It's all my fault, but extenuating circumstances exist for my apparent remissness. A decision to proceed had only been reached in the early morning hours. Acting promptly, before daybreak that is, became essential."

Seeing Wirt's frown changing to an expression of bewilderment, Brunt explained:

"The short of it is this: We are in the midst of an investigation that could have criminal dimensions. Regrettably I'm not at liberty to expound upon the matter, except that it involves that vexing problem called obeah."

Heaving a sigh of relief, Wirt offered:

"I expect those boxes contain, how shall I say..."

"The purloined documents," the chief chuckled, still a bit amused at Wirt's consternation.

"You removed them, in other words. May I inquire why?"

"You may, sir, but since I must hedge my answer, silence is preferable."

Scarcely had the files been in place, when Brunt signalled to leave.

"Sorry to say, but I'm on the jump again."

Consulting his watch he declared:

"The old story, I should be somewhere else hours ago."

Looking Wirt full in the face, he stated:

"Don't forget, help is just around the corner. My door is always open. Should you find it shut, climb in through the window. Ha, ha, ha, have a nice evening."

Wirt watched the slouching figure lumber towards the road. Before Brunt and his retinue disappeared behind a cluster of bushes, he turned around. For an instant he seemed lost in thought, while observing the botanist standing irresolutely on the top landing. Wirt could neither see the chief's smirk, nor hear his prophetic words:

"Yes, my dear fellow, you need help alright. Upon my word, you do."

Drawing a deep breath Wirt went inside. He directed his attention to the returned files; that is he tried, albeit unsuccessfully. What prevented it? The will existed, yet the mind demurred. When he caught himself gazing vacantly at a half opened drawer, he resignedly pushed it back again. There was no sense trying to perform any task, be it ever so simple and repetitive, because his thoughts reverted irresistible to Howard Brunt and his escapade. One could hardly call it by another name, or could one? Giving free rein to various notions, Wirt found each one implausible upon closer reflection. Yet he wondered whether the chief might keep two faces under one hood. His vaunted open-heartedness could be a facade to conceal a mean spirited conniver. Removing documents on the sly, possibly arbitrarily on some flimsy pretext, certainly allowed one to believe so. Then again, who knows if the removal of the files were not based on necessity? Deciding to leave the scrutiny of documents in abeyance, Wirt locked up, then started on his way home.

The Plot Thickens

Relieved, but not exactly light-hearted, he arrived at the house just as the domestics left. The smell of freshly cut grass, pleasantly pungent, touched a nerve that raised his spirit. The gardener, as always, had done a good job. Wirt liked, rather admired the old man with few worldly possessions, but endowed with enviable virtues. He unfailingly came and went silently, like a shadow, never grumbling nor importuning anyone. Strangely shy, yet decidedly headstrong, old Ransy considered the grounds his personal trust. Loath to attract attention or receive praise, he required no other guiding principles except his own. Once, at the beginning, Wirt paid him a compliment that earned him neither thanks nor smiles. Old Ransy, observing him disapprovingly, raised his head to heaven as if praying for his employer's salvation, then walked away silently.

Salina, the housekeeper, was a different kettle of fish. A more fastidious wench could not be found in the entire island with a magnifying glass. Often moody, outright surly at times, she hankered for constant approval. Wirt considered her a vixen out to sow thorns and thistles on his path. At every slight, imagined mostly, she bristled with anger and wrapped herself in offensive silence. Any hint of a request, regardless how insignificant, she perceived as a reprimand to be paid back with interest. Upon sight of him she grumbled about a string of grievances that needed immediate alleviation. How could she perform her duties under such onerous conditions, like paucity of supplies, lack of suitable kitchen utensils, and not least an absence of appreciation? Why must she scrounge and scrape together to satisfy his needs and whims? And look at Ransy, is he not a beast on two legs who treats her with utter disrespect? This–this John-a-Nokes is a source of embarrassment to the entire household. He should be sent packing, he should.

"You first," Wirt felt tempted to say, but he checked his tongue, for the recollection of an episode with Verna, the cook, still stuck in his craw. By all the saints, did not her dismissal cause a ripple, if not tremor, which made his spine tingle to this day? Murdoch got involved, even Mauch importuned him with requests to reverse his decision. Why they stuck their noses in his private affairs puzzled and angered him. Entreaties from all sides fell on deaf ears, besides steeling his resolve to give her the boot.

To begin with he had no need for a cook, though admittedly the compelling reason for her dismissal lay elsewhere. The woman, besides being a suspected snoop, possessed an aura which made him uncomfortable. Her glances, reminiscent of a jettatura's, were undoubtedly meant to inflict misfortune and injury upon him. In any case, why else would she make peculiar signs and mystic eye movements at every encounter? When he caught her fingering his personal papers, he lowered the axe. It served as a pretext, he privately admitted, but he ignored her avowals of innocence.

"I just tidied them," she protested to no avail.

Murdoch's vehement objections, as much as Mauch's untoward protests, were given the cold shoulder. Others too made a fuss. Their remonstrances ran the gamut from the sublime to ludicrousness. What, an expatriate, meaning a white man of course, a scientist to boot, without domestics? Heads were shaking, frowns met his refusal to abide by the rules. Worse, he treated time-honoured customs with levity.

"Yes, yes, Mr Wirt, that's how it is perceived. Curtailing free services, though perplexing, is one thing; refusing them outright borders on absurdity. It gives an impression of wilful nose-thumbing, it does. You will have to bear the mark of an iconoclast, and that's no small burden."

So it went. A clique of men and women, laden with the imaginary cross called convention, gave Wirt no rest. How could he, a man of stature, command respect from his peers, and deference of the natives?

"Think of it and reconsider. Don't forget, the government covers all expenses."

Others, less aggressive, viewing his attitude with a measure of tolerance, just appealed to his sense of propriety.

"If you must be obdurate, my dear fellow, so be it, but be discreet. Don't blazon such breaches of tradition abroad. Believe us, servants in this part of the world are as essential to expatriates as oxygen in air. Be careful, you might be tagged a renegade, and thus be treated with disdain."

Why a trifling matter, concerning him alone, should excite so much attention, Wirt could not comprehend; not yet anyway. But it made him think twice to carry out his intention to give Salina, the housekeeper, the sack.

Tonight Wirt resolved to take it easy; imbibe a little, read excerpts of a book, and dawdle away the hours. Today's events, as much as recent occurrences, though following him like pesky flies, were pushed to the background.

What made him stop and stare in the direction of the bedroom seemed inexplicable. More so why he instinctively started to move in that direction, which he seldom went except at bedtime. A force, stronger than habit, appeared to be controlling his feet. Then he recognised the reason for his odd captivation. The door, kept open day and night, was shut. It never happened before; in fact, he didn't even realise that a door existed. Curiosity urged him on, presentiments held him back.

"What the dickens," he called out louder than intended, subconsciously hoping that it would drive away nascent apprehensions.

It didn't work. His feet, seemingly stuck in concrete slabs, refused to cross the line that reluctance had drawn. As common sense tried to gain ascendance over fancy, darkness set in, stirring to life voices that never sounded so shrill. Giving himself a mental kick, Wirt hastened towards a nearby wall switch, which he flicked. No lights came on, even after frantically flipping others.

"What now?" he muttered involuntarily, as he stumbled through the house.

Looking outside he noticed that nearby houses and the city lay in full illumination. Fighting back onsetting alarm, he groped his way to the distribution panel, whose location had been pointed out to him. There, the main breaker had tripped, that was all. Odd to say, he hesitated to move the lever to the ON position. A dozen questions raced through his head for which answers were not at hand. Should he chance it or call an electrician? He did move the lever, after fortifying himself with several drams of brandy.

Hearing the contacts snap, seeing the lights come on, Wirt regained his composure. He went straight to his bedroom where everything appeared to be in order. Chuckling at his foolish trepidation a moment ago, he prepared to leave the room, when he caught sight of a small object on the bed. For an instant he thought a cat had chosen this comfortable spot as a lair. Ha, he would teach the little intruder a lesson. Clapping his hands, he called out sharply:

"Out you go! What, you want to be defiant? Scat, or I shall throw you out the window!"

The little beast showed neither fear nor moved an inch. Stomping on the floor, hollering at the top of his voice, Wirt approached the presumed feline. Then his face lit up, his voice became a whisper:

"Look at that," he chuckled appreciatively.

Neatly placed between the cushions sat a stuffed doll. Smiling, he picked it up to take a closer look. The smile grew broader upon realising that the doll resembled him to a remarkable degree.

"How nice of Salina, how thoughtful," he repeated deeply touched.

Clearing the lump in his throat, choked by remorse on account of his unworthy intentions, he stroked the stuffed image affectionately. What he noticed made him laugh on the wrong side of his mouth. The smiles turned to grimaces, the chuckles to hiccups. A large thorn pierced the effigy's heart. With an expletive on his lips, Wirt threw the figure out the window. Thoroughly riled he stomped onto the veranda, then shook his fist at the city beyond the river, where his treacherous housemaid presumably lived.

"Calm down, calm down," he told himself repeatedly.

It was easier said than done to quench the flames of anxiety darting at him from all sides. Conflicting emotions surged through his mind, wavering between anger, fear, and self-disparagement. One moment he looked upon the incident as mummery, nothing but a fatuous prank; the next he ascribed a prophetic meaning to it. Showering the housekeeper, together with her kith and kin, with mockery and taunts, mitigated his agitation somewhat, but failed to banish billowing misgivings thundering towards him. Despite his attempt at a brave front, Wirt felt stung to the soul; his habitual equanimity became unglued, giving way to rampant imagination.

What ears could hear, eyes could see, and the mind perceived, acquired a sinister aspect. Darkness was never so dreary and black. The voices of the night, otherwise bestowing serenity, and rendering one's thoughts agreeable, took on a strident ring, as if vying to outdo each other in discordancy. The rush of the river, inherently somnolent, now sounded ominous; it carried a message that Wirt preferred to ignore. He should not have done so, for the incident with the doll was not meant to be a prank; far from it, as he soon found out. It was a precursor of uglier things to follow.

Presently, however, while divining much, he understood little beyond the assumption that somebody tried to frighten him. Who? Not the housekeeper, Wirt decided, she had no reason to harbour ill will towards him. He always treated her well. His demeanour expressed benevolence towards her, which in a way was insincere, for he felt no sympathy for the young woman with the false smile. Besides, he resented servants around him.

There now, could she have sensed that he wanted to get rid of her? Hardly, unless she is endowed with clairvoyance; in other words could read his mind. True, she might have placed the doll on his bed on somebody else's behest, but innocently so. No, someone ill-disposed towards him was behind this silly, yet nasty trick. Again Murdoch came to mind, but Wirt quickly repudiated the notion, it stretched credulity to the utmost. No, his colleague, proper to a fault, would not possibly stoop so low. Playing around with dolls, whether they be symbolic or not, could hardly be imputed to a dyed-in-the-wool conformist, who abhorred even a whiff of levity.

Despite his chagrin, Wirt chuckled at the thought of Murdoch sitting in a dark room, sticking needles into his effigy, mumbling gibberish, and invoking mumbo jumbo to cast a deadly spell. No, it's inconceivable that stiff upper lip Murdoch would dabble in witchcraft, or collude with subordinate native women.

That left only Salina as a suspect, Wirt concluded. She, and no one else placed that doll on the bed; whether on her own volition or someone else's bidding, he determined to find out by setting a trap. Deliberation concerning the method made scant progress; they were interrupted by bouts of anger. To be more exact by the housekeeper's image that rose before his eyes. Her face, distorted by sardonic laughter, infuriated the otherwise even tempered German. Snorting indignantly, he vowed to get even with her, and anybody else partaking in this trickery.

As he reviled the treacherous housemaid, an afterimage stirred him into action. Being overly hasty, he had ignored something attached to his effigy's chest. He decided to take a closer look, which he did a few moments later. Inside, under a bright light, he could see a label sewn on, pierced by the thorn, showing the symbolic skull and crossbones, signifying death. Curbing an impulse to tear the doll to shreds, Wirt sat down to think. This was not meant to be a prank, but rather a broad hint to be on guard. Murdoch's words came to mind:

"You will never dig up a single root at Sylvania."

Strange predictions, threats really, Wirt groaned. Though uttered under the influence, they contained a sinister connotation, considering past occurrences. Many notions went through his head; some laughable, others bewildering, giving rise to suspicion. Like Murdoch's insistence to have servants in the house, despite his protest that is. Added Mauch's and other worthies' importunate meddling, one surely was entitled to sit up and take notice. Were these advisors, unsolicited mind you, driven by self-serving needs perhaps? Did they, for some reason, want him to be surrounded by domestics? Hm, strange, to say the least, disquieting really, Wirt decided. No doubt, something was in the wind, probably had been since the day he stepped onto the shore.

Against his will, Wirt became absorbed in the recent past. He went over incidents with a fine-toothed comb. Events, ordinarily deemed waggish, if not ludicrous, acquired portentous significance. Some, only dimly remembered eliciting an amused chuckle, now took on oracular dimensions. Like Murdoch's behaviour for instance, enigmatic at times, disagreeable mostly, but nevertheless judged by Wirt as being genuine; till now that is.

This assessment, upon scrutiny, evaporated quicker than gossamer in an autumn morning sun. It gradual dawned on him that he had been deceived, rather deluded himself. His colleague's arcane mannerism was not innate, but a carefully managed performance. Idiosyncrasies, thought to be inherent in an upper crust Englishman, were nothing but a facade behind which Wirt decided to take a glimpse. He did. What he saw made him gasp and cringe in shame.

"How in the name of mercy could anybody be so naive," he moaned.

Anybody endowed with an ounce of perception should have seen through the veneer of this crude effort at respectability. Murdoch played the gamut of eccentricities, ineptly to say the least, yet he fell for it hook, line, and sinker, Wirt admitted. His face darkened in disgust and disappointment on account of his lack of judgement, and Murdoch's presumed perfidy.

As the last scales dropped from his eyes, past events took on a different hue. Deemed trivial till now, some incidents had one attribute in common: they all bore the same message of skulduggery, directed in part at him. Wirt had more than an inkling that he was a thorn in the side of an insidious person, aided by Murdoch, that conspired to put him to flight, or worse, bring about his demise. Who was it?

Trying to restrain the clamour racking his mind, Wirt rose and prepared to go outside. He stopped abruptly after the first step, then turned towards the sea. The serene vista, so contrary to his inner turmoil, made him introspective. Could it be that he was the author of his own vexation? He knew from past experiences about discords in his association with others, attributable to an aversion towards convention and dependence; so he thought. This, plus his propensity for self-reliance, he noticed, was perceived by many as a personal affront. In this case the mote in their eyes, no doubt, was his scientific acumen; but more so a putative colour blindness. His treatment of natives stuck in their craws; he moved among them without a whiff of prejudice. Imputing such heresy to ingenuousness and lack of experience, well-meaning men and women, expatriates, plus a few native-born considered white, dutifully enlightened him. Upon sensing that they were talking into the wind, brows puckered, patience yielded to annoyance. They became more emphatic. Even nodding acquaintances buttonholed him, figuratively speaking, to point out, in a humorous vein mind you, that being matey with natives, meaning blacks, usually backfires.

"Familiarity breeds contempt, you know," they reminded him.

Wirt's pat response: "Humbug, my dear fellow," earned him icy stares.

Associates cautioned not so subtly:

"Treating natives as equals is synonymous with losing respect from all sides."

Pooh-poohing the notion raised eyebrows, and countenances flushed with vexation. Several men and women, inveterate high-hats, intoxicated with self-importance, snubbed him outright. Yet they could not resist casting punishing glances in his direction before turning up their noses.

Opposed to taking umbrage, Wirt found these pantomimes entertaining. He never failed to hail the pretenders at gentility enthusiastically at every encounter. Women especially seemed endowed with a knack to mutely cut him down to size with withering looks and frowning countenances.

Wirt, though disconcerted by the censure, pretended to be unconcerned; outwardly in any case. Inwardly a prickly anxiety refused to subside. Random glances and passing remarks made in his presence acquired portentous significance. His contemptuous disregard for his peers' views was but a front that failed to blot out a growing self-consciousness, especially after a tiff with Murdoch.

Wirt liked to work with his hands, not constantly, but now and then. Dreading his colleague's scathing remarks however, not mentioning those reproving stares, he generally desisted. But not one morning about a month ago. Hardly had he swung from the bed, when a mutinous disposition overcame him. He did not as usual linger over breakfast, nor admire the sun's rapid journey across the swells of the Martinique Passage, for his intention brooked no delay.

"Today, part of it anyway, I shall work in the Gardens with my own hands," he promised himself.

To blazes with Murdoch and those cavillers trying to push dying traditions down his throat that benefit nobody, besides being a fount of mediocrity. Losing no time to reach the Gardens, he unlocked the tool shed to which by chance he had a key. Taking out a wheelbarrow, spade and rake, he went to work.

Soon the fun began. Murdoch, as though divining his colleague's intransigence, not only showed up unexpectedly, but early to boot. In retrospect of the incident Wirt chuckled despite his unsettled frame of mind. Murdoch approached with strides gaining in speed and size. What he saw must have set fire under his soles, and breath into his lungs. Wirt pretended not to notice, he dug assiduously while humming a tune. Planting himself squarely before Wirt, Murdoch flew at his successor:

"I say, what do you think you are doing?"

Raising his head slowly, observing his colleague with dancing imps in his eyes, Wirt exclaimed:

"Ah, it's you. What brings you here so early?"

"Never mind that," Murdoch snapped seemingly appalled, but sensing Wirt's quarrelsome mood, toned down a bit:

"I must talk to you."

"I am listening," Wirt replied while continuing his work.

Despite being taken aback by Wirt's unwonted refractoriness, Murdoch started his lecture about the imprudence of being chummy with Negroes. Having heard that song and seen that dance before, Wirt paid little heed to the lecture. Getting into his stride, Murdoch did not relent.

"I can tell you from experience, mixing freely with the natives invariably leads to complications. Working physically side by side with them is anathema."

Had Murdoch been less emphatic about such high-flown notions, baseless in Wirt's estimation, he would have endured this tiresome sermon with equanimity. Against his will he bristled. Rising from his kneeling position, he faced Murdoch squarely, then growled:

"Why is that?"

Murdoch, grimacing as if hurt all over by such crass ignorance, seemed on the verge of exploding with anger. But he managed to control himself; yet not his countenance, which changed into a mask of annoyance.

"Take it from me, making common cause with natives lowers one's standing in the community. Respect goes out the window; one's effectiveness diminishes rapidly, especially among the workforce. In no time instructions given go in one ear and exit through the other. Soon you have to holler like a straw boss to be heeded."

"Fiddlesticks! my dear colleague. Such notions are mere biases, nurtured by unworthy sentiments. Simply put, we repress others to protect our own inferiority."

Murdoch's feelings were etched in his face. Furrowed with disgust, his eyes narrowing in disbelief, emphasising every syllable, he declared:

"You are swimming against the tide; why, escapes me. Relations between Europeans and Africans are anchored down since the days of Olim, they will not change in a hundred years."

Wirt looked squarely at his colleague, he wanted to tell him to save his breath, to cool his porridge. But being a polite man, he suggested:

"You are hoping against hope."

Murdoch stared for an instant at him as if he were an eyesore, then turning on his heels walked away wordlessly.

As mentioned that encounter took place a month ago. The tiff with Murdoch did not soften Wirt's aversion towards the

notion of disparate solitudes, based on colour of the skin. But
to avoid friction he decided to cease tilling the soil until the
reins were in his hands. He liked physical work more than
social conventions, even if partaking in it invites scorn and the
opprobrium of going native.

Wirt's reminiscences came to a sudden end; they yielded
to his present chagrin. Soon he worked himself into a regular
lather again. Flinging invectives in every direction, he gripped
the railing till his knuckles hurt. Calming down after a while,
he tried to separate fancy from common sense. Was this–this
mummery nothing but mischief, deserving an appreciative
chuckle, or a sign of an approaching juggernaut to be guarded
against? Come what may, he decided to catechise Salina sooner
than later. But hang it all, he neither knew her surname nor
where she lived; all arrangements were made by Murdoch.
Trying to get information from him might be as effective as
whistling for wind. In any case all locks would be changed
without delay. Ha, that squint-eyed slattern will not enter the
house again, he triumphed silently. Let her exercise her black
magic elsewhere.

Wirt gave a start. Black magic, that was it! Didn't Alfred
Nantes voice misgivings about acts of voodoo directed at him?
Voodoo? what next. Chimeras such notions are, nothing but
figments of an overstrained mind, he was told. Perhaps they
should have snickered less and commiserated more. Mulling
things over yielded no ready answer, except that incidents like
the present one were somehow connected with this mysterious
obeah, the vile practices of the mountain people.

As Wirt pondered over the recent past an odd queasiness
started to creep up his spine, which he tried to slough off with a
frown and a shrug of the shoulders. It didn't help much, for the
nausea not only persisted but was joined by a forlornness that
made his limbs leaden and addled his brains. Endeavouring to
curb the clamour in his head he rose, then haltingly started to
walk towards the bedroom. Rest is what he needed, nothing
like a good night's sleep will revive one's spirit.

"Tomorrow is another day," he murmured.

From the corner of his eyes Wirt noticed that the lights in
the entrance hall were still on.

"Hm, did I not turn them off?" he remarked frowningly. "I could have sworn I did."

As he approached the vestibule with trepidation, he debated with himself whether to illuminate the dimly lit corridor, for his queasiness took on alarming proportions. Just the same he decided to investigate, for his conviction grew that the entrance hall lay in darkness after he had reset the main breaker. Something was awry here, or his power of observation had forsaken him. Considering the latest events who should wonder. Pushing aside the curtain covering the window of the inner door, he took a glimpse. What he saw made him recoil and utter a cry of dismay. A hideous face, grotesquely distorted, grimaced at him. It resembled a mask of Gorgonean repulsiveness, twisted into folds of virulence, and disfigured by mockery. Thunderstruck, rooted to the floor, unable to lift a hand or stir a foot, he stared at the phenomenon, neither human nor spectre, ready to spit venom and bile at anyone approaching. But confronting that grisly apparition never occurred to Wirt, who fervently wished to get away. Yet unable to shake off his cataleptic condition, he just stood there like in a trance.

Luck was on his side; the spell was broken by loud screams outside. A cuckoo manioc was calling for rain. With one movement he pushed the bolt into place, turned on his heels and fled. It is said that fear bestows wings, which didn't exactly happen, but it sure cured his lame limbs and leaden feet. With a sprinter's swiftness he bounded out of the house through the back door, and kept running till he reached the bridge.

Gasping more from fear than exhaustion, Wirt slowed down, then stopped. Turning towards the house from which he had just escaped safe and sound, he noticed the tremor of his hands and dryness in his throat. Despite ruing his headlong retreat, he felt no inclination to return. Alone the thought of it made him moan in abhorrence. What he had just met with needed to be digested first.

Deciding to examine the incident quietly from a safe distance, he headed towards Roseau. On the southern banks of the river he found a secluded spot where he sat down to contemplate. It didn't get that far, for he quickly jumped up again. The sound made by the rippling water, which hitherto imbued him with a sense of well-being, grated on his nerves; it drove him away. Walking aimlessly through the town while repeatedly looking over his shoulders, he avoided other pedestrians. Questions overwhelmed him for which answers could not be found. The matter of the voodoo doll seemed clear enough. But that weird apparition, defying description, made little or no sense. Who switched on the light that had been left off? What aim and purpose is being pursued? The more he pondered the less he comprehended. Drawing a sensible conclusion appeared to be beyond the pale of logic.

Deep in thought Wirt walked down to the beach. The swells breaking on the shore jarred on his nerves. The sound made by the rhythmic fall disturbed his broody thoughts, besides conveying an uncanny message. In the near distance he could see the Fort Young Hotel to which he automatically directed his steps. For a moment he considered spending the night there, but quickly rejected the idea.

When he arrived at the bar and swimming pool area, a glimpse told him that the usual crowd, plus a few tourists, were in their element; namely, carousing. Being disinclined to join in, Wirt was about to steal away when he detected Dr Brodeur sitting alone at a table aside from the others. His heart leaped up; it flashed through his mind that the doctor might be in possession of the key to a vexing enigma. Overcoming his inherent reserve, he approached him.

"I am glad to see you, doctor," he burst out.

"Not for consultation, I hope," Dr Brodeur quipped good-naturedly.

"In a way, yes. May I sit down?"

Pointing to a chair invitingly, Wirt was told:

"Be my guest."

Did the doctor shrink back when Wirt sat down opposite him, or did he just move involuntarily? The wrinkles of anxiety that appeared on his face were undoubtedly real. Somewhat alarmed he said:

"You look distraught, have you seen ghosts from the past?"

"No, doctor, from the present," Wirt replied with a wan smile.

"What's on your mind?"

Wirt recounted his latest experience, carefully avoiding references to the friction between him and Murdoch. Inclining his head sideways, pursing his lips, Dr Brodeur explained:

"The voodoo doll, as you call it, can be disregarded as a practical joke, or an attempt to vent one's spleen. Some of our maroons delight in such practices when they feel slighted. I did hear about your reluctance to employ domestic servants, which could cause malignity, thereby trigger such acts."

"I agree with you, doctor; in fact, Salina, the housemaid, could well have been the perpetrator. By the way, do you know where she lives?"

A ghost of a smile appeared on Dr Brodeur's lips while replying:

"No."

He is lying, it flashed into Wirt's mind. Hiding his disappointment, he queried:

"What do you think about that demonic apparition, doctor?"

"Hm, hm, you say it resembled a human gargoyle?"

"That was my first impression."

"Apart from the head what shape did this–this creature possess?"

He doesn't believe me, Wirt suspected.

"I'm unable to say, because the entire window, fairly small as is, was covered by that leering mask of hideousness."

"You noticed neither a movement nor heard a sound, you aver?"

Nodding his head in agreement, Wirt granted:

"Remember, I was in a state of consternation already on account of that voodoo business, my perceptive faculties weren't exactly keen."

Dr Brodeur appeared to be troubled, and vexed for some reason. He gave the impression of a man wishing to be elsewhere. A pained look entered his eyes; he was evidently ill at ease.

"It sounds far-fetched," he intimated.

Looking at Wirt with a strained smile, he implied:

"Could it have been a dream?"

Shaking his head several times, Wirt asserted:

"It was neither a dream nor a spectre produced by my overwrought condition."

When Dr Brodeur, beset by incredulity judging by his facial expression, asked more pointed questions, Wirt proposed:

"I have no wish to impose on you, but would you consider coming with me to the house?"

When he noticed the doctor's pout, he quickly added:

"It's only a stone's throw from here."

Dr Brodeur consented, albeit reluctantly. They spoke little on the way; both were lost in thought.

The first surprise wasn't long in coming. As they approached the house the entrance hall, a half-open porch really, came in full view.

"I don't see a light," Dr Brodeur remarked.

"But–but, it was on when I left," Wirt stammered.

The doctor's face remained inscrutable. Gazing at him inquiringly in the light of the moon, Wirt detected not even a twitch. Yet his repeated, hm, hm, made him feel self-conscious.

Meanwhile having entered the vestibule, Dr Brodeur requested:

"Switch on the light."

Wirt, increasingly baffled, obeyed. Nothing untoward could be seen; the frightful shape had vanished.

"Hm, hm," Dr Brodeur mumbled.

Wirt tried to shake off a growing uneasiness. He gripped the door's handle. Though realising it wouldn't budge, he tried anyway.

"There," he was about to exclaim triumphantly, but groaned instead:

"I barred it from the inside, I did–I did."

"Hm, hm," the doctor mumbled.

"I don't understand, I simply don't understand it," Wirt moaned.

An awful thought struck him. Did he indeed dream it all? Had he been a victim of hallucinations induced by drugs in his brandy?

"Can I see the voodoo doll?" Dr Brodeur asked with a wry grin and a tone implying frustration.

He couldn't, because it too had disappeared. Despite rummaging through the house and grounds, Wirt was unable to locate it.

"I left it on the veranda table," he stammered repeatedly.

Dr Brodeur's kind eyes filled with pity, but odd to say his face broke out into a scarcely disguised smirk.

"Come to my office tomorrow at ten o'clock," were his last words before he left.

Wirt was speechless, smitten by the thought that Dr Brodeur considered him fanciful, deemed him a man afflicted by delirious dreams which he could not separate from reality. With horror-stricken eyes he followed the doctor's shadowy shape till it disappeared beyond the bridge.

A leaden heaviness descended upon him, dark clouds of portent approached from all sides. He never felt so abandoned as now. Thrown to the dogs by his peers, silently mocked by the natives who divined an expatriate's downfall. He shuffled to the veranda where he sat down. The city below, in semi-darkness already, reassured him somewhat. He tried to rein his galloping consternation, for after all was he not a scientist by training, and rational by nature?

"Think, Hannes, apply your ratiocinative capabilities," he urged.

Whilst he sat there hovering between dread, and nascent doubts he dared not utter, the city grew darker by the minute. As lights went out his loneliness increased, calling to life presentiments he dared not explain. Wild suspicions, which he failed to bridle, stirred his imagination. He saw himself standing at the edge of the proverbial vale of tears, unable to decide whether to step back or enter. The notion of being but ligan without a float or buoy gripped him mercilessly. Whom could he trust? Certainly not Murdoch or Mauch. Dr Brodeur perhaps; Rintoul, the banker, with reservations. Only Celia Burchard, the premier's wife, seemed worthy of confidence.

But a voice from somewhere cautioned to be on guard. She was an enigmatic woman no doubt, who exuded an aura of mystique. There were times, after having tossed one too many, when Wirt deemed her a modern day Delilah, voluptuous but treacherous.

No denying it, the coal-black woman with a matronly exterior affected him in a way not entirely chaste; in fact, her presence set his pulse astir, and evoked an image of the Venusberg. Her full body and seductive voice seemed intend to lure men to the mountain of delight and love. Yet he realised that within this feminine shell dwelled a calculating mind. No doubt she liked men more than women, but she could be equally ruthless to both, as he witnessed more often than once.

Who could forget the sudden transformation from a lilting siren to a stern mistress, should her will be opposed. Take the case of Murdoch and the Sylvania property, which in his judgement was a conundrum of the first order. Mrs Burchard's intent to have practically every tree from those grounds uprooted caused him discomfort. Transplanting several of each species in the botanical garden, very well, that made good sense. But digging up every single one looked more punitive than expedient. She had the law on her side of course, and possessed the power no less, but circumspection was lacking.

Wirt made his way to the bedroom. He might as well have remained outside all night watching the lights go out. Sleep, the healer of woes and snatcher of an errand spirit, failed in its duty; tossing about helped not a whit. Hardly had he turned onto one side when a crushing weight descended that pressed him down till he turned again. So it went all night. Only in the waning morning hours did he sink into a trance-like slumber. Just the same he sat outside at the wonted hour observing the rising sun climb over the mountains.

In the shimmer of the approaching day Wirt regained his equilibrium. Reason gradually elbowed rampant imageries aside; common sense jostled to the surface. Let them play with his nerves, or try to. Whoever was behind these monkeyshines would soon find out that getting him rattled is like biting granite.

He visibly relaxed, a smile stole to his lips, a sigh of relief escaped from his breast. Ah, life wasn't so dreary in the land of warm sunshine and cooling trade winds. What could be more delightful than sitting above a rippling river while listening to the rustle of leaves and flirting with the temptation to take a dip in the sea? The sight of women on their way to the market, being their voluble selves as always, raised his spirit. How they could laugh and engage in banter with heavy baskets on their heads and arms, tykes hanging onto their skirts, Wirt couldn't understand. Like many men he was unable to fathom the souls of women unrestrained by onerous mores and critical eyes.

The awakening bustle of the city, audible and visible from the house, made Wirt linger. While trying to suppress uncomfortable thoughts, he reflected on more pleasant aspects. Why fret on account of silly witchcraft and other trifles, he told himself. Come on, Hannes, count your blessings. You are still fairly young, sound as a bell, financially in good shape, and living in a splendorous world. The future will be a bed of roses. So, quit moping and invoking images that stifle life's vital forces. Shoo away those bogies before you immure yourself in a tower of fear. No, he wouldn't! From now on these oppressive notions were to be kept at bay. But the wish is not always the father of deeds, as this case demonstrated. Despite a brave front Wirt subconsciously realised that he whistled in the dark. Though refusing to admit it Murdoch's shadow never left his side. Try as he may his mocking face sprung up again before he managed to banish it from his mind.

Despite his feigned unconcern Wirt's inner eye saw the ominous wisp of straw hanging in the air; with reasons as it turned out. Just the same he resolved to tackle his work with all his strength and ability.

The Missing Shirt

*H*is first tasks would be the work at the Sylvania property. What about Murdoch? Let him just lift one finger to prevent it, let him try, and watch out what will happen. The days are past were his effronteries received demure acceptance. In any case, averting the removal of those trees, regardless of motives, exceeded Murdoch's orbit of power. The transplantation will begin most likely before the end of the week, prior to Mrs Burchard's return.

Having settled all that in his mind he prepared to dress for work; it was high time to be on his way. To his surprise he didn't see his shirt, which as always hung over the armrest of a chair.

"Odd," he grumbled while searching through the room.

Puzzled, yet not disconcerted, he took a fresh one from a nearby wardrobe.

The workers had already started, albeit with scant enthusiasm, as Wirt noticed at a glance. He said nothing beyond good morning. He remained silent, though noticeably vexed at the sight of men moving aimlessly around the grounds chattering away, no doubt to camouflage their idleness. I know that exercise, Wirt thought, it's called killing time. But he kept quiet, for now that is, because he blamed the supervisors, foremost Murdoch, whose indifference undoubtedly bore the responsibility for the workers' slipshod performance. That will change, Wirt decided, sooner than later, and no mistake. Little did he know it would be a Sisyphean task, requiring the patience of Job.

He made the rounds quietly, making notes and sketches, while keeping an unobtrusive eye on the crew. A few days ago he had appointed Fasot as a working foreman despite Murdoch's strenuous opposition.

"You will curse the day when that preposterous conception entered your head," he was brusquely told.

"It will be a trial, nothing more."

Well, he didn't curse as Murdoch predicted, but he rued the very thought of it in a short time. Anger, mixed with sadness, stirred his soul as he watched the workers from the corner of his eyes, pushing wheelbarrows hither and thither in a random way. Fasot neither directed the crew, nor led by example, but he made a lot of noise. What did Murdoch say?

"The natives laugh at instructions given by one of their own, they never obey them."

Perhaps so, my worthy colleague, how can it happen if none are issued? Time will tell, Wirt reckoned, right now I must attend to more vital matters. He was in a vexatious mood; all day he felt plagued by an unusual lack of concentration. His attention span, hitherto worthy of mention, had constricted to almost zero.

After he removed a file from the cabinet, he forgot what he was looking for before he opened it. Self-castigation had no effect; it helped not a whit. Going outside to investigate this or that, he caught himself standing near some tree staring at nothing in particular, while desperately trying to remember what he wanted to see. Retracing his steps failed to revive his power of recollection. He felt like a man who had sipped from the Lethian Dew. Like the magnetic needle always points towards the pole, so his thoughts reverted to the house on the hill. He was no longer master of his mind, which seemed spellbound by recent happenings. He lost control of his will; the reins were yielded to the subconscious. Before he fully realised it, he strode towards the house, where he commenced to look around. For what in particular he refused to name; initially that is, not aloud in any case. But that quickly changed, Wirt tossed affectation to the wind.

"It's my shirt I'm after. Where is it, where is it?" he exclaimed.

An inexplicable anxiety, at variance with common sense took hold of him. Reason pleaded for calmness; apprehension, fanned by premonition, urged him on. Pretending that this shirt not only fitted perfectly, but also possessed irreplaceable sentimental value, he continued the search with increasing zeal. The wrinkles on his brow deepened, his otherwise smooth features distorted from irritation when he didn't find what he sought. A voice from within attempted to make him listen to sound judgement. Stop this wild-goose chase. Why fret on account of a misplaced piece of clothing that can be bought for trifles, he admonished himself. Cold comfort that was for a man trembling from agitation, whose ears resounded from sibylline hissing:

"You must find that shirt–you must, you must. Try to remember were you left it last night."

It sounded like a command easier given than obeyed. Having worked himself into a regular sweat, Wirt stepped outside to cool off and seek respite from his distress. Nothing of the sort happened. The disquieting foreboding did neither disappear nor abate. Standing on the veranda he grilled his memory with added intensity. Ignoring the bustle below, caused by women washing clothes in the river, he tried to retrace every step and movement he made last night.

After Dr Brodeur's departure he had quickly approached a state of hysteria. Racked by doubts, suspicion, and self-incrimination, he wandered around the house, wearing most certainly the missing shirt.

"Are you sure? Yes, yes, as certain as I am standing here. Well, you drank too much, added the evening's excitement, heaven knows what occurred, you might have left that shirt in any old place," Wirt consoled himself. "In any case, why get flustered on account of a misplaced shirt?"

Annoyed by the washerwomen's uproarious laughter and raucous banter, Wirt went inside again. Hardly had he crossed the threshold when it flashed across his mind: That was it! A curse had been laid on him! What a bunch of duffers trying to hoodoo a man of science. He recalled the weird tale Murdoch related at their last, not so convivial, gathering. Granted, his colleague wasn't exactly sober while explaining the inane obeah cult, yet he appeared to mean business. The maroons of the interior seemingly practise witchcraft similar to Haiti's voodoo, he maintained. To what purpose did Murdoch relate such fanciful pieces of gossip? To pass the time, or for entertainment perhaps? Not at all, Wirt decided in retrospect. Murdoch pursued one aim, and one aim only; to lay the cornerstone of the castle of fear. He intended to strike horror in his heart. In other words, pave the way on which he would soon walk to his Golgotha.

Wirt unwittingly chortled, then curled his lips in mockery directed at Murdoch:

"You have done yourself an ill favour with this tittle-tattle, my dear colleague, it's a giveaway. You are a participant in these shenanigans."

Ha, the nerve, trying to scare a scientist, ha, again. How did it go? An item of clothing, worn close to the skin of an intended victim, is given to a secouya, who casts a spell which transforms it into a shirt of Nessus. This accursed piece of clothing is put on a corpse about to be interred. Now comes the part that could make a prophet of doom howl with hilarious laughter. What did Murdoch say? As the corpse decomposes, so does the selected victim. He dies a slow, macabre death. What a bunch of numskulls trying to frighten a man like him with such threadbare tricks. Well, they were barking up the wrong tree. Chasing him off the island with cabalistic mummeries? That notion is all horn, but no cattle.

Looking upon yesterday's occurrences as grotesque hocus-pocus, designed to confuse and drive him away, Wirt felt reassured. Tickled actually, by the thought of Murdoch's attempt to kindle the flame of fear under his feet, and sow doubts in his heart about the planned tree removal. These scare tactics steeled his resolve, thereby easing his mind.

Humming a tune he wandered through the house seemingly relaxed, looking at nothing in particular. Despite the self-deception, his hands groped in every nook and corner. In no time he ransacked the entire place for his missing shirt. Finally, as the sun disappeared beyond the horizon, he gave up. Consoling himself that tomorrow is another day, he decided to saunter down to the Fort Young Hotel for an ale or two. Should he meet Murdoch there, lets play it by ear, he told himself.

Darkness had descended. The city lit up gradually, casting shimmers onto the sea. Murdoch was nowhere to be seen, but Dr Brodeur sat with another man at a table away from the throng. He beckoned Wirt to approach. Pointing to an empty chair he said:

"Please join us."

Nodding to the man he knew by sight, Wirt sat down.

"I haven't seen you in my office yet."

"No need to bother you, doctor, I'm back in shape, the riddle is solved."

Smiling at the man he knew as Kenneth Reid, Wirt remarked:

"You knew Alfred Nantes, I understand?"

The impromptu query caught Reid by surprise.

"I didn't, we never met."

"But your wife..." Wirt let slip, before he checked himself.

"Never mind my wife," Reid advised somewhat brusquely.

Noticing Wirt's baffled stare, feeling guilty of rudeness, he added:

"Mind you, I was cognisant of his presence, but that was about all. Why do you ask?"

"For no particular reason. It's just that I consider him a colleague."

"I see."

Turning towards Dr Brodeur, Reid observed:

"It seems the fellow vanished suddenly and unexpectedly."

Dr Brodeur started to fidget as if uncertain how to interpret the casual remark. Annoyance creeping across his features, sighing wearily as if being importuned, he intimated cryptically:

"So it seems, so it seems."

Reid, taken aback by the doctor's petulant response, raised his eyebrows, then glancing at the clock over the bar he advised:

"Sorry, gentlemen, I must go. Allow me to sign the chits on my way out. Have a nice evening."

"Hm, he seems to be in a huff," Wirt noted.

Dr Brodeur remained silent, he appeared to withdraw under a cloud. Both men directed their attention to the activity before them. Men and women, growing more clamorous by the minute, disported in and around the pool as if vying for a trophy of obnoxiousness. Watching the suggestive deportment, fuelled by liquor, hearing the strident voices, grated on Wirt's nerves.

A group of German sailors, half blind to the world, gave a performance of dissoluteness that made him wince.

"Doctor, don't tell anyone that I am German."

"Shameful, isn't it?"

"They should be locked up till their ship leaves," suggested Wirt.

He was a quiet man, introspective to a fault, who abhorred ostentation. How people, some no longer young, supposedly respectable, can openly flaunt their baser instincts, eluded him.

Dr Brodeur interrupted his musings:

"You mentioned a moment ago that the riddle is solved. What exactly did you mean?"

Wirt was prepared to make his views known to the doctor, but something held him back. Suspicion, the rouser of demons and rampant imageries, bade him be cautious. He hemmed and hawed for a few moments. Then pretending to have forgotten screwed up his eyes as if trying to remember.

"To confess, doctor, it was an empty boast. While I'm no longer on the ragged edge, anxiety still lingers."

"You are referring to your unpleasant experience last night, I presume, that knotty mystery?"

"You may call it so if you wish. To me it was a slight of hand performed by a clever trickster."

"Oh?"

How anyone could embody an everyday expression with such pith, surprised but also annoyed Wirt. The doctor's monosyllable exclamation said more than a hundred words. Evidently he now as before took his narrative with more than a grain of salt.

Glancing at Dr Brodeur rebukingly, Wirt pointed out that, although being overwrought, he saw and experienced what he asserted.

"Forgive my incredulity, but can I be blamed considering the circumstances?"

"Granted, not entirely, in view of the vanished shape and voodoo doll; yet both, I repeat, were real enough," Wirt assured.

"What possible purpose could these masquerades serve?"

Observing the doctor with an enigmatic smile, Wirt remarked:

"To instil fear, panic even."

"In you?"

Wirt signified affirmation.

"But why?"

"That's my question to you, doctor."

A bit stung, Dr Brodeur raised his head while eyeing him critically. Wirt's puzzling smile possessed a quality he couldn't comprehend. His query appeared to be reasonable had it not lost innocence by a tinge of sarcasm.

Just as Dr Brodeur was about to utter a gentle rebuke, a hue and cry arose. One of the German sailors, either brutish by nature, or rendered thus by his friendship with John Barleycorn, dove with a bellow into the pool, then crawled out moaning. His face was covered with blood, a fact that did not escape the doctor's notice. In a flash he was at the prone man's side. To Wirt's amazement Dr Brodeur, the epitome of urbanity, acquiescent to a fault, became outright dictatorial. He displayed a side that Wirt had not presumed existed; he evidently was on his mettle.

Barking commands left and right, telling the sailor roughly to keep his mouth shut, he soon stanched the blood and bandaged his patient. It was a sight to behold watching this ruffian, bellicose a moment ago, timorously submitting to the will of a man half his size.

"Lucky the fellow's skull is empty," the doctor chuckled when he returned.

"Now, what was your question?"

"I tried to be frivolous, nothing more. But tell me, doctor, did you come back to the house last night?" – and took my shirt with you – he felt tempted to add, but prudently desisted.

He thanked his stars he did, judging by Dr Brodeur's reaction who bolted upright, then burst out:

"Man alive, what makes you think so?"

What indeed. It was a stab in the dark evidently hitting home. Scowling, shaking his head in a manner expressing disbelief and indignation, the doctor scoffed:

"Are you trying to be facetious again?"

"Not exactly. Someone entered the house. When I shouted from my bedroom that I shall be out momentarily, the person left in a hurry."

"Don't you lock the place at night?"

"Not so far, but I will from hereon."

Talking often unlocks doors that action cannot force. Wirt saw the light. When he left the house last night, head over heels to be exact, someone, possibly the hideously masked creature in the entrance hall, removed the voodoo doll, and later returned to steal his shirt, which might have been left anywhere.

Dr Brodeur, seemingly recuperating from his righteous anger, made a cryptic remark:

"Suppositions are built on sand, they can ruin the best man; yes, even kill."

Did the doctor read his mind, or was he merely musing?

"I don't understand."

"You will, once the truth about Alfred Nantes is known."

"Do you know it, doctor?"

An inscrutable expression appeared on the doctor's face.

"I can only surmise, not much more," he intimated.

Glancing at Wirt sideways he murmured almost inaudible:

"Best to let well enough alone."

He didn't elaborate. Mentioning an appointment he dared not miss, Dr Brodeur rose and left.

Wirt felt no inclination to follow suit. The house on the hill, his temporary home, held scant attraction tonight. Despite his annoyance because of the unabated din, he felt more at ease here than amid the tranquillity there.

"May I sit down?" someone asked.

It was Harold Rintoul, the banker. Glad to have congenial company, Wirt jumped up. Clasping the other's hands, he virtually pulled him onto a chair.

"Be my guest," he sang out. "How about supper?"

When Rintoul nodded acquiescence, Wirt extended a hand invitingly. Bowing slightly he said in his quaint accent:

"Let's proceed to the dining room, it's quieter there."

They chose a table in the far corner, deliberately, for Wirt had much to say and ask. He noticed with a smile Rintoul's high spirits, indicating that he had whetted his whistle at the Green Parrot, where undoubtedly he not only looked deep into his glass, but also into the lustrous eyes of Mrs Daphne Agar, the owner. It was no secret that he courted the sprightly widow who seemed not avers to tie the knot once more.

Rintoul, no longer young, a confirmed bachelor till he met her, considered to pop the question. Guided by the rules of a banker's prudence, he made discreet inquiries. All appeared to be in order, with one exception: Mrs Agar didn't cherish chastity. It was a fly in the ointment, albeit a small one. While looking askance at such frailties, in women that is, he closed both eyes. After all, Daphne, a widow of two years, still in the glow of life, could not be expected to remain virtuous forever.

Rintoul was evidently in a talkative mood. He spoke of this, that, plus everything, except what Wirt wanted to hear. Well, if the mountain will not come to Mahomet, then he must go to the mountain, he said to himself.

"I don't wish to change the subject, but there is something weighing heavily on my mind."

"Tell me," his guest encouraged with a knitted brow, indicating displeasure.

"First I have a question."

"Go ahead."

"Are you acquainted with obeah?"

"Not even remotely, it's a fantasy of the maroons. They are the most gullible and superstitious folks on earth. Believe me, once a notion, regardless how outlandish, enters their frizzled heads, no amount of entreaties, threats, or inducement will remove it again. But let me add, some people, known by you and me, encourage the practice of these fooleries."

"I wonder why?"

Rintoul stared vacantly at the wall, then shrugged his shoulders. He gave no answer. After a few moments silence, he queried:

"Are you still occupied with Nantes' fate?"

"I am, in a way."

"Did you ever try to sound out others, Murdoch for instance?"

"There was no need. He told me all and more about the Belgian."

"And?"

"I heard nothing favourable. Murdoch implied that he got his comeuppance. He portrayed him as a philanderer, a fake surrounded by a sea of enmity. Professional qualities were sorely lacking, according to him."

Rintoul chuckled:

"Did you ever notice how we impute our cardinal faults to others?"

"You are implying that Murdoch depicted himself, in other words?"

"Nothing less. He is, in my estimation, the epitome of a womaniser. Nantes a fake, lacking professional knowledge? Hm, that describes Murdoch to a tee. Having enemies galore? I can assert that your colleague sows dragon's teeth wherever he goes."

Wirt was on pins and needles, many questions rushed into his mind which he dared not ask; especially the one concerning Nantes' missing shirt. He distinctly recalled Rintoul referring to it with a contemptuous smirk as if to say:

"A man of science, reasonably well off, bemoaning a missing shirt?"

No, Wirt decided, that snare had to be avoided. As things stood, he wasn't exactly showered with sympathy by the expatriates, who wouldn't hesitate to brand him unstable, a man unfit for high office.

Steering the conversation towards less entangled topics, he obliged Rintoul's desire for small talk.

The First Attack

Wirt spent another harrowing night in that lonely house. Despite the locked doors, someone appeared to prowl in the dark, inside and outside. Every rush of wind or rattle at the door invoked images of danger. Several times he bound up while calling out:

"Who is there?"

Twice he climbed out of bed, gripped a sturdy walking stick and stomped from room to room, uttering bloodcurdling threats. At more composed intervals he tried to construe Rintoul's assessment of Murdoch whose competence he also questioned. How anyone could be grossly negligent, plus diffident in matters concerning his profession, seemed beyond the pale, as did the government's behaviour. The botanical garden ran to seed under Murdoch's long tenure; yet his contract was extended when Nantes disappeared. Though the pride of Dominica had become its shame, the man, a slacker if ever there was one, responsible for the decline, had been rewarded.

Wirt arrived at the Gardens before sunrise. With a spade in his hands and a strange joy in his heart, he dug here and there, while humming a tune. The trade wind sounded different today; its sough had a quality not hitherto experienced by him; it bore tidings of hope. Despite the sleepless night, which sapped his strength, he felt enterprising. A sense of freedom pulsated through his being, that lightened his step. His eyes, the window of one's soul, acquired a glint only boldness knows. He was in charge now; no power on earth could frustrate the lofty aims suppressed for months, yet refused to yield an inch. Soon these grounds, gone to rack and ruin, deplorable mismanaged, sinfully neglected, would attract visitors from around the globe. He envisioned botanists tapping, sniffing unknown flora, marvelling at the profuse, singular growth, wishing to plant some in their homeland.

Enthusiasm is toil's demise and worry's foe. Tossing vexation, real and imagined, in the wind, Wirt hastened from spot to spot. Thrusting his spade lightly in the ground, casting knowing glances in every direction, he murmured:

"This will be a good place for granadilloes; here I shall erect a bower flanked by roses and pelican flowers; there now, that's the spot for a few cashimar zombis."

Turning towards a bare, dismal plot, he promised to plant every square inch with the most exotic growth of the interior.

Then something unforeseen happened. When he thrust his spade in the earth again, a shooting pain made him double up, forcing him to his knees. As he overcame an initial fright, he tried to straighten himself, but succeeded only after several attempts. Then a blinding dizziness almost hurled him onto the ground again, but the sight of a nearby bench made him resist.

Staggering to it, while moaning piteously, he sank down. He carefully probed his back and hips for sore spots, but found none. The painful stab, Wirt decided, had an internal origin. Trying to make rhyme or reason of it led nowhere. Oh well, he told himself, why worry about something that might never occur again? Then a second, more severe seizure gripped him that paralysed his limbs and took his breath away. Curbing an impulse to cry for help, he collapsed on the bench.

The paroxysms abated gradually; then ended abruptly. Relieved, Wirt sat up again, all the while trying to find the cause for these crippling onslaughts. How a man, bursting with health and strength could be thus smitten, eluded his imagination. True, he barely slept a wink last night, but surely that would hardly be a contributory factor for these paralysing seizures.

Glancing warily in every direction, he got on his feet and sort of loosened his limbs by shaking first one then the others.

He appeared to be fit as a fiddle again; only apprehension lingered.

Meanwhile the workers had arrived; they went their way without acknowledging his presence. What a surly bunch that is, Wirt couldn't help thinking. He felt an urge to go after them and knock off those chips on their shoulders, placed there by ancient grudges and envy. But he staved off the impulse with a wave of the hand, accompanied by a shrug. Struggle on for another thousand years; grumble, pick up imaginary gauntlets; fret over self-inflicted indignities nurtured by cowardice and misconceptions. Simpletons, don't you know that you are stoking smouldering embers, inherences of inferiority, forsworn to put a crimp in your aspirations?

Let them, Wirt concluded, I have my own problems to content with. He applauded his foresight to have assigned tasks for everyone. I any case, he had appointed a straw boss despite Murdoch's strenuous objections.

Assuming an unobtrusive air, Wirt sauntered towards the workers, who unfailingly flocked together as if their salvation depended on it. Only Fasot, the foreman, stayed behind, evidently ill at ease, judging by his peevish mien. Wirt addressed him:

"Fasot, did you know Mr Nantes?"

"Yes, sir," came a hesitant reply.

"He disappeared unexpectedly, I understand."

"I don't know," he said.

Neither do I care, his demeanour expressed. Worming anything out of this fellow is no trifling matter, Wirt granted, but he nevertheless tried some more:

"Tell me, Fasot, what do the natives say about the Nantes' affair?"

The foreman looked bewildered from his spade to the palm trees and nearby flower beds; in fact, everywhere except in Wirt's direction. He knows something he wishes to conceal from me, Wirt concluded. His following comment evoked an amazing reaction from the stolid man.

"I hear rumours that Mr Nantes' unexpected departure had something to do with obeah."

Fasot started, then stuttering in patois threw down his spade and bolted.

"What the blazes," Wirt called after him nonplussed.

Ruing his imprudent remarks he went to the office where he sat idle, eschewing any type of work, while reflecting especially on Fasot's arcane behaviour. The single reference to obeah played the deuce with him; it stung the fellow to the quick. Why? What made a bland man, over sixty years old, who would sooner hurt his own than someone else's feelings, act like the wild man of Borneo?

Time to check on the crew, Wirt told himself, for he noticed that they clustered around Fasot talking and gesticulating excitedly. In all likelihood they are disputing the foreman's instructions again, he mused. Give the devil his due, Murdoch was right, they will not heed orders given by one of their own. Mind you, Fasot's faint-hearted commands, sounding more like appeals for debate, invited contradiction. No doubt, the entire gang partook in a heated argument with the foreman and themselves.

Wirt called out in his most peremptory manner that everyone should stay put and listen to what he had to say. After giving them a piece of his mind and explicit instructions in a tone that brooked no opposition, he sent them home with a word of warning:

"The next man who walks away from his assigned task will be fired."

It was a vainglorious threat, Wirt realised, since abandoning allotted work to help out somewhere else, seemed intrinsic to one and all.

Wirt locked up, then prepared to leave. On the way out he stopped to look at a mango tree that needed trimming. Someone hailed him from the street whom he didn't recognise offhand. It turned out to be Michael Mauch, the publisher, who approached with vigorous strides. He raised and waived a hand, holding what appeared to be a book.

"Just made it in the nick of time, I see," he exclaimed in his winsome lilt.

"As promised here it is."

When Wirt raised his eyebrows, Mauch remonstrated:

"Don't you remember our conversation at my place? That is the book about voodoo and obeah I had mentioned."

Wirt instinctively balked, then collecting his wits he accepted the proffered book.

"But of course, excuse my obtuseness, I'm a bit distracted today."

"Who could blame you in view of recent happenings."

Uncertain what to infer from this peculiar remark, Wirt eyed his visitor. Recent happenings, upsetting to boot? How could Mauch be in the know? Did Dr Brodeur tattle perhaps? Hardly, therefore only one conclusion could be drawn; the publisher partook in the masquerade. He either connived with, or had a hand in it.

Sensing Wirt's dubiety, Mauch quickly expounded:

"What I referred to is the fact that you are now in full charge of the botanical garden. I should think that such responsibilities, initially in any case, can distract anyone."

Extending a hand which Wirt reluctantly took, he commented:

"Congratulations, sir, welcome, its high time for a change, I declare."

Reaching in his pocket he produced a sheet of paper. Handing it to Wirt he said:

"I have prepared a sort of questionnaire for your consideration."

"Oh?"

"Nothing fancy, we just like to introduce you to our readers, who presumably are interested in your background, and more so in your future plans."

Smirking roguishly, acquiring an elfish air, he chatted unrestrained about anything entering his head. That was a pose, Wirt decided. The seemingly irrelevant discourse undoubtedly served a purpose. Why else would he cast repeated calculating glances at him as if searching for telltale signs in his demeanour?

The prating publisher's presence jarred on Wirt's nerves; he wished him anywhere except here. The fellow sounded like a hurdy-gurdy cranked to its limit, yet he unfailingly managed to weave into his palaver the island's sinister practices of voodoo and obeah. Being anxious, Wirt said less and less; he just nodded or shook his head as if on cue.

Finally Mauch prepared to leave, not too prompt, however. First he raised a paean concerning the book in Wirt's hands.

"This is the most authoritative book about voodoo and obeah, written by men that have no inclination to cause excitement, or attempt to appeal to our baser instincts."

"It's a book of facts in other words," Wirt suggested in a tone not entirely free of sarcasm.

Glancing sideways at him, Mauch expounded:

"I shouldn't say so, but most of its content is based on experience by the author or contributors, who witnessed those weird customs bordering on the occult. They relate what they had seen."

"Or preferred to have seen," suggested Wirt.

"Perhaps, but reading the book with an open mind might change your views. Far from being a penny dreadful, it does titillate at times as much as stretch one's credulity to the breaking point. Chapter thirteen should be given special attention; it's highly revealing considering that mysterious Nantes affair."

Wirt grew visible fidgety. He started to shift his feet, turn his head, and clear his throat; all to no avail. Mauch showed little inclination to stop the flow of words, he delved headfirst into the topic of voodoo and obeah, which appeared to be surprisingly familiar to him.

Wirt's discomfort changed to irritation. He couldn't stave off the feeling of being manipulated by the artful publisher; to what end only he knew. He had an inkling that something was in the wind. Mauch's recurring references to witchcraft had an ominous ring. Listening with but half an ear one would think that these vile practices were a virulent epidemic in the island. Repeated allusions to the occult, followed by fulminations, made Wirt's eyes squint, and deepened the wrinkles on his brow. Impatience triumphed over manners; he abruptly extended a hand while offering regrets:

"I don't want to be rude, Mr Mauch, but I must tend to pressing business."

"In that case I shall not keep you any longer. We can continue our conversation later, tonight perhaps, over a dram or two?"

"I must decline. As mentioned…"

"Another time then?"

"With pleasure," Wirt lied.

With these words he skipped away. Before he disappeared behind a cluster of bushes, Mauch called after him:

"Don't forget, chapter thirteen."

Wirt felt disinclined to go to the house, which he began to dread. More than ever he resolved to search for another place, distant from the rank growth that inexorably encroached upon body and soul. Although Old Ransy, the gardener, did his level best to contain the rampant march of the choking jungle, his finely honed cutlass was no match for its silent encroachment.

Wirt would have been reluctant to admit his preoccupation with the missing shirt that gave him no rest. Like a jack-in-the-box springs up when the lid is lifted, so did that picayunish garment appear ghostlike before his eyes at every turn. Trying to banish the silly matter from his mind led nowhere, for within minutes it popped up again.

One thought led to another, then finally to Murdoch and his spurious assertion about the existence of obeah, which hitherto he decried vehemently. Could this about-face be attributable to the consumption of liquor? No, Wirt decided. Granted, Murdoch was tipsy, but that in itself could hardly have been the reason to reverse convictions tenaciously held so far. Especially by a man who decried any form of superstition with frightening vehemence. Yes, something was in the wind.

Wirt stopped abruptly, then listened intently while turning in every direction. Did he hear voices trying to gain his attention? Or was it the wind that distracted his thoughts? Closing his eyes for an instant, concentrating with every fibre of his being, he could have sworn to hear sibylline whispers entreating him to be on guard. As these whispers grew louder and more insistent, Wirt clapped his hands over his ears. The oracular voices could not be shut out, for they rose up within himself, urging him to run–run. It was a strange sight beholding a respectable man moving up and down the street at a fast clip, clasping his ears while yelling:

"Shut up, shut up."

The natives chuckled; the expatriates exchanged meaningful glances. The grapevine in Dominica is short and well-routed, thus rumours travel fast among their coterie, they become more insidious at every junction.

Wirt didn't know it yet, but to some he was a marked man; denounced as unstable, therefore unfit for the position of head botanist. Before sunrise the next morning he would be disparaged by them with a glee that only sanctimony managed to invoke. By noon the entire elite will likely hear about the botanist's latest transgression, which will be grist to their mills.

"What do you expect from someone gone native," unmitigated snobs would declare.

"He is a drunkard," dipsomaniacs might assert.

"A libertine to boot," women, grown prematurely wan and wrinkled under the yoke of hypocrisy, will intimate.

"From day one I suspected it; that fellow has more than one skeleton in his closet."

Nothing unites the wearers of Moran's collar like a man who eschews conventions held sacrosanct by them; even worse, that vents his sarcasm on such inviolable beliefs. While not generally hated, far from it actually, he was nevertheless a target of the clique's gossip; malicious and otherwise. The bone, or rather bones of contention, were manifold, thus justifying criticism of Wirt in some people's mind.

"Why is he so secretive about his past? What does he have to hide?"

"Plenty," some implied with a knowing sniff.

"Probably nothing," others countered.

"Well then, how about the rumour, a legitimate one no doubt, that he and Alfred Nantes were fellow students at the University of Tübingen? They surely must have known each other, possibly still do. Just beholding his deportment, aloof to a fault, if not high-hatted, is enough to make one's blood boil."

These faults, vexatious to be sure, could have been tolerated by the circle with a shrug and a squint, but not his cardinal ones. Foremost the refusal to help carry the white man's burden. He pooh-poohed the notion expounded by a paragon of English wisdom, who looked haggard, was prematurely bald, and cadaverous.

"Having an axe to grind is quite a chore, it seems," Wirt gently mocked whenever the topic arose.

Speaking lightly of their idol hardly endeared him to the men who saw themselves performing a duty imposed by provenance. The fact that Wirt declined to help enlighten the natives was irritating, to say the least, but wanting to learn from them was the last straw.

As previously mentioned he was accused to have gone native, quite openly so. His eagerness to learn patois, thought as nothing but gibberish, appalled many expatriates. A few however, were amenable to such endeavours; yet they could be counted on one hand. While the men, foreigners that is, neither hated nor liked Wirt, the women scarcely concealed a certain affection for him. His old-world courtesy tickled their vanity; his Joseph-like bearing roused the slumbering temptress in their bosoms. They liked to be near him, engage in dallying conversation, and display a long forgotten charm. Why otherwise languid women behaved girlish and frisky in his presence, none probably knew, or even realised that they were being flirtatious. Mind you, nothing loath, they still turned the sails of the rumour mill.

"It's his own fault," they averred, "how can a man be so tight-lipped about himself."

The guesswork about Wirt's past went on. The web woven around his life thickened, as did the clouds of annoyance on account of lacking information. Undeniable he was a queer fish, an enigma to many, and a thorn in the sides of a few.

Brunt's Puzzling Behaviour

*T*hings started to gain momentum. First a message arrived at the botanical garden that Mrs Burchard's return journey was delayed. How long, Mr Garneau, who conveyed the communication, couldn't rightly say. The minister appeared to be in a snit, which he made no effort to conceal. He also advised that his department is no longer accountable for the Gardens' administration, which had been shifted to Celia Burchard who, by the way, had sent word that the intended work at Sylvania must be deferred; at least until she returns.

Judging by the minister's long face, this edict evidently found no acclaim with him. Before he left Mr Garneau made a cryptic remark that came to haunt Wirt.

"The fat is in the fire," he said with a wry grin.

"What is that supposed to mean?" Wirt called after him.

The minister kept on walking, yet turning his head he called back:

"Good luck, Mr Wirt."

Waning confidence, mixed with apprehension, induced Wirt to consult Howard Brunt, the chief of police. Contrary to his wont the chief said little. When he spoke the words lingered on his tongue as if abashed to be heard. Letting Wirt have his say with few interruptions, he inquired:

"You want to proceed with the work at Sylvania, I take it?"

"Without delay."

"Despite Mrs Burchard's missive?"

"It wasn't a missive," Wirt countered.

The chief raised his eyebrows while eyeing Wirt. Then heaving himself out of his chair, he lumbered to a nearby cabinet from which he removed a sheet of paper.

"Didn't you receive this?"

It was an official letter bearing the government's head and seal that confirmed Mr Garneau's verbal communication.

Wirt shook his head.

"Not yet," he intimated.

Judging that loophole closed, he expelled a heartfelt sigh. Considering Brunt with knitted brow, as if trying to take his measure, he grew silent. This was not the same man he knew; his jollity had given way to a starchiness that surprised and annoyed him. The mercurial wit, refreshing any time of the day, was conspicuously absent. Wirt couldn't help thinking that the chief was caught in the talons of a dilemma. Despite his bulk he looked shrunken and browbeaten.

Wirt took a deep breath, then posed a question:

"Mr Brunt, what is going on?"

For an instant the chief's genuine self almost gained the upper hand; he seemed ready to spit out what stuck in his craw. He bolted upright, but quickly slumped back again.

"Short of hoodwinking you I have nothing to say. As mentioned before we are in the midst of an investigation. This much I can say, there are serious issues hanging in the balance which concern many people."

"Am I endangered?"

"We all are, sir, we all are," Brunt replied with a rueful smile.

Turning fully towards his visitor, he suggested:

"Let's not beat about the bush, Mr Wirt. If you are trying to enlist my support for the scheduled work at Sylvania, it will be denied."

Waving a hand to stifle Wirt's intended protest, he hastened to add:

"I know, I know, this is an about-face of my attitude so far, but I have no choice considering the directive I received."

Wirt, tapping the letter before him, wanted to know:

"You mean this?"

"Not at all, it is only a copy sent along as an attachment."

Bewildered, Wirt's head came up.

"There are further government communications?"

"Indeed, but I cannot divulge another syllable."

Wirt sensed how the wind blew, he made no further inquiries prior to taking his leave. As he walked towards the door the chief advised:

"By the way, did your shirt turn up again?"

Wirt spun around. Gaping at Brunt he stammered:

"Shirt, my shirt, but how did you know?"

"My dear sir, I am not such a dolt as you might think. Remember I am the chief of police."

The chief of police, Mr Brunt? I reckon you are, Wirt mused on his way back, but you no longer look it. What dampened your exuberance and etched lines of worry onto your hitherto smooth brow? Who snuffed out the glint in your eyes and wiped the smiles from your lips? Was your expansiveness and sincerity just a pose meant to entrap? Whom, and why, I like to know. You certainly deceived me, I must admit.

Wirt was vexed, understandably so. He sharpened his knife, in the spirit that is, to stab the man imputed with betrayal. On whose side is he on? Did he switch allegiance, to Murdoch perhaps? Or had he always colluded with him? Wirt granted that he must be circumspective, but nevertheless steadfast.

Nantes came to mind whom he knew from their university days in Tübingen. They had lost contact over the years, which fact Wirt did not bemoan. He remembered him vividly. His quaint accent brought smiles to Wirt's lips, but they froze when recalling the Belgian's impulsiveness and penchant to brag. Fellow students called him Bombastus quite openly. Despite his chagrin Wirt couldn't suppress a chuckle while reminiscing when they were boys trying to be men. Time must have tamed Nantes' impetuosity; if not, marriage undoubtedly had clipped the wings of the erstwhile Pegasus.

As Wirt approached the house his anger gained momentum, yet no less his resolve. He admitted walking close to the edge of the proverbial Serbonian bog, which he vowed not to enter. There and then he decided to take the bull by the horns; in other words force the issue. Rain or shine, tomorrow he would visit the contested property. Casting the vexatious matter of a trespass to the wind, ignoring the chief's half-hearted admonition, for now anyway, he determined to test the waters.

As often happens calmness follows on the heels of decisiveness. Courage leaped to his heart; his steps became livelier; dread slunk away. He set the table for one out on the veranda prior to sundown. Sipping wine while preparing the evening meal, he hummed songs popular during his youth. In a twinkle the last mote of dust fell from his heart. The melodies had a ring only childhood's memory can evoke.

After the meal plus several snifters of cordials, Wirt opened Mauch's vaunted book. He leafed to chapter thirteen as recommended. Reading it twice, the first time with mockery in one eye and doubt in the other, the second time with rising anger. He threw the book down while announcing to the sea:

"Ha, and ha again, I smell a rat!"

These clowns, or two bit scoundrels, were undoubtedly trying to frighten him, hoping that he would show the white feather and take to his heels. Like Alfred Nantes must have done, judging by Rintoul's and Dr Brodeur's description of his mental state. Recalling from their student days in Tübingen how high-strung Nantes could be, Wirt thought him capable of fleeing helter-skelter under cover of the night in any old boat. It wouldn't surprise him to find the Belgian and his vessel at the bottom of the Martinique Passage. Let him rest there, or anywhere else, for to tell the truth he never liked the fidgety Belgian.

Reminiscing soothed his nerves; he took up the book again and read chapter thirteen once more. No doubt, that was the source of Murdoch's information about the obeah cult, which he propagated fervently on Wirt's latest visit. His sudden somersault concerning such fiddle-faddle, as he hitherto called it irately, no longer puzzled Wirt. Yes, something was afoot that reeked of subliminal persuasion directed at him; the pieces of the puzzles started to fit. Murdoch's astounding assertions about the obeah cult were meant to open a window to a world of horror. The mummery with the voodoo doll and grisly mask followed on the heels of this revelation, and was crowned by the matter of the purloined shirt.

How does it go again? A piece of cloth worn near the skin of a chosen victim is put on a corpse, after being cursed by a secouya. As the corpse decomposes in its grave so does the accursed decay. Soon he will be a walking skeleton. Ha, ha, ha! Even simple Simon would roll on the ground laughing if told about it.

Wirt Finds His Shirt

*M*urdoch's shadow hadn't fallen on the ground of the Gardens for a while. They passed each other in town the odd time, plus once or twice near the Fort Young Hotel. Both pretended not to see each other, yet Wirt couldn't refrain from casting furtive glances at his presumed detractor. He didn't like Murdoch's smug-faced demeanour, even less the sly grin, reminiscent of a cat who got the canary.

Conditions at the botanical garden were less than ideal, for which reason he had not yet visited the property in the mountains. The workers, besides moving as if toting heavy loads, displayed a constant pout. Fasot proved not only useless, but a veritable hindrance.

To make matters worse he received unsettling news from home. A letter from his parents arrived that stoked the smouldering embers of his discontent. They were uneasy, justifiably so he thought, upon digesting the contents of the letter. Inquiries were made about him with a disturbing eagerness and intrusive pertinacity. Under the pretext of an impending promotion, the questioners implied a continuous biography of the nominee was essential. No, Wirt couldn't be asked himself, accosted informants were advised, for strange reasons which were not divulged. The position in question? A momentous one, that would lead to riches, fame, and possible immortality.

These queries, bordering on interrogations, baffled and worried him. Reluctant to approach him, were they? Bah, what next? Anybody possessing a semblance of common sense, unfailingly knows that he will be notified; so why the dissimulation? To raise his state of anxiety of course, thus make him amenable to their scheme; softening him up in other words. Well, they succeeded. He found no peace of mind nor restful sleep all night. Each gust of wind or rustle in the trees made him bolt upright. Sitting there, staring into the darkness, every nerve strained, a sudden shooting pain racked his whole body, followed by a paralysing weakness. Bathed in cold sweat he sank down, rather collapsed on the bed.

The balance of the night turned out to be pure agony. Try as he may, he was unable to fend off recurring nightmares. Alfred Nantes, older and wizened, an image of vengeance rose before his eyes, scoffing mercilessly:

"Hannes Wirt, remember me? You never liked me, did you? Are you still making fun of my accent? Smirk, chortle to your heart's content as long as you can. Take a good look at yourself in the mirror; enjoy what you see, because you soon will be a ghastly sight. Savour your image before the transformation begins when you start rotting from within, as others have. Will you still be proud and haughty when you decay on your feet? You were second in our class; first by more than a full length in botany. It made you supercilious and condescending. What good will it do when the smell of death drives you mad?"

"Alfred," Wirt heard himself calling, loud, louder till the incubus got off his chest.

In the morning it took an effort to rise. He nearly had to crawl on all fours to get anywhere. Then the numbing ache gave way to panic; far more distressing than physical pangs. Wirt thought of Murdoch's prediction:

"You will never thrust a spade into that soil."

Was this the beginning of the slow, tortuous end? He snorted at the idea.

"Stuff and nonsense!" he cried. "Fiddle-de-dee twice over! That's enough, I have better things to do than wallow in misery."

Drawing himself up he dressed hastily, then went to the Gardens. After the daily tasks were assigned, although he considered the exercise futile, he decided to visit the Sylvania property.

"I will be back shortly," he advised Fasot, whose morose mien indicated that he needn't to hurry.

He and the foreman weren't exactly on hail-fellow-well-met terms; Murdoch's shadow appeared to hover between them. The fellow's days are numbered anyway, Wirt promised himself.

It is an arduous climb to reach that property, which was once part of a huge banana plantation. Wirt, weakened by mental anguish, or a fertile fancy one could say, proceeded but slowly. His stamina had been sapped by imagination, but luckily his tenacity was still intact; soon his agility returned.

In those days the road, a wide path really, could not be traversed in a motor vehicle; not entirely in any case. The best mode of travel was on foot, or with a donkey. About halfway up the salutary silence was interrupted by discordant voices that made Wirt stop and listen; an altercation seemed to be in full swing. Thinking that his presence may be welcome, he walked on. Around the next bend he perceived a small crowd of natives gathered around a donkey cart. Watching islanders entangled in a dispute is a sight to behold. They dig in with a religious fervour that sounds alarming to an uninitiated foreigner. As if obeying an inner calling they jump into the fray that isn't, for it lacks malice as much as profanity.

Wirt had witnessed these spectacles several times at the market. Although he did not understand much, he nevertheless found these free-for-all entertaining. Never interfere, he was told, because the entire lot will tackle you head on.

This one appeared to be the mother of all brawls; it reminded him of the story about King Pètard's court, where everybody talked but no one listened. He approached gingerly, although it wasn't necessary, for young and old, men and women, were tooth and nails at it; they paid no heed to him.

Suddenly Wirt froze; what he saw nailed him to the ground. Rubbing his eyes, literally shaking himself, he stared at the old man trying to lead a donkey away that was hitched to the cart. Wirt jolted into action; the driver wore his shirt.

"Hey there, that's my shirt," he bellowed, while pointing at the old man.

All eyes were now directed at him; the strident voices died away as if on cue. Rushing the wearer of his garment, Wirt gripped the shirt with both hands trying to wrest it off the terrified old man. Yelling in patois the aged but still nimble fellow took to his heels. Wirt was beside himself. Goaded by wretchedness, whipped by lingering uncertainty and pangs of fear, he plunged after the presumed thief. With part of his shirt still on his back, the rest in the hands of his pursuer, the fleeing villager sought refuge in a small ravine.

Consternation overcame the gathering, whose excited mutterings gained loudness and momentum, intensifying to shouts and shrieks. It neither intimidated Wirt nor slowed him down. He pursued the yelling man calling for help with a fury one should have thought incongruous with a confirmed pacifist and gentleman. When he caught up with the donkey driver they both tumbled to the ground.

Abruptly, as if awakening from a trance, he recoiled. Shocked by his impetuosity, overcome by regrets, he looked up. Meanwhile the younger and pluckier men had arrived. Their anger changed to surprise upon seeing Wirt on his knees, holding up shreds of his shirt while breaking out in a piteous lament:

"What have I done, what have I done? All because of a paltry piece of cloth. Good gracious, what now?"

He wanted to make amends, remunerate the poor fellow fivefold for the loss, and tenfold for his inconvenience, but the harassed villager had disappeared. The whole crowd now sidled up to Wirt; they were still chattering excitedly, some in anger, most in bewilderment.

Wirt, deeply penitent, admitted that he had misbehaved execrably, thus he wanted to apologise and pay the old man amply.

"Where can I find him?" he asked.

No one stirred, they just stared at him sullenly, but said not a word.

His resolve to continue the trip wavered. He not only lost the will to go on, but also the stomach, for the crowd became restless; they grumbled in undertones bolstered by menace.

So he went back; not to the botanical garden, but to the house. He needed time to think since he divined the danger of rapidly skidding towards a state of desperation, that will eventually render him unfit for the position held. Attacking a helpless old man to retrieve a paltry shirt, possibly given him by a well-meaning relative, will surely raise eyebrows. He was playing into his detractors' hands, who undoubtedly will get wind of his latest escapade.

Distracting News

*F*rom thereon life held few pleasures for Wirt. He was pitted by remorse on account of that dreadful episode with the villager, whom he still tried to locate. For some inexplicable reasons he neither learned his name nor where he lived, although he spread the word that he wished to compensate him handsomely for his loss and suffering. Surely in that close-knit surrounding there must be people who knew about the unfortunate incident, including the name and dwelling place of the roughed-up fellow.

When he asked Fasot about it, the foreman fidgeted as if under duress; it noticeably ruffled his temper. Looking everywhere except in Wirt's direction, he denied knowing anything, then walked away. It made no sense to a reckoning mind that someone poor, possibly destitute, would forgo what for him might be a small fortune. Well, he soon found out the reason.

As mentioned Wirt's existence couldn't be called a bed of roses. Chagrined by Mrs Burchard's continued absence, uneasy on account of Murdoch's avoidance of the botanical garden, he was beset by nagging apprehension. Added the chief's astounding turnabout, who could fault him for being pensive and distraught. Just the same he vowed to overhaul his life, beginning from today. These recurring outbursts, needless, besides undermining his reputation, had to be curtailed, or better yet must cease completely. The label hotspur, no doubt pinned on him in certain circles, must be removed from his neck. More than that; the habit of invoking chimeras at the drop of a hat has to become an act of the past. Behaving like a wild boar at the slightest provocation, imagined or real, behooved a Mohock perhaps, but not a man of science.

Wirt had sustained more than a few reverses in the past on account of his touchiness, bordering on irascibility at times. Take the matter of the shirt that should have been handled entirely different. The old man surely was not the thief, he most likely obtained it as a gift from the hands of a relative. He was still uneasy about the incident that hung over him like a Damoclean sword. He reckoned that it would hunt him for months to come. The police might get involved more likely than not. He expected a visit any time, maybe from the chief who, though well-disposed towards him, must follow regulations. He acted like a ruffian, but considering the circumstances who should blame him. The fellow cut and ran like a surprised thief. After all he owed him an answer how he came into possession of his shirt.

Nevertheless, this latest unbridled deed proved to be a bitter pill to swallow. Besides evoking emotions in Wirt, gnawing at his vitals that no amount of soul-searching was able to allay, he became preoccupied with the dubious obeah cult. Although the mere thought of it engendered a vehement revulsion, he couldn't leave it alone.

The same evening Wirt received a visit from Howard Brunt, whom he greeted with trepidation. Glancing at the chief sheepishly, he murmured:

"I know, I know."

"What do you know?" the chief inquired with surprising acerbity.

"That I behaved contemptuously, but do come in."

The chief did not come to chat, his countenance spoke louder than words, it was framed in direness. Wirt was about to make a humorous allusion but thought better of it. He asked:

"How is the old man?"

"He is dead."

The matter-of-fact reply stunned Wirt, he needed a few moments to regain his composure.

"When did he die?"

"Three days ago."

Wirt stiffened when he realised the significance of the chief's information. Three days ago that shameful confrontation took place. The old fellow's demise could hardly be connected with it, since he seemed fit when he left him, judging by his agility. Just the same, Wirt felt queasy and tongue-tied. The chief's interrogative scowl made him shudder despite the heat.

"What did he die of?"

"Heart attack, the death certificate states."

Blinking while staring at Brunt, clearing his throat several times, Wirt protested:

"But–but, the fellow was up and lively on that day."

"You should know, Mr Wirt, but remember that was before you chased him around the stump."

"I did no such thing," Wirt countered not entirely truthful.

Brunt was till standing, but Wirt slumped onto a chair upon hearing the disconcerting news. Pointing to a chair, he asked the chief to sit down. When he reached for a bottle and glasses, Brunt raised a hand:

"Not for me, I am on duty," he said.

Questions formed in Wirt's mind which he was averse to pose. What was Brunt after? How should one interpret the unusually stern demeanour of a man known to be jocund to a fault, whose witticism no one denied? How, and why did an inveterate optimist suddenly metamorphose into a doomsday Sedgwick? Wirt would have liked to know.

Brunt, screwing up his face, commented quietly:

"Perhaps I exaggerated, but from what I hear it was quite a performance. Apparently you scared the decrepit villager out of his wits."

Wirt started:

"Decrepit? The man skipped around like a streak of lightning."

Although the chief was in a dour mood, he chuckled appreciatively.

"Well put, well put, but let's go over the facts."

"Am I being investigated?"

"You are, sir."

"For what delict?"

"Assault."

"That didn't kill the old man."

"Quite so, but the aftermath might have."

"Aftermath?" Wirt echoed.

Brunt sighed as only a fat man can, his face acquired a more conciliatory mien while inquiring:

"Did you go near that place after the incident?"

"Not once."

Brunt stroked his chin pensively while trusting out his lips. The gesture implied annoyance at Wirt's reply. He changed his tack, a smile appeared on his lips.

"If the offer of a drink still stands, I'm ready to accept," he indicated.

Relieved, Wirt jumped to it. After two goblets were filled with his best, he asked:

"Is the investigation over?"

The chief's answer was another heartfelt sigh.

Meanwhile darkness had descended. In a twinkle the loud, yet friendly voices of the Caribbean night filled the air. The sounds reassured Wirt, but the chief's changed state of mind made him feel insecure. Was he laughing up his sleeve, or dared one to imagine that his erstwhile benevolence towards him had returned?

Brunt summed up:

"Let's go over it again. On your way to Sylvania you encountered a group of natives embroiled in an altercation. There you saw a man wearing your missing shirt. Rushing him you made an attempt to wrest it off his body."

"Unsuccessfully, I might add. All I ended up with was a rag of the front part."

Frowning, because of the interruption, Brunt continued:

"Justin bolted with you in pursuit. What happened when you caught up with him?"

"Mr Brunt, I explained that twice already."

"Well, then once more won't hurt."

"As I tried to get hold of him, we both stumbled and fell."

"What happened then?"

"Nothing, since I became suddenly aware of my abominable behaviour. I shrunk back, then falling on my knees I raised a regular dirge directed at myself."

Brunt appeared to be in a quandary. He stood up, walked a few steps, turned on his heels, and sat down again. He struck Wirt as a picture of irresolution. Glancing from Wirt to the sea, cocking his head a few times, he gave an impression of someone wishing to say something but didn't know how to start. The chief's peculiar deportment made Wirt itchy; he felt obliged to speak, be it only about the weather.

"Have you finished questioning me?" was all he could think of.

Wavering for another moment Brunt was about to make a comment when a loud knock at the back door prevented it. It turned out to be Dr Brodeur who was in a flurry, to say the least. Vouchsafing Wirt with barely a glance, he addressed the chief:

"Mr Brunt, I must speak to you," he panted.

Brunt observed him absent-mindedly.

"Well?" he said in a tone that signified annoyance.

The doctor started to shuffle in a manner unbecoming for a member of Dominica's upper crust, Wirt couldn't help thinking. Looking sideways at Wirt he intimated:

"Not here, let's go to my office. I have something that you should see."

Whether the chief believed him remained anybody's guess; Wirt did not. He sensed a prevarication on the doctor's part, meant to lure the chief away.

As Brunt left he glanced at Wirt in passing. His face still framed by contemplation, and intentions to say something that perhaps should remain unspoken, he commented:

"Besides answering your question, Mr Wirt, I have something further to discuss; but that can wait till tomorrow. If it suits you I shall call on you at the botanical garden, say around ten o'clock?"

When Wirt nodded, they both left.

Wirt's Visit To The Cemetery

Shortly after midnight Wirt bolted upright on his bed with a suppressed cry. That old man, what did the chief call him? Ah, Justin, he still had the better part of his shirt on his back when Wirt left him.

"So what?" a voice from within sneered. "It's no longer of any value to you, let the dead rest."

Another voice, coming from heaven knows where, protested.

"But–but, he might be buried with it. Under no circumstances may that be," sibilated that prophet of doom."You must prevent it – you must prevent it."

Bathed in perspiration, Wirt climbed from his bed. He noticed something not perceived till now: the frogs! They didn't whistle anymore, far from it. They had struck up a chorus of shrieks, derisively directed at him. He clapped both hands over his ears to drown out the obtrusive din.

As he stood there with haunted eyes, ready to flee, from what he did not know, whereto even less, there was a lull in the wind, so suddenly and wholly, that Wirt felt his skin crawl. Instinctively his hands dropped to his sides, thereby giving his hearing free rein. But there was nothing to hear; a dead calm prevailed. The frogs whistled again, but much quieter than usual it deemed Wirt. What now? He started to hear voices:

"Hannes, get your shirt, no matter what, you must reclaim your shirt!"

In a twinkle another voice, sounding like the devil's advocate, derided that notion with glee.

"What skinflint you are, Hannes, a regular dog in the manger. Let the old man have that useless rag, it's of no significance to you anymore; besides, it keeps the poor fellow warm in his grave."

It was small consolation for someone pitted by fear whose source he dared not name. Sleep was out of the question. The fickle pendulum of a distraught mind disallowed the repose that he so fervently craved. One side of him clamoured for instant action, which reason, though waning, ridiculed stingingly; it prevailed upon him to wait till daybreak prior to make a move. Despite the rancorous discord between the chimera bidding him to plunge ahead, and common sense trying to hold him back, he must have fallen asleep. Not in his bed, however, but on a chair outside, for nothing could have induced him to lay down again.

Soon he heard utterances, sounding like barked commands, answered by mocking laughter. Someone nearby appeared to be arguing fiercely. Tearing himself from a trance-like state, Wirt realised where the bickering voices originated; he had been talking in his sleep. He felt tempted to hoist a few, hoping it would calm his nerves, but he suppressed the desire quicker than it arose. Smelling of liquor or, heaven forbid, swaying in the wind, would surely evoke sneers and condemnation from his fellow expatriates.

It was now past four o'clock, two hours before the first shimmer of dawn would appear. Constraining his flutter somewhat, he brewed coffee, which he drank on the veranda, with little enjoyment however. He almost spat out the first mouthful; it had an acrid taste which burned his tongue and made him think of poison. He found no peace of mind in the balmy night under a serene, starlit sky.

Wirt, sanguine by nature, who loved solitude since childhood, for the first time in his life hankered for company; anyone would do. A beating heart and understanding soul was all he needed to reassure him that he was still among the living, and he must divert his attention from the path of despair paved by himself. The pleasing quality of a Caribbean night possessed no allurement for him. Neither the friendly shimmering sea below, nor the soporific rhythm of the falling surf affected his tortured mind; a mind endangered to lose its grip on reality.

Despite an effort to view past incidents, trifles really, with indifference, he did not succeed; quite the opposite happened. He fussed over every minute occurrences, be it imageries of his agonised mind, with a vengeance. Brunt's inexplicable flip-flop concerned him deeply; his erstwhile jovial support, proffered effusively, had waned. The welcome mat rolled out with Falstaffian flair, appeared to become threadbare. He still owed him an answer to his question concerning the investigation; besides, something seemingly weighed on the chief's mind. It's nothing important, he had implied, it could wait till the next day or later. Fair enough, Wirt granted, had his odd behaviour not given the lie to such averments. Something stuck in Brunt's throat alright, judging by his furrowed brow and faltering steps. Of course Dr Brodeur's intrusion forestalled any further communication.

There was a man Wirt couldn't make out. He left Haiti, his beloved homeland, under some kind of political duress, he claimed, accruing from that spurious voodoo cult. Wirt no longer believed everything he was told. Questions, never before thought of, now queued up clamouring for answers. Like Mrs Burchard's continued absence, which could be construed as curious, if not suspect. She left him in the lurch; whether intentionally, compelled by circumstances, or due to indifference, he couldn't say, but it certainly evoked anxieties that were increasingly difficult to restrain. Crucial decisions had to be made that brooked no delay. The minister's message, an order to desist really, baffled Wirt particularly. What were his words again?

"Mrs Burchard expressly states that no work must be done at the Sylvania property till she returns."

Why the sudden turnabout for which no reasons were given? Is this a political manoeuvre? Had legal complications arisen that were previously unknown? Or was it but the whim of a woman enjoined with an authority incongruous with her ability? No matter what, he should not be kept in the dark. This whole affair reeked of evil tidings, more so in view of Murdoch's suspect behaviour. They hadn't exchanged a word since that evening when those prophetic utterances were hurled at him. They had encountered each other on the streets, but neither one extended greetings, nor showed signs of recognition. Not with words or gestures to be sure, yet Murdoch's devilish grin, accompanied by derisive snorts, made Wirt wince. He couldn't shoo away the notion that the malediction laid on him might be fulfilled.

At the first sign of dawn Wirt decided to look for, and possibly retrieve, the remnants of his shirt. The reason for it he did not admit, neither in thought nor words; he kept that part intentionally muddled. After the workmen's task were allotted, he instructed Fasot what to say to the chief of police:

"Tell Mr Brunt I am detained by urgent business, I shall call on him this afternoon."

It was a beautiful morning till the rain arrived. What a spectacle that was, it had to be seen to believe. Ominous clouds gathered over the mountains, in no time they blotted out the sun as they descended at a surprising speed. The inevitable downpour wasn't long in coming; calling it a deluge wouldn't have been far off the mark. Within minutes creeks and brooks, meandering lazily a moment ago, turned into angry torrents; waterfalls, cascading towards the sea, sprung up here and there. The wind, gaining strength rapidly, swept the treetops, making them moan and creak alarmingly.

Then the fury stopped with a suddenness that Wirt found uncanny. The clouds dispersed, the rain stopped abruptly, and the corn levelling wind died down after a last violent surge. He had sought refuge of sorts under a tree, but just the same he was soaked to the skin, and miserable to the marrow. In no time, however, the reappearing sun dried his clothes and revived his spirit.

On his way again, Wirt passed natives whom he asked about the old man, called Justin by the chief. Their responses irritated him. Some went by without uttering a word; others shrugged their shoulders while muttering in patois. Several, especially youngsters, acted as if frightened; they accelerated their steps. An old woman appeared to be more amenable, she stopped and listened.

"I am looking for a man called Justin," Wirt said in a silvery manner.

"Justin?" she echoed with a knitted brow.

"Yes, old man Justin."

"Don't know him," she offered.

"He has a donkey," Wirt declared.

"Never heard of him."

"Hitched to a cart," he almost pleaded.

Seeing that he drew a blank, aware of her desire to be rid of him, he broke into patois, of which he scarcely possessed a rudimentary knowledge.

Was she amused? Slightly. Did she understand? Not a word, judging by facial expressions.

"He died recently," Wirt intimated.

The woman's reaction could have been best described as wary.

"What a queer fish we got here," her sideways glances seemed to say, "seeking a dead man among the living."

Intent to put a distance between her and that odd white man, she started walking. Turning around, her face lit up.

"Would you be after Manicou perhaps, who died a few days ago?"

Talking a bit more Wirt concluded that Justin and Manicou, the opossum in other words, were one and the same.

"Where can I find him?"

The old woman, looking at him with dilated eyes and a sniff, appeared to be nonplussed.

"Where can you find him?" she repeated.

"Yes, yes," Wirt intoned like an arrant fool.

"In his grave," she intimated with a hint of mockery. "He was buried yesterday."

"Buried, where?"

"In town, I guess," she suggested over her shoulders.

Upon his return Wirt neither went to the Gardens, nor paid a visit to Howard Brunt. Obeying a compelling force, he walked towards the cemetery. On the way he bought some flowers at the market to conjure up an image of someone paying homage to the dead. There were several people milling about; native women mostly. Some knelt at a grave, praying in a voice audible from one end to the other. With purposeful strides, the flowers held for everyone to see, he examined the graves, of humble appearance especially. When one came into view he slowed down to read the name on the cross or monument.

Soon he noticed that his presence caused a stir, as evidenced by sideways glances cast at him. Some women started whispering and turned their heads in his direction. Wirt became self-conscious, more so when several of the women congregated to have a chat, whose topic he could readily guess. He approached them respectfully:

"I like to leave these flowers on a grave that I haven't found so far," he explained.

"Who might you be looking for?" someone asked.

When Wirt told her, she queried:

"An old man you say?"

"Yes."

"Is he a white man?"

"No."

"Black?"

Wirt nodded.

"Where is he from?"

"A place called Sylvania," Wirt intimated.

No one seemed to know anything about him. But one of the women who had meanwhile joined them, chimed in:

"Was he buried yesterday?"

"I believe so," Wirt answered.

"Come, I will show you the grave," she offered.

He was led to a spot containing a wooden cross stuck into the loose ground. On its lateral piece the name Manicou had been carved.

Wirt Has To Act

*A*fter a despairing night, graced with scant repose but
much turning and tossing, Wirt had reached a state of
lethargy, rendering him weak in body and fickle in mind. He
felt like a shell deprived of vital organs, a comatose being
lacking physical strength as much as volition. Yet surprisingly
his judgement appeared to be entirely intact, if not enhanced.

He realised that he was fighting with windmills, battling
spectres of his own creation that were about to devour him. His
innermost self understood a simple fact: act, or meet Alfred
Nantes' fate. In other words he must retrieve the remnant of his
shirt, or at least make certain it is not in that coffin. Fleeing was
not in the cards. Escaping from one's misery isn't a trivial
matter, it requires fortitude which presently eluded him. Ever
lurking sophistry came to his aid.

"What good will it do," he said to himself. "How can one
flee from harrowing thoughts and dire images?"

No, it could not be done, every touch of queasiness would
conjure up pictures of lepers waiting for a slow, abhorrent end;
it was not a solution. Pooh-poohing this weird notion of obeah,
decrying it as blatant abracadabra is one thing, he granted, but
doubting its efficacy is another. Those invasive whispers,
visions of doom, might follow him everywhere he went.
Therefore he decided to take the bull by the horn; hatch a plan
and carry it out without delay. Resolve eased Wirt's mind and
strengthened his body, but it also impaired his reasoning.
Anyway, the combat with ghosts ended; a real battle began.

On the next morning he called on Brunt who appeared to
be on his way to the Gardens.

"Unfortunately I missed you yesterday," he remarked in a booming voice, tinged by reproach.

"You got my message?" Wirt asked.

"If you can call it that," the chief responded.

Knitting his brow, squinting in annoyance, Wirt queried:

"Didn't Fasot apprise you?"

"As I said in a way he did."

Sporting a puckish look, the chief chuckled:

"The police and Fasot are not exactly on cooing terms. But now to our business."

Brunt contemplated Wirt for a few moments; neither unfriendly nor benevolently.

"You implied that after the incident you returned immediately to Roseau."

"I did."

"Did you go back there later on that evening?"

"Of course not. What for?"

"To look up Justin."

"Why should I have done so?"

"For the same reason you attacked him."

"I did no such thing, Mr Brunt."

"Shall we say tackled him?"

"I lost my head," Wirt admitted.

Brunt started to drum on the table; as before he appeared to be irresolute how to proceed. Well, Wirt helped him out.

"Chief, here is a riddle for you. A man, not so old yet, lean as a hound, fit as a fiddle, suddenly dies of a heart failure. The reason? Because I frightened him seems to be the official inference. Weak heart, cardiac arrest? Bosh and nonsense! I say. That fellow ran like a cheetah, had his foot not been caught in a liana, I, a man in excellent physical shape, over twenty years younger, might still be chasing him."

The chief couldn't suppress an appreciative smile, for he too liked to draw the long bow.

"Well put, well put," he agreed.

Wirt spoke again:

"No, chief, that man suffered from nothing more than greed. The rascal stole my shirt, or was given it by someone with an ulterior motive."

"I don't understand," Brunt protested.

"Neither do I, except that something is amiss here; two plus two does not add up to four."

Brunt nodded while sighing as only a bulky man can.

"Quite likely, but rest assured we shall puzzle it out. If I may add, a policeman's lot is not always pleasant; like right now. Instinct tells him one thing; inherent or acquired distrust bids him to pursue an opposite path. Once more, you state with assurance that you have never been near Justin's hut, especially not later that evening."

"I do. Believe me, chief, I couldn't have found the place, at night to boot, even if guided by the star of Bethlehem; in fact, I am still trying to find the location."

Brunt said something that he appeared to be ruing the moment it rolled over his tongue:

"Somebody was prowling about Justin's dwelling that night, a white man according to witnesses."

"In other words, I."

"So they say.'

Raising a hand to forestall Wirt's anticipated protest, he continued:

"In view of earlier events, not mentioning darkness, I pay little heed to these assertions, but the lurking part I have reason to believe."

"Which you will not tell me, I suppose.'

"I can't, I can't," were the chief's parting words.

Next morning at the botanical garden, Wirt had difficulties to concentrate on his work; his thoughts invariably wandered. Did fate, in a capricious moment, contrive that astounding sequel, or had she be given a leg up by human hands? How curious, Justin, a picture of health in the morning, contracted an instant heart disease which did him in before the next sunrise. Tell that to the marines, as Americans say, Wirt snorted. What happened after he and Justin went their opposite ways appeared to be wrapped in layers of mystery.

Later on that evening Wirt visited the cemetery again. Equipped with a flashlight he made his way to Justin's grave. An eerie silence prevailed; whether in deference of the dead, or for other reasons, he felt no inclination to think about, for his mind was otherwise encumbered. Standing on Justin's grave he concluded that tomorrow night he will disinter the old rascal and remove the remnants of his shirt. A pick and shovel should do the job, for the earth was still loose. A crowbar and hammer must also be brought along, Wirt reminded himself.

Way into the night he sat in his easy chair out on the veranda. Despite an inner turmoil he managed to retain a semblance of his mental acuity; so he hoped. He took pride in his ratiocinative mind, capable of judging any situation coolly. But not the present one, by all appearances. His vaunted analytical faculties had taken a back seat. He could not focus his mind on the problem in question, no matter how strenuously he tried. One moment the splashing river hurrying towards the sea disturbed his thoughts, the next, attempts at reasoning petered out; it mingled with the noise of the falling surf.

Despite these annoying distractions, Wirt concluded that he was entering a perilous path. Being caught, and possibly prosecuted for desecrating a dead body, could have dire consequences. Apart from being declared mentally unstable, he might receive a jail sentence, if indicted and found guilty. Illegally disturbing a grave for any reason is a serious delict, he realised in a lucid moment. It also flashed through his mind that he would place himself at the horns of a dilemma. Offering no contest might earn him a severe sentence, while putting up a defence will brand him a lunatic, unfit for the meanest position; he could kiss his professional career goodbye.

Just the same, it needed to be done, for the conception of being preoccupied the rest of his life with debilitating thoughts deemed him intolerable. Hannes Wirt did not suffer from delusions in that respect, he knew his weaknesses, especially the tendency to brood to the point of nausea, capable to kill. He owned up to the fact that he must find the remnants of that shirt, eventually solve the mystery surrounding it, or enter a gradual state of vegetation. There it was in a nutshell: do or die. Right or wrong, that was his mental state presently and would be forever, unless he took matters into his hands, which he intended to do tomorrow night, if conditions were propitious.

Wirt jumped up. Chuckling he snapped his fingers at imaginary enemies. Who are they? Mauch came to mind; Murdoch however figured more prominently. No doubt, both intended to sow the seeds of despair in his heart. Murdoch's motives could easily be conjectured; he perceived in him a spoilsport, a stumbling block towards his ambitions. But what was Mauch up to? Why should a news publisher resort to such machinations? or did he? Well, he took pains to apprise him, Wirt, of the obeah cult, which fact no amount of palliation can deny. Did he share Murdoch's interest in those mystery draped uras trees? "Who knows," Wirt murmured as he sat down again.

Sitting there, a bit stung by those confounding, whistling frogs, he once more endeavoured to examine his situation with detached logic. The intention was laudable, the result dismal. Two things remained anchored in his mind: One, he must recover the remnants of his shirt; two, under no circumstances should he be caught doing it. Digging in that loose soil he considered to be no chore worth mentioning. He reckoned that three feet, at the most, of straight shovelling will expose the coffin sufficiently to lift or pry off the lid. The rest ought to be child's play, he snorted in anticipation. Time, while not running out, he considered nevertheless of the essence. In case tomorrow night proves inauspicious, what of it? The job can still be done days later. On the way to his bedroom he reminded himself that the risk is minute, the benefits incalculable. No native would go near a cemetery after darkness.

Wirt Enters The Serbonian Bog

*N*ext day Wirt heard a rumour that Mrs Burchard was on her way back. Better news had not reached his ears for a while; unfortunately it proved to be false. To say that Wirt possessed the nonchalance he tried to purvey, would have given the lie to reality. He walked stooped as if weighed down by a load, looking repeatedly behind himself. He gave an impression of a man fleeing steps ahead of an impending calamity. Unable to adhere to any task longer than a few minutes, he seemed to wander in circles, while mumbling to himself.

At noon he packed up and left the Gardens. Did he see spectres, or were those two natives again lurking about? Fasot, the foreman, did he indeed chortle to himself all morning and grin from ear to ear? Going to the house had no appeal for him; thus he decided to pay Dr Brodeur a visit; offhand he couldn't guess why. He would be hard pressed to give a reason for such an impromptu call. After all they weren't exactly lovey-dovey with each other. Racking his brains he couldn't think what to say, but that quickly changed.

Halfway across the bridge a notion struck Wirt that unwittingly made him stop in his tracks. Yes, that must be it! Justin might have died of a heart attack, but what or who induced it is food for thought. Chief Brunt implied that the donkey driver's cardiac insufficiency, aggravated by that silly chase, killed the fellow later that night. Why then insinuate, quite intrusively Wirt thought, that someone, most likely he, returned surreptitiously to Justin's hut? To do what wasn't even hinted at.

"Died of heart failure, presumably caused by excitement?

Fiddlesticks, twice over!" Wirt snorted. "No one suffering from a weak heart could have run and leaped like that latter day Ladas."

That Justin fellow, Wirt was willing to swear on the Bible, possessed the breath and endurance of a racehorse, not to mention his amazing swiftness, to which the above cited Ladas, Alexander's messenger, would have bowed his head. No, taking into account the chief's hemming and hawing, his unwonted beating about the bush, something happened in that hut that Brunt wished to tell him, but dared not. Wirt smelled a rat, which he could not identify. Well, he decided to bluff it out of Dr Brodeur.

"Can I see the doctor?" Wirt asked the secretary. "It's urgent," he added upon noticing her defensive glance, mixed with annoyance.

"Not now, he is with a patient," she advised.

Then after another askance and contemplative look, she informed him:

"I will speak with the doctor. What is your name?"

"Hannes Wirt, he knows me."

She returned, not exactly promptly, but she did take her seat behind the counter again.

"He can see you in half an hour, but only for ten minutes at the most. You can wait here or take a stroll," she suggested.

Wirt did not in the least cherish the notion of sitting opposite that morose woman; he went out in a hurry.

Walking towards the wharf, where a banana boat was being loaded, he took up the thread of his thoughts again. He felt no longer at sea, nor timid, for things started to fall in place. True, questions still begged to be answered. One statement, however, could be made unflinchingly: This Justin affair reeks of subterfuge and collusion. Why did the old fellow die, moreover, how? According to chief Brunt, later that night someone prowled around Justin's hut; he alluded to screams heard by neighbours, indicating that this someone entered the shack. Yes, Justin was being frightened to a degree that his heart stopped beating. Or had he been attacked perhaps? No doubt, the key to the puzzle lay in Dr Brodeur's hands. Wresting it from him, Wirt decided on the spur of the moment, might not be so cumbersome. On the other hand, why take the trouble if all he desired was the recovery of his shirt, burn it to cinders, then forget about it? Mind you, the matter of a criminal investigation, an indictment possibly, now as then hovered above him. Therefore he must endeavour to tackle Dr Brodeur, who in some way might serve others with a ready plan in their heads and mischief in their hearts. Whether the worthy doctor is a cog in the wheel of a conspiracy, or an unwitting dupe, Wirt was unable to determine. An innocent bystander he was not, Wirt concluded, more than one finger pointed towards guilt by association.

Take his uncharacteristic behaviour at the house. A gentleman like him, decorous to his fingertips, would hardly barge into a man's home unless driven by urgencies that cannot be staved off. Indeed, he acted like a harbinger of tidings that brooked not a second's delay to be imparted, albeit not in the presence of him, the host. What had stoked the flames of this impulsion, furthermore, how did he manage to interrupt at the exact moment when Brunt was about to make a disclosure? It seemed uncanny, unless Dr Brodeur was eavesdropping, Wirt concluded, and rushed in to prevent the chief's intended communication to reach his ears. It sounded far-fetched, yet plausible. I shall soon find out, Wirt murmured as he entered the premises with purposeful steps.

"I am not coming as a patient," were his introductory words.

"Well, take a seat anyway," Dr Brodeur invited while he took a chair himself.

"Thank you, doctor, I prefer to remain standing."

Dr Brodeur raised his eyebrows. Being an inherently sensitive man, he noted his visitor's guarded behaviour, which made him watchful.

"Doctor, I shall come to the point, if you don't mind."

"Please do. Remember I expect a patient in ten, fifteen minutes."

"Quite so, here it is: My unceremonious appearance serves one purpose; to clear up the mystery about that fellow Justin."

"Who died a few days, rather nights, ago?"

"The same. You probably know I had a... how shall we say, a bit of a fracas with him earlier on that day."

"I heard about it," came a cautious reply.

Wirt looked straight at Dr Brodeur, whose glance wandered towards the clock on the wall.

"Doctor, if I appear to be prying, forgive me, it's not done out of idle curiosity. This Justin affair has placed a noose around my neck; invisible, yet leaving weals that hurt."

"Weals?" Dr Brodeur echoed, while he jumped up as if stung to the quick.

Thunderstruck Wirt looked at the swarthy phycisian whose face grew pale.

"What are you saying, Mr Wirt?" he cried.

"I was speaking metaphorically, yet not untruthfully. I am under a cloud of suspicion which, with your assistance, could probably be lifted. Justin's death is seemingly attributed to me. I am being suspected to have triggered his failing heart to stop beating."

Dr Brodeur heaved and lowered his shoulders.

"You promised to come to the point quickly," he reminded.

"I will, doctor, I will instantly. First let me make a statement."

"Yes?"

"Justin did not suffer from heart ills."

"Oh, how do you know? Are you a medical man? Have you treated him prior to his death?" Dr Brodeur queried with a measure of sarcasm.

"Of course not. But a layman with his wits about, plus first hand experience, can be a reliable judge of matters that concern him."

Wirt observed the doctor deliberately prior to saying more:

"Yes, I tackled and pursued the old fellow who skipped like a deer. Look at me, doctor, I'm still fairly young, in excellent physical shape; in fact, there was a time, not long ago, when people called me Hannes the Swift. I was reputed to outrun a greyhound, but let me tell you, I would have never caught up with this putative heart sufferer, had he not stumbled and fallen."

Dr Brodeur asked ironically:

"What are you trying to say, Mr Wirt?"

"This: Justin was willfully…"

At that moment the secretary entered the room:

"Mrs Reid is here, doctor," she announced.

"Sorry, Mr Wirt, please contact me later, this calls for a chat, tonight perhaps at the Fort Young Hotel?" he suggested.

"Not tonight, doctor, I shall be in touch," Wirt muttered as he walked out.

Midafternoon had arrived. Wirt now as then felt scant inclination to go to his house, even less to the botanical garden. Looking with strained eyes at the formation of ominous clouds, he lost heart for an instant. He knew the signs; a downpour was in the offing.

"Oh well, let it rain," he consoled himself.

The night was still far off, besides, that loose soil would absorb any amount of water in a hurry. Thinking about Dr Brodeur clouded his brow. He seemed unwontedly on edge, constrained and brusque, there were no traces in him of that hail-fellow-well-met attribute generally displayed.

Wirt felt an impulse to return and intrude rudely as the doctor had done at his house. Yes, he should accuse him to his face of being a schemer, and no less a prevaricator. Strange, how he bridled when he, Wirt, alluded to a noose around his neck leaving invisible, yet painful weals. It sure touched a nerve in the respectable doctor; one had to wonder why.

Equipped with the necessary tools Wirt set out after midnight. He approached the cemetery with measured steps, quite convinced that no one will be abroad at this time of the night. The entire surrounding lay in darkness; the moon, as much as the stars were obscured by gathering clouds. Wirt knew what it meant; a downpour was imminent. Well, he thought, while rendering digging more uncomfortable, rain will surely keep people inside. Not that he expected any stragglers wandering about, certainly not in this area. Being out of doors at such late hours, especially in the case of natives, bordered on foolhardiness; not even drunks are that venturous in Dominica.

Just the same he couldn't suppress a lingering apprehension till he reached the confines of the cemetery. Once inside he heaved an audible sigh of relief, for no one, black or white, would dare sauntering among the dead after midnight.

Looking behind him, then left and right, he proceeded towards Justin's grave, which he located with the help of his flashlight. After he had laid down the tools he reached in his pocket for the rudimentary sketch, just to reasure himself. A frown darkened his brow. With a quickening pulse he turned every pocket inside out. Where was that confounded diagram? For an awful instant panic seized him. Struck by momentary amnesia he walked to and fro in a fit of terror.

"What is happening to me?" he moaned.

Wirt, the man of science, generally tranquil, did occasionally get into a flurry, which affected his otherwise excellent memory. That's what happened now; he couldn't recall the man's name anymore whom he intended to disinter. Straining every nerve in his body, he managed to calm down. Was he at the right place? Pointing his lit torch at the shingle once more increased his confusion and hightened his anxiety. The name Justin came to his mind, but that wasn't the one written on the cross. Cursing his well-known quirk, racking his brains, led nowhere. For the world of him he could not recall that name.

Luckily the technique of mnemonic, that astounding memory aid, came to his mind, which he usually applied to anchor objects and names in his brain. To his utter relief he came to the conclusion that Manicou, the name on the shingle, was the man he wanted.

When he prepared to start digging the clouds burst. Although expecting it, Wirt had silently prayed for a few hours respite. Heavy drops fell with a thud, soon it came down in buckets; it made him forget the matter of the sketch, whose absence caused a temporary loss of memory a moment ago. It would have been soaked by now anyway, thus rendering it illegible, Wirt consoled himself. But just the same, what happened to it? He could have sworn by the book of books that it never left his pocket. To have been taken out with other odds and ends seemed impossible in view of its sequestered place. It was put in a little sewn-on pouch within his trousers that had a zipper. Only one explanation remained; someone pilfered the sketch. That idea however made no sense. Anyway, Wirt had neither time, nor was he inclined to dwell on it.

Drenched to the skin, miserable in body, apprehensive in mind, he considered his next move. Being dripping wet was not to his liking.

"Go back to the house, dry up, change clothes, and wait for the rain to stop," his better judgement urged.

Leaving his tools behind he hastened towards his home; yet not before taking a close look at the surrounding. In the light of the torch he surveyed the sturdy cross and the attached shingle with wide open eyes. No doubt he stood on Justin Manicou's grave.

Barely did he step inside the house when the rain stopped. After he had dried himself and changed clothes he decided to linger awhile till the ground dries up a bit. The clouds moved beyond the mountains, the reappearing moon and stars lifted his sagging spirit; for to tell the truth, second thoughts about his undertaking began to manifest themselves. In other words, he heard the bell ring backwards. Despite attempts at bravado, certainly not a trait bred in his bones, he was unable to shake off a foreboding. What till now appeared to be a cakewalk, though fraught with inconveniences, took on a dubious aspect. Indistinct, ominous murmurs rang in his ears, or so he thought, till he made out their origin; it was the wind making the palm fronds sough. Emboldened by this realisation, no less angry on account of the momentary display of the white feather, he called out:

"Justin will be exhumed tonight, and that's it!"

Wirt set out again. The sky, though not exactly ablaze with stars, coupled with the wan shine of the moon, accorded sufficient light to find one's way without a flashlight. All artificial illumination had been extinguished, even the city lay in darkness. A glance at his watch told him that he still had four hours to complete the task. He went at it with might and main. Casting all caution to the wind he neither paused nor

listened or looked up. Spurred by fear of another downpour, he
dug feverishly and no less noisily.

Not too long after he reckoned that he must be nearing the
coffin; in fact, a few times his shovel appeared to have touched
wood. The sound, imagined or real, fanned Wirt's excitement;
it also tautened his tiring muscels and filled his panting lungs
anew with air. With redoubled effort and waning strength he
drove the shovel into the ground.

"There, that should do it," he exclaimed under his breath.

Wirt neither heard nor saw the approaching figures. Only
when a burst of light engulfed him did he look up. He knew
one of the men before he saw his face or heard his voice.
Brunt's inimitable form, ungainly even at rest, could be
recognised in a total eclipse. He was accompanied by a
policeman in uniform. Although unable to discern Brunt's
countenance, wherby to judge his mood, Wirt sensed that he
felt out of sorts. He appeared to be strangely irritated, like
someone trying to forget a personal slight. His voice, generally
loud yet pleasing to the ear, had a jarring ring. He sounded like
a man forced to perform an onerous duty.

"This is unfortunate, very unfortunate," he groaned, then
commanded:

"Corporal, get to work. Take notes, make the necessary
photographs, and don't forget to tag the tools."

Stepping up to Wirt he asked for all to hear:

"Do you wish to make a statement? Remember, you have
the right to remain silent."

In an undertone he remarked:

"Hold your tongue, man."

The chief's conciliatory attitude raised Wirt's hope against
hope. The proverbial sword, though poised above his head,
might not fall; but it did with a thud.

Michael Mauch, the newspaper man arrived. He was in
fine fettle; three sheets in the wind, he appeared to be a man
geared to cause mischief. Before Wirt had a chance to turn
away, or Brunt managed to raise a cautionary hand, he took
pictures from every angle. His questions, angrily rebuffed by
the chief, found no favour with Wirt, who told him roughly to
mind his own business.

"That's exactly what I'm doing," he was told.

The chief's bearing astonished Wirt immensely; he almost pleaded with Mauch to leave, but to no avail. Like a sleuthhound with the scent of a prey in his nostrils is guided by his baser instincts, so it happened with the otherwise convivial son of the Old Sod, who must have licked his chops at what he saw and surmised. Only when Brunt threatened him with arrest for interfering in police work did Mauch depart. Still slewed by the liquor he had taken, he advised at the top of his voice:

"I have seen enough."

Indeed, he had.

After Wirt undertook to report to the police station within forty-eight hours, he was allowed to go his way.

The first silvery streaks started to tinge the horizon; dawn drew near. The chief seemed anxious to leave, judging by his snorts and edgy movements. Before Wirt got out of earshot he called after him:

"Just a moment, Mr Wirt."

When he stopped and turned around Brunt aproached him. Reaching in one of his pockets he produced a piece of paper which he handed Wirt, while saying in an undertone:

"You left this at the doctor's office."

Then in his regular voice he commanded:

"Let's pack up, Clarence, time to leave."

Despite the lingering darkness Wirt instinctively knew that in his hands lay the missing sketch.

When he arrived at the house the sun pushed over the mountains, the sky aquired almost instantly that peculiar hue inherent to the Caribbean islands. The first hour after sunrise lingers in one's memory with a choking vividness. The feeling, difficult to describe, left Wirt untouched this morning.

Caroline Brise Appears

*T*oday was Sunday. Soon noisy and fervent prayers, followed by louder chants and hymns, would drown out the splash of the river. Listening to these liturgic praises, reminiscent at times of the krakamals of his forebears, never failed to enrapt Wirt; till now that is.

While paying scant attention to the throng of natives in their fineries, ready to praise the lord, he pondered about his predicament.

A peremptory rap at the door wrenched him out of it. A wild-eyed, dishevelled woman of nondescript age stood outside.

"Don't worry, I'm sober," were her words of greeting.

An image of a street beggar rose before Wirt's eyes, whom he decided to fob off with two bits and some didactic words. Yet casting a second glimpse at her made him hesitate, for the thought struck him that the tigerish figure staring at him resembled rather a street fighter than a street mendicant.

"You are the new botanist," she stated with a sardonic grin.

"Yes – yes," Wirt admitted reluctantly, taken aback by the woman's lordly air contrasting sharply with her unkempt appearance.

A song called 'princes in rags and tags' came to his mind. He had never seen such an audacious face that attracted and repulsed at the same time.

"What do you want?" he asked with more bravado than conviction.

"I have a gift for you, step aside and let me pass," she demanded.

Wirt obeyed without a word of protest.

"I am Caroline Brise," she advised with an air of haughtiness befitting a queen. "You must have heard of me."

"Never," he was about to reply, when he recalled chief Brunt refer to her as that hussy, the terror of Dominica.

"I heard your name mentioned," he admitted.

"I bet you have," she heehawed.

"What's the gift?" Wirt inquired.

From seemingly nowhere she produced a piece of cloth whose sight rendered Wirt moon-eyed.

"That's my shirt," he cried.

"Part of it, dearie, just part of it," she explained visibly amused on account of his eagerness to reclaim a soiled piece of rag. Indeed, he tore it out of her hands and pressed it to his bosom.

Caroline Brise was taken by surprise by this display of effusiveness on account of a torn piece of cloth. She couldn't help snorting in disgust while taking a step backwards, because for an awful moment she thought was going to embrace her. She, who in her own words had fought the police and others, standing up, lying down, and even when chained to a tree, abhorred mushiness almost as fervently as the authorities. She couldn't comprehend the man's maudlin behaviour; it embarrased her.

Wirt was reputed to be an oddity with a penchant for theatrics. Upon learning that he was German she decided to meet him. The reason? Some years ago she knew a man of German origin, who left a lasting imprint on her. The roving, untamed spitfire still possessed a woman's heart; the hellcat turned into a purring kitten in his presence.

The incident with Justin, or Manicou, as the locals called him, presented an ideal opportunity to make the botanist's aquaintance. Caroline, who grew up in that area, knew the donkey man since she could crawl on all fours. His mishap with Wirt, shirt and all, and subsequent death, reached her ears almost instantly; in fact, she attended his funeral, if one could call it that.

When Wirt offered her a reward she nearly spat at him, but gave him a tongue lashing instead that brought his head down and fanned the wish that she should leave. He wanted to be alone to savour and celebrate his triumph. But Caroline Brise, though eyeing the door yearningly, stayed put; something held her back from storming out. They stared at each other without saying a word. Wirt couldn't help thinking that her errand was not a charitable deed; she undertook it to satisfy a selfish motive.

Caroline broke the silence first. In a husky voice, while blushing under her dark skin, she stated:

"There used to be a German living in this house."

Wirt realised in a twinkle how the wind blew. The horror of Dominica entertained tender feelings towards this compatriot of his.

Encouraged by her softening bearing, he decided to make further inquiries about Justin's death, which now as then he deemed shrouded in mystery. No doubt she knew more about that weird incident than she was willing to admit. He expressed interest in the man she called Rudi, whom she described vividly, as only a woman in love can. He promised to convey her warmest regards to him at their first encounter. She appeared to be pleased, but only for a moment; in no time her eyes looked daggers again, her lips curled up in mockery. Out of the blue Wirt made some comments that led to a surprising discovery.

"Caroline, you said a moment ago that you attended Manicou's funeral."

"I did, but it wasn't really a funeral, we just laid him in his grave and went our way."

"There were many people present, I assume?"

"No, just myself plus two others."

"Oh? I guess the distance to the city prevented some of the older folks to show up."

Caroline, on the way out, turned on her heels.

"What do you mean by distance to the city?" she snapped.

"To the cemetery where he is buried," Wirt explained.

Drawing herself up she hurled the words at him:

"You must be daft. Don't you know that the maroons never bury their dead in the city's cemetery?"

With a scowl meant to fling him into the fangs of satan, she stormed out.

Wirt's consternation grew by the second while trying to absorb what he had just learned. He repeated her furious exclamation several times:

"Maroons never bury their dead in the city's cemetery."

Her avowal made no sense at first, but slowly an awful realisation sunk in: he had been set up.

A few minutes later another imperious knock at the door interrupted his deliberations. Wirt instinctively knew who it was. Caroline Brise had returned, probably to heap more scorn upon his bowed head, he reckoned. The decision whether to invite her in or bar the door came to an abrupt end. Caroline stood inside, facing him with one contemptuous eye, the other veiled with compassion.

"Sweetie, you are up the creek, don't deny it, you got it in the neck," she intimated with authority.

When he lifted a hand to protest, she cut him short:

"Listen to what I have to say. Old donkey-man was either murdered, or he strangled himself."

"How would you know?" Wirt blurted out.

"Keep your shirt on, dearie, I saw the welts around his neck, besides, I found this rope on the floor underneath his body," she said, pointing at a sturdy rope wound around her waist.

"Caroline, are you telling me the truth?"

"Cross my heart, I do."

Wirt was confounded beyond description. He stammered:

"But – but, this is serious. Did you make a report?"

She harumphed that notion with gusto:

"Talking to the authorities, perhaps to that overblown Englishman? Not this mother's daughter. I would sooner spike his whisky with poison, than give him the time of day. He once…. never mind about that. I did talk to Dr Brodeur however, whom I also gave a piece of this rope."

Wirt's attempt to worm out more information failed dismally.

"What a bullheaded creature you are," he almost let slip out, but decided against it. He watched her walk towards the exit with swaying hips and purposeful strides.

Suddenly she stopped while glancing at some books on the shelf.

"You have a lot of books, I see, I wonder if there is one about sleepwalking among the lot."

With this cryptic remark she disappeared.

Alone now Wirt became a prisoner of his thoughts, and in no time a fugitive from spectres of his own creation. Whichever way he looked, a forbidding wall of anxiety rose before his mind that neither hope nor faith could surmount. No doubt he had become the victim of a scheme aiming at his elimination. Of course he was the architect of his own misfortune; he played into the intriguers' hands. Unwittingly at times, on account of inherent peculiarities, but more so because of his erratic behaviour, which made him a morsel for idle minds beset by the ulcer of discontent. But then, he concluded, his idiosyncrasies thrice over would hardly have been the decisive factor of his debacle. Whoever wanted him out of the way received silent consent, if not encouragement, from a privileged coterie, united by the glue of convention, instinctively resented by him.

Despite his chagrin Wirt smiled amusedly, while thinking about his fellow expatriates' proclamation to be frank in speech and bold in action. Independent thinkers they call themselves, every inch individualists. The truth wore a mantle of a different cut. Like Menechmians of old they thought, looked, and talked alike. They wore the heavy chains of conventional prejudice which, though invisible, produced a clank that could not be muffled. All marched to the beat of one and the same drummer; with one notable exception, Wirt granted, Howard Brunt, the chief of police, who of late acted strangely.

Anyway, this was not the time to seek causes and principles of his predicament. Stick to facts and shun fancies, he told himself. Yet after each reminder wild notions leaped up from every direction. How did Brunt get wind of his intention to disinter Justin who, according to Caroline Brise, isn't buried at the cemetery to begin with. Another puzzle, insoluble to

Wirt, was the police's timely appearance. Brunt, acting on a tip, must have commissioned someone to shadow him. No other explanation, short of a miracle, would make sense. Admitted, the curse of obeah, whether imaginary or real, had been averted, but the stigma of irrationality would forever glow on his forehead like St. Anthony's fire.

"Just think of it, our botanist is a grave desecrator," people will say.

Of course the possibility of an indictment, if not conviction, loomed high. What likely defence could he offer? certainly not the truth. Caroline Brise came to mind. He envied the free spirited woman with a devil-may-care attitude. What did she say on her way out while glancing at the books?

"I hope there is one about sleepwalking among the lot."

Hm, a peculiar remark that was, it made no sense, Wirt decided. Then the connection flashed through his mind. She hinted at a probable line of defence. Offhand he deemed such notions nothing but arrant nonsense, till he recalled an incident concerning a young woman of his home town. She, as much as her kin, was of sterling character, of an aristocratic lineage, esteemed by young and old. Then the stunning news of her indictment reached their ears. The charge? Repeated theft and destruction of property. Wirt had paid scant attention to the proceedings, but in retrospect he remembered that she was acquitted. Extenuating circumstances prevailed; the authorities agreed that she had committed these crimes while sleepwalking.

Wirt pondered for hours about his embarrassing situation without reaching a conclusion. Pleading somnambulism might get him off the hook; legally that is. But disgrace would never leave him, not to mention silent sneers and spoken defamation. On Saturday Mauch's newspaper will report about his eternal shame. Broad hints would surely be headlined, slyly referring to his unsuitability for any professional job in this fair island; least of all the position of chief botanist. Such a post requires integrity, prudence, and rationality, not exactly inherent in him, some would profess. Wirt harboured no illusions about Mauch's intentions to cleverly refer to his repeated irregular behaviour, culminating in disturbing the dead. He could see it black and white that despite his acknowledged professional qualifications, he lacked essential steadfastness of character. Yes, he could hear the snickers in town and see people cross over to the other side of the street at the sight of him.

All day, plus most of the night, Wirt walked, rather stumbled, through the house in a daze. In the morning he made his way to the Gardens, more driven by habit than a sense of duty. The sight upon arrival set his teeth on edge. Murdoch and Mauch ambled about, engrossed in conversation whose topic Wirt could guess. As he came in view he heard Murdoch say:

"I told him that he, nor anyone else under his supervision, shall ever thrust a spade into that ground."

Mauch chimed in:

"By jingo, he never will."

Wirt, suppressing an impulse to beat a retreat, approached them with rising anger instead.

"Ah, there is the man we are talking about. Good morning, Herr Kollege, spent a restful night, I hope?" Murdoch inquired with a supercilious air.

Mauch, grinning from ear to ear, wanted to know:

"Have you read the book, Mr Wirt? Don't forget, chapter thirteen deserves special attention."

A desire to light into them nearly overwhelmed Wirt, yet it quickly subsided when he noticed the camera slung over Mauch's shoulder, which he grasped with both hands. Wirt stopped abruptly, he realised that another outburst of fury, on film to boot, would be grist to his detractors' mills.

After a curt nod, followed by perfunctory greeting, he went to the office. Trying to concentrate proved to be a Sisyphean task; he was unable to avert his thoughts and eyes from the two men outside.

When the workmen arrived, he unlocked the tool shed. Then, after securing the office, he walked away. It was too early to report to the police station, or go anywhere else for that matter. Riven by the cruel foe indecision, feeling his mettle choked by premonitions, he walked aimlessly through back lanes. Without realising it he arrived at Dr Brodeur's house, which also served as his pratice. He was hailed from a window:

"Good morning, Mr Wirt, how about joining me for a cup of coffee?"

"With pleasure," Wirt agreed, thankful for the diversion.

Dr Brodeur, unwontedly agitated, eyed Wirt deliberately. Not intrusively, mind you, but pensively and somewhat on edge, as if waiting for an auspicious moment to broach a subject. What did the doctor wish to divulge? How much did he know or divine? Could he be trusted as a father confessor whom Wirt sorely needed? Wirt decided against it; for now in any case, since the doctor himself seemed to be searching for a willing ear to listen to his woes; in addition he deemed Wirt unusually contradictory this morning. True, every time they met he felt at sea about Dr Brodeur's personality, that was shrouded in mystery and kept deliberately nebulous. Was he a scoundrel clothed with garments of respectability, or a saint with an aura of villainy? Wirt couldn't say, but to be on the safe side he resolved not to take the doctor into his confidence; yet drawing him out could do no harm.

As indicated, the doctor's behaviour contrasted sharply with his wonted self. He stirred about uneasily as if on the verge of committing a blunder which he would rue forever. His countenance, a portrait of harmony as a rule, deemed Wirt like a battlefield of conflicting emotions. Undoubtedly he had been accosted for specific reasons.

"Did you ever meet our enfant terrible?" the doctor asked.

"You must be referring to Caroline Brise."

"The same."

"Yes, I did, just yesterday in fact."

Dr Brodeur shifted uneasily on his chair, evidently irresolute what to say next.

"She has quite a reputation, I understand," Wirt intimated.

"Most unsavoury, I regret to admit, but undeservedly so. True, she could make a Tasmanian devil blush at times with her unbridled behaviour. No doubt she falls prey to dark forces occasionally, like all of us."

The doctor paused for an instant or two, then he made an astounding remark:

"In my estimation her demons are more benign than ours."

Wirt disguised his surprise with a smile and a nod; it was a peculiar statement to be made by an urbane physician who resented any form of boisterousness. He couldn't stave off an eerie feeling of being contemplated, appraised as it were. It made him self-conscious, especially when he caught his host staring at him several times. A heartfelt sigh, resembling a stifled moan, escaped from his chest:

"Mr Wirt, have you ever looked in the mirror and saw a strange face staring back at you?"

Taken aback Wirt muttered:

"What do you mean, doctor?"

"A face, I should emphasise, that one saw never before."

"I can't say I have," Wirt replied not exactly truthfully.

After expelling another prolonged mournful sound, the doctor's head came up:

"Well, the first patients shall arrive any moment," he observed insinuatingly.

Back on the street Wirt tried to reason out Dr Brodeur's peculiar conduct, reminiscent of a man forced into a corner. In Wirt's understanding the doctor had good reasons to be on edge. After all he signed a dubious death certificate, thereby ruling out a coroner's inquest, necessary by law under the circumstances. Heart failure, the stated cause of death, while technically correct perhaps, was rendered spurious by the omission of vital facts which bore the signs of negligence, if not villainy. The welts around Justin's neck, undoubtedly noticed by the doctor, plus Caroline Brise's information, made a sham of Dr Brodeur's declaration. Added reports of a prowler around Justin's hut that night reinforced that assumption.

Where was the piece of rope given to the doctor by Caroline? Why were the welts on Justin's neck, mentioned by her, surely noticed by him, glossed over? Did she invent these occurrences out of spite? Odd to say, Wirt believed every word that wildcat said, as did the doctor to all appearances. Besides, he had an inkling that she deliberately held back evidence to be sprung as a surprise later.

Wirt smelled the proverbial rat; the entire affair appeared to be cloaked in mystery, if not villainy. Was chief Brunt privy to the doctor's knowledge gained from his examination and

Caroline's disclosure? Of course. Why else would the doctor, delicate to his fingertips, every inch a gentleman, barge into his home, if not to impart Caroline's disquieting revelation, undoubtedly pooh-poohed by Brunt enthusiastically. It might have been easy for him to do; but what about Dr Brodeur? Did he divulge his own findings? Had he handed over the piece of rope to be dusted and fingerprinted? Regardless, the doctor, presumable a man of conscience with apprehension nipping at his heels, must surely be in a quandery. Misfortune has a habit to repeat itself. Not too long ago, by his own admission, he had to leave his homeland under cover of darkness. Would he cherish a repetition of such an escapade? Not likely, Wirt thought, yet the possibility existed, should the truth become known in the right quarters.

Contemplating Dr Brodeur's plight, Wirt forgot his own, but only momentarily, it soon assailed him again with full force. The hussy fickleness had a field day with him. What should he do? what could he do? Take to his heels as Nantes must have done, or fight it out?

Suddenly he felt a surge of excitement racing through his veins that made him halt his steps. An urge to heap hooting mockery upon himself and the world almost overwhelmed him. He saw the light at the end of a long, dark tunnel.

In a twinkle he guided his steps towards the station house. Now as then he considered Brunt, along with Mrs Burchard, his staunchest ally; although he lately appeared to be on the fence concerning matters pertaining to the botanical garden.

"Watch out, Mr Brunt, soon you shall be off your perch, make no mistake about it," Wirt snorted as he approached the station with growing confidence.

His mind was made up; he would fight it out, with flying colours to boot. Pity, that he must take advantage of Dr Brodeur's and the chief's blunders, gross negligence if considered closer. So be it. They must serve as his Trojan Horse, Wirt concluded.

A recurring thought, unfounded perhaps, had nevertheless taken root lately. Murdoch was not the kingpin in this subversion aimed at him, and Mauch even less. They might be willing tools in the hands of someone else who casts a longer shadow than either one. Murdoch's chief, if not sole concern, belonged to that property at Sylvania, trembling in the balance on account of his, Wirts, involvement. To be fair, one had to pause and think about Mrs Burchard's curious aspirations, shared by Brunt, consisting of nothing less than the destruction of those mysterious uras trees. Furthermore, were they not conspiring to chase Murdoch from the island, plus have him permanently barred? Had they not induced him to be the grindstone to sharpen their axes with? Therefore, who could blame Murdoch for colluding with others to settle his hash, especially if he, or she, is influential. Admitted, his colleague could hardly be called congenial; his standoffishnes made one's blood rise; besides, he possessed a tyrant's vein that swells up if opposed.

Just the same, Wirt granted, insidious he was not. To scheme against someone to satisfy a mean streak? Not Robert Murdoch, who liked to drape himself with probity and sing the songs of fair play. No, he, as much as Mauch, was a compliant victim of someone lashed by psychotic sentiments that feed on themselves. A silent foe, inflamed by animosity, sworn to his ruin, lurked behind the scene. Who it could be Wirt questioned as he walked up the steps.

The chief appeared to be in a snit; his eyes swept over Wirt with obvious ill humour. There is a man in the doldrums, Wirt surmised prior to uttering a word. The chief observed him inquiringly, like one does an intruder.

"Well, Mr Wirt, what brings you here?"

Cocking his head in surprise, Wirt replied:

"As promised I am reporting to the police."

"Reporting what for?"

Wirt, visibly perplexed, started to explain, when the chief interrupted:

"That request was meant for constable Clancey's ears. I know you are not running away."

"Neither now, nor in the near future," Wirt advised in a tone that made the chief perk up.

"How is the investigation going?" Wirt inquired.

"Concerning your recent midnight escapade?"

"That's all it was, a silly adventure never to be repeated, I hope."

Both men fell silent. Brunt, seemingly chafing at the bit while waiting for further comments, stared straight ahead.

Wirt posed a question:

"Chief, did you ever hear the expression 'odic force'?"

Brunt shook his head.

"It's a term coined by Karl von Reichenbach."

"What does it mean?"

"That we frequently act under the influence of a power called odyl, of which somnambulism is one."

Knitting his brow, starting that infernal devil's tatoo, the chief exclaimed:

"You are not insinuating that you dug up Justin Manicou's grave while asleep?"

"While mesmerised. Besides, it is not Justin's grave nor anyone elses, for that matter."

Brunt, confounded and no less curious, remonstrated:

"What about the cross bearing Manicou's name?"

"Put there by schemers. In any case what I did was done under the spell of odyl's forces; in other words while sleepwalking. Such occurrences aren't all that rare, if medical science can be trusted."

The chief stood up. Lacking a sophist's instinct, he resorted to slapstick humour:

"You are trying to lead me a pretty dance, old boy. If I weren't so stout I would fall in. Let's not gild the pill. You intended to retrieve the remnants of your shirt," he grumbled.

"I have my shirt; all of it."

"So why did you go there under cover of darkness?"

"I was sleepwalking. Granted I had been, still am, haunted by Justin's death, a vile murder as I see it, perpetrated to incriminate me."

Noticing the chief's sceptic mien, Wirt hastened to say:

"I had a visitor yesterday."

Brunt shrugged his shoulders, signifying lack of interest.

"Caroline Brise came to see me."

Had a pin be stuck into the portly figure, the reaction could not have been more startling. Grimacing disdainfully, Brunt said:

"Congratulations, you have met the bane of my existence. I suppose she told you all about our ongoing feud."

"Much more, chief, much more."

"So, so," Brunt grumbled with a measure of concern.

"She may be a nuisance to you, yet what I learned from her renewed my lease on life. Justin, she told me, is buried in the village of Cochrane, his place of birth. She attended his funeral."

"One cannot believe a word uttered by that alley cat; not a syllable," Brunt protested.

"I do, and so does Dr Brodeur. Why else would he have rushed to the house and rudely interrupted our conversation, calling you away, in fact?"

"The good doctor has a Latin temperament, he emotes freely."

"I concede he does, especially when assailed by twinges of conscience, and fear nips at his heels. In all likelihood Caroline Brise had just knocked at his door to apprise him of certain facts, disquieting facts, I may add. She also left in his hands a piece of rope used to strangle Justin. Undoubtedly the doctor had the wind up; who can blame him in view of Caroline's insistence to have a coroner's inquest performed, as required by law."

This was a shot in the dark that did not miss its mark however; far from it. Brunt cleared his throat angrily:

"Mr Wirt, quit beating about the bush. Why did you come here?"

"To honour my parole."

"Fiddlesticks! let's hear the real reason."

"As you wish. But first let me pose a question: Who is scheming against me, and why?"

"Murdoch, for one; why, can easily be deduced."

Shaking his head Wirt countered:

"That's what I thought at first."

"But no longer?"

"No. Admitted, he wishes to see the last of me, but this wish alone will not be the father of the deed."

"Explain what you mean," the chief demanded testily, for biblical expressions or similes were not to his taste.

"He, like other expatriates lacks the force, and more so the authority to contrive my ruin. No, the person with a shoulder to this wheel wields more power, plus is goaded by an animus out of control. An animus that not only desires my departure, but my annihilation, which only fear can engender."

"Whom do you suspect?"

"I haven't the faintest idea."

Lifting his head, grimacing woefully, Wirt groaned:

"Chief, my life has been made a living hell."

"In what way?"

Wirt started to explain. Trying to suppress the tremor in his voice and shiver in his limbs, he related his experiences with hardly a tinge of pathos, grateful however for the sympathetic ear lent him.

Brunt listened, but more courteously than attentively; initially that is. This yawning listlessness soon changed to open-eyed concentration.

After Wirt had ended his narrative, Brunt remained silent. He pursed his lips, passed a hand over his knitted brow where dark shadows flickered from temple to temple, while muscles twitched in his face. A thought appeared to gain a foothold which made him groan.

"Hm, curious, very, very curious. What you have just told me brings back disturbing memories. It sounds like a sequel to Alfred Nantes' plight who, like you, had not a single enemy in the island, except Murdoch perhaps, whom everybody gives a wide berth anyway. Strange to say, he also blamed not Murdoch for his grief, but someone in the background who harboured relentless ill will towards him. Nantes entertained a suspicion that a powerful politician or wirepuller had a private agenda to rid the island permanently of him. As we know, the Belgian, deeming the game not worth the candle, took to his heels."

Looking squarely at Wirt, Brunt remarked with emphasis:

"To my understanding you entertain no such intentions."

"Not for a moment, but I do need your good will and co-operation."

Raising his eyebrows, nodding lightly, served as an invitation to speak.

"To begin with I suggest you treat that episode at the cemetery with a yawn and a sweep of the hand. That's all it deserves in any case. My vindication as mentioned is simple and cogent: I was sleepwalking; in other words I acted below the threshold of awareness."

"Should I laugh or hoot?"

"Choose after you have digested this. I depose as follows: I was, still am, preoccupied with Justin's death, for obvious reasons. Upon learning the disquieting news from the grapevine, confirmed later by Caroline Brise, which implies that evidence has been withheld by Dr Brodeur and the authorities, subliminal forces compelled me to see with my own eyes the welts around Justin's neck, prior to demanding a post-mortem examination required by law."

"That's a tall order, my friend, but anyway I hear you loud and clear."

The Veils Are Lifting

Several days later Mrs Burchard and the premier returned. Her first question dumbfounded Wirt:

"How is the work proceeding at Sylvania? Have you encountered anything unforeseen?"

Involuntarily Wirt's face fell; he virtually gaped at her, begging silently to repeat her words, which he most likely had misunderstood. When she just looked at him inquiringly, patiently waiting for a reply, he stuttered:

"But – but…"

The wonted smile disappeared from the serene, womanly face; it yielded to a crimped expression.

"I sense that you have encountered difficulties which haven't been conveyed to me, am I right?"

Did she suffer from amnesia? Was she making sport of him? Or did she try her skill at a childish guessing game?

Mrs Burchard, growing impatient, declared reprovingly:

"Mr Garneau had explicitly been requested to promptly inform me, or the premier, of any delays or obstacles. Since we never heard a word of concern we decided to combine business with pleasure, meaning we prolonged our sojourn. Of course the ministry was always kept abreast of our whereabouts."

Wirt, stirred by rising dismay, fanned by indignation, protested vigorously:

"I am thoroughly baffled. The minister advised me in no uncertain terms of your express wish that all work at Sylvania be deferred until your return."

"He what?" she exclaimed.

"Madame, I am puzzled and perturbed. Not only were your instructions imparted to me, but a directive, written on government stationary duly stamped and signed, had been delivered to Mr Brunt; it confirmed the minister's message."

Mrs Burchard drew herself up:

"Are you saying that no work has been performed as agreed?"

Stung to the marrow, Wirt called out:

"Of course not, in view of your orders."

Celia Burchard grew silent. She gazed at the mountains where her cradle stood, and where she spent her childhood and youth. An ardent desire gripped her to take refuge with the people she had left, and whom she slighted at times.

Wirt was touched by her pensiveness, he dared not to interrupt. It would have been of little avail, since she seemed to have entered a state of deep abstraction. Signs of annoyance, wrestling with nascent suspicions which she tried to shake off, were omnipresent. Convulsive hand movements, acccompanied by flickering eyelids, foreshadowed a soul in anguish. She cocked her head ponderously, which conveyed an impression that an awful truth, long glossed over, reared its head unmercifully.

Mrs Burchard nodded in recognition, then asked in a quavering voice:

"Mr Wirt, will you accompany me to Howard Brunt's quarters?"

He hesitated not one moment to comply with her request. As they walked up the steps she came to a halt, then turned to gaze at the mountains once more. Never in his life had Wirt seen such a mournful countenance, as she slowly scanned the lush, forbidding terrain. Gradually a resigned smile flitted across her face.

"The pieces of the puzzle are falling into place. The green-eyed monster has struck again."

Mystified by her cryptic remark,Wirt looked at her.

"You know the expression, I suppose?"

"I do, but the connection evades me."

"The beast jealousy that loves and hates at the same time has bared its fangs once more. I am defeated a second time;

Murdoch wins again. Assisted and goaded by the premier, my husband, he will have his way unless you stick with us."

"I pledge to do exactly that."

Then Mrs Burchard said something that stuck in Wirt's memory for years:

"Hannes, why, oh why, could you and Nantes not have been dark, old and ugly? Why must both of you have blue eyes, plus an abundance of blond hair, and a fresh complexion?"